The BABY BLITZ

USA TODAY BESTSELLING AUTHOR

LEX MARTIN

Copy editing by RJ Locksley

Proofreading by Julia Griffis, The Romance Bibliophile

Cover by Najla Qamber Designs

Model Photograph by Perrywinkle Photography

First Edition

ISBN 978-1-950554-07-2

ABOUT THE BOOK:

Two pink lines won't change the bad blood between us.

I haven't always hated my brother's best friend, but Michael Oliver gets under my skin and brings out the worst in me. He knows how to push my buttons, and I relish pushing all of his. He betrayed my trust years ago, and I've made it my mission in life to aggravate him until he admits he was wrong.

When his sister's wedding brings us together, Michael suggests a truce for one night. If only he weren't so handsome and smart, maybe I could resist the allure, but I've always been a little impulsive, and this man is my ultimate temptation. After years of pent-up frustration and unrequited love, I finally let down my guard, and that's all it takes for us to combust.

But like all bad decisions, the morning after brings a reckoning, and I leave his hotel room swearing to never waste another moment of my time pining after him. Who needs that grumpy jerk warming her bed? Not me.

I don't let myself think about that steamy night together, or how it pained me to hear about his football injury, or how much I know he wants to get drafted so he can help his family. Because I'm cutting Michael out of my life for good.

Only the two little pink lines mean I can't forget him. Even if I desperately want to.

∽

The Baby Blitz is a companion standalone to *USA Today* best-selling author Lex Martin's sensational college football romance novels, *The Varsity Dad Dilemma* and *Tight Ends & Tiaras*. Readers will love this sensual multicultural romance featuring a scorching-hot college football player and the feisty, but slightly nerdy girl next door—the one he swore he'd never make a move on.

Will Michael make the right decision if he has to choose between Maggie or fulfilling his dream of playing professional football?

I burn, I pine, I perish...
—*The Taming of the Shrew* by William Shakespeare

PROLOGUE

MAGGIE

ON A LIST of dumb things I've done, this is the most idiotic.

I crawl deeper behind the couch. There! Behind Luke's chemistry book I spot my sweatshirt, the one that used to belong to my dad. The one Luke swore he didn't have. The jerk probably didn't even bother looking for it when he dumped me last week.

The retro lettering that spells out Van Halen, my dad's favorite band, is faded, like my memories of him, and as my current predicament indicates, I'll do anything to get it back. Even set aside my pride to sneak into my ex-boyfriend's man cave and crawl on my hands and knees over greasy hamburger wrappers.

I'm over Luke, though. I let myself be mopey for a few days before I resorted to baking an assortment of holiday cookies that my family gobbled down without bothering to ask why I was trying to eat my feelings one gingerbread man at a time. I'm blessed with the Morales genes, so even though I've consumed my weight in junk food this week, I'm still as skinny as the half-melted peppermint stick I flick off my precious sweatshirt.

Jesus, Luke's a slob. I don't know what I saw in that boy.

After I dust myself off, I stare up at the window I wiggled through a few minutes ago. I'm wondering how the hell I'm going to hoist myself up to the ledge when the basement door bangs open and a stampede of high school boys storm down the stairs.

Panicked, I dive back behind the couch, where I nearly crack a rib on a forgotten can of soda.

"Holy shit. I still can't believe we're in the playoffs!" my brother Sebastian crows.

"You're the man!" Luke bellows.

I roll my eyes. Luke's an idiot. But he's not wrong. My brother *is* the captain of the basketball team, and he *did* make that buzzer-beater.

I'm the opposite of Sebastian, my tall, handsome older brother. While he's athletic, I'm athletically challenged. While he's tall and muscular, I'm short and twiggy. While he can fix almost anything, I'm most likely to have broken it in the first place.

Three enormous bodies toss themselves onto the old couch that groans under their weight. I barely keep from squeaking because the back of the couch now presses into me, and it's hard to breathe back here among the dust motes and moldy leftovers.

Someone coughs. "Statistically speaking, I figure we have a thirty-five percent chance of winning this year."

I chuckle inwardly. Michael Oliver, or Olly to his friends, is the biggest nerd, and that's saying something because I usually head up that team.

Olly is stupidly attractive. Like Luke Skywalker in that old *Star Wars* movie poster he has hanging in his bedroom, but with muscles. Blond hair. Big dimples. Giant blue eyes fringed with long lashes. And while he plays sports, most notably football, he's not a total jock. He doesn't party like those other idiots. He takes school seriously. He's a little socially awkward, but I love that about him. He's just himself.

I had a crush on Olly for years before I realized he probably sees me as a kid sister. But that's when Luke moved here, and I vowed to get over Olly.

Except my brother made a stupid declaration to his friends this fall that his "baby sister" was off limits. Like I'm some infant instead of a junior in high school and only one year younger.

Which is why Luke and I had to sneak around. I'll admit the sneaking was half the fun. I'd thought things were going well when, out of the blue, he declared "it's not you, it's me" and broke things off. I might've bought that if he hadn't been the one to pursue me. Who does that and then suddenly has a change of heart?

"Boys!" Luke's mom calls out. "Pizza's here. Somebody needs to come pay!"

"I'll get it," Sebastian offers before his clodhopper feet go stomping up those stairs again.

"Olly, man." Luke clears his throat. "Before Bash gets back, I want to thank you for the heads-up about Magnolia last week."

I freeze when I hear my name and pray they don't say anything horrible. In the movies, things never go well when the heroine eavesdrops.

My prayers go unanswered.

"No problemo. I don't usually pass along gossip, but I heard it with my own two ears, and I didn't feel right keeping it from you." *Keep what from him?* "'Sides, there's nothing I hate more than a cheater. Even though, well... I hate to think of her like that."

What. The. Hell. Is Olly talking about *me*? Am *I* the cheater in this scenario? Because I was nothing but faithful to Luke. I even stopped hugging my guy friends because I didn't want to make him feel weird.

"I still can't believe Maggie would do something like that. I had no idea. And it's not like I can ask her brother. You know how protective he is with her." Luke cracks his knuckles, which, for the record, is one of his more annoying traits.

"I don't blame you. Frankly, I wouldn't believe it either if I hadn't been there." *What is he talking about? Been where?* "But she said it herself. She's been hooking up with some guy from St. Gregory's."

My eyes squeeze shut as realization hits me. That's the cover story I told my brother. Minus the hooking-up part, of course, but I couldn't tell Bash I was heading out to lock lips with his buddy. And Olly must've overheard me and made some dumbass assumptions.

Luke clears his throat. "Not gonna lie. I was really into her." *Aww, Luke!*

At least now that I know what's going on, I can explain and clear the air. Luke and I can get back together, or at least part as friends.

I just read that men mature fully a whopping eleven years after women, but that's no excuse for Olly. He's supposed to be the smart one out of Bash's buddies. How could he think I'd have it in me to betray my boyfriend, or anyone for that matter?

"Nah. You can do better, man. Maggie's pretty, I guess, but any chick who would lie to your face like that is not worth the time."

He "guesses" I'm pretty. We all know what that means.

My eyes fill, and I try to blink away the tears. Hearing how Olly really sees me is somehow worse than Luke's grunt of agreement.

It's not like I think I'm some beauty queen or anything. My mom says I'm a late bloomer, which is code for not having any boobs. And my butt is pretty small too. Would it be wrong to say a rosary and ask Jesus for better endowments?

I clench my jaw and barely resist leaping out from behind the couch to smash this crusty chemistry book on Olly's smug mug when Luke says, "I'm over it. Fucked Virginia ten ways to Sunday last night. Maggie had decent tits and all, but Virginia's..." He growls like an animal. "Virginia has two giant handfuls of beauty. Why I was wasting my time dating a virgin is beyond me. Senior year is the time to get laid, am I right?"

Virginia. His best friend. The one he swore was "just a friend."

Before the other dumbass can respond, my brother returns with dinner.

The guys stuff their faces while I cry quietly behind the couch and vow to get back at Michael Oliver.

They say revenge is a dish best served cold.

And I plan to serve it.

1

OLLY

FOUR YEARS LATER

"I was thinking I should hire a dancer... from Heavenly Hunks," my sister says.

All the girls cackle, and I nearly choke on my coffee.

I slam down my mug. "Y'all know I don't really work there, right? For the millionth time, that's a *stock photo*." My ex-girlfriend Amelia set up that shoot last fall. She said it would be "great exposure." Somehow, a billboard of me on the main drag of Charming, advertising a strip club, isn't the kind of exposure I had in mind.

Those assholes seem to be doing a whole series. The first one popped up before the holidays. It featured me in a Santa hat with something about putting a Heavenly Hunk under your mistletoe. In the latest one that went up last week, they gave me a bow tie to ring in the New Year.

I glare at my sister Kayla when she keeps joking about it. "Doncha think it'd be pretty gross for your own brother to show up as the dancer at your bachelorette party, sporting a thong and shaking his banana?"

My mom can barely contain the mirth in her eyes as she darts around the dining room table, serving everyone her famous cinnamon rolls. "Don't be such a prude, Michael. It's just a joke."

I look to my father at the head of the table. I can't see him over the newspaper, but his shoulders are shaking. At least he has the decency to not laugh out loud.

But my sister's friends are snorting and giggling and making crude gestures at me when my parents aren't looking. I've never catcalled a woman before, and this moment right here is why I never will.

"Here, have another cinnamon roll," my mom says, as if vast quantities of carbs and sugar will solve all my problems.

I have more than one at the moment.

And I'm not even talking about that damn billboard or the ex-girlfriend who was behind it.

I hold up my hand as I struggle to stand. "I'm good."

"Oh, honey, don't go. They're just teasing." My mom holds out her oven-mitted hands.

"I know. We're cool. Just want to check on Gramps before I leave."

My mother's bright blue eyes study me, and I feel like a ten-year-old kid with his paw in the cookie jar instead of a twenty-one-year-old man. "Your father will drive you back to campus when you're ready. Tell Dad I'll bring down his lunch in a bit. Careful on those steps."

"Ten-four." I wobble over to my crutches and yank them into place, annoyed I can't drive myself.

Life is not going as planned, starting with the bone-jarring injury I got in November that basically wiped out my dream of getting drafted. But Coach Nicholson is encouraging me to use my last season of eligibility to give it one more try. Since I redshirted freshman year, I can return to Lone Star State and play another season even though I'm ready to graduate at the end of this semester.

Because, let's face it, I won't be ready for the combine in March, and if I'm not there to show I've recovered and I'm in top shape, I haven't a shot in hell of getting drafted in May. Not after I missed the last three games on the heels of a lackluster season and so much fucking team drama.

The guys turned it around and ended on a high note, but I didn't play those games. I'm glad my buddies will have a decent chance of getting drafted, but damn. The thought of going through another year of college football after months of rehab sounds exhausting.

"Hey, Beulah," I call out as I wobble across the overgrown lawn of my parents' small farm. My mother's goat ignores me to chew on someone's ratty tennis shoe. I knock on the rusty door of my grandfather's trailer.

"Come in! I hope you brought some food. A man could die back here from starvation."

I chuckle as I carefully make my way up the stairs. "Gramps, it's me."

Rheumy-eyed, he looks me over. "Who's my favorite grandson?"

"That would be me." I lean over to hug him, hating how frail he feels. "You taking your medicine?"

"Your mother would have my balls in a sling if I didn't. Although I don't know how we'll afford my insulin any longer. Gonna go bankrupt with those prices."

"We'll find a way. 'Cause look on the bright side—it would be worse to die of a diabetic coma."

He clicks the TV remote with one hand while he gives me the finger with the other. "No one likes a smartass."

I smile. At least he has some dexterity.

But my good mood evaporates as I take in his trailer. I know my mom and sister come back here to clean and help out, but it hurts to see how threadbare his furniture is getting.

From what my parents have told me, every penny of Grandpa's retirement fund and a good chunk of my family's savings is going toward his medication. It's why I'm sick over not being ready for the draft. Gramps needs that money. He shouldn't be living in a dilapidated trailer in my parents' backyard.

My mom plays it off, but I watched her clip coupons for an hour this morning. A dollar just doesn't stretch as far as it used to.

After living a frugal life, my parents should be going on cruises and kicking back like their church friends, but they're more stressed out than ever. I'm painfully aware it's my turn to be the breadwinner instead of needing more money for textbooks.

By the time I get ready to head back to Charming, my sister's friends have all left. Kayla crushes me in a goodbye hug.

"Did you save the date?" she asks as she leans back.

"Yes, ma'am. Wouldn't miss your wedding for the world."

"You didn't say anything about my invitation. Isn't it beautiful?" She pulls one from her back pocket and waves it in my face.

"Very nice."

"You know who designed it, right?"

"I have no idea, but I'm pretty sure you're gonna tell me." Ever since Kayla got engaged over the holidays, she's been obsessed with weddings.

"One of my favorite people," she singsongs. I wait for her to spill it, although I have no idea why she's being mysterious. "Magnolia Morales." I can't hide my scowl, which makes her huff. "Why are you like this? Maggie is sweet as pie."

"Maggie's a brat. Half the time, she pretends like she barely knows me. Get this—she tells people we 'met in a class,' like we didn't grow up together. Do you know what that girl did to my truck in high school?" It pains me to remember.

Kayla cackles at my expression. "Don't be dramatic. Maggie *accidentally* left a tuna fish sandwich in your car, and you've been butthurt ever since."

"Accidental, my ass. She pulled that shit in May over a long weekend when it baked in the scorching Texas sun while we were all at the lake. And don't forget the time our economics teacher thought I was cheating. Maggie had asked me for a pencil. She could've spoken up. Defended me. Instead I got a zero on that test." When my sister doesn't say anything, I feel the need to underscore the importance of that exam. "It's the only zero I've ever gotten." Crickets. "It could've hurt my G.P.A."

My sister frowns at me like I'm being a little bitch and pats my chest. "Okay, big guy. Don't get all huffy-puffy. I don't know why you two have a beef, but Maggie's only been a sweetheart to me. She did my invites for free. No one does anything for free these days. I tried to pay her, but she said I was her little sister's favorite babysitter and will always get her friends-and-family discount."

That was nice of her, damn it.

For some reason, I don't like having reasons to appreciate Magnolia.

She and I didn't always bicker. When we were younger, we were friends, but that changed my senior year.

I still get a twinge of guilt over breaking up her relationship with Luke. How was I supposed to know she wasn't really sneaking around behind his back? I've always been a little rigid when it comes to certain things, and I've worked hard to not be so strait-laced, but back then, I couldn't let that fly.

Trust me—Magnolia has made me pay for that mistake.

She'd never believe me, but she was better off not dating that guy. Aside from the fact that Bash would've freaked out if he'd found out Luke and his sister were hooking up, Luke was the biggest player in our group of friends. The way he talked about girls was worthy of PornHub. Magnolia didn't deserve that treatment.

In retrospect, I could've handled it more gently, but I was young and dumb and not great with interpersonal relationships. I've taken a shitload of communication and psych classes to improve my "robotic outlook on life." That descriptive gem came compliments of a girl I dated in high school. Those words stung, but it opened my eyes, and I've since tried to do better. To be better.

Now that I think about it, had Maggie been my girlfriend, I'd have put up a bigger fight than Luke did. He just accepted that Maggie was seeing someone else—which, for the record, she did in fact say. If she hadn't been lying in the first place and just told Bash the truth, he could've been the one to handle things.

After I tug on my coat, Kayla helps me stuff myself and my crutches into the passenger side of my grandpa's old truck.

"You bringing a date to my wedding?" she asks as she runs around to the other side to warm the engine for Dad.

"Probably not."

"You still upset about Amelia?"

"Nope." Maybe.

Deep down, I know my ex and I weren't well suited. She was a model and stunningly beautiful. This will sound horrible, but dating her made me feel like I wasn't that middle-school geek anymore. The sex was pretty amazing, and we had fun together, but all of my friends hated her, and I can't say I blamed them. Amelia's idea of a good time was causing drama, which is the polar opposite of my goals in life.

Still, it was tough to crash and burn like that because the end was ugly.

"Hmm." My sister looks me over, and I sigh.

"I thought we were done with the inquisition."

"Can I set you up with someone for my wedding?"

Christ, no.

She clasps her hands together. "Pretty please?"

Kayla knows she has me at a disadvantage because I'd pretty much do anything to make her happy. "Fine. It's your wedding."

She squeals and reaches over to squeeze me in another hug. I'm about to tell her she can set me up with anyone she wants *except* Magnolia Morales, but she knows better. Kayla had a front-row seat to one of our disagreements a few years ago. Doubt she'd want that kind of tension at her wedding.

As Kayla gets out, my father ambles toward us. "What's she trying to finagle you into doing?"

I laugh because we all know Kayla's ways.

Before I can respond, the CB on the dashboard roars to life and my grandfather's voice fills the truck. "This is RogerRabbit. Who the hell is gonna feed me before I die? Over and out."

Gramps used to be a trucker, and the only way he agreed to live on my parents' property was if they installed a few CB radios around so he could easily communicate with us. He didn't want "no fancy fucking phone."

My mom bangs open the front door of the house, turns her head toward the backyard, and shouts, "I'm coming, old man!" Balancing a tray of food in one hand, she heads over to my dad. They pause in front of the car as he leans down to rub her nose with his and whisper something in her ear that makes her blush and giggle like a teenage girl.

"Ugh, they're gross." Leaning in my door, my sister makes a choking sound. "I heard them going at it last night. Almost puked."

Wincing, I hold up my hand. "Overshare, dude."

I definitely don't want to hear about my parents' sex life, but I'm grateful they're still in love and have each other. Bash and Maggie lost their dad when they were in middle school, and it wrecked them. That's why they moved here to Heartland Hills, a small town in the Texas Hill Country.

They lived next door to us for a couple of years. Bash, Maggie, and I spent long summers trampling through the tall grass, catching frogs, and building forts. Those were some of the best summers of my life.

I rub my chest. Sometimes I get a weird ache when I think back to those days.

On the way back to Charming where I attend Lone Star State, I stare out the window and watch grove after grove of mesquite and cedar and oak trees roll on by. Unfortunately, now that my sister has been in my ear, I can't stop thinking about Maggie.

Even though she annoys the hell out of me, if Magnolia wasn't so dang mouthy, she'd be a stunner with her thick black hair, dark brown eyes, and that adorable sprinkle of freckles across her nose. And when she glares at me over the rim of her glasses, well, sometimes I forget what my name is.

She might've been scrawny when we were kids, but she's one hundred percent woman now with curves upon mouthwatering curves. I saw her working out at the gym last semester and nearly swallowed my tongue. She was wearing a sports bra and these little gym shorts that...

Mentally, I come to a screeching halt and remind myself she's firmly in the no-fly zone. Her brother Sebastian made sure of it. In fact, Bash took each of his friends aside senior year and told us he'd lop off our balls with a rusty razor if we got near Magnolia. At the time, I'd already vowed to myself I wouldn't check her out. Bash trusted me around her, and I'd never do anything to jeopardize that.

As someone with a sister, I get it. No one wants their horny friends making eyes at their sibling.

So I make a point to not look at Maggie Morales.

Even if I sometimes want to.

2

MAGGIE

STRETCHING AS FAR as I can go, I reach for the last box of discounted macaroni on the top shelf as I calculate what's in my cart already and how much more I can afford before I get paid on Friday.

My cracked phone blares my mom's ringtone, and I scramble to answer it. "Mom, what's wrong?"

Her warm laughter immediately puts me at ease. "Why do you always think something's wrong when I call?"

I can think of a number of reasons, but listing them off in the middle of the grocery store isn't going to help my mood. "Y'all are okay, though? Frannie's good?"

My little sister is autistic, and my mom sometimes has a hard time juggling everything at home.

"Francesca had a great day." Thank God. At least someone did. "She's doing so much better now that we got her off processed foods. But that keto stuff means she loses weight too easily, so she needs to eat more."

The diet isn't keto, but it cuts out certain carbs, so I get what she means. I eye my grocery basket and put back a few things. "I can send you more money if you need it."

Frannie's diet is expensive. Why is it that healthy food costs a small fortune? I'd ask my brother to pitch in, but he's had some major car repairs lately, and he's still trying to pay that off. Plus, he's starting law school soon and needs the cash as much as I do. I figure someday when he's a hotshot attorney, it'll be his turn. I'm just holding down the fort in the meanwhile.

"No, Magnolia. You need that money. I just wanted to let you know we got invited to Kayla's wedding. I can't go, of course, because who's going to watch the kiddo? But it was so thoughtful of her to invite us."

Single moms have it so hard. They're the unsung heroes of our society. "You're awesome, Mom. I love you."

"Love you too, *mija*." She always rolls with my non sequiturs. Finally, she asks, "Did you mail the property tax check?"

Today it really hit. How hard it's going to be to afford the utilities and my textbooks after I sent that check. And this was only the first half. I owe the other half come summer.

My eyes sting. "I'm sorry. You can say it. Tell me it was a mistake."

"I'd never do that, honey. You did what you thought was right. Your daddy would be so happy to know you're taking good care of that house."

Hearing this makes me more upset. My father was born in that house. His older brother Hidalgo inherited it, and when he passed recently, he left it and a few assets to me for some reason. That old Victorian is huge and decrepit. I love it with my whole heart and soul because it's a link to my father, but it's bleeding me dry. It's sucking out the money I should be using to buy my sister her special food and help my mom with her rent.

"I'm so stupid," I whisper. "Why didn't you knock some sense into me?"

Genius that I am, I thought I could renovate it and make it nice for my mom and sister to move into. Since the house was paid off, I thought I could afford everything, but I'm slowly realizing I'm not so great at flipping houses.

Plus, it's more expensive than I thought to repair, and the property taxes are ridiculous for something that looks straight out of a horror movie. I've had to hustle all year with side jobs just to write that check I sent last week. I'm a junior in college. Why didn't *any* class *ever* teach us about property taxes?

I hate to say it, but Sebastian was right. I should've sold my uncle's house when I had that offer last year. It would've broken my heart to let it go, but I wouldn't be struggling right now.

I couldn't sell it now even if I wanted to. I've started projects —ripped out tile and baseboards—that I haven't been able to fix yet. Who wants a half-finished house with zero curb appeal and a mountain of weeds?

My mom tries to reassure me, which only makes me feel guiltier. Since my dad died, she's worked her ass off to send me and my brother to college. To try to get all the extra therapies for my sister because Frannie's local public school is small and doesn't have many resources.

After I get off the call, I catch sight of my reflection in the produce area. My eyes and nose are bright red even though I didn't shed a tear. I just got emotional, but that's all it takes for my face to go full-on Rudolph. I'm not one of those people who can play off getting upset. At least I'm wearing my glasses, which might mask it a little.

With a sigh, I look at my grocery list and scratch off a few items I know I can't afford.

I let myself have one splurge and grab a couple of apples from the discounted box—they're not too bruised—and head for the checkout.

Worst-case scenario, if you really need money, you can always donate blood.

I wonder how much that pays.

High-pitched giggles snag my attention, and I spot my arch-nemesis, Michael Oliver, hobbling through the store on crutches. I don't have time to feel bad for him and his injury because he has two girls tripping over themselves to help him with his cart.

He looks up just as I haul ass around the corner and hide behind a cereal display.

Thankfully, I don't think he saw me.

That guy never has anything nice to say to me, and I'm in no mood to deal with him. Glancing down, I take stock of what I'm wearing. Old jeans. A ratty t-shirt. A tattered coat. And let's not forget the red nose.

I say a little prayer that I can get home without another run-in with that guy.

Resigned to wait it out, I scoot back so I can rest my rear on the bottom shelf next to the oatmeal. I open my phone and see I missed a message from my friend Sienna.

Can you babysit tomorrow?

Dear God, yes.

Sienna is engaged to Ben, who has a super-sweet toddler named Lily. Not only do they pay me well, they always feed me, and I could use the free meal. I used to get more hours with them, but then Ben's aunt and uncle decided to move closer to help with Lily.

The only downside to babysitting is I risk running into Michael, since he lives across the street with his football buddies, but he tends to give me a wide berth when he knows I'm at Ben and Sienna's.

Knowing him, he'll assume I designed Kayla's wedding invitations to annoy him, except the truth is she's one of my favorite people. I get it—I'm dumb for not charging her for the work, but she's not loaded. She and her fiancé have been scrimping and saving to tie the knot. The least I could do was make a small contribution to her special day. In contrast to her brother, Kayla's always been sweet to me, and even though Michael gets under my skin like a bad rash, his family is awesome.

After a few minutes, the coast is clear. There's no sign of Michael and his giggling escorts, so I head for the checkout.

"How's it going, Edith?" I always try to learn the names of the checkout attendants. I've come to this grocery store every week for three years. It seems rude not to know who these people are.

"It's going. How've you been, Maggie?" She gives me a tired smile.

We chat while she rings me up. She pauses to help another cashier for a minute before she returns.

I'm so busy wondering if tomorrow night's babysitting gig will get me enough gas for the rest of the month that I don't hear what Edith says. "Sorry, what?"

The grimace on her face should tell me this isn't good news. "Your card was declined."

"It has to be a glitch. I should have enough. Can we run it again?"

"Of course."

I zip my card through, punch in the PIN, and start praying, only to see that hated word pop up on the credit card screen: 'DECLINED.'

Oh, hell. "Maybe I have some cash." If Moses parted the Red Sea, a few bills could magically pop up in my purse. They say God works in mysterious ways, right?

No such luck. I pull out a handful of lint, three dimes, and an unwrapped but tattered piece of gum.

A low, deep voice interrupts my panic attack. "Do you need money?"

I close my eyes. Why does it have to be him?

When I don't respond, Michael leans closer. So close I can smell his fresh scent. "Magnolia, I can help."

The way he says my name sends shivers down my arms. I open my eyes and turn, and there he is. I don't know why, but it's always a shock to my system when I see him. Like I'm being slowly killed with low-voltage electricity.

His two clingers watch me with annoyance. Probably because I'm sucking up time with their precious Olly.

"Michael." I clear my throat. "Thanks, but I'm good. I'll just put everything back." Tears fill my eyes as I apologize to Edith, who gives me a sympathetic nod.

"It's okay, honey." She looks around briefly and then hands me the apples and two boxes of macaroni. "Go ahead and take these. I know you're good for it."

That makes the tears come faster. I've been trying so hard to pay for everything, to be responsible, and I can't even balance my damn checkbook correctly. "No, really. It's okay." I swipe at my eyes and take all the bags and put them in my cart. "I'll return the groceries. Put them back where they belong."

Michael says my name again so forcefully that I still. Then he grumbles, "Why are you so damn stubborn? I said I can help you."

Finally, I face him. He studies me from head to toe. Probably notices the hole in my old Chucks and how my jeans are torn because I accidentally ripped them when I was trying to hang a door, not because I bought them fashionably shredded. My hair is in an ugly, tangled bun, and by now my face looks like I have scarlet fever.

I try to whisper to him, but his entourage leans closer to eavesdrop, so I grab his shirt and pull him close to me. Between clenched teeth, I grit, "I don't need you to come to my rescue, okay? I'm not your responsibility."

His eyes narrow. "Sebastian would want me to buy you food, dingdong."

Of course. The only reason he'd help me is because he's best friends with my brother. Not because we used to be friends.

I stand there while he wobbles on his crutches and tosses a few twenties to Edith. Humiliation burns every inch of me as his two friends whisper to each other.

"Do you need a ride home?" he asks. "It's raining out."

"I'm good."

"Does that mean you actually have a car, or are you planning to hoof it home in the freezing rain and risk pneumonia?"

I look down at my tattered Chucks, unwilling to mention my twenty-year-old Ford Focus. It's old as hell and sometimes doesn't want to shift into gear, but it runs. "I'm glad to see you have so much faith in me." Resigned, I meet his eyes. "Some things never change, huh?" Before he can respond, I motion to the groceries. "Thank you for the food. I'll pay you back. I promise."

If I have to go without heating my house, I'll pay him back.

Unlike him, I always keep my promises.

3

OLLY

MY HEART always feels like it's going to pound out of my chest when I'm at the doctor's office. The smell of disinfectant and the stuffy air in the patient rooms instantly remind me of those days right after my injury, when I wasn't sure what the prognosis would be.

Dad sits in the corner with his face in the newspaper. His remote exterior doesn't fool me. I know he's as invested in my recovery as I am. He and my mom have attended every one of my games and scrimmages since I was in peewee. If I'm playing football, they're in the stands. There hasn't been a game where my mom hasn't lost her voice from cheering for my team.

The fact that he made the forty-minute drive to take me to this appointment speaks volumes.

While they couldn't afford my surgery, they made it happen. It makes me that much more determined to recover and get back on the field so I can pay them back. Their farm is in shambles, and it's because all their money goes to me and Gramps.

"The swelling looks much better," Dr. Curtis says as he gently probes my knee. "You're lucky. A grade two tear is rare."

People keep saying I'm lucky. That I only partially tore my

ACL. That it didn't require grafting from some other area of my body to repair.

Missing the last part of the season doesn't feel lucky, but I'm trying to focus on being grateful, so I nod at him and force a smile. "Think I'll be back on the field for training this summer?"

My dad lowers the newspaper to listen.

Dr. Curtis gives me one of his deadly serious stares. "With any surgery, I hesitate to make any declarations, but I'd say you have a good chance of being ready to do *some* training in June."

Fuck. That's six months away. He's given me the estimates before, but I keep hoping for a miraculous recovery.

When I don't say anything, he taps on his clipboard. "That's a conservative estimate. I'd rather take things slow than move too quickly and risk getting hurt again."

"Makes sense."

"Technically, with your kind of injury, it can take between four to six months to return to training, and six to eight to return to competitive sports. Depends on the patient."

Please let it be four months. I have to be ready to go when the season starts next fall.

"The good news is you're done with crutches."

Finally, something positive.

He pats me on the back. "Take it easy, Michael. The worst thing you can do is overexert yourself before you're fully healed. Trust the process. Our physical therapist will go over the additional exercises I want you to do until our next appointment."

"How much longer do I need to wear the brace?"

"Probably four more weeks, except during your stretches."

After I'm done talking to the therapist, I jot down a few notes in my phone and ease off the table.

My dad hands me my coat. "About what we expected. Just gotta do what the doctor says. Slow and steady."

Slow and steady sucks, but Dr. Curtis is right. I don't want to injure my knee again.

"Wanna get some Dairy Queen?" my dad asks as he holds open the door.

I laugh. "It's January."

"Sounds like a good time for a Blizzard. Your mom doesn't let me get them anymore. Says it's bad for my cholesterol or something."

Fuck it. "Yeah. Let's get some ice cream."

After we enjoy our desserts, he pulls up to my house. I lean over to give him a hug. "Thanks for coming, Dad. I appreciate you taking me to those appointments."

My natural state is anxious as fuck, which I've mostly overcome through the years with sports and intense training, but now that I mostly sit on my ass, I'm getting reacquainted with that old state of mind.

"No problemo. Don't tell Mom about Dairy Queen."

"Ten-four."

Instead of going home, I hobble across the street to Ben's. It feels good to not need crutches, but I'm still terrified one wrong move will hamper my recovery.

Ben's girlfriend Sienna opens the door, and a big smile lights her face. She wraps me in a hug and shouts, "Lily, look who's here!" When she lets go, her head tilts pensively. "How are you feeling?"

"Better. How was Mexico?" She and Ben have been back for two weeks, but between me mostly staying with my parents and doctor appointments, I haven't seen them since they went on vacation.

"Amazing." She waves her engagement ring around. "So nice to traipse off with my fiancé."

I chuckle. "Glad you guys got some time away. Lily missed you guys."

"We missed her like crazy too." She lowers her voice. "But I'm not going to lie, it was nice to get away with Ben for a bit. Thanks for helping Ben's aunt and uncle while we were gone."

"Didn't do much. Just sat on your couch and iced my knee while Lily tried to get me to eat her half-chewed food."

Out of my peripheral vision, I see a little head of hair zip past the coffee table. "Uncle Olly!" Lily wraps herself around my leg, and I laugh, grateful for the knee brace.

"Come here, monkey." I scoop her up and kiss her chubby cheeks. "Did you tell Sienna about all those Disney movies you made me watch while she and your dad were away?"

She nods solemnly and turns to Sienna. "Where are da pics?"

"Lily is obsessed with our engagement photos. Here, baby." Sienna hands them to her, and Lily wiggles out of my arms and drags me to the couch, where she pats the seat next to her.

She hands me photo after photo of the guys serenading Sienna last month. Little fingerprints dot each print.

As I look over the images, Sienna and I discuss her new business. "I'm sinking every penny I have into it, but I think it'll be worth it in the end," she says proudly.

"I don't doubt it'll be a success."

Lily hands me another pic.

"Does it matter that we're getting these grubby?" I ask Sienna.

"Those are her own set. She can manhandle them if she wants. Lily, show him your favorite."

It's a photo of me scowling at my housemate Johnny, who has me in a headlock. Ben is down on one knee proposing to his girl, and we're in the background looking like asses.

"You'd think Johnny would've been more careful with you since you were in a leg brace and crutches," she says.

"Caution is not his style."

"I like dis one," Lily says, handing me a photo of Maggie and Sienna, hugging and grinning at the camera.

It almost hurts to see Maggie so happy after what happened the other day at the grocery store. She acted as though I'd offered to shave her head instead of buy her groceries. We weren't always so antagonistic with each other, but I have no idea how to get back to our old friendship. I'm not sure it's even possible.

"Oh!" Sienna hops up and runs to the kitchen and returns with an envelope with my name on it. "After Maggie babysat the other day, she left the money I paid her with for you."

I'm not surprised when I open it and find sixty dollars with a Post-It that says, *Thanks for the help the other day. Sorry for snarking at you.*

I'm shocked by the apology. Grateful she paid me back because I need to buy a textbook with the cash, but surprised nonetheless.

I clear my throat and limp my way over to the kitchen. "Can I ask you a question?"

Sienna turns back to me as she unloads the dishwasher. "Sure. What's up?"

"Is everything okay with Magnolia?"

Sienna doesn't say anything at first, just watches me. "As far as I know. Why?"

If I tell Sienna what happened with Maggie at the grocery store the other day, Maggie will be horrified. She'll think I betrayed her trust again. I've never seen her cry like that, and it broke my heart to see her so downtrodden. I wanted to wrap her in a hug, but I think she would've kneed me in the balls if I touched her.

I groan as I scrub my face, indecision gnawing at my insides. "No reason. Just... making sure."

"I know you two have had your differences, but..." Sienna

studies my face for a moment. "If you're worried about her, you could just stop by her house and talk to her."

She makes it sound so easy.

Trust me—I've considered it. But I can't drive for a few more weeks, and it would be weird to make one of my roommates take me. I never know how to explain what's going on between me and Maggie.

I consider calling Sebastian, but that would make it worse. He's a senior at UT now, and he'd haul ass up here to investigate and freak out his sister.

"Worried about who?" Ben heads toward me, and we do this little fist-jab, back-slap thing.

"No one. Good to see you, bro."

"Same here. Missed you, man."

He asks about my doctor appointment and prognosis. After I relay everything I discussed with Dr. Curtis, I tell him my plan. "As much as I hate this, I'm going to use my last season of eligibility. Talked to my counselor the other day. I'll be a fifth-year senior come August." Saying that out loud is embarrassing. I always thought I was a smart guy, and while there's no shame in doing what you need to finish school, it definitely dings my pride to not graduate on time. At least I've got a full ride, and Coach says my scholarship will get funded in the fall, so I'm beyond grateful.

Ben nods thoughtfully. "That's a solid plan. You'll get beefed up again over the summer once you're healed and back on the field."

I give him a look. "You saying I'm out of shape?"

"No, darling, I'm not," he teases. "Your ass looks great in those jeans."

I bat my eyelashes at him. "Doesn't it?"

Sienna giggles and wraps her fiancé in a hug. Lily hops off

the couch and runs toward her dad, who picks her up and covers her in kisses.

I'm nowhere near the point of being able to afford a family of my own, but someday I want what Ben and Sienna have. I foolishly thought Amelia might be the girl for me, but I was looking at her through rose-colored glasses. I've since learned I shouldn't confuse sex with love.

That night, I toss and turn as I debate what to do about Magnolia. If her credit card was declined and she gave me the cash from her babysitting gig, what does that leave her with?

I don't have much to give her, but maybe I can find someone who can help. Without her knowing, of course.

Because if she thinks I'm behind any kind of gift, she'll never accept the assistance.

Stubborn woman.

4

OLLY

"Why am I doing this again?" my roommate Johnny whispers from behind an overgrown bush.

"Because I asked you to."

He squints at me. "You're really not gonna tell me what's going on?" I glare at him, and he holds up a hand. "Don't Hulk out. I told you I'd do it, and I will. Which house?"

It's possible he'll screw this up, but I don't feel like I have other options. "That one over there." I point to the bungalow across the street from Magnolia's. Twenty minutes ago, a woman pulled into the driveway, and she and a man went inside. There are kids' toys on the porch, so I figure a family might live there. Maybe Magnolia knows them.

"And you want me to say what again?" he asks as he hefts the box of groceries higher.

Jesus Christ. "Pay attention this time. Tell the lady or whoever answers the door to take those to Maggie's house. Explain how she needs to pretend that she got an extra delivery of groceries she doesn't need, so she thought she'd see if any of her neighbors could use them. Offer the woman a pair of tickets to a game next fall, if she's on the fence. The most important thing is Maggie can't know the food is from us."

"And you think Maggie is gonna believe all that? She's a sharp chick."

I shrug. "She might not, but I want to try."

I'm staring at Magnolia's door, wondering what the hell is going on with her, wondering if her family is okay, when I feel Johnny watching me. "Ah, I get it." He pats me on the back so hard, I almost fall over.

"Get what?"

"You like her, and this is your weird, socially deficient way of telling her."

"I don't like her. Half the time, I can't stand to be around her. But..." I don't know how to explain it. How she gets under my skin. How I can't decide if I'm coming or going when I'm with her. How I'm tired of worrying about her. "I feel like I owe her, okay?"

I blame that dumbass Luke. If I hadn't gotten involved, Maggie wouldn't hate me now. The kicker is Luke didn't deserve my help. He turned around and cheated on his new girlfriend just before we left for college.

"Whatever, bro. I'm just happy you're not still moping over Amelia. Be right back."

I never *moped* over Amelia exactly. Mostly I was pissed I'd wasted my time.

He jogs over to Maggie's neighbor's house, and my heart hammers in my throat as the door opens. Johnny starts talking and points across the street. The woman nods back and smiles, which is promising.

A few minutes later, my roommate hands her the box of groceries and heads back to our bush on the corner. "She said it's no problem. Said she'd go over after she's done making dinner."

"You told her what to say? How she shouldn't make Magnolia feel like a charity case? Because she'd hate that."

"Yeah, yeah. All that."

"And the neighbor knows to keep it anonymous?"

"Maggie will never know you sent it. I promise."

Finally, I let out a breath. I don't know why this matters so much to me. It's not like Maggie would starve. She could always go to Sienna's house if she were desperate.

But would she ever admit she was in trouble? To anyone?

I hobble back to Johnny's car. For my own mental health, I have to stop obsessing about this woman and trust if she needs something, she'll go to her brother or friends. Johnny's right. She's smart, and she's gotten this far without me meddling in her life, so unless I hear from her, I'm gonna butt out.

We slam the doors shut and take off to grab a bite to eat.

"So, Romeo," he jokes. "Does this mean you're a free man, or is Maggie Morales your new ball and chain? Clarify it for me."

I nod slowly as I stare at the wild weeds growing in Maggie's yard and make a decision to get on with my life in more ways than one. "I'm a free man. Why? What did you have in mind?"

5

MAGGIE

MARCH

Dubious, I stare at Sienna's closet. I knew this wouldn't work.

Sienna gently pushes me out of the way, unhooks a raspberry-colored silky confection, and hands it to me. "Try it on."

"It's never going to fit." Sienna does yoga six days a week. The kind where she twists herself into a pretzel. She's svelte. Petite. I hit college and instantly gained that freshman fifteen, plus a few more I'd prefer not to count. I regret all the times I wished I wasn't so skinny growing up, because those extra pounds have landed on my ass. I work out plenty, but I probably like enchiladas a little too much to pull off that dress.

"You'll never know if you don't give it a shot."

My shoulders slump. "Am I crazy for doing this? Kayla called me at the last minute and begged, and I felt bad turning her down."

Michael's sister called me last weekend in a panic and told me her bridesmaid broke her leg and couldn't fly in from Florida. She asked me to take her spot so she could keep her party even with the number of groomsmen. Which means I need to figure out what to wear and book it to Austin tomorrow for the rehearsal dinner.

I had planned to head home to Heartland Hills for the weekend to babysit Frannie so my mom and brother could attend the wedding, but Mom says she'd rather I go and be a part of Kayla's special day.

Sienna shrugs and lifts the dress to my shoulders. "It means you get a hotel room for the weekend, all paid for. Free food and a party? Hell, yeah, I'd go. Want me to take your place? I'm sure Michael's sister wouldn't mind a stranger in her wedding photos."

I laugh. "Okay, you've made your point. I'm being silly."

"It's sweet that she asked you. I had no idea you were close to his family." Her lips twitch as she tries to hold back a smile.

Last fall, I eventually broke down and told her Michael and I met in middle school and grew up together, but she knows he's a sensitive subject for me.

Part of me hates that I haven't run into him since that grocery store episode in January. I keep thinking I'll see him here, but it's almost like he makes a point to avoid me.

I guess I thought he'd sent me that box of food as a peace offering. Who goes to all that trouble of approaching someone's neighbor if you're not trying to do something special for someone? It took some prodding, but eventually Diana admitted some college guy put her up to the food delivery. I mean, it had to be Michael, right?

I baked him a pie and left it on his front stoop to say thanks, but never heard back. His silence hurt more than I care to admit.

If anything, it proved I need to forget Michael Oliver once and for all. Whenever I let myself think we'll be friends or... something, he hurts my feelings. It's not worth putting myself out there for him.

The Baby Blitz | 35

Besides, if we did become more, I'd probably end up disappointed anyway.

I've had a few boyfriends over the years, but I always break things off because I don't feel like we connect on a significant level. Sometimes I worry it's me. That, deep down, I don't give anyone a chance.

Except I want a loving, deep relationship. Like those decadent, eight-course meals I see served up on those cooking shows, complete with those bite-sized crème brûlée tartlets. But all I get served are stale, gas-station donuts and burnt coffee. Those donuts always look good from behind the glass, but once you get in your car and take a bite, you're instantly smacked with buyer's remorse.

I'm tired of taking chances. The right guy will have to sweep me off my feet and jump into the deep end of the relationship pool for me to put myself out there again.

Realizing that Sienna is waiting for me to say something, I explain how much I love Kayla. "She's the big sister I always wanted but never had. Kayla would braid my hair and let me play with her makeup. Do my nails and tell me about the boys she was dating. Let me stay up late. She was always great with Frannie when she babysat." I run my finger over the dress. "I did her wedding invites over the holidays."

"It would be really meaningful if you were in her wedding. You should do it." She lifts an eyebrow. "I bet Olly will look hot in a tux."

I feel myself turning lobster red. I shrug. Try to play it off, but I'm probably not fooling anyone. Yes, Olly will be devastatingly handsome in formalwear, but the man could wear a paper sack and I'd find him attractive. Unfortunately.

Chuckling, Sienna nudges me with her elbow. "While we're on the subject, you should be in mine when Ben and I tie the knot next year."

"Shut up." I've never been anyone's bridesmaid. "Are you asking me to be a bridesmaid?"

"You're one of my best friends. You've helped me and Ben so much. Of course I want you to be my bridesmaid."

I'm stunned to hear she considers me such a good friend. I can't remember the last time I had a BFF. Probably before we moved to Heartland Hills. My dad had died, and we'd moved to a new town. I remember being so overwhelmed and sad. I had people I hung out with, but I don't think I ever really let my guard down with anyone.

Until Bash brought Michael home one day. He was my first friend in Heartland, which made his betrayal hurt that much more.

I squeeze Sienna in a huge hug. "I'd be honored!"

As she shares plans for her own wedding, I undress and try to squeeze into her dress. Hesitantly, I look in the full-length mirror.

She claps wildly. "You're gorgeous! Look at you."

"I want to remind you that I'm headed to a solemn church function and not a nightclub."

"Kayla's only requirement was that you wear something in cranberry. And it covers all the pertinent parts. Although you do look cold."

I glance down to see my nipples poking straight through my bra and the thin fabric of the dress. "My mother would die if I showed up in the wedding photos with high beams."

Sienna drags me to the bathroom. "Have I ever told you what you can do with Band-Aids? And you'll need more than one dress for the weekend. Don't even argue with me about this."

6

OLLY

My sister guides us through the hotel like she's a cruise ship director. I like seeing her in all her pre-wedding glory.

She turns to face me, our parents, and Gramps. "Just a reminder. You need to get to the church by four, and the rehearsal dinner is at the restaurant afterward."

Because our family is strapped for cash, she's called in a million favors to do this on a shoestring budget, but her fiancé Joe pitched in, which is why we're staying in a decent hotel this weekend.

As Kayla hands out the keys to our rooms, she jots down notes on her clipboard. "Gramps, your room connects to my parents' room, so if you need anything, they're right there. Same for you and..." Kayla's voice fades when my date Vanessa walks up and gives me a hug.

Vanessa and I haven't been dating long. Just a few weeks, but she's a nice woman. Not crazy and emotional like my ex Amelia, who chucked a bottle at my head when I broke things off.

I'm taking things slow with Vanessa. I see how jumping into bed with Amelia made me throw caution to the wind, and I'm too old to make rash decisions when it comes to dating. That's how life-altering mistakes are made.

Just ask Ben, who knocked up his high school girlfriend. He adores his daughter Lily, so I know he doesn't regret what happened, but if he could erase all the angst Janelle's dropped on his doorstep, he would.

I'm curious to see how Vanessa will take to my family. They mean the world to me, and Amelia met them once. Let's just say it didn't go well. I should've taken that as the first sign we were doomed.

Before I can introduce Vanessa, the sliding doors to the hotel open, and a gust of wind has us all turning to see who's arrived.

I freeze when I spot Magnolia.

She wheels her small suitcase up to our group and hugs Kayla. Like a mute, I watch as she bear-hugs every member of my family. Well, everyone except me.

My mom squeals—I shit you not—*squeals* when she sees Maggie. Even Gramps, who hates being fussed over, grins when he hugs her. I'm talking full-out googly-eyed like the Cheshire Cat after popping a few mushrooms.

"Sorry I'm late," Maggie says, her eyes traveling over our group, barely pausing on me. "Traffic was obnoxious."

I haven't seen her in months. Only caught flashes of her running in and out of Ben's house, but after how everything went down in the grocery store that day, I decided she didn't need me meddling in her life.

But now I feel like an ass for not checking on her sooner. Is her situation better? Is she making ends meet? Did she get those groceries from her neighbor that Johnny swore she'd deliver?

Maggie's long, black hair is down and windblown. Her brown eyes are sparkly and bright. She looks so damn beautiful. And she's wearing... Christ.

Vanessa clears her throat, and I feel a hot flush steal down my neck when I realize I'm checking out Magnolia in front of the woman I brought home to meet my family.

I place my hand on Vanessa's back. "Guys, I want to introduce my..." Friend? Date? Girlfriend? Fuck. After an awkward silence, I regain my ability to speak. "This is my date, Vanessa."

My sister makes a face at me. *What?* I mouth.

She turns to Vanessa and shakes her hand. Everyone is polite. Says hi. But the greeting is particularly reserved after how they gushed over Maggie.

My eyes gravitate toward her again. Gramps has one arm over Maggie's shoulders and is telling her some joke that has her completely absorbed.

As we all move toward the elevators, I force myself to talk to Vanessa, but the whole time I'm trying to ignore the sight of Maggie in that form-fitting dress that puts all of her curvaceous assets on display.

Kayla gets my parents and Gramps settled in their rooms while Vanessa, Joe, Maggie, and I wait in the hall.

"It's been a million years, Joe," Maggie teases Joe. "Thought you'd be retired before you popped the question."

He laughs and shakes his head. "I forgot how you love to bust my balls."

Hell, I forgot they knew each other.

Maggie smiles. "Kayla used to talk about you nonstop when she'd babysit my little sister. She told me a long time ago that you were the one."

His eyes grow soft. "I've always been in love with her."

Kayla pops her head into the hallway. "You'd best be talking about me."

"Who else could I possibly love to the point of obsession?" he says before he kisses her forehead.

They smile at each other in such a tender way, I have to look away. It feels like we're intruding on a private moment. I glance at Vanessa, who's shifting awkwardly and edging away from the group.

Maggie, though, hooks her arm through Kayla's. "Y'all are sweet. Good thing you're getting married tomorrow, or the stork might beat down your door before you make it to the minister."

Kayla blushes and gives Joe a look, but before I can tease her, my sister clears her throat and ushers us to our rooms, which are just across the hall.

She swipes the key to mine and opens the door to suite 301. "I guess this is your room and, uh, Vanessa's." Kayla gives me a weird look. "And good news! Maggie is just next door!"

Maggie and I look at each other, and she gives me a big, fake smile. "Awesome."

I don't know what's going on, but I have the distinct feeling I've done something I shouldn't have.

7

MAGGIE

WITH A KNOT IN MY STOMACH, I watch the door to Michael and Vanessa's room shut. What was I thinking? That he'd be by himself this weekend and excited to see me? That he'd want to hang out? That he'd fall at my feet once he saw me in Sienna's dress? That we'd, what, have one of those hot wedding hookups I'm always reading about in the grocery aisle?

I let out a cynical laugh. I feel stupid. Like, 'crawl under a rock and hide for the next year' stupid. When did my hatred of him become this untenable craving? Why did he have to go and do nice things for me? I had him all boxed up as someone who didn't give a shit about me. But then he went out of his way—twice—to help me. Only to later ignore my attempt to thank him.

Michael Oliver is literally making me go insane one slow interaction at a time.

"Sorry about that." Kayla tugs me down the hall.

Ugh. What did she see on my face just now? Kayla is wildly perceptive, unlike her numbskull brother.

I pointedly ignore her suggestion that I was uncomfortable just now. "Have I told you how excited I am to be in your wedding? Just think, K. You're getting the fairytale you always wanted." Her eyes get watery, and I shake my head. "None of that. You can't cry. If you cry, I'll cry. It'll be a vicious cycle."

She laughs and wipes her eyes. "Deal."

I drag my suitcase into my room. It's clean and bright, and I'm already in love with the king-sized bed. "I'm gonna starfish on that mattress the moment you're gone."

Kayla stares at the door along the back wall.

I look around, spot the bathroom, and then turn to look at the door that appears to connect my room to...

"Is that Michael's room?" I whisper.

She winces. "Maybe?"

Great. Now I get to listen to him bang his girlfriend all night.

Lowering her voice, she explains how she had planned to set him up with the bridesmaid who broke her leg. "I thought it was kismet." She juts out her lower lip. "I thought this meant the stars were aligned for you two to make it to the Promised Land."

"Promised Land?"

She tilts her head toward the bed. "I'm pretty sure he forgot he told me I could set him up on a date this weekend."

Perhaps hearing him with his girlfriend is what I need to get him out of my system once and for all. Michael Oliver is not meant for me, and the sooner I learn this lesson, the better.

At the church, Kayla and Joe introduce the members of the bridal party to each other, and then we do a quick run-through. Who am I paired with? Michael, of course.

As each couple walks down the aisle as though Kayla and Joe just got married, I gingerly hold his arm.

"How've you been?"

I'm so stunned he's talking to me, I trip. He steadies me with a hand to the small of my back. Vanessa watches us with a frown on her face.

"I'm good. Thanks. I'm not used to these heels." Sienna packed every single outfit along with matching shoes for the entire weekend. The only clothing that belongs to me is my underwear, and even that's new. Sienna said I couldn't wear these dresses with cotton underwear and made me buy some silky numbers that she said would eliminate panty lines.

"You, um, you look beautiful."

I stop in the middle of the aisle and stare at him. "Did hell freeze over just now and I missed it?"

"Shut up, smartass." He laughs and tugs me toward the back.

"You can't curse in church," I hiss. My mother would have a coronary if she heard him just now. "Look what you did. Now I'm gonna have to say a rosary for you."

His shoulders are shaking, and I'm smiling for some reason. His mom pops out of nowhere and snaps a photo of us. "Aww, look at that. You two are getting along."

Vanessa joins us, and I let go of her boyfriend's arm. She looks out of place, and since I know how that feels all too well, I decide to help her feel welcomed.

"What's your major, Vanessa? You're a student at Lone Star, right? I think I've seen you around campus." She's very attractive with striking red hair and brilliant blue eyes. All the women I've ever seen around Michael have always been gorgeous. Which makes sense because he's ridiculously handsome, especially like this, in a suit.

"Communication." She sniffs and, clinging to Michael's arm, turns away from me.

Okay, then. Maybe she doesn't want to be friends.

One of the groomsmen, a guy by the name of Greg, asks if I need a ride to the restaurant for the rehearsal dinner.

"She can come with us," Michael says.

I'm once again shocked. Is he only being nice to me because we're in a church? Or did his mom threaten life and limb if he wasn't civil to me this weekend?

Judging by Vanessa's expression, she's not excited by the idea of me tagging along. Being cooped up with them isn't my idea of fun either.

"Actually, I'd love a ride," I tell Greg before I turn to Michael. "That way you guys can enjoy your date."

Michael and I have one mode, and it's awkward as hell. No need to torture his girlfriend with our weird vibes.

Throughout dinner, I sit next to Greg and try to concentrate on what he's saying, but my attention keeps drifting to Michael and Vanessa across the table. Their evening doesn't seem to be going well. She's stiff and silent as she picks at her food.

I have no idea how long they've been together. I make a point to never ask Ben or Sienna about him, but now I wish I had because I'm dying to know if this is serious.

Michael gets up and talks to one of the restaurant staff briefly, and I take the opportunity to give him a once-over.

His injury must have healed because he's no longer sporting crutches. His hair is neat and combed out of his face, except for that one lock of hair that has never acquiesced to any styling product and falls rakishly over his left eye. He's lean and tall and fills out his suit like nobody's business.

Greg coughs, and I jump in my seat, uncomfortably aware that I've been staring at Michael for untold minutes now.

Someone taps their silverware against their glass, and the table quiets. Kayla's maid of honor stands and welcomes everyone and explains that we'll go around and share a few things about the couple. Hearing so many people toast Kayla and Joe fills my heart. When it's my turn, I stand and smile at the happy couple.

"Kayla, you were one of the first people I met when my

family moved to town. It was such a sad time for us because my dad had just passed away, but you always brought sunshine and laughter to our home anytime you babysat my sister, who was just a toddler at the time. I have so many memories of you making my mom smile when I didn't think that was possible anymore."

She wipes under her eyes, and my throat tightens. "Anyway, before I turn into a soggy pile of tissues, I just want to say how much I love you and Joe and how excited I am that you're getting your fairytale. Thank you for letting me be a part of your wedding. I'm so honored." I hold up my glass. "To Kayla and Joe and happily ever afters."

Silently, I pray I can find what they have someday. But it feels so far out of reach, especially that night as I lie in bed and listen to Michael bang his girlfriend on the other side of the wall.

Talk about stamina. It goes on forever. *He must be good to make her moan like that.*

Squeezing my eyes shut, I try to block them out.

You just have to get through this weekend, and then you'll never have to see him again. He does a good job of avoiding me, so why wouldn't he continue to do so when we're back in Charming?

I snuggle the cold pillow, and I promise myself this is the last time I get worked up over Michael Oliver.

8

OLLY

THE KNOCK on my door has me groaning. What time is it?

I roll over in bed and reach for my phone on the nightstand. Eight in the morning. I don't have to be anywhere until ten.

"Michael," my mother calls out from the hallway. "Honey, we need to switch back. Our room was too cold, and your dad couldn't figure out how to work the thermostat. We need to hurry before the hairstylist gets here."

Christ. Just what I want to do this morning. Wake up before my alarm and haul my shit back across the hall.

"Yeah. Okay. Give me five minutes," I yell and roll over.

"Don't fall asleep, Michael. I'm serious."

I check my phone. No text from Vanessa, but I'm not surprised.

There's a message from Ben, though. **You should be here, man. Sucks that you're not.**

The combine. Ben, Johnny, and a few other teammates got invited.

I should be grateful for my sister's wedding. It's a good distraction. Although this weekend is not going as planned.

After I tug on some shorts and shoes, I toss my toiletries in my bag and drag my sleepy ass across the hall and back to room 301, which originally was mine. My mom opens the door. "Darling, shouldn't you get dressed before you come out here?"

I shrug. "Do you want me to move your suitcase?" I drop my stuff in a chair. Mom liked the view from my room, so we switched before heading to the rehearsal yesterday.

My dad grabs her from behind, and she giggles and playfully swats at him. "Not in front of the children."

I grab my phone and ignore my parents' flirting until they're gone. But then I spot my mom's favorite lip gloss on the night-stand and head over to 302 to return it.

As I'm swiping the keycard to get back into my room, the door next to mine opens, and out sweeps Maggie wearing some silky, floaty burgundy concoction that makes her look like a princess with her beautiful long hair.

I smile at her, but her reception is decidedly less friendly than it was yesterday. "Hey. How'd you sleep?"

Her eyes narrow at me so sharply, I almost take a step back. "Why? Did you enjoy keeping me up half the night?"

"What?" The emotion on her face catches me off guard.

"Was that payback for something evil I did to you in high school? Consider me warned."

"What are you talking about?"

"Never mind," she mumbles as she stalks off to my sister's suite down the hall.

I don't think I'll ever understand that woman. Flustered, I resolve to stay out of her way. Kayla doesn't need me and Maggie arguing in the middle of her wedding. When Sebastian texts and asks me to keep an eye out for his sister tonight, I'm worried she might stab that eye with a sharp utensil based on the looks she gives me.

By the time I'm standing on the altar, my brain hurts from

trying to figure out what the hell Maggie was bitching at me about.

My eyes slide from my sister to her disgruntled bridesmaid, who's watching the ceremony with a rapt expression.

Maggie loves Kayla. It's obvious she adores my entire family. Is it weird that I wish that affection included me?

Afterward, I escort her down the aisle. I'm admittedly tongue-tied. I never know what to say to this girl, and if I attempt to be courteous, I'm afraid she'll impale me with the very pointy heel of her shoe.

When we reach the courtyard, she releases my arm. I'm about to ask if I did something new to offend her, but I save the question for later when I spot her mom headed for us.

"*Mija!* Don't you look beautiful!" Mrs. Morales says before she turns to me. "Michael, *qué guapo eres!*"

Little Frannie pops out from behind her skirt, and I smile as I watch Maggie scoop her into a hug. "Oh, my goodness! Did you sit through that entire wedding, as quiet as a mouse?"

Frannie nods. "I was good. Really good."

"You sure were, honeybunch. I might have to make you a batch of those organic oatmeal bars you love before I go back to school."

Mrs. Morales smiles. "She had her coloring book. It really helped. Plus I brought those fidget toys she loves."

"Are you guys staying for the reception?" I ask as I lean down to give Mrs. Morales a hug and Frannie a high-five. Frannie only lets her mom and sister hug her, and it's important people respect that.

"I don't want to push our luck. I didn't think we'd be able to pull this off, but we sat in the back. I just wanted to see Kayla's wedding and see you two all dressed up. Can you scoot together for a photo? Every time I visit my daughter, she's wearing torn overalls and has paint in her hair. I need to commemorate this special occasion."

"I don't always have paint in my hair," Maggie grouses as she steps next to me.

Her mom looks at us and motions to get closer.

I whisper to Maggie, "I'm going to put my arm around you. Don't knee me in the balls."

"I can't promise anything."

I almost smile at her acerbic response.

As soon as I drape my arm over her shoulders, I regret it. She smells so damn good, I have to fight the urge to bury my nose in her neck. But spotting her brother Sebastian reminds me why that would be a bad idea.

"Dude!" He holds out his fist, and we do a hand gesture-chest bump combo we came up with when we were in middle school. "Look at you in a tux!"

Then he puts his sister in a headlock. She stands there patiently until he's done giving her a noogie.

"You know I'm not ten, right?" she says before she elbows him in the ribs and smooths down her hair.

"You'll always be my baby sister, turdlette."

"You're barely a year older, Hershey squirt."

I chuckle at their nicknames for each other.

He shrugs. "If I don't look out for you, who will? Speaking of which, you look tired. What's going on?"

Now that he mentions it, I can see it too.

She glances at me and then her eyes dart away. "The people next door kept me up all night."

"Ah. A hotel bang. Got it."

Who had the room on the other side of Maggie? After moving rooms twice and hauling suitcases for several members of the bridal party last night, I'm not sure who's in what suite anymore.

Mrs. Morales gasps. "*Mijo*, we don't discuss those kinds of things *en la casa de Dios*."

After we chat with Bash and Mrs. Morales for a while, my sister herds us together for photos. I'm about to ask Maggie if she'd like a ride to the reception, but Greg beats me to it.

I watch him help her into his car. Sebastian walks up on me silently like a fucking ninja and slaps me on the back. "She's all grown up now. Guess we can't worry about her forever. But if he hurts her, I'll beat his ass."

The whole drive to the hotel, I'm thinking about what Bash said. Is that true? Is he over freaking out about guys making a move on his sister? He was a little psycho about it when we were in high school, but it had to do with how his dad asked him to watch out for Maggie while on his deathbed. I couldn't disrespect that.

When we line up to have the bridal party introduced, I grit my teeth when I find Maggie still talking to Greg. He's all up in her space, and she's letting him.

It's a pleasure to break that up.

"Sorry, guys, but my sister wants us paired with our bridesmaid. Otherwise, the DJ won't have the correct names for the intros."

Greg gives me a look like he thinks I'm full of shit, and I smirk because I'm the lucky asshole who gets to dance with Maggie in a few minutes. Maybe I can figure out what's going on with her.

"Catch up with you again later?" he asks Maggie, who nods.

She and I stand next to each other. Silent and stiff. Awkward as always.

I fucking hate it.

We watch Kayla and Joe twirl around the dance floor. My sister's smiling and staring up at Joe like he's the center of the universe.

I clear my throat. "So you like Greg?"

"What's it to you?" The chill in Maggie's voice makes Siberia sound tropical.

"Just making idle chitchat."

"No need. You can go back to ignoring me."

I face her. "When have I ever, in the history of you and me, *ever* ignored you?"

She rolls her eyes. "Perhaps 'ignore' isn't the right word. Maybe I should say you *avoid* me."

"I don't avoid you."

"Sure. Let's go with that."

The parents are now dancing with the bride and groom. We have a minute, so I grab Magnolia's elbow and tug her into a nearby hall. "What's your problem?"

"My problem?" she hisses. "Didn't you know? It's always been you. You have some damn nerve, acting like you and Vanessa didn't keep me up half the night. Pretending you didn't know your room was right next door to mine."

I still, my feet rooted to the ground. "What are you talking about? Vanessa left last night."

She scoffs. "Someone was howling, 'oh, Daddy, hit it harder' on the other side of my wall. I seem to recall you had that room. In fact, I saw you open that door this morning, half-clothed, so don't lie."

Oh, shit. I laugh, relieved as hell, now that I understand why her feathers are all ruffled.

"Michael Oliver, don't you dare laugh at me." Her face is flushed, and she looks like she might deck me. She's beautiful in her fury. Ready to bust me up if I'm not careful. Makes me want to kiss the hell out of her.

I hold up both hands. "Just listen, okay?"

"Michael Oliver and Magnolia Morales!"

Her eyes get huge when we hear our names boom over the loudspeaker. "That was our intro! Crap."

I grab her hand as we press pause on our bickering and race out to the dance floor.

"Somewhere Only We Know" by Keane plays in the background as I pull her into my arms. She's stiff and obviously still pissed at me.

"Relax, Maggie. I'm not gonna bite you."

It's a strange experience to finally hold her. I might've been Bash's friend first and initially viewed Maggie as a little sister, but I remember the day that changed. From the moment she strolled up on my lawn on a blisteringly hot summer day with a scraped knee when she was thirteen and I was fourteen, I've wondered what it would be like to make this girl mine. To hold her when she cried. To be the reason she smiled. To have the words to make her laugh.

I ruthlessly locked away those urges. Sebastian was my best friend. In our small town world, you don't mess with your buddy's little sister. At the time, I didn't know exactly what that meant. I just liked the way Maggie always smiled when I caught her looking. Like a toy secreted away in my pocket, I wanted that.

Except I learned to look away when she turned my way. Pretended I didn't light up inside when she was around. Dated other girls when I wondered what it would be like to ask out Bash's beautiful sister.

It's something I try not to think about—what might have been.

When Maggie doesn't respond, I lean close to whisper in her ear. "Vanessa wasn't enjoying herself, and she obviously didn't click with my family. We both agreed it was best to go our separate ways. So she left last night."

Her wary eyes meet mine, and she studies me for a long

moment, probably to see if I'm telling the truth. "So you're telling me that wasn't you having an extra-loud hotel bang next door?"

"Hate to disappoint you, but it wasn't." I chuckle and then groan at what that means. "You heard my parents going at it like horny teenagers." I explain how we switched rooms last night and then switched back this morning.

She stops dancing. "If you're lying to me..."

"I swear to God, you heard Wendy and Ted burning up the sheets."

Our heads swivel to stare at my parents, who are dancing, swaying slowly and staring into each other's eyes like they're thinking about all the dirty things they did last night.

"Gah!" Maggie covers her ears. "I can't un-hear all of that."

Laughing, I pull her into my arms again. "Mags, I know you're slightly traumatized. We all are the first time we hear Wendy and Ted in beast mode. You'll need to avoid making eye contact for a while."

She giggles and rests her forehead on my chest. I have the strangest urge to kiss her hair.

Maggie's face is flushed, and she can't stop laughing as we finish the dance. When the next slow song comes on, I don't let her go, and she doesn't try to get away.

"How about this?" I whisper in her ear. "Let's call a truce. Just one night where we don't bicker or fight or try to get even. Call me crazy, but let's pretend we're friends."

Her hands lock around the back of my neck as we sway to the music. "A truce, huh?"

"What's the worst thing that could happen?"

9

MAGGIE

THE WHOLE TIME we eat dinner and dessert, I'm acutely aware of Michael's presence next to me. His knee presses into mine, and I smile.

"Just admit you left that tuna sandwich in my car," he says in my ear.

"Will you be mad if I tell you I did it?"

"No. I'm sure I did something shitty to deserve the retribution."

My smile widens. I'm not used to having Michael agree with me. He usually argues for the sake of arguing.

He motions to my brother, who is sneaking off with one of the bridesmaids. "Another wedding hookup on the books, ladies and gentlemen."

I laugh. "Those are supposed to be the best kind of hookups," I say as though I have any experience with these sort of things. I don't, but I've read plenty of *Cosmo* articles on the topic. "Everyone goes their separate ways the next day, so there are no awkward run-ins later. Half the time, it's a great excuse to do what you've always wanted to anyway."

"I mean, how are you supposed to resist all of this romantic stuff, right? Candle lights and slow songs."

"Booze and cake."

He nods and holds up his empty glass to mine, and we clink. "Booze and cake. That's romantic shit right there."

"Absolutely. There's no resisting it," I say slowly as I look into his captivating blue eyes.

"As if that's even possible," he whispers as he stares at my lips.

The rest of the night is spent dancing and laughing with the bridal party on the dance floor. And while Gramps asks me for a slow dance and Greg takes me for a whirl once, Michael gets the rest of the slow songs.

With the dim lights, a little champagne, and the romantic backdrop, I'm having a hard time keeping my walls up. I have to admit that I'm having more fun with Michael than I've had on any date.

Not that this is a date exactly.

Just a truce.

Which reminds me.

"Michael Oliver, did you have groceries delivered to my door via my neighbor, or did I imagine that?" The deer-in-the-headlights expression on his face makes me laugh.

"Will you be mad if I admit that was me?"

"Why would I be mad?"

He shrugs. "You like to do things on your own. Didn't want to mess with your girl power vibe." Girl power vibe? "Plus, we'd had that horrible conversation at the store. Didn't want to upset you again, but at the same time, I couldn't stop worrying that maybe you needed some groceries."

I'm momentarily speechless. As we sway to the music, I dust off some lint on his tux. "You know, I baked you a pie and left it on your doorstep to thank you. Did you get it?"

He stops moving. Tilts his head. Growls. "Johnny ate my damn pie!"

His outrage puts another smile on my face. "It probably wasn't even that good."

"Everyone knows you're a damn good cook, Maggie."

Little flutters fill my belly at the compliment, and I make a mental note to bake him another one.

When Kayla and Joe take off, everyone lines up outside with sparklers. Everyone except for my brother and his bridesmaid, who are probably upstairs getting freaky. Which... I'm not gonna think about. Realizing I overheard Mr. and Mrs. Oliver going at it like animals is enough for me to handle for one weekend.

Finding out it wasn't Michael and Vanessa banging away sent a shockwave of relief through me. I was ready to deck him for tormenting me like that. It's always been hard for me to think about him dating other women, but actually hearing it was torture.

Which makes me realize I care about him way more than I should.

I sigh as I watch Joe twirl Kayla between the two rows of sparklers. I want that. Someone who'll be my person. Someone who doesn't care how wacky I can be sometimes. Someone who wants me no matter what.

Before Kayla hops in the limo, she yells, "Don't forget about golf tomorrow. Tee's at ten. If I'm late, though"—she waves her thumb behind her—"you know why!"

Everyone laughs as we watch them speed away.

A warm hand tugs at my wrist, and I turn to find Michael, who pulls me close. "Wanna hang out?"

Now that everyone is returning to the ballroom or heading home, standing out here in the dark with Michael feels particularly intimate. "What did you have in mind?"

He thinks about it a minute. "I heard there's a jacuzzi on the back patio. We could go for a midnight swim?"

I laugh and run my finger over his bow tie. "I didn't bring a swimsuit. Would you have any objection to me taking a dip in my underwear?"

A devilish grin spreads on his lips. "Meet you at the pool in ten?"

This is going to be either the best decision I've ever made or the worst.

"See you in ten."

As THE COOL air cuts through the wedding fog, reality sets in.

Am I really going to do this? Have some quasi-clothed swim session with Bash's little sister?

This is Magnolia Morales we're talking about. Not some football groupie who parties at the house every weekend and wants to let off some steam.

Maggie. Who's hated me for years.

Stone-cold fox Maggie, who slowly drove me crazy tonight in that little dress of hers.

I'm sitting on the ledge of the jacuzzi, having a crisis of conscience, when the sliding doors to the pool area open.

My mouth goes dry when Maggie steps out of the shadows in a thin robe and a shy smile. She holds out towels in one hand and a bottle of champagne in the other. "Think your sister will mind I snagged a beverage?"

I cough, my throat totally dry. "Not at all."

Was I dumb enough to question my good luck a moment ago? Because I'd have to be a fucking fool to walk away from this. Thank God for the Texas weather, because if it was any colder, I never would've thought to do this.

I pat the ledge next to me. "Water's warm."

She hands me the bottle, drops the spare towel, and slowly unwraps herself.

I'm gonna be honest here. I've imagined what Maggie would look like unclothed a few times, and my imagination never did her justice.

The robe falls to the ground revealing a pair of gorgeous, high, round breasts, covered in a thin, semi-translucent bra. A curvy waist. A dainty pair of panties in that same thin material. Muscular, smooth thighs.

But then she unwinds her hair from the updo, and it comes tumbling down in a mass of curls.

Jesus Christ. She's gorgeous. Literally the most beautiful woman I've ever seen.

And she's out here tonight with me.

I lean forward to hide the instant erection tenting my swim trunks.

Before I freak her out with my body's reaction, I slide into the water. As she dips her toe in, goosebumps break out on her skin, making her nipples stand at attention, and I wonder what it would be like to pull those luscious buds into my mouth. Graze them with my teeth. Lick them until she cried out.

Can a man die from anticipation? I think there's a strong likelihood.

As she slides into the water like a mermaid, I pop open the champagne because I need a drink.

Full confession: I'm not a hundred percent sure Maggie is into me.

Maybe she has a wild side I've never known about, and taking a dip in the middle of the night in her underwear is not a play to hook up.

Maybe she's had a stressful week and just wants to relax in the jacuzzi.

Maybe she didn't know I was flirting with her on the dance floor. It's possible. Hell, most of the men at the reception did double-takes when she walked by. There's no good reason I'd catch her attention.

After the cork goes flying, I chug a few sips.

"Are you nervous?" she asks quietly, and I finally turn to look at her. Her thick hair bubbles up in the hot water and floats around her like mist.

I always try to be truthful, so even though I'd love to play it cool right now, I go with honesty. "Yes, I'm nervous. I don't want to do anything that ruins our truce." I take her hand and pull her closer. She surprises me when she straddles my lap. My hands land on her waist. Her arms drape over my shoulders.

Dark, serious eyes study mine. "Maybe we should seal our truce with something," she says softly.

"A handshake?" I tease as I brush her nose with mine before I tuck my face against her shoulder. Fuck, she smells so good. Like ripe strawberries and temptation.

She snuggles closer and presses her hips to mine. My erection nestles against her stomach, and I close my eyes, hoping I'm not moving too fast.

"I mean, we *could* shake hands," she whispers in my ear as she presses her beautiful tits against my chest.

I let my hands slide down her hips to rest on her ass, which gloriously fills both of my hands. "Or..."

"Or... maybe we could try something sweeter."

My mind instantly goes to what's behind that thin strip of fabric between her thighs. That seems pretty sweet to me. "Mags, everything about you is sweet. Gonna need you to be a bit more specific."

She grazes her teeth on my neck. Swipes my skin with her tongue.

For the love of God. I don't think I've ever been this turned on before.

"Maybe we seal our truce with a kiss," she says in my ear.

It must be the champagne, because I throw caution to the wind. "Can I choose where to place that kiss?"

We're nose to nose, the dark night drowning out the rest of the world, and I'm about to kiss *the* Magnolia Morales when a flashlight beams in our faces.

"Kids, the pool area closed two hours ago," a stern voice says. "Gonna need y'all to get out."

11

MAGGIE

LAUGHING, we run hand in hand through the hotel. We're both wet, so we're slipping and sliding on the tile as we cling to our towels and bottle of champagne and each other.

"Oh, my God, watch your knee!"

"Ten-four." Michael pauses. "But it doesn't hurt."

"Okay, then hurry up!"

My heart races when I hear the magical sound of the keycard unlocking his door. We're barely inside his room when he pushes me against the wall and kisses me.

The world stops spinning on its axis while my heart pounds. It's finally happening. I'm finally kissing Michael Oliver.

And it's every bit as magical as I'd always hoped it would be.

In my frenzy to get closer, I dig my hands into his hair, hike my leg over his hip, and suck on his tongue.

A groan rumbles his chest as he thrusts his huge bulge against me. And when I say huge, I mean, holy crap, that thing might affect the Earth's gravitational pull.

"Fuck, Maggie. This is crazy."

I don't know if that means he thinks this is a great idea or the worst, but he doesn't stop kissing me, and that's all that matters.

His big hand finds my breast, and he gives it a squeeze. I shiver against him, overwhelmed by finally being the object of his attention.

In the low light streaming through the large window on the opposite side of the room, I can make out the bed.

Sliding out, I fling off my bra before I flop back on the crisp sheets. Thankfully, I remembered to remove the Band-Aids from my boobs before I snuck down to the pool area. "Come here and warm me up. It's so cold, my nipples are going to pop off."

"We can't have that. I'll warm you up." But he doesn't budge, just stands over me and stares.

I do a little staring myself. Michael might've been injured, but he's obviously working out whatever he's allowed to because he's ripped. Big, broad shoulders. A beautifully sculpted chest. Rock-hard abs. Thick thighs.

Let's not forget that other thick part of him I'm dying to explore.

"You've come a long way since band camp," I tease as I flip my hair back.

He smirks. "I could say the same about you."

"You didn't know I was alive back then."

As he moves over me, he tilts his head. "I wouldn't say that." He starts to lower himself, but winces.

"Your knee?"

"Pinches a little."

I push him back with my palm. He immediately flops onto his back, so I crawl over him and sit on his stomach. "Does it still hurt?"

His eyes are lasered on my tits that peek out from behind my curtain of damp hair. "I... what?"

Laughter spills from me. "You're a boob man, huh?" I grab mine in my hands and squeeze my nipples.

"Jesus, Maggie. You've already exceeded all my dreams about

you. Not sure how much more I can handle."

I watch him for a moment. Is he pulling my leg? "You had dreams? About me?"

"So many. A ridiculous number of dreams." His hands graze my thighs, and I shimmy back until that giant bulge rests beneath me.

"Dirty ones?" I ask as I grind down on him.

He smirks and thrusts up. "The kind that left me with damp sheets in the morning."

Shock and delight spear through me. I try to play it cool, but I doubt I'm fooling anyone. "Starting... in college?"

He looks down, glances up at me, and shakes his head. "Before that. Way before that."

I frown, wondering how I missed his interest. I was in love with this big idiot for years before I decided to move on with Luke. Luke, whom he sabotaged.

Definitely going to need to investigate that at some point, but not when I have this blue-eyed Adonis almost naked beneath me for the first time. I remind myself of the nice things he's done for me this year. That's enough for me to table the Luke discussion.

All of a sudden, I want to know what tonight will mean. If we'll be more than just a crazy hookup at his sister's wedding.

But if one night is all he wants, would that change anything?

I drag my hand down his sculpted chest as I think about it.

No. Nothing changes.

That reckless, eager part of me wants this, whatever it is, however I can get it. Even if it's only one night.

"Everything okay?" he asks softly.

"Someone said something about warming me up. Now I'm wondering if that was just an empty promise."

"Get over here."

And he drags me down until my lips meet his.

12

OLLY

Maggie's luscious body presses against me, and she lets out a moan that makes me so fucking hard. I flip her under me, and she cradles me between her thighs.

"What about your knee?"

"It's fine. I promise."

If it's not, she's gonna have to sit on my face because there's no way I'm forgoing this particular pleasure. I kiss my way down her body. Lick her collarbone. Nibble on her beautiful full breast. Pull it between my lips and suck in time to my thrusts.

Her hand fists my hair, and I smile against her, surprised that I like that bite of pain. By the time I work my way lower, she's panting.

She must use a scented lotion because every inch of her smells like delicious ripe berries. I drag my lips over her hip bone and lick the inner crease of her thigh. Her whole body goes taut. When I glance up, the sight before me has me reaching down to give myself a good hard tug.

Maggie's laid out before me like a decadent dish. Lush hips. Tiny waist. Full tits. Tight, bite-sized nipples pointing straight up. Her thick hair splayed out beneath her.

Gorgeous.

The scent of warm woman draws me back to the task at hand—making Maggie lose her mind.

I'm a very goal-oriented person.

I drag my finger over her mound. Her underwear is so thin, it's already mostly dry from the jacuzzi. Except in one spot.

"Your panties are soaked." Fuck, that's hot.

Before she can say anything, I lick the damp fabric, her sweet scent making me crazy the moment I get a taste of her. I gently tug the panties until they slip between her slick lips that I suck one at a time.

Her knees come up on either side of my head as I lick all around that mound. Over her hot opening.

I'm gonna tease us both into early graves if I'm not careful.

"Michael," she gasps when I graze her swollen clit.

She shivers and quakes beneath me, which breaks my resolve to go slow. I slide her panties to the side and give her a long lick that has her mewling in the darkness.

I slip one finger in her tight, wet heat. Then two. Her back arches, and I watch as she pinches her nipples.

Christ, she's incredible. Who knew that under all that acerbic humor was this spicy little vixen?

I pump my fingers into her as I lave her swollen clit. With a gasp, she fists my hair and holds me to her as she screams. Pulsing on my fingers and tongue, she comes long and hard.

"That's it, baby." I work her down from her climax and laugh when her arms and legs flop to the bed.

"You've killed me. I'm dead."

Gently, I remove my hand and lick her cum off my fingers.

When I look up, I see her watching me. "You're a dirty boy. I like. Now come here."

I crawl up the bed and sprawl out on my side. Resting my

head in my hand, I take in the ethereal creature lying in my bed. A dark flush stains her cheeks, and her eyes are drowsy.

Leaning down, I kiss her. "We can call it a night if you... if you're tired." My balls might explode, but I don't want to pressure her if she's not comfortable doing more.

"Shut up and lie back."

Laughing, I obey, because she's hot as fuck when she's bossy. A naked Magnolia crawls over me. "Condom?"

Please, God, let me have one in my suitcase. I point toward my bag. "Toiletry bag."

I watch her trot her beautiful ass across my room, but when she bends over, I groan and kick off my swim trunks. With a tight fist, I jerk off while Maggie shakes her round bum one way and then the other as she looks for the foil package.

Finally, she holds up her hand. "Found it!" She settles over me again, rips it with her teeth, and tries to roll it down my length. "Why doesn't this work?" Frustration furrows her brow, but I'm distracted by watching her handle my cock.

My brain cells eventually kick in. "Maybe it's backwards."

She flips it around. "You're brilliant."

I am, aren't I? Because I'm pretty sure this is the smartest thing I've ever done.

When she sinks over me like a wild goddess, all tousled and slick and very, *very* tight, my breath catches in my throat. It's a heady realization that I, a lowly man of no means, might be able to bang the fuck out of this gorgeous woman.

Thank you, universe.

Time to make her come again.

Slowly, she lifts herself up and down, and I watch those beautiful tits bounce. Her wild, damp hair clings to her skin.

She's a vision. So beautiful. So sensual. A fantasy come to life.

Reaching under her, I grab the round globes of her ass and

help her ride me. I bring her down harder. Faster. She moans and reaches between her legs to frantically rub her swollen clit.

The bed squeaks and lurches under our weight. We're a tangle of limbs and slick skin and desperation to get closer.

It isn't until she's chanting my name and pulsing around my cock that I finally let myself go. I moan her name and hold her tight as my release hits.

We're a cosmic explosion. An interstellar collision of heat and particles that's all-consuming.

And somewhere deep inside my chest, I know I'll never be the same again.

13

OLLY

Is someone knocking?

Groggy and half-asleep, I squint into the harsh morning light, and I'm immediately reminded of exactly what happened last night.

Maggie is sprawled over me. Her tits are pressed to my chest. One slender thigh is tucked between mine. And one round ass cheek rests under my palm.

Is it possible to wake up like this every morning of my life? I chuckle to myself as I spit out a strand of her hair.

She shifts and groans and wiggles closer, which my morning wood finds enticing.

"Babe." I kiss her forehead. "Mags. We probably need to get up."

I can hear my phone buzzing on the nightstand. How it made it there, I'm not sure. Last night is a blur of sex and champagne and laughter.

Christ, last night was incredible. In between all the sex, Maggie and I talked and talked. It felt like a dam unleashed in my chest to finally connect with this woman.

"I can't move," she rasps against my chest. "You broke me."

"Are you sore, sweetheart?" She feels so damn good in my arms. I'm loath to move.

She grinds on my thigh and lifts her head. "Not *that* sore." With a mischievous grin, she reaches under the sheet and takes me in hand.

A loud knock on the door has us both jumping.

"Olly, dude! Get your ass up," Sebastian shouts. "Your girl-friend's here."

I freeze, unsure what troubles me more—having Maggie's brother on the other side of that door while his sister was seconds away from jerking me off, or Vanessa returning. Why is she back? I thought we were done.

"You said you broke up!" Maggie whispers as she yanks the sheet to her chest.

"We did. Boy Scout's Honor." I hold up three fingers. I'm an Eagle Scout. I take that shit seriously.

Bash bangs again. "You up, man? Let me in. We gotta talk."

My eyes widen. He might have said he needed to let his little sister grow up, but that probably doesn't mean he wants to walk in on her naked in his best friend's bed.

"Your brother is gonna kill me, Magnolia. Get up." I leap out of bed, freaked out by the twinge in my knee. Did I overexert it last night? Jesus, how hard did I thrust? "What the hell did I do?"

Gingerly, I test my knee. I'm pissed I lost my head in a frenzy of lust. Is there anything more important than my recovery? As amazing as last night was, if I fuck up my knee, my football career is over. All of the plans I've made for my future and the future of my family are over.

Bash is mumbling about Coach Nicholson, but once I make sure my knee is okay, just a little sore, I start running toward the bathroom. Maggie's got a wild-eyed, panicked look in her eyes that needs no explanation. I motion over my shoulder in what I hope she understands is a signal for 'I'm gonna wash off the smell of sex before your brother kills me and buries me in a field.'

I race into the bathroom and take the world's fastest shower. I don't even wait for the hot water to engage, just pour soap all over myself and rinse it off. I'm out in sixty seconds—after I'm sure I no longer smell like Sebastian's little sister.

I'll tell Bash what happened, but I need a day or two to process everything. I'm not good at spur-of-the-moment decisions. Wrapped in a towel, I step back into the bedroom, ready to tell Maggie that maybe we should wait until we're back in Charming to tell Sebastian about us, but she's gone, the door to her room closed.

Even better. I'll deal with Bash, get rid of Vanessa, and then I'll hunt down Maggie. She's probably more freaked out by her brother showing up first thing in the morning than I am.

I open my door, and Bash laughs at me. "Put some clothes on, you savage."

He hands me a coffee and strolls into my room. Panicked, I look around, eyes widening when I realize the headboard is sitting askew and there's an empty condom wrapper on the bed. I need to get him out of here, because there should be two more of those, and I have no idea if they made it to the trash.

"Sebastian," I say to get his attention. Fortunately, he turns toward me and away from the bed. "Let me dress, and I'll meet you downstairs in ten." He gives me a look, probably because he's seen me naked in the locker room plenty of times. There's no room for modesty in there. I make a face. "Gotta floss. You really shouldn't neglect your gums."

"Just thought you might want to talk about the Coach Nicholson news."

What news?

Before I can ask, he pats me on the shoulder. "And by the

way, while we're alone, just wanted to thank you for hanging out with Maggie last night." Guilt settles in my gut like a boulder for not coming right out and telling him I have a thing for his sister. "I know she drives you batshit. Thanks for doing me that favor."

Internally, I wince. Thank God Maggie already went next door. Who knows how she'd interpret that? I need to tread carefully with her. We've antagonized each other for years. It'll take time to build her trust in me, and if she hears her brother, it might undo some of the headway we made this weekend.

I'm two seconds from confessing all of my sins, in the most G-rated form I can manage, when someone else knocks on my door.

"Olly, it's me." Vanessa's voice settles over me like the call of doom.

Why is she here? We said all we had to say the other night.

And then it hits me. How I tried to let her down easily by saying if she wanted to talk some more, we could meet up again. I meant back in Charming. Not here at my sister's brunch.

Can this morning get any worse?

14

MAGGIE

WITH MY EAR pressed to the door between our rooms, I hear everything. How Bash made Michael hang out with me this weekend. How Michael acts like nothing happened between us. How he has no intention of telling my brother about us. Probably because he's still dating Vanessa.

She's in his room now. "Thanks for inviting me to brunch, Olly. That was so sweet of you."

I could puke.

In a rage, I toss on some clothes and fling everything else in my suitcase. How could he? I should march in there and tell my brother what happened, because he'd kick Michael's ass into the next town if he knew the truth.

Angrily, I slam my suitcase shut and admit to myself that I could never let that go down. Last night might not mean anything to Michael, but it meant everything to me. And to find out he was just sowing his wild oats? Cheating on his girlfriend? Leading me on? It's devastating.

For the first time, I thought I was really connecting with a man, with someone I could see in my life. Finding out he's the worst kind of scum has me trembling.

He said it himself. *What the hell did I do?*

Maybe he feels bad for cheating. He should, that lousy rat.

That had to be what he meant by those words, right? What else could it mean?

Because if he isn't dating Vanessa, why didn't he correct my brother?

When the voices dim and I realize Michael isn't coming back to explain why his ex showed up at his hotel room, I'm apoplectic.

I feel so fucking stupid. Why did I think he was a different person? He bought me groceries, and I let that erase years of animosity. Was last night merely a way to get back at me? To get the last laugh? I have a hard time thinking he'd sink to that level, but perhaps I'm being naive.

Not for the first time, Michael Oliver has pulled the wool over my eyes.

Never again.

15

OLLY

MY MOUTH DROPS OPEN. Coach Nicholson just accepted a three-year contract. *With another team.*

Had I been answering my phone last night, I would've heard. I have a million messages from my teammates, but I was so wrapped up in Maggie that the rest of the world dimmed.

Vanessa's brow crinkles. "I figured you might want to talk about it." She and Sebastian and I are seated on the terrace of the hotel's restaurant. I keep looking around, waiting for Maggie to show up. Hoping she won't think something more is going on between me and Vanessa.

I have no idea what I'll say to her or Sebastian. I should just go with the truth. That I'm crazy about his sister.

Vanessa clears her throat. "My dad says you should come over for dinner this week."

Why would I want to do that?

She must see the confusion on my face. "So you guys can talk about what this means for your scholarship, silly."

It takes me a full minute to connect the dots, but when I do it nearly stops the beat of my heart.

Her father is the athletic director.

And while the incoming coach makes the final decision about how those eighty-five scholarships get distributed to the one hundred and fifteen players on the team, the AD *might* be able to have some input. I know all of this based on the coaching situation last year.

Holy shit. Talking to Maggie is the least of my problems right now.

Sebastian gives me a hard look for some reason. "Good thing your girlfriend is looking out for you."

My insides twist like I've been knifed by this falsehood. I can't even take a drink of my coffee because I'm nauseous.

Worse? Vanessa beams at him like we're actually still dating.

Am I going crazy? Did Vanessa and I not have a conversation two nights ago where we parted ways amicably? Why is she here playing the devoted girlfriend all of a sudden?

I open my mouth to correct Sebastian and clarify things for Vanessa when my parents and several members of the bridal party join us on the terrace.

I scan the group, eager to see Magnolia and tell her what's going on with my situation. Use that as the opportunity to show Vanessa that I've moved on. Instead, I spot Greg, who gives me a head nod. I follow him off to the side.

"Hey, man." His voice lowers. "Saw Maggie on the way out this morning. She looked pretty upset."

Oh, shit. Did she leave? Jesus Christ, I've messed this up already.

He smirks. "She gave me a message for you."

My stomach sinks. This can't be good.

He smacks me on the back, and his smile turns brittle. "She said you should go to hell."

∽

Pacing my small bedroom back in Heartland, I can't believe I'm resorting to this—taking advice from my roommate Johnny. But Ben and Sienna are out of town, my sister is on her honeymoon, and it's not like I can get advice about this from Sebastian.

"You're so fucked, man," Johnny says.

I freeze with my phone next to my ear. My life must be car-wreck level devastation for him to say those words. "You're supposed to be my wingman. Why would you say that?"

"Were you really planning to tell the AD's daughter that you're now sleeping with Bash's little sister? Are you insane? One word to her father, and he could zap your scholarship into oblivion." He takes a big puff of what I'm guessing is a fat joint and in his stoner voice says, "Gotta play that shit cool, bro. No need to wreck your career over a woman."

On one hand, he makes sense. Maggie and I are barely a blip on the map. It was one night. One scorchingly hot night.

On the other, this is fucking Magnolia Morales we're talking about. Now that I've had a taste of her, I don't think I can get her out of my system. I'm not sure I want to.

Furthermore, I'm not the kind of man who can date another woman simply because her father might negatively affect my career if I don't go out with his daughter. I try to have integrity. It's why I broke up with Amelia last fall.

"Keep shit in player mode," Johnny continues. "No need to lock yourself down. You're young. Be free. No one would fault you for keeping your options open."

I frown. I could never do that. It's like he doesn't even know me.

"And you haven't heard from Maggie?" he asks on another puff.

"Shouldn't you lay off the weed?"

"I waited until the combine was over. Now I'm giving myself two days to get high and get laid. Then it's back to training. You know the drill. Besides, it's spring break. Gotta live a little. All work and no play makes Johnny a dull boy."

It's his life. And as I've learned, Johnny likes to learn things the hard way. "I've left Maggie a million messages. She doesn't pick up when I call and doesn't text back. Leaves me on read."

"Brutal."

Thank you. Finally, some sympathy.

I scrub my face. "I actually girded my balls and asked Sebastian for her number. He patted me on the back and told me I was a good friend. Like I'm doing him some big favor being friendly with Maggie. I felt like such an ass."

"No doubt." Why am I having a heart-to-heart with Johnny? He's terrible at this. "Want my advice?"

Why else would I be calling you, dude?

"Stay away from Magnolia. Have you considered that Sebastian deliberately gave you the wrong number?"

If that's not a headfuck kind of question, I don't know what is.

Does Sebastian really think I'd be bad for his sister?

"So I shouldn't resort to standing under her window and begging her to talk to me?"

"Fuck that. No way, man. Keep your shit together. Rehab your knee. Bag some babes. Find your inner chi."

I don't even know what the hell he's saying right now.

Before I forget... "Hey, asshole, remember when you found that random pie on the porch? That was for me. Maggie made it to thank me for the groceries."

"And it was damn good. Sorry you missed it." He doesn't sound sorry at all.

When I get off the phone, I'm no closer to figuring out what's going on with Magnolia or what I should do to get her to talk to me than I was an hour ago.

"Honey, it's dinner time," my mom calls from the other

room, reminding me I won't be back in Charming for several days.

Gramps is having several toes amputated, and he'll need around-the-clock care. He was waiting for Kayla's wedding to pull the trigger, but his doctor called this morning and said he shouldn't put it off any longer. I need to stick around to help my parents take care of him and make sure Gramps is stable, which means I won't get a chance to grovel under Maggie's window for a while.

I just hope she responds to my texts before then so I don't go out of my mind in the meanwhile.

16

MAGGIE

WITH VICIOUS MOVEMENTS, I scrub the floor. I'm on my hands and knees, covered in sweat and grime, determined to focus on the task at hand. I'm going to finish renovating the hardwood on the second floor if it kills me.

But thoughts of what happened last weekend hover in the back of my mind like a lingering migraine.

Because it's been nine fucking days.

Nine. Days.

And still no calls from Michael.

In my weaker moments, I've cried or obsessed over how incredible the sex was.

In my stronger moments, I've fantasized about getting one of those voodoo dolls, dressing it like Michael Oliver, and plucking off all of his limbs.

Could I dig up his number and call him? Sure. But I have too much pride to break down and do that. He was the one who paraded another woman at the brunch within *hours* of fucking me. After telling me how special he thought I was. After saying he'd always liked me.

After I foolishly thought he was what I'd been looking for,

the kind of man I wanted long-term.

Was everything just a ruse to get me in bed?

Was he telling me the truth about overhearing his parents going at it, or was he really banging Vanessa?

That thought really sent me over the edge.

Just when I started to calm down, Sebastian called and gave me all the details about Michael's "great girlfriend." He went on and on about how Vanessa was such a sweetheart and so beautiful and how she was looking out for his bro's best interests.

I was tempted to tell Bash how his "bro" fucked his little sister into oblivion Saturday night. Three times.

In fact, I just got over the whisker burn on my thighs.

I've only slept with boyfriends—three to be exact—and none of them worked my body the way Michael did.

And that's the rub. How could the sex make me levitate in pleasure if it was just a wham, bam, thank you, ma'am?

Seeing as how he didn't call me, I guess we'll never know.

But the nail in the coffin came yesterday afternoon when I saw him and Vanessa seated in the corner of the Rise 'N' Grind Coffee House, looking as cozy as could be. Chitchatting and smiling. Blissfully unaware that I was plotting to slash their tires.

I didn't, of course—I'm not a psycho—and I only let myself fantasize about that for a few hours before I went to the gym and worked out until I could barely move.

If there's an upshot to being incensed, it's how much energy it's given me to work out and repair my house. I'm trying to get as much done as I can before my new internship starts. I'm not sure how I'll juggle everything, but at least being busy might keep my mind off that douchebag.

The weather has gotten cold again, so I've given up on my plan to weed my yard. Hopefully I won't get another notice from the city about it. Apparently, some of my neighbors are less than pleased with the state of my property. But seeing how the yard is covered in frost, there's nothing I can do about it now.

And since I can't afford to prime and paint the exterior of the house, which is dependent on the porch I don't have the funds to repair, I have to settle for fixing what I can.

Thus the floors.

In the weeks following the wedding, I don't hear from Michael, but you know who does call? Greg.

17

OLLY

THREE WEEKS, fifty-seven texts, and a dozen calls later, I'm over it. Magnolia obviously has a bug up her ass and no amount of groveling will change that.

By the time I got back from the spring break I spent cleaning up my grandfather's vomit, I had second thoughts about standing under Maggie's window and shouting apologies.

Because what could she really be pissed about? I told her shit with Vanessa was over, and I meant it. Instead of having dinner with her father, I went to talk to him during his office hours.

I ran into Vanessa when I got back from Heartland and explained, again, that we were only friends. She said she understood, but still wanted to hang out. Which... Now I'm wondering, why not? Since Maggie has all but told me to fuck off.

Was Maggie mad I didn't tell Sebastian I'd had her on all fours and railed her over the side of the bed? Upset I didn't run over and bang on her door moments after having my world fall out from under me with news about Coach Nicholson?

I don't pretend to understand women on a good day, and

Magnolia Morales has me at a total loss. Considering what we did that night, couldn't she do me the courtesy of returning one of my calls?

After wondering if Sebastian had tried to sabotage me and deliberately give me the wrong number, I reconsidered. He's been super-chill. When he gets upset about his siblings, his composure is the first thing to go. At the end of the day, I don't think he'd be underhanded like that.

I'm not sure how I'll handle running into Maggie. I keep expecting to see her at Ben and Sienna's, but Sienna told me Maggie got an internship and can't babysit anymore. I wonder if that's her way to further avoid me.

Damn, I've never been ghosted before. Can't say it's a pleasant feeling.

"Chill, dude," Johnny says from the chin-up bar next to me. "You go any harder on those weights, you're gonna hurt something."

With a grunt, I drop the dumbbells.

"What am I missing?" I ask myself. "What could she possibly be that upset about?"

"Jesus H. Christ. Are you still hung up on Magnolia? Bro, grow a pair. She's not interested. She got what she wanted." He waves at my crotch, which makes me want to punch him in the face. Because that's not like Maggie at all. "And she moved on. In my own way, I admire her ability to not get attached." Pointing at his phone, he smirks. "Would it be okay if I called her?"

I clench my fist. "Over my dead body."

The asshole chuckles. "Just kidding. I'd never do you dirty like that."

An hour later, I'm on my way home when I can't fucking stand it any longer. I haven't a clue what I'll say to Magnolia if she picks up, but I want to try one last time.

I pull over to the side of the road and, with my heart in my throat, dial her name.

Four rings later, someone picks up.

"Maggie, don't hang up. Please hear me out."

A deep, masculine voice clears his throat. "Is this Michael?"

"Who the fuck is this?"

He snickers. "Just a friend. Listen, Imma do you a solid. This is not Maggie's number."

I freeze and try to process his words. I double-check who I dialed, and sure enough, it's Maggie's contact info on the screen of my phone. "What do you mean? I've left her a million messages. Were they all going to you?"

"Yup. And I gotta say, your night sounded hot as hell." He lets out a whistle. "But I think your girl Maggie got her one-and-done and ghosted ya."

I'm going to be sick. "She didn't give me her number."

"See? Case in point."

"No, that's not what I mean. Her brother gave me her number. And I guess... I guess I punched it in wrong. Or I misheard. I don't fucking know except it's been weeks now. Jesus, if she wasn't pissed at me before, she is now."

"Tough cojones, brother. Listen, by any chance are you Michael Oliver, the running back on the team? You go by the nickname Olly?"

I close my eyes and tilt my head back. Great. Just what I need now. For my dirty laundry to be aired out across town. "Who wants to know?"

"Just a fan. I'm Samuel, by the way. I think we had bio together freshman year."

"Hey, man. How's it going?" It takes every ounce of energy in my body to be friendly.

"By the sound of it, better than you. Hey, we're having a little shindig over here tonight. Wanna come over and toss back some beer?"

Fuck it. "Yeah. Sure. Think you might want to help me figure out how to win back a girl who probably hates my guts by now?"

A deep chuckle rumbles out of the phone. "I'm a plotting master. Get your ass over here, and we'll figure it out."

18

MAGGIE

NOTHING ABOUT THIS FEELS RIGHT. Greg smiles at me across the table, and I try to return the gesture.

We're having dinner at this new restaurant. The lights are low, and the candlelight on the table is romantic. I guess I'm not in the mood for this right now.

It's been three weeks. I shouldn't be thinking about Michael, but I'm ashamed to say I am.

The way he smiled and made me laugh. How he gave me shit, which made me want to serve it back. The push and pull of our banter.

Now that my anger has quelled, I think about our night together even more, if that's possible. How he held me, the way he made my body fly apart, the sounds he made when he came.

How he looked at me.

Let me ask you this—how can a man look at a woman like he wants to gobble her down whole and then not call afterward?

Thinking back on our pillow talk sends me into another downward spiral.

How do you share your hopes and dreams and fears when you're naked in a woman's arms and then ghost her? He told me about his injury and rehab and how he wants to get drafted to help his family. Was it all meaningless?

"Maggie, would you like a different kind of wine?"

It takes me a second to realize the waiter is standing next to the table. Greg repeats his question.

"No, it's fine. Thanks." I take a tiny sip. It tastes so tart, I shiver. But I was raised not to complain about dinner if someone else is treating. As someone who came from a poor family, my mom taught me to try to appreciate what's offered, even if it isn't to my liking.

If I eat first, perhaps I'll be in the mood for some wine.

The food smells delicious, but when I take a bite, it tastes off. I manage to finish half of my dinner. It keeps me from needing to talk. Greg seems content to carry on the conversation.

I nod and smile and try to pay attention, but truthfully, I'm not feeling it. Greg's a nice guy. He's one of Joe's old roommates, so he's a little older. Handsome. Settled. Has a house. A good job. All things I appreciate, but we seem to be missing that spark.

Either that, or I'm broken.

After dinner, Greg leans forward until we make eye contact. "Can I say something without you getting upset?"

With that opening, I brace myself for him to tell me I'm a terrible date. "Sure. Go for it."

"Are you still hung up on Kayla's brother?"

My eyes instantly water. What the hell? I'm not a big crier. There's no good reason why I've suddenly turned into a watering pot.

Embarrassed, I use my napkin to dab at the corner of my eyes. "Maybe? But that seems pretty stupid since Michael never called me." I sniffle and shake my head. "I know I gave him that message, to go to hell, but in my emotional state after the wedding, I figured that should've made him call me immediately. It sounds ridiculous now. I hear myself and think I sound like a nut job. We just have a long history of making each other crazy, of antagonizing each other." Ashamed, I glance at my lap. "It's childish."

I don't want to be this person anymore. The one who holds on to every single slight. Maybe if I hadn't reacted like that the morning after the wedding, Michael would've called me, and I could at least have some closure.

I've never had a hookup before, but if this is what it feels like, I'm over it. I'm tired of games. If I ever meet another man who does it for me, I don't want to be that crazy girl who goes off the rails over every little thing.

Not that what I suspect of Michael is insignificant. Only it would've helped to talk things through. If he's really a cheating bastard, it would be nice if he said it to my face so I could find a way to move on.

Even though I saw him with Vanessa right after spring break, the truth hasn't sunk in. Why I'm having trouble letting him go is a mystery. Shouldn't I have more pride in myself?

Greg hands me another napkin. "Would it help if you knew for certain he was over you?"

I freeze even though everything in my body trembles. "What do you mean?"

"If I could prove to you that he's moved on from whatever you two had, would that help you?"

With a knot in my throat, I nod, even though I'm pretty sure I'm going to hate what comes next. Do I want to know with certainty that Michael is, what, fucking other women? The thought turns my stomach, but now that Greg has thrown down the gauntlet, I can't go back. This is what I was just telling myself I wanted, but now that it's offered to me, I want to curl up in the corner and cry.

Standing, he motions for me to scoot over in the booth, and he sits next to me. "Don't shoot the messenger."

Then he's on his phone. Typing something in. Scrolling.

It's a website. "The Lone Star Stud Report." I've heard people talk about it. Everyone is so obsessed with football around here that anything those athletes do is fodder for gossip.

The blog lists all the team's top players, their girlfriends, their hookups, and their legal problems. As the school was mired in a huge controversy with our last coach, I'm not surprised by some of those details.

He scrolls down until he gets to the O's.

Michael's ad-hoc bio notes his injury, surgery, and expected recovery time. It notes his scholarship might be in jeopardy since the team is getting a new coach.

I hadn't thought about that. Even though I'm still upset with him, I'd hate for him to lose his scholarship. I know how hard he's worked to get where he is now, and it would devastate him and his family if things don't pan out.

There he is in all of his Heavenly Hunks billboard glory. I wince and wonder if he hates that sign.

But my sympathy shrivels up when I get to the rest of the photos. They start with a few of Michael's ex, Amelia, who's an elite model. She's gorgeous. Blonde, tall, and rail-thin. I'm pretty sure I could jam her entire body into one of my pant legs. There's a pic of her in her underwear in Times Square on a neon billboard, which makes me uncomfortably aware that my jeans are too tight.

Next up is Vanessa. There are three photos of her and Michael at different parties and one from the coffee house where I spotted them after spring break. This girl doesn't have a bad angle. No wonder he went out with her.

Then there's a photo from last night. I know because it's

dated. Whoever's putting this blog together should get a job at *TMZ*.

Michael looks drunk. His eyes are bloodshot, and two blondes are in his lap with their arms wrapped tightly around his neck. Everyone has a huge grin.

I push the phone away. "I've seen enough."

That pasta I had lurches. I swallow hard and try to breathe through it. Take a few sips of water.

"You okay?" Greg asks gently.

I can't respond right away, but then I nod. "I'd always rather have the truth than get smoke blown up my ass, so yes. I'm okay." Or at least, I will be.

When Greg drops me off at home, he gives me a long hug. "Can I call you again sometime?" he whispers.

Why not, right? Michael's moved on. Why shouldn't I?

19

OLLY

MAY

SIENNA'S DAD slaps me on the back. "How's your rehab going, Olly?"

He rented out El Toro, the best restaurant in town, to celebrate Sienna's graduation, her new company, and Ben getting drafted to Houston. I keep scanning the room, hoping to catch a glimpse of Maggie, but if she knows I'm here, there's a chance she won't come.

"Great. My doctor says I'm on track." He says no such thing, but I've inferred as much since he hasn't told me otherwise. And I need to hype myself up so I feel like I can handle the season. So I tell everyone what they want to hear. What I want to hear. Not "I'm cautiously optimistic."

The white lie bothers me, but the last thing I need is to be brutally honest with Alex Escalante, the school's biggest booster. Because if someone overhears me and that shit ends up on that stupid blog, the Lone Star Stud Report, I might have to kiss my scholarship goodbye.

I have no idea how those people know so much about me.

Why the hell do they care who I'm dating? My roommates think it's hysterical. Because they all know my love life is the most boring out of the household.

Why? Because from the moment I saw Maggie at my sister's wedding, she's all I can think about.

Even if she is dating that asswipe Greg.

How do I know? Because I saw them.

I'd planned out everything I was going to say to win her back. Samuel even wrote it down for me as we talked it out. He gave me a great pep talk about how nothing mattered except getting my girl. His party had gotten wilder than he planned, and we had to stop so I could sign a few autographs and take pics with fans, but I'd been all smiles. I had shit figured out.

Only to show up at Maggie's the next night and see her make out with Greg on her porch.

Full disclosure: I don't know *for sure* if they were making out.

It was dark out there, and I was hiding behind a bush, but what else would they be doing out there, late at night? If she'd been mine, I'd be making out with her. Hell, I'd have her in bed with her feet in the air, introducing her to the Holy Spirit.

In that moment, the cold hard truth slammed into me. I'd lost her. All because I hadn't gotten my head out of my ass and raced home from the wedding and demanded she talk to me. I should've stood under her window until she listened.

Reluctantly, I turn my focus to the party. Most of the team is here, and I congratulate my friends who were drafted last month. I put on my best face and pretend I'm not depressed as fuck that I'm not going pro with them in the fall. That I have to suffer through another year of living in a house full of smelly guys who leave their shit everywhere.

Don't get me wrong. I love them like brothers. I'm just tired of living like a college student. Tired of my grueling schedule and having to balance classes and training and games.

Not that going pro is a cakewalk, but if I'd been drafted, I'd have that paycheck and a nice apartment and not have to worry if Gramps can afford his insulin. I wouldn't have to come down to the kitchen and find that one of my roommates had eaten my leftovers or accidentally puked in my gym bag instead of the trash can.

My eyes snag on the vision waltzing through the front door. Magnolia.

Her hair is down, and she's wearing a little sundress. She's so beautiful, she takes my breath away. But her cheeks look hollow, like she's lost weight recently.

Is she having money trouble again? Is she not getting the groceries she needs?

Why the hell haven't I grilled Sienna more? She's been strangely silent on the topic of her bestie.

She and Sienna hug, but the two of them look somber for some reason. Next week, Ben and Sienna will be moving to Houston. The girls are probably sad to be separated.

I feel like a thirsty man dying in the desert, steps away from a drink of water. But Ben and Sienna's party doesn't seem like the appropriate place to break the ice with Maggie. For all I know, she'll toss her drink in my face.

After a bit, I see her head toward the bathrooms. This is my chance. I follow her and wait in the hall.

She's in there for a while. Then I hear it. The puking.

Is that Maggie?

I pace outside the bathrooms, wondering if I should go in there, when I spot Ben's aunt Teresa. "Tía," I say, because we all call her Tía. "Can you check on Maggie for me? She's in there, and it sounds like she's getting sick."

Teresa and Maggie have spent a lot of time together at Ben's taking care of his daughter, so she isn't a stranger.

After a moment, Teresa sticks her head back out. "Come help me."

I follow her in and find Maggie sprawled on the floor next to the toilet, dry-heaving. "Jesus, Maggie. What's wrong?"

I scoop her hair back and get a good look at her face. She's pale. Really pale. And covered in sweat. This close, I can see dark circles under her eyes.

"I'm fine," she says, but when she wipes her mouth, her hands tremble hard. She starts retching again.

"Did you get food poisoning or something?"

Her eyes fill with tears. "I don't know. I've had this bug I can't seem to kick."

Teresa scoots in behind me and hands me a wad of damp paper towels. "Wipe her face."

I do as I'm told, grateful to have a job. Gently, I dab Maggie's forehead. "Do you need to go to the doctor's or the ER?" She looks mortified to have me in here, but if she's sick, I want to be by her side.

"I... I don't know."

Teresa rattles off something in Spanish. Maggie shakes her head. Then Teresa asks, "*¿Estás embarazada?*"

Why would she ask if Maggie was embarrassed? Of course she is. She's hurling chunks in the middle of a party.

But Maggie's eyes widen. "I don't think so. I mean..." She glances at me and then lowers her voice. "I got my period last month. It was light, but..."

Oh, shit. Teresa didn't ask her if Maggie was embarrassed. Teresa asked if she was *pregnant*.

Then they talk about "la regla." Again, I'm at a loss. I took Spanish years ago in middle school, and I think that word means "the rule," but judging by the context, I'm off base.

In a daze, I go out to the bar, order a glass of ice water, and return to the women's bathroom. Maggie is off the floor and not so deathly pale anymore, thank God.

I hand her the drink as I mull over what I heard a few minutes ago. She got her period *after* we were together.

So that means if she's pregnant, it's not mine.

I'm instantly relieved.

Then wrecked.

I definitely don't need a kid right now—I need to put one hundred percent of my time and energy into the team and my rehab. But this also means Maggie is probably having Greg's kid.

Fuck.

Besides my knee injury, I've never felt this kind of devastation. Because if I know Maggie, she'll try to make it work with that guy for the sake of her kid.

Being benched for three games last season, I can tell you there's nothing like watching your team from the sidelines. Seeing what you want to do but being unable to help.

It's the same with Maggie. If this kid were mine, I'd be by her every step of the way.

But that role's not for me.

I clear my throat. "Is Greg here? Do you want me to call him for you?"

Her head jerks back. "Why would I want to call Greg?"

"Because you're... possibly pregnant... with his baby," I say.

Her expression goes flat. "That's what you think? That I hopped from your bed straight into his?"

I open my mouth, to say what, I don't know, but Teresa clicks her tongue. "Best to speak carefully, *mijo*." She turns to Maggie. "Who's this Greg person?"

"A friend's old roommate. Someone I went on *one* date with."

Okay? *We* didn't even go on a date. Maggie and I just tore each other's clothes off like a pair of savages. It can happen.

Although thinking that's what went down between her and Greg sets my teeth on edge.

For some reason, my expression pisses her off more. "I'm pretty sure sex is a prerequisite for pregnancy, and I never slept with Greg. I never even kissed him. In fact, you're the only man I've slept with my entire junior year."

Relief sweeps over me so hard, I have to brace myself against the wall. I smile at her like a dumbass. "Really?"

"You're happy about this? About the possibility you knocked me up?"

Well, when she says it like that, it's a lot to process. But I'm too relieved she's not having another man's baby to say much.

"What will your girlfriend say?" she asks sharply.

I scratch my head. "What girlfriend?"

"Oh, my God, not this again." As she pulls out her phone, Teresa waves goodbye and steps out of the bathroom. Maggie taps on her phone and waves it in my face.

When I see that blog, I curse under my breath. I should sue those dicks.

Conveniently, Maggie pulls up my info. "Hmm. Let's see. You're currently dating Vanessa, right? Or is it these bodacious blondes? It's hard to tell you're even in this picture, seeing how their tits are pressed to your eyeballs."

I smile again. "Are you jealous?"

But my smile evaporates when her eyes well with tears. "Why didn't you call me? After the wedding? After everything we did. It's because I told you to go to hell, right? I was upset. Vanessa had showed up, and I figured you guys were still dating. You said we were a mistake, and when my brother said your girl-friend was there, you never corrected him. I figured you were cheating on her. Were you? Were you cheating? Are you really a douchebag?"

My God, no wonder she hates me. "I would never say you

were a mistake. Hold a gun to my head and test this theory. I swear to you. And I'm not a cheater. Never have been, never will be. And I did call you. In fact, I called you a dozen times, but—"

"Bullshit."

I have to pause my groveling because a woman is trying to use the bathroom. I grab Maggie's hand and pull her out behind me, but instead of heading to the party, I tug her to the back alley. Given the stench coming from the trash, this is a bad idea. Maggie instantly starts retching again.

"Fuck." I wrap her in my arms and walk us to the other side of the building where the breeze is fresh. "I'm sorry. I wasn't thinking."

When she can speak again, she shakes her head. "You don't owe me anything, okay? If I am pregnant, it's not your problem."

"The hell it isn't. Maggie, I know you don't have a lot of reasons to trust me right now, but I swear you're not going through this alone. Whatever your decision, whatever you want to do, I'm on your side. But please let me show you just one thing. Because I need you to believe me."

A long pause ensues before she warily nods.

"I asked your brother for your number. I must've typed it wrong or heard it wrong. But here are the texts." I pull up my text thread to Samuel.

Tears stream down her face as she stares at my phone, and it kills me not to wrap her in my arms.

"Who's Samuel?" She sniffles.

"Some random guy. A friend now, though. He's the one who got all of my texts and phone calls."

My heart beats erratically, knowing she's finally reading my messages. Will they be too much? Will they overwhelm her? Will I sound like an ass? Mentally, I think back to what I wrote.

Maggie, baby, call me back. Please let me explain what happened after the wedding.

I can't stop thinking about you. Pick up the phone. Let's talk.

Our night was incredible. Wasn't it? Why won't you return my messages?

"So you didn't ghost me?" Her lower lip quivers, and that's the only excuse I need to hug her.

"Come here."

"But—"

"Shut up and come here." I squeeze her tightly. Breathe her in. Say a prayer that I can finish untangling this mess I've made. "No, I didn't ghost you. I would never do that to you. Want to hear something funny? I thought you were ghosting me. After I left you a million messages and you didn't reply, I thought you were telling me to fuck off."

"We suck at this," she mumbles into my shirt.

"We do, but when you're at the bottom, you can only go up from there, right?"

20

MAGGIE

FROM THE PASSENGER seat of Michael's car, I eye the pharmacy like it's a viper waiting to strike.

"Look, I know you're a 'rip the Band-Aid off' kind of person, so let's go in there and get a pregnancy test," Michael says. "At least we'll know what we're dealing with."

I turn to him, surprised. "How do you know this about me and Band-Aids?"

"Because once, a long time ago, you and I used to be friends. You always told your mom you wanted the bad news first."

"And you remember this?"

His eyes travel over my face, and I hate that it's probably red and swollen from puking, but he gives me a tender smile. "I remember a lot of things about you."

A part of me hates that he's being so nice. While I can admit he probably didn't deliberately set out to make me miserable this spring, I'm tired of nursing a wounded heart, and right now I don't have the energy to deal with that kind of injury again. We should probably table that discussion about our grievances to deal with the matter at hand, but it doesn't mean I've forgotten.

I feel the need to make that clear. "Just because we're in this situation and you're helping me right now doesn't mean everything is water under the bridge. I don't... I don't know how to get over all of this."

He nods. "I understand. We'll talk some more. Let's figure out if there's gonna be a little Maggie or Olly joining us first. Then we'll go from there."

Why does he sound so damn reasonable? "How are you so calm?"

"There are worse things in this world than having a baby." He shrugs. "Besides, if I'm gonna have a kid with anyone, it might as well be with an awesome woman like you."

And then he goes and says stuff like that.

Tears leak from my eyes like I'm a broken faucet. I swipe at them with the back of my hand. "Before that day I ran into you at the grocery store, I hadn't cried in almost a year. Not since I accidentally hammered my thumb instead of that nail. And I didn't break down because I was emotionally overwrought. I cried because I'm bad with hammers."

"I don't know. You were pretty good with *my* hammer." He chuckles.

"Michael Oliver, this is not a good time for sex jokes!"

Still laughing, he comes around to help me out of the car. When I stand, he doesn't back away, just stands in my space and takes my hand. Leaning down, he looks into my eyes, his expression now serious. "We'll get through this, okay?"

And then he walks me into the pharmacy.

A soft knock almost makes me drop the pregnancy test. I place the thing on my vanity and open the door.

"I'm waiting for the results," I tell Michael as I resume pacing across my small bathroom.

He hooks a thumb over his shoulder. "Why is there a hole in that wall?"

I almost ask which one, but then I see where he's pointing. "There's a curtain in front of the hole. Why did you move the curtain?"

"I was wondering why there was a random curtain in the hallway."

I put my hands on my hips. "I got overly ambitious, okay? I wanted an extra light fixture because this hallway is kinda dark, especially at night. Only there's no outlet. So I thought I'd add one. Except by the time I punched out that hole, I realized I probably shouldn't be doing anything electrical. Because, you know, death."

"So, uh, do you have a lot of little projects like that around the house?"

He has no idea. It was dark when we got home, so he can't tell this place is a giant mess. "A few here and there," I say slowly.

His lips fold as he looks away. At first I think he's upset, but then his shoulders shake.

I poke his chest. "Are you laughing at me?"

His face goes blank, but his shoulders keep going. "Not laughing. No. Definitely not."

After a minute, I sigh. "I guess I am a little ridiculous."

"The last thing you are is ridiculous. Maybe ridiculously beautiful? Or ridiculously clever? Or ridiculously hot?"

I smile up at him. "You can be charming when you want to be."

His eyes drop to my lips, but the back door slams shut, and he frowns. "Is someone here?"

"Probably Felipe."

"Felipe?"

"My Airbnb rental guy."

"He's renting a room from you?"

"That's how Airbnbs work." I stick my head in the hallway, and there's Felipe. "Hey! Did you need the bathroom?"

"If you don't mind. Please and thank you." He folds his hands before him and does a little bow.

I stick the pregnancy test in my pocket, grab Michael, and tug him out to the living room.

"Seriously, Maggie, who was that?" he asks when we're alone.

"Felipe. He's an exchange student who's renting my casita."

"You're living with a complete stranger?"

"No. He's living in my casita. I told you already."

"I'm really fucking confused right now." He drops down onto the couch and places his head in his hands.

"There's a nice-sized shed in the backyard that I converted into a casita." When he doesn't say anything, I try to explain. "It's a real estate thing. It has a bed, small kitchen, and TV. A window unit for air conditioning. Nothing fancy. But my friend Charlotte took these amazing photos of the place, which helps me maintain a good occupancy rate. There's an issue with the bathroom right now, and my plumber can't get here until Monday, so Felipe has to use the toilet in the house. Anyway, it helps me pay the bills."

When Sienna lived with me, I used her rent to pay for that shed. I watched the contractor do everything so fast, it made me feel a bit too ambitious, like I could do more repairs myself instead of hiring people to do them.

Let's just say I've overestimated my abilities.

"I'm still stuck on you living with a stranger. If he's coming into your house, you're basically living with him. It's dangerous."

"Felipe wouldn't hurt a fly."

"He might not, but you have no way of knowing what kind of people live back there. Are they all students?"

"Mostly." Now's probably not a good time to tell him about Randy, who had a shoe fetish, which I only discovered when I came home early and found him dicking my favorite pair of sandals.

"Fuck, Maggie. How am I going to sleep at night if I'm worried about some psycho hurting you?"

I look at my lap and admit the cold, hard truth. "I can't afford this place without that income, and even with it, it's a stretch."

A serious stretch. An almost impossible stretch.

Worst-case scenario? I might lose this house, but I'm working my ass off to not let that happen.

"Does your family know you're renting your house out to strangers? Does your brother? Because I can't see Sebastian being cool with it."

"Seeing how Bash can't pay my bills while he's busy studying for the LSAT, I figure it's none of his business."

Michael sighs and nods. "I get it. I do. I'm just gonna be worried about you. How did you end up with this house anyway?"

"It belonged to my grandparents. My *abuela* lived here for fifty-three years. Gave birth to my dad on the second floor. My dad's older brother Hidalgo ended up with it, and when he passed, he left it to me for some reason. Not sure why, since I'd only met him once or twice as a child, and he hadn't spoken to my parents in years because he and my dad had some big falling-out. All I know is Hidalgo liked me more than Bash, since my brother bit him when he was little."

Michael chuckles. "Your *abuela* was sweet. She used to pinch my cheeks."

"I forgot you knew her." It warms my heart to know that they met each other.

Abuela was the reason we moved to Heartland Hills from El Paso after my dad died. My mom wanted me and Bash and

Frannie to see her more often, since she was our last connection to our father.

As I look at the faded paint and worn-out furniture, I remember the look on my grandmother's face when she'd talk about this house.

"At first, I wanted to flip it and get my mom and sister to move up here. Mom's been struggling with her rent and helping me and Sebastian through school and paying for all of Frannie's therapies. But the property taxes are killing me, which I hadn't taken into account. Housing in Charming has had skyrocketing sales in the last few years, and it's made my property tax bill balloon. So even though I don't have a mortgage, everything else adds up quickly—the upkeep, repairs, utilities, and taxes, along with the money I need for school."

When he doesn't say anything, I fidget with the hem of my dress. "Do you think I'm crazy? Sebastian does. He says I should've sold the house and moved on."

"I think you're amazing. I couldn't sell my grandmother's house either."

Michael stares at me so intensely, I have to look away. And then I remember what's in my pocket, and my heart goes into a frenzy. "Should we look? I'm scared."

I pull out the pregnancy test. Michael moves over to sit next to me and wraps his arm around my shoulder. My head fits perfectly under his chin. It's such a random thing to notice, but I'm trying not to freak out, and there's something so steadying about this man.

Closing my eyes, I rest my forehead against his chest.

His low voice rumbles in my ear. "Whatever it says, you're going to be okay. Like I said, I'm here for you no matter what. Together, we can handle this."

I hand him the test. "You look."

He's quiet for a long moment, but then he lifts my chin and

gives me the sweetest smile before he kisses my forehead. "How do you feel about being my baby mama?"

A million emotions rush through me. Fear that I'm in over my head. Dread that I won't know what I'm doing. Dismay that this is all happening so fast.

Elation that Michael is the father.

I take a deep breath and try to stay calm. "It's a big commitment. Like, twenty years. More if they don't leave home for college."

He chuckles. "I can handle twenty years."

Swallowing past the lump in my throat, I nod. "Then so can I."

21

OLLY

GASPING, I sit straight up in bed. I'm covered in sweat, panting like I just ran in for a touchdown. Except the panic racing through me is definitely not from making a great play.

What the hell am I going to do? I'm going to be a fucking father. I don't even have my own health insurance. I'm on my parents' plan.

In the bathroom, I flip on the harsh light and blast the cold water and splash my face.

I didn't lie to Maggie. I'll be there for her no matter how this all goes down, but it doesn't mean I'm not scared shitless. But if I'm afraid, she must be terrified, so there's no way I'm going to portray anything but a stalwart conviction we can get through this.

It's six a.m. I won't be able to fall asleep again, so I throw on some gym shorts, grab my phone, and wander down to the workout room. The benefit to living in a house of football players is that we have great amenities. I get some tunes going on my phone, plug in my headphones, and turn up the treadmill to a slow jog. If this injury has taught me anything, it's the need to warm up and start slow.

It's what I should have done with Maggie. We should've started with some nice dates. I should have wined and dined her, shown her that I've grown up and that I'm serious about her.

What did I do instead? Fucked her so hard we broke the headboard and got her pregnant after what she thought was a one-night stand.

Holy shit, I've knocked up my best friend's little sister.

There's a one hundred percent chance Sebastian is going to kill me. If I were in his shoes, *I'd* kill me.

If Maggie and I could've gone slow, if I'd dated her, I think Sebastian would've been cool. But I don't see how he's going to take this news well.

After I warm up, I go through the series of stretches my physical therapist taught me. Then I jump back on the treadmill and crank it up until I'm sweating and able to work off some of this anxiety.

By the time I head upstairs, the sun is up and the guys are moving around in their rooms. Johnny's sitting on the kitchen counter in his underwear, eating cold pizza. He waves it at me. "You work out already?"

"Yup." I chug water and ignore the sting of sweat in my eyes.

"You gonna miss me next year?"

I tilt my head one way, then the other. "I don't know. It's possible."

"Don't lie. You know I'm the best part of your day."

I crack a smile. "Who's gonna bust my balls when you're gone?"

"That's what I'm saying."

Most of my roommates are graduating and moving across the country for football or jobs. I slap Johnny on the shoulder. "Proud of you, man. Who knew you'd be such a great kicker when you smoke so much weed?"

"This is true. Even my mother's shocked." Johnny got drafted. He's headed to Arizona. I'm gonna miss this crazy bastard. "Gonna smoke a giant bong tonight and go cold turkey. Don't want anything to mess up my big ride."

"That's a solid plan."

"You know how they say a cat has nine lives? I feel like I've already used at least seven. Rider has a kid. Ben does too. You got injured. And the joke is I'm the biggest fuck-up of us all, and look at me. I'm the one who woke up in someone's yard, buck naked, with wildflowers in my ass, and I somehow managed to get through it all unscathed. Doesn't seem fair, but I'm not looking the gift horse in the mouth. I'm gonna get my shit on straight before I test fate one too many times."

"You're not a fuck-up." Him thinking this way is half the problem. "Just needed to spread your wings and live a little. No fuck-up I know would babysit as much as you do."

"That's beautiful, man." He pretends to wipe a tear. "But let's not forget Ben and Rider *made* me babysit their snotty kidlets."

I chuckle. As if he doesn't love those babies.

It's on the tip of my tongue to tell him about Maggie being pregnant, but we said we'd keep it under wraps until she could get in to see the doctor and confirm everything. I feel like I'm going to burst with the news. One minute, I'm elated. *I'm having a kid with Magnolia Morales, one of the most beautiful, smart, and feisty women I know.* The next, I'm losing my shit.

What if my knee blows? What if I don't get drafted next year? What if I do get drafted but suck ass? How the hell am I going to afford a kid?

Does this mean Maggie and I should get married? Should I offer? Will she laugh in my face?

"You okay?" Johnny asks. "You're paler than usual."

"When do you leave for Phoenix?"

"Two weeks. Why?"

"We should talk before then."

He lifts an eyebrow dramatically. "Isn't that what we're doing now?"

"Got some stuff going on right now. Can't discuss it yet, but I could use someone else's perspective."

He scratches his nuts and smiles. "I'm your man."

It makes me laugh. I should probably go to Ben, but he and Sienna have a million things going on right now.

"Wanna go for breakfast?" he asks. "That pizza was just a snack."

"Yeah. Let me shower. Give me ten."

By the time I get cleaned up and return, I'm surprised to see Maggie in the kitchen chatting with Johnny.

She smiles hesitantly. "I brought you guys donuts."

This woman is having my kid. Just seeing her leaves me dazed. Her thick hair is in a ponytail, and she's wearing blue jeans shorts and a t-shirt I'd love to strip off of her. Today she's sporting those sexy-as-hell glasses. Now that I've accepted this thing between us, I want to fuck her until she can't stand straight.

Slow, asshole. You gotta go slow this time.

Johnny opens the box. "She wouldn't let me have one until you arrived." He takes a round donut and is bringing it to his mouth when I slap it out of his hand.

It tumbles back into the box. "What the fuck was that?" Johnny asks.

"I'm doing you a favor." I turn to Magnolia, suddenly suspicious. We said we'd table the discussion of our grievances, but that doesn't mean she won't try to get even in the meanwhile. "Did you put mustard in these?"

She starts laughing. "No, weirdo. I haven't tried to sabotage your donuts since junior year of high school."

I turn to find Johnny chomping away at a chocolate-filled donut. "Those are my favorite."

Maggie rolls her eyes. "I know. That's why I bought them for you."

"You remember that chocolate-filled donuts are my favorite?" I dated Amelia for months, and I'm pretty sure she had no clue.

"You also like Boston cream, but they didn't have any of those."

With his mouth half-full, Johnny asks, "So are you two over being butthurt? Does this mean you're dating or something?"

Maggie blushes and shrugs. "Or something."

She's having my kid. I'd say it's more than something.

22

MAGGIE

AFTER MICHAEL and Johnny scarf down a few donuts, I tug on Michael's shirt. "Could we, um, go talk?"

He turns to Johnny. "Raincheck on breakfast?"

Johnny holds up his thumb while he shovels another bite into his mouth.

Once we're in the other room, I whisper, "Johnny's funny. You two must've gotten in a lot of trouble over the past few years."

"Too many times to count." Michael looks around the living room, which has boxes stacked in every corner. I'm guessing some of the guys are moving out. "Wanna sit by the pool? We're less likely to be interrupted there."

"Sure." I wipe my sweaty palms on my shorts. I almost threw up on the way over here, and I don't think that was from the baby. Michael makes me nervous, like there are crazy-ass butter-flies doing a samba in my belly.

The backyard looks straight out of one of those frat movies. A huge yard and pool. A jacuzzi. An enormous grill. My eyes go back to the jacuzzi as thoughts of our night together barrage my mind.

Michael leads me to a bench under an oak tree. Deliberately, I turn away from the jacuzzi. It's hard enough to focus around this man.

"I thought we should clear the air." I glance down at my hands. "Talk about your sister's wedding and the fallout after. And... I think I should tell you all the shit I've done to get back at you after what happened with Luke in high school. I'm not proud of myself. I get, uh, impulsive sometimes, like how I ended up with all those holes in my house, and it seems like you're on the receiving end of that. Well, you and my sheetrock. I just want to start this"—I wave at my stomach—"with a fresh slate. If you're amenable."

I finally look up at him, and he gives me that soft smile that makes me want to crawl into his lap. "That's a great idea."

"Can we start at the beginning? I feel kinda dumb going this far back, but if I could understand this better, maybe it would help me make sense of why you always set me off in high school."

He balances his elbows on his knees. "It's not dumb. Say what you want to say. You and I have always danced around shit. It's never worked out well for us."

"Exactly." I wipe my palms again on my shorts and swallow past the surge of nausea. "Can I ask why you told Luke all that shit about me? You and I have yelled at each other about it, but we've never sat down to discuss it like rational adults. Back then, I thought you and I were friends, good friends even when we were younger. It was really crushing to hear all those things you said."

His brows furrow. "Luke always swore he never told you what happened."

"He didn't. I overheard. I have a tendency to overhear things I shouldn't. That night, I was wedged behind his nasty couch because I had to get my dad's sweatshirt back. You guys returned before I could hightail it out of there, so I hid while y'all ate pizza and snuck Luke's dad's beer stash."

"Fuck." He rubs the back of his neck. "I'm sorry. I know I've apologized in the past for this, but that was a really shitty thing for me to do."

"You yelled an apology. Well, after I yelled at you."

He winces. "Yeah, not my best moment." Shaking his head, he places his hand over his chest. "I'm sorry, Maggie. I had no business meddling in your relationship with Luke. I've worked hard to not be so black and white in my decision-making, except back then I was wound tight. I was surprised to hear you were going out with someone behind Luke's back, but I thought he had a right to know. I was following my conscience."

Silence grows between us. "I'm not going to lie—hearing that you thought I could cheat on someone was really devastating. I wish you had just asked me what was going on." I clear my throat. "Before you and Bash started high school, you promised we'd always be friends, promised you'd have my back. It was crushing to find out you didn't mean that."

"God, I was an ass. You're right. That's exactly what I should've done. Sweetheart, I didn't mean to hurt you. And I get why you embarked on a campaign of retribution."

Somehow, that makes me laugh. "I wanted to make you cry uncle."

"When my truck reeked like tuna for the entire summer, there might have been some stinging eyes. Torture I totally deserved."

"Wait." I squint at him. "Weren't you the one who suggested Ben fake-date Sienna? How was that being honest?" I overheard Ben and Sienna discussing it once.

"That was different. Ben's ex, Janelle, had already lied to him for years about their kid. In that case, turnabout was fair play.

Ben needed to protect himself, and I figured pretending to date Sienna would give him the barrier he needed with Janelle."

"That... actually makes sense."

He smiles at me, and a strange, peaceful sensation settles in me, one I haven't felt in a long time. Not since my family lived in El Paso and my dad was alive.

He coughs. "Luke ended up being an idiot, so I'm not going to apologize for *everything*."

"So you're saying you ended up protecting me?"

"I'm saying at least he cheated on someone else and not you." That does shed light on things. "Plus, he violated bro code. Bash made us all promise not to make a move on you. He said you'd gone through a lot after your dad died, which I knew, and we were all horn dogs. Luke was the worst. But Bash once told me how he sat with your dad in the hospital, and your dad made Bash swear he'd always look out for you and Frannie and protect you. I knew how seriously he took that."

Looking down at my lap, I think back to that horrible time. "My mom stopped letting me see Daddy because I'd started getting nightmares about him dying, but I wish I could've visited him more before he passed."

"Pancreatic cancer, right?"

"Yeah. It all happened really fast. One day we were a happy family barbecuing in the backyard, and the next we were packing up everything we owned and moving to Heartland because Dad was gone."

Michael wraps his arm around my shoulders, and I sink into his embrace. "Since we're laying everything on the table, I should probably confess that once you started dating Luke, I realized I'd lost my chance with you, and it pissed me off. Granted, at the time, I didn't know I was feeling jealousy. I just knew I hated seeing you with him."

I'm not sure I should let him off so easily. "I don't know. You told Luke he could do better than me. And then you said, 'Maggie's pretty, *I guess*.' We all know what that means—you didn't think I was attractive."

He groans and covers his chest with his hand. "I was an idiot. You've always been a stunning woman."

"You *were* an idiot. I had a huge crush on you for years. I gave in to Luke's overtures because I thought you saw me like a little sister."

When he moves back to look at me, his eyes are wide with disbelief. "I'm having a hard time believing this. You liked me?"

"Yes! All the guys pretended to be so cool. You were always yourself. Smart, cute Michael Oliver with the big blue eyes and dimples. The guy who always picked me up and dusted me off when I fell off my bike. That was before you got your big muscles and turned into a smoke show."

The first time I saw him without his shirt in high school, I almost tripped over my own two feet. How had he gone from that scrawny kid when we moved to town to a brawny, tall, golden god? Football.

"I was one of the biggest nerds in the school, and you thought I was cute?"

I shrug. "You were the hot nerd who started to ignore me."

"When did I ignore you? You've said this before, but I don't know when that happened."

"You always ignored me when I was with Luke. Maybe even a little before that."

He frowns. "I guess I didn't handle my feelings well, huh? I'm sorry I was a dick to you. Luke liked to brag about his conquests, and I was loathing the day when he'd start talking shit about you. I think I was bracing myself for the eventuality that you guys would sleep together. It was making me crazy."

"I never slept with Luke. I was a virgin until college."

"No shit?"

"Luke dumped me and banged that girl he swore was just a friend ten seconds after we broke up. It was a while before I trusted anyone enough to date again."

"I'm so sorry. I hate that I had a part in all that. No wonder you despised me."

I blow out a breath. "I don't think I *despised* you."

"Just disliked me enough to sabotage my donuts."

"And zip-tie grocery carts to the door handles of your car."

"I knew that was you!"

"Did you get my sandwich?"

He pauses to think. "The plastic wrap?"

"Yeah." His senior year of high school, I snuck a slice of cellophane-wrapped cheese into his lunch with the words "Not Sorry" written in sharpie on the plastic. "Did you eat any of it?"

"Half the sandwich. Until I realized it didn't taste quite right."

I laugh. "It took you that long to figure it out?"

"I was a growing boy with a big appetite." The way he says that, the way he's looking at me with those heated eyes, makes me think he's talking about more than food.

"I'm sorry about the whiplash thing." I cringe when I remember how upset he was.

"At least it wasn't during football season. You didn't mean to rear-end me that hard, I suppose."

"I really didn't. I'd just gotten my license, and I thought it would be funny." I fold my lips, embarrassed. "And I'm sorry about your bumper falling off."

It's really a wonder he doesn't hate me after all of the crap I pulled on him over the years. Now that I think about it, him coming to my rescue at the grocery store a few months ago was really sweet of him. I didn't deserve his kindness.

Which makes what I have to say that much worse.

My stomach knots as I spit out the words. "Listen, I did one more thing..."

"It's fine. No more confessions. I probably deserved whatever it was. Let's just move on."

"Are you sure?" I'd be lying if I said I wasn't relieved.

"I don't want to hash things out forever. You and I have wronged each other in many ways over the years. The past is a clean slate. Let's get to more pressing matters, like what happened after the wedding."

I'm exhausted just thinking about what's left to talk about. I hold up a finger. "Can you feed me first? I wasn't hungry earlier, but now I'm pretty sure I could eat a small buffalo."

He winks. "Your wish is my command."

23

OLLY

MAGGIE TAKES a big bite of her bacon and egg sandwich. I'm relieved to see she has an appetite. We're sitting outside the Horsey House, an ancient diner that serves killer breakfast around the clock.

"I feel bad that you bailed on Johnny to eat with me," Maggie says.

"He had pizza before he downed three donuts. Pretty sure he's fine. He and I have plans tomorrow anyway. We're good."

"Are you going to miss him and Ben? They're your best friends, right?"

I don't know how she knows this, since she and I have never hung out in college. I've only really seen her in passing. "Did Sienna or Ben tell you that?"

"I could tell from watching you talk to them that they mean a lot to you. You have the same camaraderie with them as you do with Sebastian."

Hearing his name makes the food in my stomach drop like a rock. "Your brother's gonna be so pissed when he finds out what happened. How I got you pregnant." Saying those words out loud makes me freeze. How was I that dumb? After my friends had baby scares, you'd think I'd be more careful.

"Let's hold off on that until you and I have a grasp on everything. If he sees I'm okay with this, he'll handle it better. He just doesn't want me to get hurt. Are you planning to hurt me?"

She asks me so earnestly, my chest squeezes. "No. Never."

After setting down her sandwich, she wipes her hands with a napkin. Fidgets with her straw. Looks away. "As much as I hate to dig into more ugly stuff, we really do have to talk about the wedding. You're saying you won't hurt me now, but I heard everything you said to my brother that morning. The walls between our rooms were really thin."

Fuck. I just cannot catch a break with this woman. "What did you hear? Let's go through it all. I don't want us to have secrets." Didn't I say back in January that I didn't want any more drama? And yet it follows me and Magnolia around like a stray after a free meal.

"I heard Sebastian say that Vanessa, your *girlfriend*, was there, more than once, and you never corrected him."

No wonder she had Greg tell me to go to hell.

"That was me panicking. It's stupid, but I figured if Bash thought I was seeing someone else, then he'd never guess I was railing you the night before. Plus, there were condom wrappers everywhere. The headboard was crooked. I just wanted to get him out of my room."

She laughs, her cheeks an adorable shade of pink. "Shockingly, I get that." She nibbles her plump bottom lip. "So if I go up to Vanessa right now, she'll agree you guys haven't been intimate since then?"

"Mags, she and I have never had sex. We kissed once or twice —weeks before that wedding. I don't think it did anything for either of us. I guess I thought if I tried harder, I could make that spark happen, so we kept going out. And then I saw you at the wedding and lost my head. But it's what I needed to realize I didn't like Vanessa like that, which is why she left after the rehearsal dinner. I couldn't see us sharing a bed that night."

"And your parents really slept in the room next to mine on the first night? You swear they're who I heard?"

"Ted and Wendy have legendary lays. Ask my sister. We're both planning to get therapy about it at some point."

She laughs, but it turns into a moan. "Please tell me you had the sheets changed before we, you know..."

"Of course I did."

"That's a relief. Okay, what about when Sebastian thanked you for hanging out with me? Was he the reason you talked to me that night?"

"I talked to you because you looked so beautiful in that dress, my head was gonna explode. Sebastian texted me before the reception, hoping to set up a rendezvous with one of the bridesmaids. I don't think he wanted to leave you alone, but..."

"But Bash wanted to clear the runway so he could make his move, the dog."

I laugh, nodding. "Probably. I'll say this—you were already on my mind. I didn't need a lot of encouragement to seek you out."

Her eyes go serious. "Then why didn't you just come over after that weekend? I don't live that far from you."

"I stayed home for the rest of spring break and helped my parents with Gramps, who had a surgery. By the time I got back to Charming, I'd already sent you a million messages. Since I hadn't heard back, I started to second-guess everything that had happened between us."

"Is Gramps okay?"

"Yeah. He's had some issues with his diabetes, but he's doing better."

Her head tilts and all of her hair cascades down her shoulder. "I'm sorry I assumed the worst about you."

My mom always says never ask the question if you don't want to hear the answer, but I have to know. "Which was?"

"That I was a smash-and-dash. That perhaps a one-night stand was your way to get back at me for all the shitty things I've done to you over the years." She doesn't cry, but her face gets red with emotion. She shakes her head. "I don't want to be that person who always assumes the worst when it comes to you, Olly. You don't deserve it."

To hear her call me Olly again after all these years makes me want to scoop her into my arms and spin her around. She and Bash gave me that nickname when we were in middle school.

The waitress stops by to refill our drinks, and I use the distraction to study Maggie, who smiles at the waitress and thanks her. Amelia never thanked the wait staff. Neither did Vanessa, now that I think of it.

Once we're alone again, I ask the question I'm dreading. "Where do we go from here? Have you decided what you want to do?" My heart is in my throat as I wait for her response. I never knew I wanted a baby like I want this one, but I do. With my whole being, I do. But Maggie's the one who has to carry it for nine months.

She whispers, "I want to keep it, which I know will be tough because I have another year of school, but no matter how at odds we've been over the years, this baby is special to me because it's part of you."

Her eyes fill with tears, and it about kills me. I take her hand and tug her toward me until she's out of her chair and in my lap.

"That's probably the best compliment anyone has ever given me," I say softly as I kiss the top of her head. I hug her to my chest and ignore the stares of the customers around us. "Does this mean you'll give me a chance to be more to you?"

She sniffles and sits up to look at me. "How much more do you want to be?"

Everything, Magnolia. I want to be everything to you.

24

MAGGIE

MICHAEL CLEARS HIS THROAT. "I want to be as involved in your life as you're comfortable with."

Is that because of the baby or because he wants to be with me?

As sweet as he's being, after how messed up things got since his sister's wedding, I can't say I'm ready to jump into dating him. If he even wants that.

I move back to my seat and turn my chair so I'm facing him. "Are you talking about being a co-parent, or are you talking about us?"

He mulls that over for a minute. "Both. I definitely want to be in our baby's life, and I'd like to see where things lead between us."

"Don't take this the wrong way, but we don't even know how to be friends, much less parents. And I'm feeling gun-shy after how sideways everything went after we hooked up. Could we focus on the co-parent thing for now and being friends? Would you be okay with that?"

"Does that mean you're cool with dating other people?"

My gut reaction is *fuck that*. Do I want my baby daddy dating other women? Of course not. But can I ask him not to see other people if I'm not ready to go there with him?

I breathe through that sudden burst of anger. I don't want to lash out at him. Setting boundaries is a good thing, I remind myself. "Would I be excited for you to date other women? No, but I can't exactly ask you to be celibate."

"Yes, you can. You can ask me not to see anyone else." His statement hangs in the air.

"Is it weird that I'm absurdly jealous of these nameless, face-less women you haven't asked out yet?"

A breathtaking smile spreads on his face as he laces our fingers together. "I don't wanna see you date anyone else either."

"In a few months when I'm as big as a house, no one is going to want to date me, not even you."

"Impossible." He squeezes my hand. "I bet you're going to be even more beautiful."

I glance at my lap, feeling shy all of a sudden. "So we'll, what? Take things slow? See where things go? Focus on our friendship?"

He nods. "Yeah. We're only gonna be stuck with each other for the next few decades or so. Let's get off on the right foot."

Perhaps this won't be impossible. "Are you free on Wednesday afternoon? Think you could make an OB-GYN appointment with me?"

He doesn't hesitate. "There's nowhere else I'd rather be."

I hadn't thought this through clearly, because now that I'm wearing a gown made of paper and have my legs hiked up in stirrups, I'm rethinking the wisdom of inviting Michael to join me today.

He turns to give me the privacy to change and hike my ass up onto the exam table, but when Dr. Perkins sticks her fingers in me to do whatever she has to do, Michael is *right there*. He's sitting on a stool a few feet away, staring at his shoes like they have the secrets to the universe etched in the canvas.

When she asks about my last period, I explain the weird spotting and how I thought it was just light that month.

"That happens with a lot of women. And unless it's heavy, less like spotting and more like an actual period, or accompanied by cramping, it's normal. Did you have cramping?"

"I had one sharp pain down there early on, but otherwise no."

"Could've been the implantation of the sperm."

Huh. You learn something new every day.

When the sonogram technician enters the room, Dr. Perkins grabs a giant wand. "Now for the fun part. This is where we get to hear the heartbeat."

Michael's eyes get comically huge. "You have to probe her with that thing?"

I laugh. It's completely inappropriate, but *please*. "Don't even pretend your weapon is much smaller." I mean, he's definitely thicker.

The man goes bright red. "Mags." He tilts his head toward the doctor and technician, who are both trying to hold back their smiles.

I roll my eyes. "My baby daddy has it going on. There. I said it."

"Jesus, Maggie."

"Look, if we can all sit around while the doctor asks me about discomfort in my *vagina* and shoves a giant phallus up my hoo-ha, I can admire your endowments."

He chokes on a laugh and then reaches over and grabs my hand and freaking kisses it.

Dr. Perkins smiles. "A transvaginal ultrasound will give us a really good idea of your due date. It sounds like you're almost in your second trimester, though, so next time, we'll do an external ultrasound." She has the technician wheel a giant cart closer. "You guys are a cute couple. How long have you two been together?" she asks as she squirts a bunch of lube on the wand.

"Oh, um... We're not really... I mean..." How do I explain we're focusing on being friends?

I squirm as she inserts the wand.

Olly squeezes my hand. "I've liked this woman for years, so even though this is new for us, I've had a thing for her for a while. Even when she was contemplating slashing my tires."

How is he so damn sweet? I smile. "How did you know I wanted to slash your tires? Not that I would actually do that. But after I saw you with Vanessa, I might have fantasized about it for a day or two."

He chuckles. "Why am I not surprised?"

Olly looks so handsome sitting there in a blue button-down and slacks. He dressed up to take me to the doctor's, for Pete's sake.

Suddenly, a fast whirring sound fills the room, and I turn toward the doctor.

"That's your baby." After a moment, though, her smile morphs into a frown, and then she has the technician tweak something on the monitor. They whisper to each other, and I start to freak out.

Olly stands next to me, leans down, and whispers, "Everything's okay. I'm right here."

"Actually," Dr. Perkins says slowly, "here is your *other* baby. Congrats! You're having twins."

And that's when Michael Oliver, an elite athlete and my baby daddy, whispers, "Holy shit," and passes out cold.

25

OLLY

Popping open a beer, I collapse back on the couch.

At least I didn't get a concussion or hurt my knee when I passed out yesterday. I guess there's a first for everything.

"So yeah," I tell Johnny as I rub the bump on the back of my head, "we're, uh, having twins."

He stares at me and busts out laughing. "Shut the fuck up. That's a good one! You had me going there for a second. I mean, what would *you* do with twins next year while you're trying to play football? We barely have time during the season to scratch our balls, much less date anyone. Plus, you gotta watch your knee. Throw being a father into the mix and it's pure insanity. I don't know how Rider and Ben survived that shit."

When he says it like that, I wanna puke.

I've already passed the fuck out. What's a little vomit?

He gets up and starts searching the room. "Are you filming? Is this a going-away prank?"

"Dude. I'm serious."

He must read it in my expression because his eyes bug out. "No shit?"

"Swear to God." I hold up my hand. "Maggie's pregnant with twins."

She and I agreed we could tell Johnny, Ben, and Sienna. They're our closest friends, and they're all moving away, so who would they tell? Johnny collapses on the couch. "Talk about a blitz, man. The hits keep coming for you, huh?"

I think about what he says. "I'm not gonna pretend I'm not overwhelmed, because I am. But my mom always says babies are a blessing. Will I freak the fuck out before they arrive? Probably. Will I stress out over how the hell I'll afford everything? Absolutely. Will I worry that Maggie and I can handle the stress? Most likely. But I'm gonna try my hardest to be the man I need to be for her and the twins."

"That's beautiful, man." He pounds his chest. "I felt that right here."

"Shut up."

He laughs. "I'm serious. You're gonna be a great dad. If anyone can handle fucking *twins*, it's you. You babysat for Rider all the time, and Poppy was still a baby. Lily was older, so Ben had it easier, but not by much."

Johnny tosses a ball into the air as I drink my beer and wonder if I can pull off what I need to come August.

"So are y'all gonna move in together?" he asks.

"We agreed to take things slow. Focus on our friendship." And deal with practical issues like money. Maggie has some crappy student health insurance, which barely covers anything beyond co-pays for doctor appointments. All I can do is pray I get drafted so I can afford those maternity bills.

"Don't ya think the train already left the station on that? Your super-sperm flew right up the mothership, docked, and spawned. You should move in with her, and y'all should fuck the shit out of each other while you can. 'Cause everyone knows once the babies arrive, you ain't getting laid again." He taps his temple. "That's some solid Johnny Johnson advice right there."

I'm slightly terrified he's right, but that's not something I plan to discuss with him.

I motion across the street. "Let's go to Ben's. I can't believe they're leaving tonight." It's going to be strange to not have him and Sienna around anymore.

When Johnny and I get there, Ben answers the door. "I hear congratulations are in order."

He slaps me on the back, and we do the bro-hug thing. Over his shoulder, I spot Maggie talking to Sienna, both of them in tears.

"What's going on?" I ask.

"Sienna's pissed she won't be here for the delivery. Don't be surprised if that woman charters a flight back to Charming come December."

I lean closer to him and lower my voice. "So why are they crying?"

He shrugs. "Women cry all the time. I don't always under-stand it. When Sienna's sad, I feed her, snuggle her, and offer a back massage. Makes her feel better every time."

Johnny smirks. "You mean you snuggle her until she fucks you."

Ben jabs a finger in Johnny's chest. "Don't talk about my woman like that, or I'll tell everyone about the time you crapped your pants."

"You wouldn't."

"Watch me."

"Okay, kids, enough." I separate them and pull Johnny into a headlock. "Apologize to Ben."

"Sorry, bro," he says as he picks his nose with his middle finger.

Laughing, I let him go when he waves the booger finger near my face. I'm gonna miss these two dumbasses.

Everything's packed up except some of the furniture. The girls are sitting on the couch, and it looks like the tears have stopped, so I head over there.

Maggie's face is splotchy, but she smiles when she sees me. "Hey, I was just telling Sienna about the ultrasound."

"Did you tell her about my swan dive at the end?"

"Not yet. Here, you tell her." She pats the seat next to her, and I sit down and drape an arm over the back of the couch and turn toward her and Sienna, who's bug-eyed. It's an expression everyone seems to have around me these days.

"What?" I ask.

"I'm still stunned about recent developments here." She waves between me and Maggie. "Last year, you guys had a screaming match in my front yard and now you're having babies. Plural. It's a lot to take in."

You're telling me.

Maggie gives me a sheepish smile before she turns back to Sienna. "We've apologized to each other for all the bad stuff. We're ready to move on and be adults. No more mustard-filled donuts."

Sienna howls with laughter. "I love the pranks she pulled on you, Olly. Who knew Maggie was such a little deviant? When we interviewed her to babysit for Lily, she had her letters of recommendation alphabetized and tabbed."

"I don't mess around with childcare. My little sister is autistic, and when my mom leaves directions for Frannie, she really needs the babysitter to follow it. So I take that seriously. But when it comes to getting back at the guy who drove off my boyfriend"—Maggie gives me a look—"I guess you could say I played a little dirty."

"You were too good for Luke anyway. Don't even pretend you

weren't." I lean close to her and whisper, "And for the record, that's not the only time you liked it dirty."

Maggie elbows me, and I chuckle.

Sienna juts out her lower lip. "I'm sad I won't be here for the Maggie and Olly show. You two are such a cute couple!"

"Well..." Maggie fidgets with a strand of her hair. "I wouldn't say we're a couple exactly."

What she means is we're not a couple *yet*.

I aim to make this a priority.

It's just a matter of time.

Maggie continues. "We're taking it slow. Learning how to be friends. For years, all we did was bicker. I don't want that for our kids. They deserve better."

When she says it like that, how can I deny that's the best route? Didn't I just say I wanted to take things slow with Maggie? But when I'm around her, I want to *be* with her. I want her in my bed and in my life and central to all things.

Sienna takes her hand. "That sounds very mature." Then she turns to me. "Are you planning to stay at the Stallion Station? Or are you getting a bigger place?"

That's a damn good question.

"I hadn't thought that far." I can't afford a bigger place. My scholarship covers housing, and the Stallion Station, which is what everyone calls the football house, is one of the options. I could probably swing a studio apartment, but I'm not sure where I'd put two infants. The dresser drawers?

"It'll be hard to take care of the twins there," Sienna points out. "There's zero privacy. And don't get me started on that downstairs bathroom. Plus, what happens when there's a party, but you haven't slept because you've been on baby duty?"

Maggie gives me a worried look. "You could stay with me on those nights, I guess. I have extra bedrooms. If you don't mind a hole in your wall or drafts."

"Would it be so bad if Olly moved in with you full time?" Sienna asks slowly. "Take it from me, the season is going to bust your balls. You two are going to be slammed. Living together will give you a chance to see each other at least once a day. You might not be able to squeeze that in otherwise. And what happens when you're eight months pregnant and living there *all by yourself* and having to climb those steps? I'll be worried about you."

I wipe the sweat off my brow. Jesus, Sienna is freaking me out. "I'm amenable to whatever Maggie wants to do."

My not-girlfriend turns to me. "Would you want to move in? I promise I won't be all up in your business. We could still work on the friend thing."

What if I *want* her in my business? But after all the shit that happened this spring, Maggie is skittish.

No, she's pregnant and scared and needs you to be her friend.

It doesn't matter what I want. What matters is what she needs.

"I'm game for whatever you want to do. If you're comfortable with me there, I'll move in next week."

The furrow between her brow smooths out. "Okay, roomie."

Internally, I sigh. I've been upgraded from not-boyfriend to housemate. I suppose it's a start. At least I can keep the creepers who rent her casita away from her.

"Yay!" Sienna claps and hugs Maggie for some reason. "Sit tight. I have a gift for you."

"But you're the one leaving." Maggie laughs with delight.

Sienna runs off to her bedroom and returns a minute later with a small package that she hands to Maggie. "To remember me by."

"Stop. As if I'm going to forget you." Maggie unwraps the jewelry box and pulls out a dainty gold necklace with a butterfly.

"It reminded me of you. I know you have a lot on your plate, but think of it this way—if nothing ever changed, there'd be no butterflies. And you're going to be a beautiful butterfly, mama."

That does it. They both start bawling and hugging again. I squeeze Maggie's shoulder and excuse myself to the kitchen, where the guys slam down pizza.

But I watch the girls from the other room and wonder if I can be what Maggie needs.

I wanna try.

26

MAGGIE

IN AWE, I watch as four giant, sweaty men traipse in and out of my house.

Olly introduced me to Cameron, Billy, and Diesel, fellow teammates who are moving into his old place. The guys are helping him haul his furniture over here and settle everything into a bedroom upstairs.

As I'm pouring some boring decaf coffee in my to-go mug, I overhear them talking. I should probably remind Olly that I have excellent hearing.

"Why are you giving up the Stallion Station again? Your girl is hot and everything, but bro, you'll be missing out on our workout room, the pool, hot tub, *and* all the parties." He lowers his voice, and I'd bet anything he's reminding Olly about the girls who frequent those festivities.

"Not everything in life is a party, Billy."

"But there are *holes* in the wall. I nearly killed myself on a rotten floorboard on the porch. I don't mean to be a dick, but this place reminds me of that haunted mansion in *Stranger Things*. You know, the one where everyone almost died?"

I cover my eyes with my palm, wishing I could crawl under

the couch. I hate that Olly's friends are seeing my house with all its warts.

They can't appreciate the blood, sweat, and tears I've already put into this place. How I stripped and re-finished the floors on the second floor. How I scrubbed every inch, even the walls. How I re-grouted two of the bathrooms and painted several bedrooms.

I suppose it's not enough. They don't see what I see.

Someday, it'll be a gem. Someday, everyone will look at this house and wish it were theirs.

It's not there yet.

The hallways are too dark, and as that asshole noted, I need to replace rotting floorboards on the porch and front steps. The windows need to be washed, and this place is drafty during the winter. Don't get me started on the laundry room downstairs, which makes the *Amityville Horror* basement look like a vacation getaway spot.

Why *does* Olly want to move in here? The football house is much nicer than mine.

He's obviously just doing this for the babies. I rub my tummy and try to keep the tears at bay. I've felt a million different emotions since I found out I was pregnant, but the one I'm experiencing at the moment is guilt.

Am I ruining Olly's future? Would he do better this season if he stayed with the guys? Would that help him focus on football more?

I've always been kind of a loner, and I'm not crazy about the idea of *needing* Olly's help. And it tweaks my pride to hear what the guys think of my beautiful house. I make a mental note to try to fix all the major repairs before the babies come in December. How I'll swing that, I'm not sure.

Now I regret not starting repairs with my bedroom and bathroom. I figured it would motivate me to fix things if I woke every morning to a water-stained ceiling and ugly tile. That was dumb.

Once I'm sure my emotions are locked down, I grab my purse and head upstairs to the bedroom across the hall from mine.

I clear my throat, and the four giants turn my way. "I have to go to work, so..." I unhook a key from my ring and hand it to Olly. "That's yours. I'll be back this evening. Help yourself to whatever." Not that I have much food in the house, but they could probably make sandwiches if they get hungry.

"Where do you work?" Cameron asks.

"A small advertising company. I thought it would be cool like *Mad Men*, and I'd help design ads, but I'm sorry to say I just make coffee, take notes, and file."

Billy turns his back on me to assemble the bed.

"I'll walk you out," Olly says.

"It's okay. Stay with your friends." Staring at the back of Billy's ugly head, I add, "Since you're 'giving up the Stallion Station,' you should take advantage of your freedom while you have the chance. You know, before I chain you to a pipe in the basement or something."

Damn, that sounded catty.

Cameron barks out a laugh, and Diesel smiles. "I love a woman with a little snark."

Olly hooks his arm over my shoulders with a chuckle. "Come on, Mags. Don't bloody my friends before they get to know your sparkling personality."

"Ha-ha."

He walks me out to my car. After I unlock my door, I turn to him. "You don't have to do this. I was perfectly fine here by myself before"—I wave at my belly—"and I'll be fine after. Worst-case scenario? I can take care of myself and anyone else who comes along on my own."

His brilliant blue eyes go soft. "No one said you couldn't. But would it be so bad if I were here to help?"

Staring at my shoes, I shake my head. "I just feel guilty. Like I'm tearing you away from what you really want. From your friends and... everything else." Is he going to miss all of those hookups? I'm nauseous thinking about it.

Because the reality of this is starting to set in—I'm starting to fall for him. But because I'm a practical woman, I know the odds are stacked against us. I really don't need my heart shattered on top of everything else.

He tilts my chin up. "I can't be what you need if I'm staying at the football house. Sienna was right about how demanding the season will be. Training camp alone means I'll be gone for three weeks. We're required to live on campus for that."

My gut tightens at the thought I won't see him for so long. As much as I want to think I'm an island, deep down, I don't want him to go. "You'll tell me if you change your mind?"

"I won't change my mind."

"Because of me or the babies? If you're just doing this for the kids, I need to know so I don't make more of you being here."

His thumb brushes my lower lip, and chills rush up and down my arms. "I'm gonna be really honest, whether or not you're ready to hear this. I *want* to be with you, Magnolia, however I can have you. You said you want to go slow and work on being friends, and I'm down with that, but I think we could be so much more together. So no, this is not just for the babies. This is because I've always felt a pull toward you, even when we were younger, and no one I've dated in those intervening years has come close to knocking me on my ass the way you do."

I choke on a laugh. "Is that a compliment?"

He kisses my forehead. "It is. You make me crazy, but in the best way. Let's let our lives settle in together, okay? Be friends, like we said, and see where things lead. I just need you to give me a chance. To not lock me out before we get started."

That sounds terrifying. Letting Olly into my heart on top of everything else will be either the best thing to ever happen to me or the worst.

Please, God, let it be the best.

OLLY

As I wait for the coffee to percolate, I open the fridge. What the hell does this woman eat? Is she part mouse? Because all I've found so far is a block of cheese, some lunch meat, and a box of crackers. She knows how to cook. Her brother used to come to school with some of the stuff she'd make. Is this empty refrigerator because of money?

Someone clears her throat, and I turn to find Maggie looking adorably rumpled in a matching pink pajama set and fluffy slippers. "Morning." She waves. She freaking waves at me.

We're still in this awkward stage where we don't know how to act around each other. If we were really together, I'd kiss the hell out of her, but we're more like roommates at the moment. I'm waiting for her to relax so I can be more affectionate with her. If I could snap my fingers and send us back to where we were the night of my sister's wedding, I would. She was so playful and sweet and sexy.

She's sexy now, don't get me wrong. But she's obviously uncomfortable.

"I made some coffee. Want some?" I ask.

"Yes, please. Oh, is it decaf? I can't have full caf."

"Damn. I forgot. Sorry. I'll pour this out and make you decaf."

"Don't do that. Coffee is expensive. Please enjoy it. I can make some herbal tea."

"Speaking of money, I can pay rent. I talked to the housing office yesterday, and they said I can use the funds allocated for the football house to pay you. I just need you to fill out a form."

I expect her to be happy about the news, but she frowns. "Maybe just give me half of that money and keep the rest."

"Why would I do that?"

"Because like Billy said, this place is a mess, and you're not getting any of the amenities you had at the football house."

Fucking Billy. "Think of it as both of us investing our money in something for the twins."

She thinks about that a moment. "Really?"

"Yes, really." Before I forget, I grab a notepad off the counter. "I'm going to get groceries later. Why don't you jot down whatever you want me to get?"

"I don't need anything."

This woman is going to kill me. "What do you plan on eating this week?"

She shrugs. "Ham and cheese on crackers. Some soup. Why?"

"You need more than that. You're gestating *two* babies, Magnolia. You can't treat yourself like a starving college student."

"I just... I can't pay you back right away."

Did I not just offer to pay her rent and she was trying to return half of it? She's making me insane.

"I don't expect you to pay me anything. I want to get us groceries because we need them. I'm in training and burn a shit ton of calories. You're pregnant and need to eat more than a damn Triscuit."

"Why are you raising your voice at me? I'm doing the best I can. Half the time I can't eat anything because it comes right back up, so what's the point? I'll try to eat something later, okay?" She storms off and slams her bedroom door.

I hang my head. This is not going as planned.

I've never lived with a woman before, much less a pregnant one, but I get the feeling I need to tread lightly.

Hoping not to piss her off anymore, I make her tea and peel the one piece of fruit in the house, an almost too-ripe orange, but it's sweet and hopefully won't turn her into the Exorcist. I place the mug and fruit on a plate with a few crackers and carry it upstairs. Gently, I knock on the door.

"Mags. Open up. I have your tea. It's attached to an apology, so you don't want to miss this."

The door cracks open, and a teary eye peeks through. "You made me tea? After I freaked out like a lunatic?"

"Yes. Here." I nudge my way in and take in her room. Appalled that my room is nicer than hers, I try to keep that judgment off my face. But what the fuck? Why is she sleeping in a disaster zone? There are huge water stains in the ceiling, at least one hole in the wall, and based on the way that light just flickered, some electrical issues.

Even though Billy was being an ass when he helped me move in, until this moment, I didn't think anything here was that bad. Sure, the porch is a mess and the yard needs a serious mow, but I haven't been in every room. The hallway bathroom is clean and bright. My room has a fresh coat of paint. Why doesn't Maggie sleep there? For a woman who made it her mission in life to make me suffer, why didn't she give me this room?

"Don't say it," she whispers.

"Say what?"

"That this room is a hot mess. I know it is. I haven't had a chance to renovate two of the bedrooms or the master bath."

I freeze when I finally make sense of what she's saying. "You're doing everything yourself?" I figured she was hiring contractors.

She sighs. "Trying to, but this shit takes time. They make it look so easy online. No one tells you that if you don't get the right primer, the old paint will seep through the new coat or make it look orange. No one tells you that if you use the wrong top coat, it'll peel right off. No one tells you how much dust you'll have when you re-tile a bathroom, and you'll have to clean the rest of the house all over again if it's not enclosed." Her voice drops to a whisper. "No one tells you how hard it is to get paint out of your hair."

I try not to smile because Maggie's obviously upset, but I love her can-do spirit. I set down her food delivery on a rickety dresser. "Come here."

She doesn't budge an inch, so I stalk over to her and wrap her in my arms. "You're doing an amazing job. I took a very nice shower this morning in your beautiful bathroom." I'm not even joking. "Did you re-grout the one in this hallway?" She nods, and I kiss her temple. "Incredible."

"Your friends think my house is ugly."

"They're idiots."

"They see *Stranger Things*, but I see the Granville House in *It's a Wonderful Life*. You know the house Mary loved so George bought it?" She wipes her eyes. "It has charm and character."

I know exactly what she means. I love that movie and can immediately picture the scene where George serenades his new bride even though the roof is leaking.

Magnolia is a big romantic. How did I not know this?

"This place is incredibly charming, Mags. All it needs is a little TLC."

"That's what I've been saying."

"Can I help with some of the repairs? Only what you're

comfortable handing off. I've done a lot on my parents' property. I can be handy when I need to be."

Her big brown eyes peer up at me warily. "Aren't you busy with training?"

"Not so busy that I can't take on a few projects before training camp starts next month. I'm only taking one class this summer."

"Working on the house won't hurt your knee?"

"My knee is feeling great. Been eating my Wheaties."

She chuckles, and I consider that a win.

Now we just need to rack up a few more victories, and we'll be on a roll.

Maggie has to learn to trust me. I have the perfect plan to win back her trust.

MAGGIE

GROGGY, I adjust my glasses, stumble out into the hallway and into Olly's bare chest. He's fresh out of the shower, and all he's wearing is a few droplets of water and a thin white towel.

Holy hell, he's a beautiful man. His blond hair is damp and his big muscles glisten. My appetite comes roaring back. I'm not sure how else to explain the need to lick off those water droplets one by one.

"Sorry, Mags. Forgot my clothes in my room. I've been meaning to mention how much I like those glasses."

He stares at me, and I wonder if I look like a giant geek, but he might as well get used to the stripped-down version of me.

He clears his throat. "Are you hungry? I was planning to make an omelet after I get dressed."

Am I hungry? Why, yes, I am.

Michael Oliver is not on the menu, Magnolia.

"Sounds good." I hurry down the stairs and bury myself in the fridge, where I take a second to cool off. This pregnancy thing has me freezing one minute and burning up the next. Living with Magic Mike doesn't help.

He comes down a few minutes later wearing a snug t-shirt and worn but well-fitting jeans. I'm not sure when Olly turned into my very own brand of catnip, but he's never looked more handsome. He's somehow even hotter now than in the tux he wore for his sister's wedding.

Pretty sure "taking things slow" doesn't mean mauling him until he cries out for mercy.

I make some fully loaded coffee because I know that's what he likes, and I microwave a cup of water for some herbal tea.

Underneath the maelstrom of emotions I've been wrestling with since Olly moved in, I feel bad for stomping off last week when he got on my case about what I've been eating. Once I cooled off, I could see where he's coming from. I hate that he brings out the worst in me. I turn into a sniping child with him, and that's not how I want to be as a human, much less as a parent. That's not how my mom and dad were with each other.

Not for the first time, I worry about my mom's reaction. She always wanted me to get my career in order before I settled down in any kind of relationship. I can't help but wonder if she'll be disappointed by this pregnancy.

"Did you sleep well?" he asks as he whips some eggs into submission before pouring them into a pan with browned butter. It smells delicious.

I haven't gotten around to restoring the kitchen yet. It has an ancient oven, a thirty-dollar microwave I bought at a yard sale, and an old farmhouse table. It needs a complete overhaul, but I can't afford it yet. I spent all of my money on the casita so I could get some rental income, which I then use to pay the bills.

"I did, yeah. Listen, I have a little surprise for you. Can I kick you out of the house for a bit this afternoon?" I want to do something to thank him for his encouragement. For the last two weeks, he's filled the fridge with fresh veggies and fruit. He bought me an assortment of crackers, so I don't have to eat the stale ones in my cabinet. He found this holistic recipe for morning sickness and bought all the ingredients and makes it for me when I don't feel well, which is often.

We also talked about the most pressing repairs I need to finish on the house, and he had me write a list of things I want him to do. I guess having a partner isn't so bad.

His bright eyes turn to me. "A surprise?"

I laugh at his expression. "Yes, so I need you to skedaddle."

After breakfast, which I'm able to keep down, I haul out the mower, but before I can get it started, Olly takes it out of my hands. "I got this."

"I just need the area around the casita cleared up. I have a new renter coming this evening."

"Sure. No prob."

At noon, though, he's still at it. The backyard is huge and completely overgrown, but he's made a sizable dent. I make a giant jug of lemonade and take a glass out to him. "Please stop. I feel bad that you're working so hard." This wasn't on the to-do list I made for him.

"I don't mind, but I need to shower again and head to campus. Will you be okay for a while?" He's sweaty and hot, and I lean close and try to get a whiff.

"Totally fine."

"Did you just sniff me?"

Busted. "Yup. I blame the aliens in my belly."

He hooks an arm around my shoulders and nuzzles his sweaty face in my neck. I squeal and try to push him off, but he picks me up and hugs me to him. I almost moan with how good he feels. Solid and strong. Sturdy.

And sweet Mother Mary, he smells good.

My nipples are so hard, they nearly slice through my bra and t-shirt.

When he finally sets me down, we're both breathing hard.

Why did I want to go slow? I wonder as I pant. I almost ask him if he's as turned on as I am, but I bite my tongue.

Once he's out of the house, I rub one out in the shower, which makes me so drowsy, I almost head back to bed, but I manage to make my appointment with Dottie in town.

"Thanks again for these invitations, Maggie. My daughter is going to love them!" She claps her hands excitedly.

"Happy to help." Dottie waits tables at the Farmhouse, a restaurant downtown. I ran into her last week at the stationery shop, and she said she wanted some baby shower invitations and thank-you cards made. She couldn't afford the prices the shop wanted, so we worked out a trade.

"Are you sure you won't let me pay you? This doesn't feel right."

I motion toward the dusty pile of workout equipment in her back bedroom. "I'm sure all of that is worth more than the work I did for you."

"When my son moved to Dallas two years ago, he said he'd take this with him. I've given him plenty of chances to get it."

"He won't be upset when he visits and finds it gone?"

"I told him what I was doing. He said it's fine. His apartment has a lovely workout room."

Like Olly's old place, I think guiltily. Olly now has to hoof it to campus or meet up with the guys at the football house to get in his daily workouts. "Too bad you don't have a treadmill you want to get rid of."

Dottie pauses with her Diet Coke in the air. "But you know who does have one? Bob Pearson."

That name sounds familiar. "The guy in overalls? Always walking around town with a goat?"

"You've met Elsie? He's obsessed with that damn animal. He'd bring her into the restaurant if I let him. But yes, he has a treadmill he wants to get rid of. I'll give you his address."

"Could I just call him?"

"The old geezer doesn't have a phone."

That's how I land weights and a treadmill for Olly all in the same day, but I have to find someone with a truck before I can pick up the treadmill because it'll never fit in my Ford Focus.

Half of our friends just moved away, and the only person I can think of with a truck isn't particularly fond of me.

This isn't about you, Magnolia. This is about Olly. You can eat a little humble pie to do something nice for him.

After I load up the weights, talk to Mr. Pearson, pet his goat, and pull up to the Stallion Station, I'm exhausted. I never should've masturbated this morning. I feel like all of my energy deserted me through my clit.

I take a deep breath and knock on the front door. Cameron answers. "Hey, Maggie. What's up? Olly's not here right now."

"I'm actually trying to track down Billy. That's his truck, right?"

"Yeah, he's here," Cameron says hesitantly. I'm sure he didn't miss my animosity toward his teammate when they moved in Olly.

"I have a favor to ask." Wincing, I add, "I might need your help too." It's tempting to use the pregnancy card, but I remind myself we said we'd wait to tell more people.

Two hours later, Billy and Cam are dripping in sweat and straining to squeeze the treadmill up the stairs. "Will you hate me if I yell 'Pivot?'"

Neither of them laugh. So much for my *Friends* joke.

"You promised pizza, right?" Billy grunts out.

"Yes! I put in the order on our way here."

I make several trips from my car to the house and haul the weights and bars and athletic-looking stuff I don't understand. The doctor said I could carry a bag or two of groceries, which means I have to watch how much I lug around. I'm definitely testing the limits today, but I'd rather get this done myself than beg the guys to help me again.

By the time I've dumped everything in the living room, Billy and Cam have carried that ridiculously heavy treadmill upstairs and set it up.

"Here's your pizza." I set out some paper plates and soda I'd give my left nipple to drink, but I'm trying to avoid anything with artificial colors, sugar, and caffeine, which leaves little else to enjoy in life, quite frankly.

Billy and Cam double-fist those slices like they've been caged and starved.

"It's solid of you to do this for Olly," Billy says with a mouthful.

"You're a good girlfriend," Cam adds.

I don't have the energy to explain that I'm not really Olly's girlfriend. More like exhausted baby mama.

Olly says he wants to be with me, but I suspect that's obligation talking. He's a good guy. He wants to do right by me. As much as I'm attracted to him, as much as I wanted to scale him this morning, I'm scared we'll ruin things before the babies get here, and then I'll really be alone.

It would be better to be friends because friends don't leave you high and dry. I saw how hard my mom struggled to make ends meet because my dad died. I don't want that kind of life if I can help it, which means Olly and I need a solid foundation.

I leave the guys to the pizza and return to hauling weights from the living room and up the stairs.

Good God, they're getting heavier. After several treks, I have to take a break. I sit and lean over until my arm rests on the steps above me and close my eyes. I don't know how long I'm there when I hear Olly's voice.

"So you just left her here on the stairs? Why was she carrying weights again?"

Yikes. He sounds pissed.

"We didn't know she was hauling weights," someone says. "We were out back in the kitchen."

I try to sit up, but because I fell asleep on the staircase, everything hurts now. "Hey. I'm okay. They were helping me."

Judging by his scowl, Olly doesn't believe me. I wipe the drool off my chin. How long was I asleep?

"I have your surprise." But then I realize half of it is still sitting in a pile by the sofa. Shit. "It's not quite done yet. It took longer than I thought it would." I smile awkwardly. "Would you close your eyes and let me finish?"

I try to stand, but my legs are asleep, so I wobble. Olly's there in a flash, and then I'm in his arms. "Maybe you should lie down." He stomps up the stairs, kicks my door open, and gently puts me on my bed.

"Please let me finish your surprise." The doorbell rings, and I drop my arm over my face. "It's probably my Airbnb person." I did not coordinate this well.

I drag myself off the bed, past Olly, and down the stairs where Billy and Cam are goofing around with the weights.

"Don't bother with the door," I mumble to myself. "I'll get it." I open it and freeze when I see who's on the other side.

"What the fuck? Don't tell me this is the shithole I've rented." Olly's ex Amelia Larson struts in wearing designer everything and a golden tan.

This can't be right.

"You're not Nigel." I would've remembered if I'd rented my casita to a woman.

"I'm certainly not. Nigel, my stepfather, books everything for me. My soon-to-be-*dead* stepfather, I should say." When Amelia lays eyes on Olly, though, her whole demeanor changes. "Oh, my big boo! I haven't seen you in so long!"

She flings herself at him like they're saying goodbye at the airport.

So much for my damn surprise. Because this one takes the cake.

29

OLLY

I'M GONE for a few hours, and when I get home, the apocalypse descends. First I find the guys eating all of our food in the kitchen. Then I realize Maggie is asleep on the goddamn stairs. Only to have the doorbell ring and find the succubus on the other side.

I peel my ex off me. "Why are you here?"

Amelia juts out her lower lip. "Don't you miss me? It's been ages."

Do I miss the nonstop drama? Not at all. And the longer we're apart, the more grateful I am that I broke up with her when I did.

Maggie sheepishly holds up a finger. "I think she rented the casita. For the next two months."

Oh, fuck, no. "This isn't gonna work out, Amelia. You need to find someplace else."

In true Amelia fashion, she ignores me and looks around the living room, her pert little nose wrinkled and hoisted in the air. "Please tell me you don't live here, Olly. This place looks like a crime scene. Oh, my God, it *is* a crime scene! Isn't this where your teammate attacked that bitch, what's-her-face?"

Sienna is one of the nicest people I know. The fact that Amelia hates her says a lot.

Maggie looks mortified. I'm wondering how fast I can get my ex out of here. "Amelia, don't you live in LA now? Didn't you graduate?"

She rolls her eyes. "I have a few more classes I apparently need to take, and my fucking manager won't release my money until I graduate."

Her poor mother manages Amelia's career. That's a job I'd never want.

It's funny how a little time away from someone makes you more objective. I used to really dig this girl. Amelia and I started dating before her modeling career took off. She was nicer and more down-to-earth back then.

"Look, this obviously isn't where you want to be. Why don't you find something else? We'll refund your deposit and send you on your merry way."

Maggie hangs her head and whispers, "I already spent that money."

Swear to God, I feel my temple throb. "What could you have possibly spent that on so quickly?"

She flinches like I struck her. Before I can apologize for being an ass, her eyes narrow. "Designer clothes and hair treatments." She waves at herself. "Obviously."

Her ponytail is falling out, and she's wearing faded blue jeans cutoffs and flip-flops. The woman looks adorable, but I have a feeling that's not what she wants to hear right now. "Mags, I'm not trying to be critical—"

"Are you guys dating?" Amelia asks, talking right over me. She gives Maggie a dismissive once-over and turns to me. "I thought you hated her. What did you tell me that day? You said she was a whiny, pain-in-your-ass brat who pouts when she doesn't get what she wants."

Fuck.

The devastation on Maggie's face cuts me to the quick, and I curse the day I met Amelia. I'm sure Maggie's said crap about me too over the years, but she doesn't need Amelia shoving the past in her face.

Maggie sniffles and bites her lower lip, her nose bright red, but she refuses to look at me. Quietly, she asks Amelia to follow her, and Maggie grabs her keys and takes my ex out to the casita. The moment the doors close behind them, someone clears his throat.

I turn to find Billy and Cam. I forgot they were here.

Billy crosses his arms over his chest. "I may not have been a fan of you moving here at first, but your girl worked all afternoon to get a treadmill and weights set up in one of the spare rooms. I didn't even know about the weights until you came home, or I would've helped her."

I close my eyes, frustrated that I can't seem to do anything right around here. *That's why she fell asleep on the stairs.* Out of pure exhaustion from trying to do something nice for me.

"What do I do?" I'm not sure why I'm asking Billy and Cam. Neither of them have girlfriends. I miss having Johnny and Ben to bounce ideas off of. Not that Johnny ever had a girlfriend, but sometimes that stoner gave good advice.

Cam slaps me on the back. "Time to grovel, brother."

30

MAGGIE

IGNORING the throb in my chest from that emotional smack-down, I unlock the casita. Thankfully, I turned on the window air-conditioning unit, so it's not five thousand degrees in here.

"It's really small." Amelia looks around like a snake is going to hop out and bite her on the ass. Perhaps that's wishful thinking.

The casita is the prettiest part of my property. It has beautiful hardwood floors, sage-green cabinets, a sparkly new bathroom, and decorative baskets I'm tempted to steal for my house. There's a reason this place is always booked. It looks great in photos.

"There's the bed and closet. If you unlock this lever, you can use this platform as a desk. Through there is the bathroom, which has a shower. Here's the kitchenette, which has a microwave and refrigerator. If you need a stove, you can use the one in the house."

Dang. Why did I say that? I'm so used to offering it to my guests that it rolled off my tongue.

"Do I get a key to your house too?" she asks as she dangles the keychain in my face.

"Just knock. I'll let you in. Or I can give you my number, and you can text, which is helpful if you know ahead of time that you need something."

"Awesome. Just what I always wanted. Needing to head into a different house to cook."

I'm guessing that's sarcasm. "Look, your stepfather wasn't honest with me either. Let's just make the best of this. You can go your way, and I'll go mine."

"Is it going to be weird, though? Me staying here? You knowing that I've slept with Olly many, *many* times?" She twirls a glossy lock of blonde hair. "That's gotta be strange, huh? And I mean, we've done it *everywhere*. My car. A shower. A cabin on vacation. My place. His place. A bathroom at a banquet. The man could not keep his hands off me. He once fucked me so hard, my neighbors knew his name by the time we were done."

I open my mouth, only nothing comes out.

She pats my arm in faux sympathy. "I have some great diet tips if you need some. If your sex life isn't as slamming as mine was with Olly"—she folds her lips briefly and then lowers her voice—"it might be because you're carrying some extra junk in the trunk. Olly likes them skinny. Just look at that redhead he dated. What was her name? Vanessa? Now she's really beautiful."

By the time I stumble out of the casita, I'm wondering why I was dumb enough to think this could work. I'm clearly not Olly's type. Add this pregnancy to the equation, all the weight that's going to pack on, and the fact I'm so disoriented when I'm with him, and it spells disaster.

I somehow manage to not cry even though I feel like that woman slowly stripped me of my skin, Hannibal Lecter-style. When I enter my living room, Olly jumps up off the couch. "Maggie, I'm sorry about all of that. Thank you for—"

I hold up my hand. "I'm not feeling great. I'm going to bed. Maybe we can talk tomorrow."

Or next week. Or possibly never.

Because right now, I want to crawl into my bed and never come out again.

31

OLLY

WHAT THE HELL did Amelia say to Maggie? She looked like death warmed over when she returned to the house last night. And when I got home from my workout this morning, all of the weights in the living room were gone. I meant to ask her where she wanted them last night so I could move them for her, but she went straight to bed.

I didn't nose around the house to check out the treadmill because I had a feeling Maggie might want to show me herself, but she's been MIA all day. When curiosity finally gets the best of me and I creak open the door to one of the spare bedrooms, I feel like an utter ass for snapping at her yesterday.

The guys said she got me a treadmill. I figured it was something rinky-dink because how could Maggie afford a nice one? And yet there's a beautiful gym-grade machine right in front of me. Dumbfounded, I turn in a slow circle. There's a workout bench. Those weights. Several bars and dumbbells. She even set up a full-length mirror, the kind you find in a gym, and in the corner is a small sound system and speakers.

Damn, this is great. I don't know where she is or if she's still upset, but I need to see her. I decide to text her.

This workout room is the coolest thing anyone has ever done for me. Thank you so much!

Twenty minutes later, she responds. **Glad you like it.**

That's it. That's all she says.

Fuck this.

I dial her number. When she picks up, I start talking. "What time are you gonna be home?"

"I get off at five."

That's right. She has a part-time job. I forget sometimes. "I'm taking you out to dinner."

"But—"

"No arguments, Magnolia. Please let me do this."

She eventually relents, thank God. Whatever Amelia told her last night obviously put her guard up, and Maggie and I have to get on the same page if we want any hope of surviving the season, much less the NFL. If I make it that far.

I flex my knee and test for soreness. I've been religious about my workouts and icing my injury to help stave off any inflammation. Because I want the training staff to see that I'm recovering well, I've done most of my workouts at the team's workout room instead of with the guys at the football house.

Since Maggie went to such trouble to do this for me, though, I should probably do a few of those workouts here so she doesn't feel like her gift was a waste. It wasn't, of course. Having a home gym is incredible, but I hope the trainers don't think I'm slacking.

When she gets home, her somber eyes tell me she's not excited to hang out, which sucks. "Do I have time to change?" she asks.

"You look great in what you're wearing, but yeah, there's time if you want to freshen up." As she passes me, I grab her hand. "Hey. Thank you again. I'm serious about that gift being one of the nicest, most thoughtful things anyone has ever done for me."

That gets me a small smile. "That treadmill isn't brand-new, but it's barely been used, so I thought you might get some mileage out of it." She looks down. Shrugs. "I just wanted to thank you for the groceries and thoughtful things you've done for me since you moved in."

She looks so shy and uncertain. I pull her into a hug and kiss her cheek. "Thanks, Mags. You're awesome."

When she comes back down the stairs an hour later, she looks so fucking sexy, my tongue almost rolls out of my body. "Damn. Hot mama." She's wearing some little wraparound dress that hugs her curves, which have gotten curvier since the wedding.

Adorably, she blushes. "I figure I should take advantage of dressing up before I don't fit in my clothes anymore. I'm already pushing the limits of decency in this outfit." She tugs the fabric at her gorgeous cleavage.

"Don't feel the need to cover up on my account," I tease.

She rolls her eyes but laughs.

Thankfully, we don't run into Amelia on our way out.

"Do you still love Italian?" I start my truck and roll down the window. My old Chevy doesn't have air conditioning, but it's a mild evening.

"I do, yeah."

We drive through town, which is quiet since it's June. I keep glancing at Maggie, enjoying how she looks in my truck. I'd love nothing more than to scoot her across the bench seat and into my lap.

Lorenzo's is small but quaint. Low lighting and candles and those little twinkle lights set the mood for a romantic dinner.

After we order our meals, she frowns. "I feel like everything lately is all about me. How I'm feeling and whether I'm hungry or nauseous. I don't want this—us, whatever we are—to be one-sided. So let me ask, how is your knee? Is rehab going well? How are you feeling about training camp?"

"My knee is feeling great."

"Is that the answer you give your coaches, or is that the truth?"

I chuckle. I like the no-holds-barred version of Maggie. "It feels tight sometimes. I'm not a hundred percent yet, but I've been working my ass off to be in the best shape I can be given the circumstances. In truth, I'm apprehensive about camp because if I move wrong, I can undo everything, and my season, along with any hope I have of making the pros, will be over. I probably won't get a full medical release until the fall, but I want to do my best in the meanwhile and show my coaches they should have faith in me. It's definitely stressful. Shit can all go sideways in a flash."

"It can't help that you're getting a new coach. Ben really liked Nicholson."

"Nix was a good guy, for sure. Better than that ass we had before him. Fingers crossed we get someone awesome."

She crosses her fingers and gives me a sweet smile.

"How's work going? Have they given you any fun projects?" I ask as I dig into my meatball sub.

"I'm still serving coffee I can't drink and filing, so no." She shrugs and takes a small bite of her chicken piccata. "It's fine. As long as they pay me, I don't care what they have me do. I can still build my portfolio with side gigs."

"Do you get a lot of freelance projects?" My sister's wedding invitations were beautiful, so I know Maggie does great work.

"I'm starting to, yeah. Mostly through word of mouth."

This woman works so hard. She takes classes, renovates her house, has that Airbnb rental, *and* freelances. "It's cool that you're able to do so much freelance design."

"I don't know that I'd call it *design*. I'm not an art student. I just happen to like fonts and know how to use a few cool programs. I wish I could draw or do calligraphy, though, instead of having to rely on a computer."

I swear, the more I get to know Maggie, the more interesting she gets. "You should add that to your 'someday' to-do list. Because it seems to me that if you're able to learn how to re-grout tubs from watching YouTube videos, you can probably learn these other skills you're interested in."

The brilliant smile she sends me does something strange to my chest. "Yeah. Someday."

I don't mention all the things I want to do with her.

Someday.

32

MAGGIE

THE SCENT of cedar and earth fills the air as we pull up to the Point, a huge hill that overlooks a valley. With the waning sunset, everything is awash in a golden hue.

"This is beautiful," I say.

"Have you ever been here before?" Olly asks as he hands me the cranberry gelato he ordered from the restaurant.

"No, but I had a roommate freshman year who used to come here with her boyfriend to make out." He smiles and takes a bite of his dessert. When he doesn't say anything, it makes me wonder. "Why? Have you brought other girls here to do the deed?"

"I've never brought anyone here."

I let out a relieved breath. That bitch Amelia really got into my head last night, and I'm having a hard time shaking it off. But I was going to lose my mind if Olly admitted he'd brought her here too.

Of all the casitas to rent, why did Amelia's stepfather have to pick mine?

"Hey," Olly says softly. "Where'd you go?"

He grabs my hand. Mine looks so small in his. "I hate

bringing this up because we've had a really great evening, but one of our big problems has always been letting things fester instead of just discussing them, so I want to be open about this." Shifting in my seat so I face him, I rip off the proverbial Band-Aid. "Last night, Amelia asked if it was weird having her around since, you know, you banged her brains out. She listed out *every* location you two ever had sex, in case I was curious."

His expression turns thunderous. "Are you serious?"

"I would never ask anything like that. Trust me, I don't want to know that you guys got freaky in a cabin on the lake or in the bathroom at some fancy gala."

He winces, and by his expression alone, I can tell she was telling the truth, which depresses me more. I'd half been hoping she was lying or exaggerating.

No such luck.

I switch the gelato to my other hand so I have a reason to let go of his. I'm too annoyed to hold hands. "So... sorry I was upset last night, but between her showing up on the doorstep and me not having your workout room ready after hustling all afternoon to get it done, I just wanted to drop into bed and pull the covers over my head."

Letting out a groan, he leans forward and scrubs his face with both hands.

Now that he's not looking at me, it's easier to say things I might not otherwise. "I'll just admit I was almost sick with jealousy. I hate that this sounds like a copout, but I'm so hormonal, some things that would never have bothered me before make me crazy now. Like how Amelia said I'm not like all the beautiful, thin girls you date."

"Fuck."

"Given that I'm having twins, I'm only going to get farther from your ideal, so that's a depressing thought. Six months ago, if someone had said those words to me, I would've held up both middle fingers, but now... now I guess I'm sensitive about my body. My boobs hurt all the time, my jeans are tight, and my belly is starting to jut out." I turn to stare out the open window. "And I know you think I was irresponsible with my money because how else would I blow Nigel's deposit, right? But I had to write a big check for the property taxes. I pay them twice a year, and it almost empties my bank account each time. I feel like all I do is work, but it's not quite enough."

"Magnolia." That's the only warning I get before he unbuckles my seatbelt and slides me over into his lap. "I'm sorry I snapped at you last night. I was pissed the guys let you carry weights and didn't notice you fell asleep on the goddamn stairs like you'd passed out from exhaustion."

"That wasn't their fault. You should've seen how hard they worked to get the treadmill up those stairs."

"I hope you didn't spend too much on it."

"Only spent two hundred on the treadmill, which I thought was a great deal. The rest was a trade."

"What do you mean?"

"I did some baby shower invites and thank-you cards for a friend. In return, she gave me the weights."

"That was really fucking sweet of you." He brushes his thumb over my bottom lip. "I love my workout room. Thank you for going through so much trouble for me."

"It was no trouble. I know how much you're giving up to live in my house, so I wanted to try to make it up to you."

"I'm not giving up anything to be with you."

I scoff. "Don't tell me you don't miss living with your team-mates or that you enjoy driving across town to work out."

His eyes bore into mine. "Moving out of the football house is no hardship. Sure, I enjoyed the camaraderie, but living with several giant, stinky manchildren who don't clean up after them-selves is not the jackpot some think it is."

I laugh and look down, but he lifts my chin. "There's no place I'd rather be than with you, okay? We're having twins. *Two* freaking children. They're as much my responsibility as yours, and yes, this year will be tough, and I'm sure we're going to argue and lose our shit from time to time, but I just need us to commit to eventually coming back to the table to talk, okay?"

Olly's steady expression immediately calms me. "Okay. Yeah, I can do that."

"As far as Amelia is concerned, she's just pissed I broke up with her, so that's sour grapes talking. Don't listen to her."

"Can I ask what happened between the two of you?"

He thinks about it a minute. "The more success she achieved, the meaner she got. And she leaves a mountain of devastation in her wake. It didn't help that she hated my best friend's girlfriend. It's ironic Amelia brought up that douchebag who attacked Sienna, since that was in part Amelia's fault for being a busybody. We ended up getting in a huge argument because of it, and I broke things off. And then, afterward, she really betrayed my trust, so I can say, definitively, that I'm not interested in anything she has to offer."

I'd be lying if I said I wasn't delighted to hear he's over her.

Since we've never discussed it before, now that we've brought up previous girlfriends, I'm dying to know more. "Have you been in many serious relationships?"

He shakes his head. "Not really. I usually broke things off if they didn't understand my commitment to football. That has to come first. That's the whole reason I'm at Lone Star in the first place. If I blow football, I blow my scholarship, I let down my family, and I let down myself. For a giant nerd who barely knew his left foot from his right, figuring out that I was good at this one thing made my whole life make sense."

"I get that. But Olly, you're good at a lot of things." I brush a long strand of hair out of his eyes. "Weren't you a math whiz in middle school? Didn't you win all those academic competitions? I mean, you're a horticulture major, aren't you? That's major smart people stuff right there. I'm pretty sure if you didn't have football, you have a dozen other things you could do. Don't get me wrong—I have nothing against the sport, and you do look pretty hot in those tight white pants, but no one would love you less because you didn't play." His stunned expression makes me laugh. "What?"

"I'm not used to you lavishing me with compliments."

"Shut up." I shove him. "Don't get used to them."

We sit and watch the sunset. I lean back and drop my head on his shoulder. It feels so good to just be with him.

Once it's dark, he whispers, "In the future, can we talk about money and big expenditures? It's not that I want to tell you what to do. I just think if we work as a team, if we put our heads together, we can get more done and solve the larger problems."

"I hate when you make sense."

He laughs and nuzzles my neck. The air has gotten cool, and I shiver in his arms.

"Can I confess something?" It's hard to speak when he nibbles on my ear, but I nod. "The only reason I haven't fucked you into oblivion on every flat surface I can find is because you want to go slow."

When I don't respond, he clears his throat. "Which I am completely down with. I think it's smart not to jump headfirst when we have so much going on. I'm going to be an optimist and say it's good that Amelia gave us shit. If we can't handle her crap, I don't know how we'll survive the NFL. At the end of the day, I'm gonna need you to trust that I'm not going home with other women. That I'm not tucking dollar bills into strippers' G-strings after games and living a double life. To trust that when I take a photo with fans, there's nothing nefarious under the surface." He turns my face so I have to look at him. "I can't say what's going to happen down the road. I'm not a fortune-teller. But I can promise I'll always be faithful. That you can count on."

My eyes sting, and I nod. "Thanks. I appreciate my monogamous, non-boyfriend, baby daddy committing to me like that."

He chuckles. "Maybe we should upgrade?" Ducking to run his nose against my neck, he whispers, "We could be monogamous, special friends who kiss."

"That..." He licks my skin, and everything in my body lights up. "That sounds reasonable. Just kissing, though, right?"

"Just kissing. Until you ask for more."

My body is screaming for more, but before I turn my face up to him, I promise myself that kissing is the only thing on tonight's menu.

33

OLLY

BEAUTIFUL, sweet, feisty Maggie is in my arms, and all I want to do is devour her.

When she turns those big brown eyes up to me, I could smack myself for not pursuing this sooner. For not dealing with our shit so we could be friends and work toward something more years ago.

Because this woman is incredible. I can't think of anyone else I'd rather be partners with when it comes to our children. She's gonna be a fierce mama bear.

I'm crazy about her now. I can't imagine how much more enthralled I'm gonna be when she's accompanied by our two little humans.

She gives me a shy smile and lifts an eyebrow. "Are you going to force me to make the first move?"

I glance down at her plump lips that are stained red from the gelato. "My dessert was lemon-flavored. Think cranberry and lemon go well together?"

She licks her lips. "I guess we'll find out. Maybe we'll discover our new favorite flavor."

With those words, she tilts her head up. I meet her halfway.

The moment our lips touch, she sighs.

I want to tell her this kiss feels like all the planets in the universe just aligned. That what we have is undeniable.

I lick the sweetness off her bottom lip, and she opens for me. Reaching up, I tangle my hand in her thick hair and pull her closer. When her chest presses against mine, it takes everything in me not to lift her to straddle me.

"You taste delicious," she whispers as she wiggles in my lap.

My straining erection digs into the zipper of my jeans, and I place my hands on her hips to still her. "Careful. You're sitting on the baby-maker."

She giggles, and I hug her to my chest.

I wish we could stay here along this stretch of road, overlooking the valley where the cicadas chirp. Away from school and football and crazy exes. Where it's just me and Maggie, and we can drown out the noise by taking a drive.

It's quiet here, and I can think. Everything is telling me I have to make this work with Maggie. We have to learn to draw down our defenses and trust each other.

Or we won't make it.

Going slow might kill me, but if it gives me a chance to build something real with her, I'm game.

When we get home, I walk her upstairs, press her to her bedroom door, and kiss her until she's panting. "Remember," I tell her between licks to her pouty lips, "*you* have to ask for more."

I can tell she wants to ask me for it now, but I'm not looking to break down barriers she's not ready to remove of her own volition. We'll get there. Eventually.

Even if it kills me.

The moment I'm in my bedroom with the door closed, I pop open my jeans, sending my erection bouncing against my stomach. I'm already sticky from pre-cum, which I slick over my length.

Leaning against my bedroom door, I close my eyes and roughly jerk myself off to my favorite fantasy—that one magical evening Maggie and I had together at the wedding before all hell broke loose. I've thought about that night more times than I can count. I sometimes wonder if she ever touches herself to those thoughts as well.

I see it like a slow-motion film flickering in the darkness.

The way Maggie rolled on the condom and sank over me, sending me into a frenzy. How her beautiful tits bounced in my face as she squeezed my cock in her tight, wet heaven.

And when I reached between us to roll her clit, she sat back, spread her legs, and let me watch my cock thrust in and out of her.

That's all it takes for me to come all over my stomach.

Panting, I lean against the door and hope the beautiful woman across the hall is thinking about me too right now.

When Maggie gets home from work the next day, I sit her down on the couch. "Hear me out."

Her eyes widen. "Now you're scaring me."

I lean over and kiss her until the furrow between her brows disappears. "My parents want me to come home this weekend to celebrate Kayla's birthday, do a Fourth of July picnic, and eat vast quantities of baked goods." Here comes the scary part. "Would you like to join me?"

She blinks slowly. "You want me to go home with you?"

"Yes. As... my girlfriend. I figure if we ease the parentals into this thing slowly, they won't be as shocked when we tell them you're pregnant. What do you say?"

She's quiet a long stretch that has me worrying she'll bail, but then she rolls her eyes. "Why do you always make so much sense?"

"It's my special power."

"But if we tell your parents, we should probably also stop by my mom's, and I'm worried she'll figure out what's going on."

"We have to start somewhere. Maybe hanging out with Ted and Wendy will help us work on this couple thing we're doing, so by the time we see your mom, we're not so uptight."

"I'm not uptight."

I toss my arm over her shoulder and pull her close. She's stiff as a board. "Babe. Relax. You look like you're about to get audited."

"Oh, God. Now that I'm adulting, that's my biggest fear. Why don't schools teach you anything about doing your taxes?"

I chuckle and kiss her temple. "So what do you say? We'll visit the fam, get a nice little barbie going."

"Please don't pretend you're Australian. It's a *bar-be-cue*." She draws little circles on my chest. "What about my brother? I'm not ready to deal with him yet. Just breaking the news that we're together is a lot for me."

Maggie and I were at each other's throats for years, so I get where she's coming from. "Then let's hold off on Sebastian."

"Have you spoken to him lately?"

"We've texted a few times, but haven't really talked since the wedding. That's pretty normal. We'll go months where we do our own thing, and then we'll hang out back home or meet up in Austin."

She nibbles her bottom lip. "Are you worried about how this will affect your relationship with him?"

"Us being together?"

"That and... you know."

"The babies?"

"Yeah."

I think about it. "If he and I hadn't been friends for so long, possibly. He can have a bad temper for sure, and he's really protective of you. But if he can't handle us dating, or if he really thinks I'm so terrible for you, then what kind of friend is he? It's not like I'm a dirtbag."

Her eyes soften, and she kisses my cheek. "You're right. You're a great guy, and if anything, he should be on our side. I'm being paranoid. He's a big boy. He can deal with it."

"You know what I can't deal with, though?"

"What?"

"I haven't gotten my quota of kisses today." I yank her onto my lap and kiss her until her cheeks are rosy.

Because I need to get her used to actually *dating* me and not just being roommates.

34

MAGGIE

My palms are sweaty, and I'm nauseous. "Are you sure this was a good idea? What if I puke in the middle of dinner and they guess I'm pregnant?"

Olly threads his fingers through mine as he drives. "Then they guess."

"How are you so calm about this? I'm freaking out."

"Relax. My parents love you."

I know how hard Olly has worked to get where he is now. How many things he's sacrificed to play football. And I just don't want his family to think I'm going to derail that plan.

If they find out I'm pregnant from the get-go, how can they *not* think I'll ruin his focus?

When we pull up to his house, I take a deep breath. "Stay close in case I pass out."

He chuckles and helps me out of his truck. "It'll be fine. Wait and see."

I love this about him. How he's always so damn calm. Between my dad dying when I was a kid, my mom always struggling to make ends meet, my sister needing so much hands-on attention, and my high-strung brother, calm does not run in my genes. I always feel like I'm on the brink of disaster.

When we're on the porch, Olly puts his hand on the small of my back. "You ready?"

He looks at me expectantly, and I don't want to let him know I'm a wimp who wants to scurry back home before anyone sees us, so I nod. And jeez, the smile he gives me makes me feel bad for not being gutsier.

"We're here," he yells as he pulls open the screen door and walks in, tugging me behind him.

The Olivers live in a modest, one-story ranch with a definite seventies vibe. Dark wood paneling and curio cabinets and doilies decorate the living room, which is packed with people.

"Michael! Over here!" someone shouts.

When we reach the kitchen, Olly stops and pulls his arm around my shoulders. I feel like my heart is about to pound out of my throat. It doesn't help that smelling all this food is making me sick to my stomach.

I rub my belly. *Come on, babies. Don't make me hurl!*

Kayla, Wendy, and Ted freeze when they see us. And they don't say a word as they look from me to Olly and back again.

Kayla is the first one to break the ice. "Holy shit. Are y'all together? Like, *together*?"

Heat rushes to my face, and I squeak as Olly hugs me. If I weren't on the verge of puking, I'd hug him back.

"Yup! I am officially dating Magnolia Morales," he says proudly. "Wanted you to be the first to know."

Jesus. Olly and his declarations.

I laugh and bury my face in his chest.

Wendy claps and runs up to us, tears me out of Olly's arms, and hugs me. "You're really dating my son? This isn't a big joke?"

I smile. "I swear this is not a prank."

Kayla is next in line for hugs. "Please tell me this bit of mystery happened at my wedding."

Olly nods. "For once, you actually deserve all the credit, Kay. Had Maggie and I not been paired up that weekend, she'd probably still be fantasizing about slashing my tires."

"Ha-ha, funny man." I elbow him in the gut, which, *ow*. Those are some hard muscles.

Ted smiles and hugs his giant son. "Gotta get the good ones before they swim away, I always say."

Aww, his dad is sweet.

Wendy covers her mouth. "Honey," she says to Olly, "I didn't know you were bringing anyone, and Uncle Al and Aunt Sherry are staying the night." She turns to me. "I hope you don't mind squeezing on a full bed with Michael, because otherwise I don't know where to put you."

A full bed is smaller than a queen, which means my giant boyfriend will take up most of that space.

Based on the look Olly gives me, he thinks this is a fantastic idea.

I'm sure my cheeks are blazing when I tell his mother the truth. "I don't mind sleeping with Olly."

Am I ready for this? I'm not sure.

But I want to be ready.

35

OLLY

IT'S AWKWARD as fuck to have my mom walk us to my bedroom. She gets out extra blankets and sets them at the foot of my bed.

"Maggie, if you need anything, just let me know. It gets cold here at night, as you know, so make sure Olly keeps you warm." And she winks at her on the way out.

Did my mom just give me the thumbs-up to bang my girlfriend? Why, I think she did. Weird, but strangely cool.

I let out a breath when the door closes. "If that wasn't a seal of approval, I don't know what is." I flop back on my bed and tuck both hands behind my head.

"Going slow does not mean having sex with you at your parents' house," Maggie whispers as she unzips her bag. "Your bed probably squeaks anyway. The whole house would know with the way you go at it."

"Are you saying I'm an enthusiastic lover?"

That adorable blush fires up her cheeks. "We broke the headboard at the hotel. Take that for what you will."

"You're probably right. We shouldn't have sex." I shrug. "With the way you scream, my parents will dial 911 before they realize we're just doing the diddly-doo."

But maybe Maggie will let me stick my hand in her panties. A guy can dream.

"Diddly-doo?" She laughs, and I yank her over me. She lands with a shriek, and I shush her.

"Would you like me to demonstrate?" I press my erection against her thigh, and her eyes flutter closed. "You'd have to be berry, berry quiet," I say in my Elmer Fudd voice.

She laughs again and sits up, straddling me. Her little sundress slides up her legs and tugs at her generous cleavage. Holy shit, she's a fox. I try not to notice how beautiful she is because she makes me a little crazy, but damn. Maggie is a five-alarm fire.

I slide my hands up her thighs and love the shiver that makes her nipples poke through. I'm about to sit up and suck on one of them when someone knocks on the door.

Maggie leaps off me, tangles in the blankets, and heads for the floor. I jump up and grab her just before she lands, turning at the last second so I hit the ground first. She drops on top of me, knocking the wind out of me. I wheeze and try to catch my breath.

For the record, landing on a hardwood floor is not the same as the field in full football pads.

Either that, or I'm rustier than I thought if I can't handle a bit of fluff falling on me.

And that's where Kayla finds me and Maggie, tangled in a heap on the ground, when she sticks her head in my door. "Wow, you guys don't waste any time, huh?"

Maggie's worried face fills my vision as she pats my head and shoulders. "Are you okay? I'm so sorry."

I don't give a shit about the rest of me, just my knee, which I gingerly stretch out. At least I landed on my back, but if Maggie had banged into my knee, that really would've sucked. I definitely need to be more careful.

And what? You'd let Maggie, who's pregnant with your twins, land on the floor, jackass?

No, I admit to myself. I'd launch myself over the bed to save Maggie all over again, damn the consequences.

When I can breathe again, I ask, "Are you okay?"

"Yeah, I'm not hurt or anything. Someone broke my fall." She grabs my face and kisses me. "Thank you for your quick reflexes."

For some reason, that simple, sweet kiss makes me breathless again.

"Aww, you guys are so cute!" Kayla squeals from the doorway, making Maggie flinch. "Who could've known you two would make a great couple? Oh, that's right. I did! Go me!"

"Go *away*," I grunt as I pull Maggie down for another kiss, which she dodges, probably because my sister is standing there. She wobbles to a stand and then offers me a hand, which almost makes me laugh. I could topple her over if I'm not careful. But her expression is so sincere, I grab what's offered, making sure not to give her too much of my weight as I stand.

My sweet baby mama stares up at me with an emotion in her eyes I can't quite make out.

Kayla clears her throat. "Sorry to interrupt your little afternoon delight sesh, but I need y'all to come out to the living room. Joe and I have some news we want to share."

When my sister clears out, I turn to Maggie and tug her dress to cover an adventurous nipple that wants to pop out.

I'm very curious about that nipple.

She shakes her head as she checks herself out in the mirror mounted above my bureau. "I'm a mess." Tugging, she does something mysterious to her bra that plumps those beauties.

"I just want to make something clear. You should always feel free to get dressed around me."

Rolling her eyes, she elbows me playfully. "Same goes for you, Mr. Oliver. If you expect me to prance around naked, turnabout is fair play."

Does she think this is a deterrent?

"Michael Oliver!" Kayla shouts from the other room. "Get your ass in here!"

I grab Maggie's hand, and we book it to the living room. Today is the get-together for Kayla's birthday, but more family is coming tomorrow for the July Fourth barbecue. I don't know how we're gonna squeeze in additional guests, but that's not my problem.

The living room is crowded. Gramps is camped out in the recliner. When he sees us, he motions to Maggie and gives me a thumbs-up.

I never realized how important it would be to have my family love the woman I was with, but it's a huge relief to have everyone be supportive.

My mom brings out a huge cake, and we sing "Happy Birthday" to Kayla, who's sitting in the middle of the living room on Joe's lap.

When we're done singing, Kayla smiles. "I know this is the part where I'm supposed to make a wish, but mine is already coming true. Joe and I are having a baby! Our little spud is due in November!"

Holy shit. My sister is having a kid the month before we have ours. That's really fucking cool.

Everyone's clapping and hugging my sister and congratulating Joe. Kayla lifts her baggy shirt to show us her growing baby bump. Kayla's tall like me, so she hides it well. It makes me wonder what Maggie's bump looks like. All I seem to notice these days is her boobs. I really need to pay attention better.

Kayla explains how she held off telling people because she

and Joe wanted to wait for a family get-together, and this one was the first opportunity since her wedding.

I hang back with Maggie and drop my arm over her shoulders. That's when I realize she's crying.

"I'm just so happy for them!" She can't wipe the tears fast enough.

I kiss the top of her head and whisper, "You'll get your turn. My mom's gonna want to throw you a huge bash. Get ready."

Her face is red and blotchy, but I've never seen a more beautiful woman.

When it's our turn to congratulate my sister, she takes one look at Maggie and lifts an eyebrow. "Are you okay?"

Maggie nods and pulls her into a tight hug. "I cry at Hallmark commercials these days, so yeah. I'm fine. Just really psyched for you guys!"

My sister gives her a funny look, but I break in before Kayla starts connecting the dots. "Does this mean I get to be an official uncle? Finally!" I give Kayla a noogie and shake Joe's hand. "Hell of an aim, brother. Did this happen on your wedding night?"

"Olly!" Maggie looks mortified. "You can't ask things like that."

"Can I embarrass my sister, who sat on my head and farted on me when I was a child? Why, yes, yes, I can."

My sister pinches me, and I yelp, which makes her snicker. "Actually, we got a little ahead of ourselves, and I found out I was preggers right before the wedding, but I was headed for the altar, so who cares? As long as I had this man locked down tight before I pushed out his kid, we're good."

Her words give me pause.

Because Maggie wanted to go slow, I hadn't thought much beyond getting us to the point where we were officially together.

Now I wonder if Maggie wants to get married. She's having my babies, so I think we should at least discuss it.

Or will asking her freak her out again?
Right now, it's a toss-up.
But I think I want to ask.
Not because she's pregnant, but because I love her.

36

OLLY

GRAMPS HOBBLES over to me as the party starts to break up. "Finally got your girl, huh?"

"Finally?"

"Don't pretend you two haven't been sniffing around each other for years. Maggie liked you from the time she was yea tall." He lowers his hand to indicate when she was younger.

"I wouldn't go that far."

He shakes his head at me like I'm an idiot. "Well, don't fuck it up."

"Thanks for the vote of confidence."

"I know what it's like to be young and dumb. Just put her first —well, first after football—and you should be fine."

Football has always come first. That's never been an issue, and it's scary as hell to consider I have something, or rather someone—soon to be some*ones*—who will have to be my top priority.

Wanting to change the subject, I motion toward his foot. He had to have three toes amputated, and his diabetes made the surgery and recovery riskier. "I'm glad to see you up and about.

Mom texts me updates every few days. Says you're a pain in the ass, but feeling better."

His gruff laugh makes everyone look over at us. "I'm not keeling over yet. Still gotta ask that old bird over on Main Street out on a date."

"Really?"

He nods and rubs the whiskers on his chin. "It's good to have a bucket list. I keep adding to it so I feel like I have a reason to live."

"Aren't your kids and grandkids reason enough?"

"Eh. Sometimes."

I laugh at his wry expression. My dad joins us, and we park our asses in the corner and debate who the school might sign on as coach and the pros and cons of each selection. Lone Star is supposed to announce the new guy any day now.

Waiting has me on some sharp needles. If we get another Coach Krugman, he'll cut me zero slack for having a pregnant girlfriend. I need a coach who isn't gonna be an asshole. It seems like a frivolous thing to pray for, but I find myself pleading we get the right person for the team.

When Gramps goes to his trailer, I help him get settled and then head off to find Maggie, only to realize she went to bed already.

My mom places her hand on my arm. "Is Maggie okay, honey? She looked so tired. And I love her to pieces for being so excited about Kayla's pregnancy, but Maggie seemed a little more emotional than I'd expect her to be."

I want to tell her, *Not for a woman who's pregnant with twins*, but I don't. "She has a lot going on right now. She's a little stressed. It's nothing she can't handle." It's true. Maggie is fierce as fuck. It's one of the reasons I think I've always liked her.

"I'm going to give her a box of peppermint tea, because stress is bad for her arteries."

"Oooo-kay." My mom and her remedies. But if it'll help Maggie relax, I'll make it for her.

When I crack open the door to my bedroom, the lights are out, and Maggie is sound asleep. She looks peaceful. I remember waking up to her the morning after the wedding and wanting more of that.

My heart beats hard at the thought that I'm really close to figuring this out with her. We could make this happen. Be a couple. Parents. Lovers. Husband and wife.

Terrifying shit. But also incredible.

As quietly as possible, I kick off my jeans and t-shirt. I keep on my boxer briefs and slide under the covers and spoon her warm body. I smile into her hair as she sighs and wiggles back against me.

I've missed this. Just holding her in my arms feels phenomenal.

She's wearing some fuzzy pajama set with pink flamingos. They're old and faded but soft. I've just fallen asleep when she gasps and yanks herself out of my arms. "Oh, my God, it's so hot." And strips off her clothes.

She flops back in a thin bralette thing and panties, and I finally see it in the low light of the moon streaming through my window—her baby bump.

I immediately reach for her. "This... this is incredible." I rub her belly, and she closes her eyes and smiles. "I can't believe you haven't shown me your belly." It's small still, but different than how she looked a few months ago.

Leaning down, I kiss that silky, bare skin.

Her hand threads through my hair and lightly scratches my head. "Will you say that when I'm covered in stretch marks?"

"Stretch marks are beautiful," I whisper. "It means your body changed to accommodate our two humans. Like Sienna said, you're like a butterfly. So yes, I'll still say that."

She reaches for me, and even though I'm tempted to launch myself on top of her, I'm determined to go her speed. I sprawl out next to her, and she rolls over to face me.

"Can I confess something?" she asks quietly. When I nod, she looks down shyly. "Pregnancy makes me really..."

"Tired?"

"Yes, that, and..."

"Nauseous?"

"Definitely, but also..."

She bites her bottom lip, and I laugh. "Horny?"

"So horny." Adorably, she covers her face and mumbles into the bedspread, "I've never wanted sex so badly in my life."

"Funny, but I happen to have just the thing to accommodate this need." We both laugh, and I tug her closer. "Your speed. We'll always go your speed, baby. Whatever you want. I can help you take the edge off, and then we can go to sleep. We don't have to do anything more if you're not comfortable."

"Really?"

"I might need to take a bathroom break to jerk off, but yes."

She giggles and licks her bottom lip.

Christ, I'm already hard.

But then she whispers, "Could *I* maybe jerk you off?"

That's when I go from having a chub to a full-on heat-seeking missile.

The second she's in my arms, she groans.

"Shh. Remember the part about being *berry* quiet."

"No Elmer Fudd when we're naked," she declares as she slides off her bralette thing.

Words desert me as I take in the beauty in my bed. Maggie's long hair is spread on my pillow, and her full tits beckon me.

Teenage Olly gives me a high-five.

Ducking down, I draw a pert nipple into my mouth. I take a handful of tit in one hand and squeeze gently. "Okay, but no screaming." With a smirk, I reach down with my other hand and rub her clit through her panties. "Which, if I recall, you are apt to do."

My dick throbs when I realize how wet she is already. Slipping my fingers under the fabric of her underwear, I slide around her swollen clit slowly until her back arches.

"Can I lick this pretty pussy?" A gentleman always asks.

"Please."

I tear off her panties and groan when her legs drop open. Mesmerized, I watch her hand dip into the shadowed valley between her legs. Her touch is eager, a swift swirl, and I'm frozen as I watch the erotic vision before me.

But when she pushes two fingers inside, it's too much. I slide down my boxers and take myself in hand as I watch her. I'm supposed to be doing something, but for the life of me, I can't remember what.

"Christ, you make me hard, Magnolia." I get more turned on when I realize her eyes are glued to my hand as I shuttle up and down my cock. "Do you touch yourself like this when you're all alone?"

She nods.

"Do you think of me?" I ask.

"Yes."

"What do I do?"

Her chest heaves as those sultry eyes meet mine. "You fuck me hard."

I swallow. How have I stayed away from this woman for so long? She's my kryptonite.

Pushing her hand away, I take a long, slow lick from her slick hole up to that pretty pearl.

Her gasp is muffled. I look up her gorgeous body and realize she's covered her mouth with one hand. She writhes on the bed when I press two thick fingers inside, and it only takes a few thrusts as I lick her to make her come.

Her little muffled cries almost send me over the edge. After I work her down, I squeeze my dick hard to back away from the ledge.

The smile on her sleepy face keeps me from asking for more.

After I wipe my face with my arm, I lean up and kiss her forehead and then slide out of bed.

"Where are you going?" she asks, her voice raspy.

"The bathroom. I figured you must be tired. We've had a long day."

She pats the space next to her on the bed. "Come here, Michael."

The way she says my name no longer carries disdain. Tonight, it sounds like a promise.

I sit next to her, my heart pounding when she rolls over so her face is almost in my lap. She turns her head up to give me a devilish smile. "I'm sorry I can't go deep for obvious reasons, but let's see if you like this."

Pretty sure I'm going to love anything that involves Maggie and my dick.

She takes me in hand and gives my tip a swirl of her tongue that has me groaning. She shushes me with a giggle.

Quiet. Right.

I lose all verbal skills the moment she sucks me into the warmth of her mouth. She doesn't go deep, and I wouldn't want her to. I'm just thrilled her morning sickness isn't an issue at the moment.

She pauses to lick her hand, places it on the base of my dick, tugs me in a rhythm that makes my toes curl, and then she tongues my slit.

"Fuck, Maggie." I grip her hair hard. "Shit. Sorry."

With a mouth full of me, she smiles. "Is okay." I slide out with a pop. "You can pull my hair. I kinda like it."

My dream girl likes when I fuck her hard and pull her hair.

I wonder if she'll let me smack her ass.

Trying not to come, I attempt to distract myself by checking out her rounded bottom, but that just makes me want to lean over and bite it.

"Mags, I'm gonna come, so you might wanna..."

She slides off me.

Before I give in to the twinge of disappointment that she took her mouth off me, she fucking straddles my lap.

"We're already pregnant, right?" she whispers. "We should make the most of this. I'm negative. I had every test known to man done at the OB-GYN appointment."

"I'm good to go, too." In a sex haze, I watch as she slowly lowers herself onto my eager dick.

I've never gone without a condom.

Her tight, wet heat makes my cock pulse.

I grip her hips to still her. "You feel so fucking good, Mags. Don't move or the ride will be over before we get outta the gates."

When I don't think I'll embarrass myself, I grab her ass in both hands and yank her as close as she can get. Her big tits press into my chest, and I lean down to nibble her shoulder. Her neck. That little spot behind her ear.

By the time we kiss, I'm ready to fuck.

Two thrusts later, though, the loud squeak of my bed has me cursing.

"What if we do it on that?" she asks, pointing to the faded, wing-backed armchair in the corner.

Never losing our connection, I hoist her in my arms, trudge across the room, and settle into the chair.

She groans the moment I'm seated and immediately starts moving. "Yes, yes," she chants.

Her beautiful tits jiggle in my face, beckoning for attention. I grab one and squeeze, which has her fluttering on my cock.

"Can you come again?" I grunt.

"Maybe. This angle is really working for me."

We should take this chair back to Charming with us.

I reach between us and rub her clit while she bounces on my lap. Unable to resist the temptation of those rosy nipples, I suck one into my mouth, which sets her off.

The fluttering tight ripple on my cock is nothing like I've ever felt before. I press my mouth to her shoulder as my release overpowers me.

"Oh, my God." She groans. "I can feel that. You pulsing." Maggie shivers and shakes in my arms as I come.

As incredible as tonight has been, as good as she felt without a condom, it's nothing compared to having Maggie drape her sated body over me in bed when we're done.

37

MAGGIE

A KNOCK on the door has me cracking my eye open.

I'm sprawled on top of Olly, naked. In his childhood bedroom. In his parents' house.

"Kids, brunch is in ten!" his mom shouts from the hallway.

I yank up the sheets, mortified that Mrs. Oliver might see us like this. Her son doesn't budge.

"Olly!" I whisper-hiss. "Olly! Wake up. Your mom wants us to come eat."

He yawns and smacks his lips. "Not hungry. Had some late-night pussy for dinner."

Said pussy pulses when I think of all the naked things we did.

Olly's golden head of hair is messy, and thick strands fall over his sleepy blue eyes. "Come back to bed." His gruff morning voice is so sexy. He tugs on my sheet so it slips to my waist. Judging from the way his attention goes directly to my boobs, sleep isn't what he has in mind.

"Do you think *they'll* think we had sex in your bed?" I whisper.

He takes one look at my face and laughs. "Uh, yeah. Especially if you blush like that."

I cover both cheeks with my palms. "I can't help it. If I get upset, my face flushes. If I get turned on, I turn red. If I get embarrassed, I look sunburned."

Judging by the hungry look he gives me, he doesn't care.

When he reaches for me, I back away. "If we were back home, we could spend all morning in bed, but not at your parents' house. They'll hear us!"

He tucks both arms behind his head and watches me gather some clothes. I turn my back because I'm suddenly self-conscious. Even though he's licked me from stem to stern, in the bright light of morning, I feel a little out of my element. I'm not excited about how the baby weight is settling on my butt and belly.

But I desperately need a shower. I reek of sex and questionable decisions.

I duck into his bathroom and break a record with how quickly I shower and dress. My hair goes up in a messy bun. Three swipes of mascara on either eye, some lip balm, and a dab of powder, and I'm ready for brunch.

Olly is wiping his stomach with a tissue when I exit the bathroom. "Did you just jerk off?" I ask.

"Yup." He gives me a huge smile. "Thought about you blowing me, and I went off like Vesuvius. Thanks for the visual." He gives me a weird little salute.

Oh, my God. My face fires up again, and he laughs.

I cross the room, put my hand on the doorknob, and take a deep breath.

"Magnolia."

Is it crazy I love how he says my name now? I glance over my shoulder, and my heart skips a beat at the gorgeous man who looks like he wants to devour me for breakfast.

"Come here." He crooks his finger, and I can't resist his call.

He leans up for a kiss. It's an achingly sweet thing for him to want. Either that or pregnancy has made mush of my brain.

I meet him in the middle, his lips softly grazing mine. With a sigh, I run my hand through his hair. His blue eyes are so bright this morning. "You're a mess. Get dressed. I have to eat something before your gremlins make me hurl." With one more parting smooch, I head out to brave the family.

When I close the door behind me, I lean back against it and close my eyes.

You're in over your head.

Why did I think having sex was the right thing to do last night? I wanted to take things slow, and at the first real opportunity to get naked, my clothes came flying off.

Because you love him.

I place my hand over my heart and hope Olly and I can withstand whatever comes our way. Because if anyone has the ability to break me, it's the man on the other side of this door.

The smell of bacon makes me so ravenous, I could eat my fist. Pregnancy is weird. I get morning sickness all the time, but I also get nauseous from hunger too.

Hesitantly, I head for the kitchen where Mrs. Oliver is plating up a mountain of food.

Please, God, please let me keep down the meal.

Gramps, Mr. Oliver, Joe, and Kayla are already seated.

"Morning," I say as I reach for a glass of orange juice.

"How'd you sleep, honey?" Mrs. Oliver asks.

"Yeah, Mags, how'd you sleep?" Kayla asks with a smirk as I'm taking a sip.

I choke and cough and clear my throat. "Fine, thanks." I

ignore the mischief in Kayla's tone and pretend I'm an idiot who doesn't understand innuendo.

"Who wants some pancakes?" Mrs. Oliver places a huge platter on the table, and in a flash, Olly is at my side and flinging them onto my plate and his. His mother laughs. "It's like you came out of nowhere. Really, it's a remarkable skill, Michael."

He taps his nose. "I have an internal pancake detector. Very handy."

I smile at him. He's stupidly charming when he wants to be.

His hair is damp, and he's wearing a white polo and worn jeans that hug his muscular thighs. He slumps down into the chair next to me, leans over, kisses me, and starts shoveling food in his mouth.

Unaccustomed to public displays of affection, I look to his family to gauge their reaction. His mother is trying not to smile, his father is reading the newspaper, and Kayla is doing something dirty to a sausage link and whispering to her husband.

Gramps is the only one watching me. He gives me a wink and demands bacon.

Everyone's fine, Magnolia. Relax.

As though he can sense my nerves, Olly reaches for my hand under the table and gives me a squeeze. It's a sweet gesture.

I'm realizing now how damn thoughtful this man is. I'm glad I didn't see it sooner. I don't need to fall for him any harder than I already have.

That thought makes me choke on a square of pancake.

"Honey, are you okay?" Mrs. Oliver pats my back. "I bet you're starving, and that's why you choked on your orange juice and the pancakes. Ted, I told you brunch was too late for the kids."

Mr. Oliver finally puts away the newspaper. "Wendy, everyone's fine. Stop fussin' and get some food before your son eats it all."

She trots over to her husband, and he leans his head back to whisper something to her, which makes her laugh. She brushes a kiss on his forehead and sits next to him.

Those are some couple goals right there.

I've always loved the Olivers. They accepted me tagging along with Bash and Olly whenever those two were running off to cause trouble. And when they ditched me, as those dumbasses sometimes did, Mrs. Oliver would let me hang out with her in the kitchen. We'd make the boys brownies and cookies, all stuff they barely thanked us for when they eventually returned from causing mayhem.

"Breakfast is delicious, Mrs. Oliver. Thank you for having me over."

"Oh, Maggie, please call me Wendy. I've known you too long for us to be formal."

I nod with a smile and nudge Olly. "Did you know that your mom taught me how to bake?"

"No shit?"

"Son, language." Mr. Oliver gives his son the hairy eyeball.

After taking a bite of bacon, I explain how I ended up spending so much time with Wendy. "Remember when you and Bash thought it would be fun to tip over the cows in Mr. Palmer's pasture? Only his bull nearly gored you? Your mom got me hooked on baking that day."

He laughs and reaches for my hand again. "I forget how long you've been around."

"Since before you had hair on your balls, kid," Gramps barks out.

"Dad!" Wendy yells. "Too much information!"

I chuckle. "Olly and Bash were in love with Ginnie Essex that summer."

"Wow. I forgot about her." He shoves a whole strip of bacon in his mouth.

Suck it, Ginnie. I won him fair and square.

"Young love is fickle." Wendy hands the plate of pancakes to her husband.

Gramps pounds the table. "Are we gonna ignore the elephant in the room? Pretend we don't know what's going on?"

My mouth drops open, which is bad because I'm suddenly nauseous. I swallow down the flood of saliva in the back of my throat and pray I don't puke on this beautiful brunch. I can't believe Gramps would out me and Olly for having sex, but what else could he be talking about?

Mr. Oliver sighs. "Bruce, we wanted the kids to enjoy breakfast before we started talking shop. Your daughter insisted."

Gramps gives him a look of disgust. "Is anything more important than Michael's season? No. So eat your damn pancakes so we can discuss this."

"What's happened?" Olly's relaxed demeanor instantly evaporates.

Ted hands him the newspaper. "Lone Star State hired Richard Santos."

A long silence ensues.

"The Saint? *The Saint* is coaching the Broncos?" Olly scans the broadsheet.

"Three-year contract."

No one says anything.

"I'm sorry, but is this a good thing or bad?" I ask. Judging by Olly's intense expression, I'm guessing it's not good.

He tilts his head one way, then the other. "It's good... if..."

"If you stay out of trouble," Mr. Oliver adds. "Santos is known for being tough but fair. He doesn't tolerate any shenanigans." He points at his son. "So no 'fiestas.' He benched three players last year when police broke up a party. He doesn't like his players to have any distractions."

That doesn't sound so terrible.

I turn to Olly. "I guess it's a good thing that you're not living at the football house anymore then, huh?"

Another beat of silence.

"What?" several voices ask simultaneously.

Wendy leans forward to grill her son. "Since when, Michael? Where are you staying? And why haven't you said anything?" Her eyes shift to me and then narrow on her son. "You'd better not be living where I think you are."

Oh. Shit.

I close my eyes.

Olly never told his family that he moved in with me.

38

OLLY

THIS MORNING WAS GOING SO WELL.

Guess I should've prepped my girlfriend about my cover story a little better.

I peek over at Magnolia, who's doggedly staring out her window as we drive home. After breakfast, we hung around as more family arrived for the afternoon barbecue and fireworks, but I could tell she felt uncomfortable even though she was trying hard to smile and be social. It didn't take much to talk her into cutting out early.

"Are you sure you don't want to stop by and see your mom?"

She shakes her head. "With my luck, she'll take one look at me, know I'm pregnant, and drag me to church to say a rosary, so no, I'm not ready to let that cat out of the bag yet. I did enough damage this morning." I try to grab her hand, but she pulls away and glares at me. "You could've told me you hadn't explained you were living with me. I can't believe you let me go in there without knowing this critical information."

"You're right. I'm sorry. It slipped my mind."

"Your parents were pissed. All of that 'honey' this and 'honey' that dried up faster than Texas in a heat wave."

I wince. She's right. As much as my parents love Maggie, Wendy and Ted are *not* fans of me living with my girlfriend.

My dad didn't have a chance to pull me aside for a lecture since family started arriving for the July Fourth barbecue, but I could see it in his eyes. I expect he'll call this week to lay it on me.

Maggie makes this little squeaking sound, and I look over and her eyes are shiny. "They're not going to like me anymore, Michael. I love your family, and now they hate me."

I feel like a dick for not preparing her better. After I make sure there's no one behind me, I pull over and throw on my hazards. We're on a backcountry road, so it shouldn't be a problem. "Come here."

"No." She swipes angrily at her tears. "I messed up everything with your parents, and now you have a coach who's a hardass. If he doesn't like distractions, he's certainly not going to be thrilled you have a pregnant girlfriend. A girlfriend who's pregnant with *twins!*"

Fuck. I hadn't thought about it that way.

I try to keep the emotions off my face, but she must see what I'm thinking because her face crumples. In between sobs, she says, "Maybe... maybe you should m-move back into the football h-house before we screw up your s-season."

A little piece of my heart cracks when I hear her struggle through that sentence. Maggie hasn't stuttered since she first moved to Heartland.

I unbuckle my seatbelt and pull her toward me. She doesn't resist long, and I hold her until she calms down.

"I don't know what we should do, okay?" I brush the hair out of her face and wipe the tears. "I don't have the answers. I only know that we have to be strong for one another and the babies." She nods, which I take as a win. "Let's do this one step at a time. We can't meet the coach until training camp, so I'll do a little reconnaissance in the meanwhile and ask some former team-mates for advice."

Her shiny eyes meet mine. "That... sounds good."

Thank God I pulled that out of my ass because it's killing me to see her cry. I just fucking wrangled her into a bona fide relationship. I can't have this thing implode two seconds into it. And judging by how unnerved she is by my family's reaction to us living together, marriage is out of the question for now.

I take her chin in my hand. "Just don't give up on us. You and I, we're good. It's everyone else who has to come to terms with this, okay?"

She bites down on her bottom lip, silence stretching between us. For an agonizing moment, I'm worried about her response, but then she nods. "Okay. I won't give up."

39

OLLY

THERE'S nothing like getting your ass chewed out by your parents. I hold the phone away from my ear, but I can still hear my mother squawking. Ted already took a turn.

"I may have given you the wrong impression by letting Maggie stay in your room. I was excited to see you with her after the string of women you typically date, but just because I accept you probably have sleepovers on campus doesn't mean I think you two should live together. You're making a mistake to rush into this, Michael. We've made all these sacrifices for you to go to school, get your degree, and play football. Not play house. You don't need that kind of distraction."

Peeking through the blinds, I make sure Maggie is still outside. The woman has supersonic hearing, and she'd be devastated to hear Wendy freak out.

As much as I love and respect my mother, this is pissing me off. I can fully admit my parents saved all their pennies to help me play football growing up, but I got a full scholarship and paid my own way to college. While I've needed help from time to time, I'd say I've been pretty responsible.

With one exception.

I stare down at my pregnant girlfriend, wishing I could snap my fingers and make everything better. I'm tempted to tell my parents the truth, but I'm pretty sure finding out Maggie is having twins will send them into hysterics.

And not the we're-so-happy-to-be-grandparents kind they had for my sister.

Even though they never say it, I know my parents are counting on me hitting it big so I can help them financially. I want to help them—that's not the issue. They've always been generous with me and Kayla, and I have no problem reciprocating. What's mine is theirs.

But what if I can't pull it off? What if my knee isn't ready when the season starts? What if I don't get drafted and can't help with their mortgage and Gramps's medical bills? Add twins to this equation, and I'm totally fucked if I don't have a great season.

"Mom, can you just trust me? I've always been a good son, right? I never got in trouble, always got good grades, always did what I was told. All I can say right now is I'm trying my best." I need to get off the phone before I blow up at her, which will not make this any better. Do I really need to tell my parents I'm a grown-ass man? I'm tempted to remind them they were younger than I am now when they got married.

"Oh, honey, I know. It's just—"

"Listen, I gotta go. I'll talk to you soon."

I rub the bridge of my nose, hating that I need to make more phone calls. I promised Maggie I'd talk to some of the guys, and she's just as anxious as I am to have some stability.

So I hang up and call Ben.

After I explain what happened with my family over the weekend and my concerns about Santos, Ben blows out a big breath. "That's a tough one, bro. You know how much shit Coach Krud gave me for having a kid. Maybe Maggie's right.

Keep the pregnancy quiet while you feel out Santos. Give him a chance to get to know you first."

That's not what I want to hear.

We talk through the pros and cons for a while, but Ben's overall suggestion is to get the lay of the land with the new coach before I make any announcements.

Will the other guys have a different perspective?

But the words are barely out of my mouth when Johnny tells me to "get my ass back to the Stallion Station, ASAP." And Rider tells me I should keep football a priority if I want to have any kind of future for my kids. In his words, "Babies are expensive as fuck."

So... what? I leave Maggie and move back in with Cam and the guys? There has to be another way to deal with our situation.

Dread settles in my gut at the prospect of sharing the advice the guys gave me, but we promised each other to be as open and honest about this as possible. Because we're screwed if we can't trust each other.

Maggie might be putting on a brave face, but I can tell being pregnant scares her. And I think the stress of staying with my family caught up with her, because this morning she couldn't keep down her breakfast.

I pour two peppermint iced teas and head outside, where she's trying to pull the weeds out of what's supposed to be a garden.

"Shouldn't you be taking it easy?" I ask gently as I hand her the drink.

She wipes the sweat out of her eyes. "I'm too stressed out to take it easy, and the yard is a mess. I don't want to get another citation from the city. It's so embarrassing to know my neighbors report me." She glares down the street and sips her tea.

"Want me to mow the rest of it?"

"It needs more than that. The mower won't even get through

the side yard. And I was hoping to plant some flowers along the front and clean up the walkway, but I'd rather work on the garden. I feel like if I can get one thing done in this yard that makes me happy, it'll keep me going. Sometimes you have to do something for yourself, you know?"

I understand exactly what she means, and it makes me wonder if this decision about football is about what's best for my family back in Heartland, the babies growing in Maggie's belly, or myself.

Wish I fucking knew, because this shit is twisting me all up inside.

I swallow, my throat feeling thick. "Can we talk? Let's sit on the porch." I offer my hand to help her stand and smile at the sight of her in overalls. I love this about Maggie. She never puts on airs to try to impress anyone.

When you play on a team of elite athletes, there's a lot of dick-swinging. Someone's always trying to have the most bravado or the biggest bark. It's exhausting. Even some of the women I've dated felt the need to brag. Amelia never shut up about her modeling gigs.

Maggie's quiet confidence is really attractive. This woman can do anything. Grout a bathroom? No problem. Sand a floor? Done. Design some wedding invitations? In a heartbeat.

Reaching up the side of the porch, I put down our now-empty glasses and turn back to her.

"You know what might be cool? In the back, we could espalier some pear trees. It would still give you plenty of room for your garden, but then you'd have some fruit at some point." I point to the section of the yard.

"What's espalier?"

"A technique of pruning and tying the trees or bushes so they grow flat and you maximize production. I watched a documentary on it once. A French monk in the sixteen hundreds discovered the trees near the monastery walls produced the most fruit, and this really cool technique was born."

"Sounds riveting," she teases.

I yank her into my arms and tickle her. "Are you giving me shit?"

"Just kidding!" She squeals and tries to wiggle away, but I lift her, pin her against the house, and kiss her until she moans and wraps her ankles around my waist.

After how upset she was yesterday, I'm thrilled she's letting me kiss her. I didn't ask to sleep in her bed last night, and she didn't invite me. I kinda felt like she wanted some space. Although now I'm not so sure that's what she needs.

Someone coughs behind me.

I press my forehead to Maggie's shoulder. It's just that kind of day, isn't it? That cough sounded distinctly feminine, and there's only one person who would be interrupting us right now.

Reluctantly, I let Maggie slide down me, adjust my junk, and slowly turn around. "Amelia. What's up?"

"I saw a snake." She talks to Maggie as though I'm not there, which is fine by me. I still haven't forgiven her for that Heavenly Hunks bullshit.

Maggie's eyes widen. "When? Where? God, I hate snakes."

"Over there, and it rattled."

I'm at the point in my relationship with Amelia where if she told me the sky was blue, I'd haul my ass outside to check first before I believed her. This woman loves making drama. She probably saw a garter snake or lizard. Hell, it could've been a shadow.

"Thanks for the warning. I'll be on the lookout. In the meanwhile, perhaps you shouldn't wear flip-flops."

Amelia rolls her eyes like this is the biggest inconvenience of her life and stomps back to the casita.

Maggie watches her with a furrow between her brows. "That girl hates me."

"I wouldn't lose sleep over it. She hates everyone." It took me a while to see that. I swear she was a different person when we first started talking. Was she hiding her true self, or did success turn her into such a mean girl? Hard to say.

Maggie and I head up to the porch and sit on the front steps. I lace my fingers together and hope I can find the right words. So I lay it out. Share the advice the guys gave me.

When I'm done, Maggie's expression is surprisingly stoic. "I think they're right. You should keep our situation quiet, let Coach Santos get to know you, and in the meanwhile, you should move back to the football house."

Fuck. This sucks. "And you're okay with this?"

She swallows. Shrugs. "What am I supposed to say? If you tell your coach I'm pregnant, he might use that as a reason to think you're unfocused or, worse, irresponsible. Plus, you're recovering from a serious injury, which might encourage him to use other players instead of you. If you live with me and struggle even a little during the season, your parents might think I'm the reason. You saw the look on your mother's face yesterday. She acted as though I'd drowned a basket of puppies in a river. And, if you stay here, it's not unreasonable to think Santos will hear about it. People talk."

Everything she says is rational, but my gut is screaming this is a terrible idea. "Mags, I hate you being by yourself in this big house. What if you need something? What if there's an emergency? What if I just want to see your face first thing in the morning?"

Her eyes go shiny. "You can come visit me. I'm not saying you can't still sleep over whenever you want, but maybe your main base should be the football house."

Back to living in a household of party animals. Not how I want to spend my *fifth* damn year of college.

I try to look on the bright side. "That's if the guys haven't already rented out my room to one of the other players." Maybe I can't move back. My parents can't be pissed at Maggie if my spot's already filled.

Maggie takes my hand. "Your teammates are welcome here. In fact, if anyone wants to swap with you and take your room here, tell them I have a treadmill and weights."

Awesome. 'Cause I really want one of my asshole friends living with my pregnant girlfriend.

But Maggie is sincere and so sweet to offer, all I can do is give her a hug. I never tell her it sears my gut to think of another man taking my place.

40

MAGGIE

Breathe through it, Maggie. Don't cry.

I hate how this pregnancy has turned me into an ugly crier. It stops here.

I swallow several times and blink fast as I chop some fruit for a smoothie.

This isn't the end. You told Olly to go. You practically shoved him out the door this morning.

In the background, Cam and Billy grunt as they haul Olly's bed down the stairs. After that's all loaded in his truck and dropped off at the football house, they return with Cam and Billy's crap.

"So we can take any of the rooms upstairs?" Billy asks.

"Any room that isn't mine, yeah. Make yourself at home." I hold up a hand. "Can I ask why you're doing this? I thought you hated my house."

Billy rubs the back of his neck. "Sorry I was a dick. I don't hate your house. It's starting to grow on me, especially once you added the workout room. That's pretty dope, considering you don't work out."

I cough. "I work out. Perhaps not as much as I should, but..."

Cam slaps Billy on the back. "Ignore him. What Billy means to say is that instead of having to share a room at the football house, we get our own rooms here and private bathrooms, all of which is great. It'll be quiet, and we'll be able to study in peace. Plus, Olly told us we could borrow his landing pad whenever there's a party, so if there's a pretty little filly who wants to keep us company…"

He lets that statement hang, and I chuckle. They don't call it the Stallion Station for nothing. "So you have a love shack for hookups if you need one. Is that what you're saying?"

"As long as we promise to wash the sheets, Olly said it wasn't a prob, since he'll be here with you on those nights."

Olly really is a great guy. The better I get to know him, the guiltier I feel for all the shit I gave him over the years.

Cam steals a blueberry and pops it in his mouth. "And since housing is maxed out this semester, it was easy to get your place approved for funding, so you'll get paid."

I'm not going to try to talk them into only giving me half, like I did with Olly. I'm not an idiot. I need the money. It's a huge relief to have that income. I actually might be able to pay my January property tax bill without working myself into an early grave.

Olly stomps in. "What's the holdup?" He lifts his white shirt and wipes his face, and I'm treated to his ripped, tan stomach.

"The guys were just telling me how excited they are to bang their girlfriends on your bed."

He makes a face, and I laugh.

Olly points at Billy. "Swear to God, I'm buying a blacklight to make sure you assholes wash the sheets." He hooks an arm over my shoulders and wipes his sweaty face on my neck. I squeal and shove him away, but he pulls me back. "Don't even pretend you don't like it when I'm sweaty."

His sexy, gravelly voice makes goosebumps break out on my

arms. I let my head fall back on my shoulders as I look up at him. He tilts his down and grazes my lips with his.

"Going to miss you," I whisper.

"Yeah, training camp is gonna suck. You have all of our phone numbers if you have an emergency, right?" He rubs my belly, and I smile. My back is to his friends, so they can't see. I'm really starting to show, and I know we'll have to tell them soon. Baggy clothes will only get me so far. I'm guessing he trusts his friends can keep a secret, or he wouldn't have let them move in here.

I nod. "I have them in my notebook and on my phone. Plus your parents' numbers. God help me if I have to call them."

"Sheesh, you guys." Billy gags a little, the jerk. "He's only going away for training camp, not to Albania. You'll see him in a week."

I'll see Olly on Sundays, but for the next three weeks, he has camp, and I'm twisted up about the whole thing.

Olly didn't want to move out. I didn't want him to go either, but I feel like the deck is stacked against us this fall. I know when I'm swimming upstream. Why make our lives more difficult than they already are?

"Who wants pizza?" I ask as I get the ingredients out of the fridge.

"Homemade?" Billy asks as he rubs his hands together.

"Yup! My mama's recipe." The dough is made from a box, but he doesn't need to know this.

Olly crosses his arms. "That's another thing. You two need to keep the fridge stocked. I don't want Maggie going hungry because you two or your friends decimated her supplies. You feel me?"

Cam pats Olly on the back. "Don't worry, bro. We'll watch out for your girl."

That night, the guys gorge on homemade pizza with all the

fixings, and then Olly and I curl up in my bed. He might be officially living at the football house, but he has clothes and toiletries here too, so he can stay over anytime.

"Sorry I didn't finish cleaning out your basement," he mumbles against the back of my neck. I love when he spoons me.

Things were weird after the barbecue at his parents', but once we discussed it on my porch, I felt better.

Which reminds me that I need to talk to my mom and brother. Bash loves Olly. I don't see how us being together will upset him. As for the babies, well, he'll just have to suck it up and accept our situation.

"You got a lot done. I hate going down to the basement, and if it were up to me, there'd still be a million boxes of Uncle Hidalgo's stuff, collecting dust and spiders." I shiver.

"It's weird that you have a basement. Most Texas houses don't."

"Please don't say that. I already feel like a demon is gonna pop out of that closet in the corner by the washer and eat my innards."

He chuckles and pulls me closer. As he does, his big hand rubs up and down my stomach. "Wait until I'm home, and I'll do your laundry. You don't have to go down there. Fuck, I should've added a better handrail for those stairs."

Smiling, I close my eyes. I'm digging how protective Olly is about me. "I'll be fine. But I wouldn't object to the handrail when you have the time. There's no rush, though. I love the pear trees you planted. Hopefully I won't kill them in the next three weeks."

"Hey, we forgot to do your lotion." He hops out of bed, turns on the bedside table lamp, and reaches for my baby belly moisturizer, which is supposed to help with stretch marks.

My eyes take a little jaunt up and down his smoking hot

body. Olly's golden brown from working in my yard. His shoulders are broader than ever, and his thighs are thick with muscle. He's been working his ass off to get ready for football. I'm so proud of his determination.

And yes, I'm going to miss the off-the-charts sex we have, but I'm particularly blue when I think about not waking up in his arms.

I lift my tank top, and he straddles my legs. He usually just rubs some in, but tonight, he leans over me and starts whispering against my stomach. "Hey, fellas. It's your dad." His eyes meet mine, and I smile. He's been ecstatic since he found out we're having two boys. I run my fingers through his hair. "Your mama and I are so excited to meet you. I'll be away at training camp for a few days, so I want y'all to be on your best behavior. No morning sickness, you hear me? Mama needs those calories so she can grow you big and strong. She's gonna give me a full report when I get home."

"Think they can hear us?"

He pops open the lotion, squirts some in his palm, and warms it in his hands. "Yeah, I do. I watched a whole documentary about it. I was gonna save this as a surprise, but I bought you a bunch of classical music and headphones to play for the boys. It's supposed to build neuroconnectors or something."

"I put the headphones on my belly?"

"Yup."

You learn something new every day. "That's really cool. Thank you."

He rubs the lotion on me with the intense focus he has about everything. When he's done, I sit up and strip off my tank top because if this is my last night with him for a week, I might as well make the most of it.

His eyes laser in on my boobs. He flings the lotion off the

bed, and his hands go to his favorite part of my anatomy. "Jesus, you have great tits."

He's already hard against my hip, so I reach down and rub him through his boxer briefs. "Is it weird to say I love your cock? At first, it's an intimidating size, but you have a way of wedging it in just right, and it always makes me see fireworks."

"Feel free to talk about my dick anytime you want."

I laugh and pull him down to me. His whiskers abrade my skin when we kiss, but I don't care. He smells so good, like his shower gel and sexy man. I want to remember everything about him. How he smells. How he tastes. How he feels when he sinks deep into my body.

I keep telling myself nothing is going to change between us. That what we have is good and solid, but what if I'm wrong?

Everything might change when the season starts.

It doesn't take us much to get hot and heavy, and before long, we strip out of the rest of our clothes. He settles between my thighs, and his hard length nudges against my entrance. Taking himself in hand, he swipes his head up and down through my wetness until I'm panting.

"Hard or soft tonight?" he asks.

I run my hand along the bristles on his cheek. "Surprise me."

He responds by licking my bottom lip as he slowly sinks into me. "Clear your Sundays for the next three weeks. You have a standing appointment in this bed."

Arching back to make room for him, I groan at how deep he goes. How thick he feels. How I don't know where he ends and I begin. "I might have withdrawals in the meanwhile."

He moves slowly at first. He's a big guy—everywhere—so it takes a minute to get used to his size. But sweet Jesus, he feels good. I don't know if this is a pregnancy thing, but all I have to do is think about him getting naked and everything south of the border starts to pound.

"Baby, you're so wet already."

"You turn me on." I kiss him. "You've always turned me on."

For some reason, that makes him stop. He looks down at me, his eyes a deep, dark blue. "Always? Even in high school?"

"Yes, you turd. Even in high school. When you dated *all* those other girls." I pinch him, and he laughs. "Don't remind me."

His eyes go serious. "We have a lot of time to make up for, don't we?"

I brush a strand of hair out of his eyes. "Yes. And you're stuck with me now, so you'll have plenty of opportunities to grovel at my feet."

He laughs, which sends him deeper and makes me groan in delight.

A second later, he flips us over so I'm on top. He loves watching me ride him. I love making him come apart.

Olly's so beautiful and sweet and almost too perfect to be true. And when I'm with him, I feel beautiful, as though he doesn't see how I'm hauling around the extra baby weight.

"Enjoy this now, because when I'm eight months pregnant, you're doing all the work. There's no way I'm bouncing on your dick like a pogo stick then."

He reaches between my legs and gently rubs my clit. "You don't have to bounce now. Although your tits are mesmerizing when you do." He punctuates that by thrusting up, and I gasp at the intensity.

I lean back with my hands on his thighs while he works his magic, each thrust sending me higher and higher. When I'm close, he sits up, slides his hands under my ass, and pulls me up and down on his thick cock.

"This angle. God." I bite his shoulder when I come.

My peak sets him off, and his whole body tenses as he pulses deep in my body. Sex is definitely more intense and intimate without a condom.

For a few minutes, all we can do is pant and catch our breath. He holds me to his damp body and runs his rough palms up and down my back.

I don't want to move. Just want to soak up how good it feels to be in his arms. Want to remember this on the mornings when he's gone.

When I wake the next day, his side of the bed is empty and the sheets are cold.

I snuggle deeper into the blankets and hope, more than anything, that we can weather the fall in one piece.

Football won't tear us apart, will it?

41

OLLY

I DON'T KNOW what I expected today, but standing single file to shake Coach Santos's hand wasn't it.

His handshake is firm, his eye contact direct. Everything about Richard Santos says he's a straight shooter.

"How's your knee feeling, Michael?" he asks, even though there are still fifty guys waiting behind me.

"Much better, thanks." After Coach Krugman called me "hey, you" for half the season, I'm surprised Santos knows my name out of the gate.

"That's what I want to hear." He pats my back, and I let out a breath. Maybe this won't be so bad. Krud terrorized us last year, so I'm hoping our streak of bad luck has run out.

As I look around, I see a lot of new faces. Aside from the team of people who got hired with Santos, there are incoming freshmen and a ton of transfers. It's strange not to see any of my old roommates. I miss those idiots.

Billy and Cam sit next to me, and Billy leans over and says, "Your girlfriend baked us cookies. Left them for us on the kitchen counter."

"She did?"

"Yup. But you obviously didn't see the bag with your name on it."

Cam shoves him back. "This asshole ate yours *and* his own. They were delicious, by the way. In case we haven't told you lately, we love Maggie."

I smile. Yeah, she's pretty awesome. I didn't wake her this morning. I tried to, but she was sleeping so soundly, I figured she needed her rest. It's hard to breathe when I think about not seeing her the entire week.

She's so fucking sweet to bake for me and my friends. I turn a menacing eye to Billy. "If you eat the food my woman made for *me* again, prepare for pain."

He snickers, the little shit.

After a team meeting where Santos introduces himself, the other new assistant coaches, and their many accolades, he pauses to scan the conference room. "There's a reason I'm called the Saint. It's not because I'm perfect or don't make mistakes." He waves a thumb behind him. "My staff can attest to that." His assistants chuckle.

Coach nods his head. "I went to college and did stupid things just like you. Only I was lucky enough to grow up during a time where there wasn't social media that documented my stupidity for the world to see. This is where I want to caution you to watch who your friends are and who you hang out with outside of football. Because if you're going to get in trouble, it's generally not when you're here, and as we all know, your mistakes are far more likely to get documented on a world stage than mine were at your age. One stupid mistake can cost you everything you've been striving for since you fell in love with the game." He holds up a finger. "Trusting the wrong person can cost you everything."

The Lone Star Stud Report instantly comes to mind, and my stomach churns. I hope Coach doesn't see that anytime soon.

I've been holed up with Maggie and training this summer, so there's nothing new on my "stud profile," but that dumb blog never removes anything, and I'd hate for Santos to see that Heavenly Hunks billboard. At least the advertisement has changed so my stupid, larger-than-life photo no longer welcomes you to town along the main drag of Charming.

Coach raises his voice until it has an almost religious quality to it. "This team has been humbled. To go from winning a National Championship two years ago to not making the play-offs—is there any greater fall from glory? It reminds me of Icarus getting too close to the sun. I don't say this to humiliate you. You didn't choose your last coach, nor did you pick me. But I want to challenge you to keep your humility, because if you can come to the field with a humble heart, ready to learn, I can make you great again." He looks straight at me. "I can take you where you want to go. We can win again. *You* can win again. This team has some of the best elite athletes college football has to offer, and if we work together, if we work as one, the sum will be greater than the parts, and we *will* kick ass on that field. Who's with me?"

The guys cheer and stomp their feet, and Santos cracks a smile.

"That shit gave me goosebumps," Cam whispers.

Santos is intense. Maybe we need that.

We're instructed to head to the field for drills, but one of the trainers pulls me aside. "Coach wants to see you." He chuckles at the expression on my face. "You're not in trouble. Santos is talking to everyone recovering from an injury first. Wants to make sure we're on the same page about how to get you back in action."

I wait outside Coach's office with a few other guys until it's my turn. When I sit down, Santos has several file folders on his desk neatly arranged and color-coded. He taps a pen on the top one.

"Michael, you've had quite a career so far. A decent high school player who redshirted freshman year. Made some adjustments to your game and had an explosive comeback as a sophomore, rushing over a hundred yards in eight straight games and breaking Lone Star's rushing record. After a shaky start as a junior —understandable given the situation with Krugman—you were on the road to the draft when you busted your knee and needed ACL surgery last December. Tough luck there. Where are you at with your rehab? How are you feeling about your progress so far?"

"I've achieved all of the milestones my physical therapist gave me. I got a green light to be here this summer."

"I don't want to disappoint you, but I believe in being upfront. I have no plans to play you before October."

I pray my face doesn't reflect the riot of emotions going through me, but what the fuck?

I'll need every chance I can get this fall if I hope to be drafted in the spring. I can see the writing on the wall—just because Santos says he'll play me doesn't mean I'll start. Or even get much game time. That speech this morning could be all BS. He wants to hype the team and win games. I still need to prove myself.

"Sir, with all due respect, if Adrian Peterson can return to the NFL nine months after an ACL surgery, if Joe Burrow can be a hundred percent after full reconstructive knee surgery, I don't see why I can't do the same. Not that I'm comparing myself to those guys. Just that if I'm careful and committed, if I'm dedicated, I'm hoping I can overcome the odds too. I'm running at full speed and started cutting drills last month."

"Those are all good signs, but it's imperative we not get ahead of ourselves. Because if we don't rehab your knee properly, you stand a forty-five-percent chance of sustaining a career-ending injury."

I know the statistics inside and out, but hearing them out loud makes me want to shit my pants.

Except I know what I'm made of. What I'm capable of doing. How hard I've worked these last several months. I haven't busted my ass through a lifetime of competitive sports to fall short at the finish line.

"Sir, I hear what you're saying. I just want you to know I have a comeback in me."

He watches me while silence fills the room. "Let's see how training camp goes. Judging by the fact that you're a straight-A student, a leader on the team, and, from what I've heard, have been religious about meeting with the trainers in the off-season, I suspect you stand a much greater chance of overcoming the odds. Even the athletic director has good things to say about you, although between us, Liam is disappointed you're not dating his daughter."

I don't know what to say about that. "She's a lovely person, but I didn't really click with Vanessa in a romantic way."

"Don't worry. I won't hold that against you. Liam wanted me to assure you that your scholarship is not in jeopardy. I'm not one of those coaches who will cut funding for players who get injured doing what's asked of them."

"Thank you. I appreciate that." He has no idea how grateful I am to hear those words.

He folds his hands on the desk. "But when it comes to your rehab, we have to be careful. If I push you too hard or if we do something you don't think you're ready for, I need you to speak up. I need you to trust me to do right by you."

Speak up.

It's on the tip of my tongue to tell him about Maggie. To tell him we're having twins, but if I say anything, will that ruin his initial impression of me?

"Yes, sir." I hear Maggie telling me to hold off and give Santos a chance to get to know me. It's what we agreed to do.

Then why do I feel like shit for not bringing her up?

"Did I also see that you're an Eagle Scout?"

"Yes, sir."

"So am I, which means I expect great things from you."

His words do not make me feel better.

At least that damn billboard ad isn't up anymore. Because I'm sure *the Saint* would have plenty to say about it.

That night, when I collapse in bed with a bag of ice on a crappy dorm-room mattress, I wish I could curl up with Maggie. As much as I love football, she and our babies are more important, and I need to kick ass this season so I can secure our future.

42

MAGGIE

IT'S SO STINKING HOT, I don't want to budge, but I promised Kayla I'd make her baby shower invites. I have a sneaking suspicion her parents had her call me to feel out where things were with me and her brother. It stings to think his family is so down on me right now.

Five days into camp and I'm finally getting used to the empty house. At first, I kept looking around for Olly. He and I talk every night, but he sounds so worn out that I try not to keep him on long.

I'll be honest—it sucks to be alone again. I miss seeing Olly camped out on the couch with his textbooks or working out upstairs. Coming out from the weight room sweaty and flushed. Making eyes at me like I'm a tasty morsel.

I rub my belly and stare at the ultrasound on the fridge that was taken this morning. I sent the pic to Olly, but he hasn't responded yet. The guys don't have their phones with them during the day, so I'm not bent out of shape over it. I know he wishes he could've come with me.

Baby A and Baby B are getting big. It's starting to freak me out that I've gotten this far without telling my mom what's going on. I keep practicing what I want to say, but it never sounds right. Everything went downhill with Olly's parents so quickly that now I'm panicked about telling my family anything.

I know Mom's going to grill me about how I'll handle my classes while nursing two babies. I have no freaking idea how I'll juggle everything. In addition to finishing his last semester, Olly will be prepping for the spring combine and the draft. Can I expect any help from him? Will I have to beat him over the head with a dumbbell to make him pitch in, or will he find a way to carve out time for us?

I grab my old laptop and wait for it to turn on, which gives me time to grab a glass of ice water and change into something cooler. Since the guys are at camp, I'm all alone, so I pick a paper-thin tank top and shorts. There's no one here to judge my baby belly and extra weight.

The design is fun, but how can you not enjoy storks and baby rattles? I'm sure Kayla will invite me to the party, but I'm not sure I'm ready to face her parents again so soon.

I'm almost done with the design when the doorbell rings. It's probably a delivery. I ordered a bigger bra because I'm busting out of everything I own.

But when I open the door, I freeze.

"*Mija.*" My mom and sister are standing on the doorstep. "Surprise! Frannie and I were missing you something fierce, and we decided..." Mom stops to gape at me. "What's going on? Why are you..." She points at my stomach.

"Pregnant?" This is not how I wanted to unleash this news on my mom.

"I was going to say swollen." Her eyes widen. "*Dios mío.*"

Once the news settles, my sister starts jumping up and down. "You're having a baby! Yay!"

At least someone is excited. I hug them both and settle them in the living room while I get us something to drink. Frannie is twirling around from corner to corner when I return.

"*Niña, siéntate.*" My mom points at the couch until my sister sits and then she turns to me. "Magnolia, are you going to tell me how this happened?"

"Mom, you have three kids. I'm pretty sure you know how this happened."

"Don't be a smartass. You know what I'm asking you." My mother never curses. Once she leaves here, she'll beat herself up about it.

Frannie bounces on the couch cushion. "Mommy, you said ass!"

I sit next to my sister and hand her a fidget toy. "It's green. Your favorite color."

Her eyes widen. "Can I play with it?"

"Yuppers. If you promise to stay seated."

"I can do that."

"I know you can." I squeeze her in a hug. "Missed you, bugaboo."

My mother presses her glass of ice water to her forehead. "This is why you haven't come to visit this summer."

"I'm sorry. I didn't know how to tell you. I was overwhelmed."

She clears her throat and whispers, "Do we know who the father is?" as though Frannie can't hear her.

"We do. He's a good guy." The best. "If it means anything to you, he's been on my case to tell you for a while." I almost spill the beans and admit it's Olly, but he wanted to be with me when we broke the news to my mom. Either I'm using that as an excuse, or I'm a chickenshit.

"At least someone has good sense." She wipes at her eyes.

Ah, damn. I made her cry. "Why don't we all meet up on Sunday, and we can all talk then?" That's Olly's day off. I'm sure he wouldn't hesitate to visit my family with me.

"Haven't I always told you that you could come to me for anything? Haven't I always been there for you? *¿Porque no me dijiste? No entiendo.*" Why didn't you tell me? I don't understand.

My eyes sting, and I look down at my feet. "I was embarrassed, Mom. I was sure you'd be disappointed in me."

"How could you disappoint me, Magnolia? You send *me* money to help with Frannie's therapists. You're the reason she can eat organic food. You help *me* pay the bills. It's supposed to be the other way around, *mija.*"

My throat gets tight, and I sniffle, refusing to let myself cry. Frannie hugs me tight, and I decide to break the news. My mom loves Olly. Hearing he's the father hopefully won't send her into a tailspin like it might Sebastian.

"Mom, listen, you already know—"

"Knock, knock!" yells a female, who then bangs on the door, making me jump in my seat. I swear Amelia has the worst timing.

Lord, grant me strength today. When I open the door, she takes one look at me and her mouth drops open. "You're not fat! You're pregnant! Bitch, why didn't you tell me? Holy shit, it's Olly's, isn't it?" Jesus. I forgot what I was wearing. I tug at my tank top, but there's no hiding the bulge under it. "No wonder he's dating you."

I grind my teeth together, hating that there might be a tiny bit of truth in her words.

Would Olly and I be together right now if I weren't pregnant? I honestly don't know.

Behind me, my mother is silent. Until she stomps to the door and stands in front of me. "The father is Michael Oliver?"

I blow out a breath. "Yeah."

"Sebastian's best friend, Michael Oliver? The boy you hate?"

"I wouldn't say I hate him." Why is everyone so hung up on that? "I mean, not anymore."

"When did this happen?"

Is my mother really asking me when I had sex with Olly? "Mom, come on. You don't really want the details, do you?"

Amelia cackles. "You used to hate Olly. And then he knocked you up. Hysterical. Guess payback's a bitch, huh?"

This woman does not know when to shut up. "Olly's not like that."

"Sure. He's perfect." She rolls her eyes. "Anyway, listen, the assholes in the registrar's office are making me take one more semester, and since your casita is cheaper than campus housing, my parents want to know if I can stay on through December."

I really hate this girl, but knowing I'd have the casita booked for the fall would be a huge financial boon. Although I'm not sure I can stand being around her for several more months. "Let me think about it."

"What's this?" Frannie is waving the ultrasound in the air. I take it from her and remind her she promised to stay seated. She flops on the couch.

"This is the ultrasound."

Amelia jumps in my face. "Please let me stay. All of my friends graduated, so I don't have anyone to get an apartment with." When I don't answer right away, she pouts. "Why are the guys allowed to move in here, but I can't stay in the casita?"

"What guys?" my mom asks as she takes the ultrasound from my hand.

Amelia has the biggest damn mouth on the planet. "Two football players who are paying me rent."

"Not Michael?"

"No. Two of his friends, Cam and Billy. They're nice guys."

"Magnolia, I don't understand. Why are his friends living

here but not Michael? In a few months, you'll barely be able to get up and down those stairs. You're going to need him to be here." She looks more carefully at the long strip of images in her hand. "And why is there a Baby A and Baby B in these photos?"

I wince. "Mom, how do you feel about twins?"

43

OLLY

"Fuck, you feel so good." A bare, wet Maggie in my arms is just what I need after the last week of camp. She arches in my arms, splashing water over the side of the tub.

I pull her down to me so her back rests against my chest. With one hand, I grab her beautiful round breast. My other hand disappears in the bubbles between her legs. As I swirl her clit the way I know she likes, I suck lightly on her neck.

"Yes! Yes!" Her cries echo off the walls of her bathroom as she comes, squeezing my cock so tightly, it sends me over the edge.

She lets out a long groan as she stretches out over me with a relaxed sigh and rests her head on my shoulder. I kiss her neck again, not ready to get out of the tub.

When I got home this afternoon, she seemed shy and uncertain. Stressed from dealing with her mom. She said her back was sore, and I figured a warm bath would help. I didn't mean for this to turn into sex, but seeing how relaxed she is now, I can't say I regret it.

I rub her stomach, which seems to have become so much

more prominent in the one week I've been gone. I hate that I'm not here to see the day-to-day differences.

She nuzzles against me. "The best part of doing it in the tub is not having to do the cum run to the bathroom." We both laugh as she threads her fingers through my hair.

"I like getting you messy." I tug on her earlobe with my teeth. "I'll rinse you off before we go to bed."

"Can I ask you something?" Those beautiful brown eyes meet mine. "Do you think we'd be together if I hadn't gotten pregnant?"

Her damp hair slides down her shoulders, and I almost groan at how sexy she looks. Her nipples are rosy red, slick with water, and her face is flushed. She looks like a damn mermaid. "Would we be quasi-living together? I'm not sure. But we'd definitely be dating because I can't get enough of you."

She nibbles her bottom lip, which makes me wonder what's bothering her. "It's just that Amelia said—"

"Stop right there. Whatever Amelia says cannot be taken at face value."

"I know what you mean. I do. But she once pointed out how you go out with model types, and I'm not that. Especially now."

Fucking Amelia. Is she really making my pregnant girlfriend feel bad about how she looks? "Mags, have you heard of the refractory period? It's the time immediately after a man comes, where he needs a few minutes or more to get it back up again. Men need time to recharge their dick batteries."

"Dick batteries?" She laughs.

"Yes, but look at this." I thrust my erection against her. "I'm ready to go. Again. You do that to me. You're the only woman who's ever done that to me. The cock knows."

Maggie scoots over, and said appendage bobs up out of the water. She runs her hand up and down my length. "We should use him like a divining rod. I could put a question out before Mr.

Cock-a-Doodle-Doo, with two answers, yes or no, and we could ask the magic dick rooster what we should do."

"Magic dick rooster?" It's weird to be laughing with her while she's stroking my cock, but I find that Maggie makes me laugh at weird times. I like how sex is always fun with her. I just plain like who she is and who I am when I'm with her.

"Does the dick rooster need another ride?" she asks, a mischievous look in her eyes.

"Definitely."

Forty minutes later, after we've fucked like our lives depended on it and then cleaned up the mess we made, we flop in bed. I pull her naked body flush with mine.

"Missed you so much this week," she whispers. "I'm glad we get one night together before you have to go back."

"I hate being away for so long."

"Are you sure you don't mind visiting my mom tomorrow?"

"Not at all. Sorry things went down the way they did, but it sounds like she took it well. Now we just have to tell my parents about the pregnancy." Really not looking forward to that. I keep the thought to myself, though, because I know Maggie is weirded out about my folks now. I don't blame her.

I expect a nice, quiet lunch with her mom and sister the next day, but we get a text an hour before we get there that tells me that's not going to happen.

Maggie thumps her head against the window of my truck and groans. "Oh, shit. Your parents are joining us."

'Oh, shit' is right.

Because I have a feeling they're not going to take the news of our pregnancy well.

～

"How did you let this happen, Michael?" My mom's shrill voice is worse than nails on a chalkboard.

"Well, Mom, I'm sure you've taken biology. When a man takes his piston and—"

"Michael Theodore Oliver, you know full well that's not what I mean."

"Son," my father interjects, "we don't see why this has to change the game plan."

He doesn't see why this changes everything? The fact that Ted and Wendy don't get what's going on is maddening.

Mrs. Morales keeps wringing her hands, and Maggie is fighting back tears.

"Look, it's done. Maggie and I are together, and while my shit's at the football house, I basically live at her house, and this is why. Because she's pregnant. With twins. I can't in good conscience abandon her while I play football, can I?" Not that I would want to. After a week away from her, I'm loath to leave her side again.

"Michael, how in the world will you keep your focus on football?" my mom asks. "I'm not saying you can't see Maggie, but this is not good for your game, especially after your injury."

Fat tears stream down my girlfriend's face, and she brushes them away with the back of her hand. I hate seeing her cry. "Mom, Dad, maybe y'all should go. You're getting Maggie upset, and that's not good for her or our sons."

My mother stills. "You're having boys?"

I'm too pissed to talk, but I nod.

Maggie sniffles. "Would you like to see the ultrasounds?" She pulls them out of her purse and hands them to my parents, who honestly don't deserve to see them.

"Oh." My mom covers her mouth as tears fill her eyes. She rests her head on my father's shoulder as he wraps his arm around her.

After a few moments, Wendy gets a tissue out of her purse and blots her eyes. "Maggie, Michael, I'm sorry. I'm just feeling blindsided. We're happy for you, though."

She sounds *thrilled*. After an awkward cup of coffee, Wendy and Ted leave.

I don't see how my parents can be out of their minds with excitement for my sister's baby but not ours. What happened to 'babies are a blessing?' Do they really think this will ruin my future?

As soon as the door closes, Mrs. Morales turns to us and apologizes for inviting them today. "When I ran into your mom at the grocery store this morning, I told her I was excited about the twins. I assumed she knew. I'd hoped we could plan a baby shower and coordinate making you meals after the delivery. You'll need help with babysitting and laundry. *¡Dios mío!* Two babies! No one knows how much work kids are until you have them."

Maggie sighs. "I'm sorry I didn't tell you about Michael's parents not knowing about the pregnancy. Breaking the news to you while Amelia was there stressed me out, and I couldn't think straight."

Mrs. Morales wraps her arm around her daughter's shoulders. "You don't need to apologize. I understand."

"We're doing our best," I add, wanting to back up Maggie. "We just have a lot on our plate."

Her mom turns to me. "You both are smart and capable. If anyone can handle the challenges ahead, I know in my heart you and my Magnolia can."

She's so sweet. I grab her in a big bear hug. "Thanks, Mom." She laughs. "Can I call you Mom now? Your daughter says I'm stuck with her, so I'm guessing that means I'll be around a lot more now."

Mrs. Morales smiles. "I always hoped you and my daughter would end up together."

I lean down to whisper, "I did too."

She pauses. "Have you told Sebastian yet? I need to know if I should keep my big mouth shut."

"Actually, everything has happened really fast, so Maggie and I were trying to just date and be together without adding other factors. That's why we delayed sharing the news about the twins."

"I completely understand, *mijo*. You don't need to explain it to me. This is your private business. You tell everyone when you and Magnolia are ready. I won't say a word to Sebastian about the pregnancy. You do it in your own time. Trust me—he'll understand."

I hope she's right.

44

MAGGIE

THE DEAFENING SCREAM in my ear nearly makes me drop the phone. "You're pregnant! Holy crap! That's why you were crying when I announced my pregnancy at my parents' last month, wasn't it? Please tell me this development happened at my wedding."

Kayla's exuberance does a lot to dull the hurt over how her parents reacted. "Kayla Oliver, I will not be telling you when your brother and I did the deed."

She howls with laughter, and it makes me smile. "You know what this means, right?"

"That in a few months, I'll be pushing out two humans?"

"It means our kids are going to grow up together, and you and I will be sisters in spirit."

My throat gets tight. "You were always the sister of my heart." After a beat, I sigh. "Your parents didn't take it well."

"They'll get over it. You'll see. They're just worried about their golden child getting off track, but Olly's always had an internal compass. It's like that boy popped out of our mother wearing a football uniform."

I bite my lower lip. "I'd hate if our situation messed up his season. This is his last chance to make the NFL."

"You can't see me, but I'm rolling my eyes. Now listen close, Magpie. You just worry about growing those babies in your belly and let Olly do his thing. He's a big boy."

I'm still thinking about her advice a few hours later when my friend Charlotte Darling comes over to take pictures of the casita for my Airbnb listing.

She leans over to show me the image in the viewfinder. "Those flowers are gorgeous. They add a lot to the curb appeal of your casita."

"Thanks, Charlie. I thought so too." With her blonde hair tied up on her head and the sunlight behind her, she looks like a fairy. She and I met at the bookstore last year when we were both reaching for the same planner and immediately hit it off.

"You're going to have this place booked up through the next year with these images."

"Your pics are always fantastic. It's one of the reasons this place has such a great occupancy rate."

She smiles shyly. "I can't really take credit. You make everything look like a Pinterest board."

A loud sigh interrupts us. "Is this circle jerk over now? Can I go back inside?" Amelia pops her gum.

"Yes. Thank you for your patience," I say sarcastically. She's pissed because I haven't extended her rental agreement through the fall semester, which starts in a few days. Why should I? Amelia gives me grief every chance she gets. Her breaking the news to my mom about Olly being my baby daddy was the last straw.

When she's gone, Charlie makes a face. "She stresses me out."

Girl, same.

"Before I forget, I want to show you some photos of Olly and my sister." I get out my phone and scroll through the images until I get to the pics I took on our last visit home. Fortunately, his parents didn't show up this time. "Check it out."

She peers over my shoulder. "Is he... are they having a tea party?"

"Yup!" I scroll down until I find a shot of Olly dancing with Frannie. "Here they're twirling. It's my sister's favorite thing to do." Olly wore the tutu over his jeans without complaint. If I hadn't been in love with him before then, that moment would've sealed it.

Charlie holds her hand over her heart. "Oh, wow. Where can I find a man like that? I've had the worst luck in the romance department."

Smiling, I run my finger over Olly's handsome face. "He and I grew up together. Made each other crazy. Not in good ways. And then..." I almost say 'he got me pregnant,' but stop myself. It's getting more difficult to remember we're not telling people yet. But it's been challenging to come up with a better plan, since he's had football camp twenty-four seven since early August.

"And then," Charlie says slowly, "you got pregnant?"

My eyes cut to her. She's staring at my belly that I didn't even realize I was rubbing. "How did you guess? Do I look huge?" I've been wearing these oversized shirts and watching YouTube videos on how to hide your pregnancy. I don't know what else to do.

She folds her lips. "You don't look huge, no. I just went through this with my sister where she was trying to hide being pregnant, so I know what to look for." I'm not sure if she said that just to make me feel better. Taking my hand in hers, she adds, "Plus, you have this glow. I don't know if it's talking about your boyfriend or the baby or what, but you look beautiful."

"Really?" I sniffle. "That's a really nice thing for you to say."

"She's having twins!" Amelia shouts from inside the casita. "There's no way to miss her being pregnant!"

"I hate you!" I yell back.

Charlie's eyes are comically wide as she watches my back-yard drama. She clears her throat. "Twins. Wow. That's so cool." Looping her arm in mine, she smiles. "We could do a pregnancy shoot if you wanted."

"That's so sweet of you, but I can't afford it right now."

She tilts her head. "What if you helped me with my website? It's all drag-and-drop, so there's no programming or HTML. But you have such a great eye for design, and it would be a huge help. In return, I could do a pregnancy shoot for you."

"Let's do it!" Swapping services is my favorite thing.

After Charlie leaves, I get out my aggression on the backyard weeds. The side yard is out of control. Olly keeps promising to do this for me, but I hate reminding him when he's been so busy.

Using the weed whacker, I hack at the taller growth. I just need to get it low enough to run the mower over it. Sweat stings my eyes, and I blink to see. I'm not sure if I hit a rock, but the trimmer dies after ten minutes. Damn.

I toss it on the ground and lower myself to my knees to see if I can fix the problem. I'm tired and hot and feeling a little woozy, which is why I don't notice the rattling sound right away.

But when I do, my heart stops.

A giant rattlesnake is two feet away, and it's *pissed*. That sucker is coiled and ready to strike.

I try to scramble back but land on my ass.

That's when it lurches at me.

Screaming, I squint my eyes closed because there's no time to move.

In that half-second, my whole life passes before my eyes. How I might lose the babies. Olly. My mom and Frannie and

Bash. My crazy house. Everything I've been working so hard to achieve. Gone in a flash.

Thwack.

I'm panting, waiting for the pain to kick in.

When it doesn't, I crack open one eye.

Wait. What?

I blink several times to try to make sense of what happened and why the snake is lying on the grass in two pieces.

"You're welcome." Amelia tosses a shovel on the ground and stomps back to her casita. "You have to let me stay in your shack now. Because if it weren't for me, you and your little Oompa-Loompas would be dead."

Holy shit, she's right.

Amelia Larson, the worst person in the world, just saved me and my babies.

45

MAGGIE

FIVE MINUTES AGO, Olly came home from camp in a great mood.

That was before I told him about the snake.

"What the fuck happened?" The blood vessel in Olly's temple looks just as angry as the rest of him.

"Don't curse at me. I'm not one of your bros." I completely understand why he's upset, but yelling at me won't change what happened.

"I'm sorry. You're right. I don't mean to take this out on you." He pinches the bridge of his nose. "But am I hearing this right? You were almost killed by a rattlesnake in our own damn yard?"

"That sounds terrible." He gives me a look, and I stand straighter because I won't be intimidated by his nasty scowl. "But yes. A rattlesnake almost bit me, but Amelia rescued my ass, and now I have to let her rent the casita for the fall semester because she saved my life."

I'm out of breath after spitting out all of that.

Squinting, he stares at me. "This isn't one of your pranks? Like that time you broke into my locker and spread peanut butter in my gym shorts so it looked like I took a giant crap?"

I laugh uncomfortably. "Forgot about that. But no, I swear it's not a prank. I haven't done a prank on you... in a while." Guilt niggles me for the last one I did, which wasn't really a prank exactly, but I don't think Olly would agree.

After a long, tense silence, he heads out the front door.

"Where are you going?" I yell.

"I want to see it."

I speed-walk after him and direct him to the metal trash can next to the driveway. "It's in here."

When he lifts the lid, he lets out a string of curses and glares at me again. "This motherfucker is huge."

It is, and as I stare at it, I'm terrified about what could've happened.

That's when I finally break down. "I know. I was so scared. I couldn't get out of the way fast enough." Giant sobs spill out of me, and he pulls me into his arms. "I'm sorry I didn't just wait for you to clear that area, but what if it had bitten you instead? What would I do without... without you? And damn it, I promised myself I wouldn't cry anymore!"

"Baby. It's okay. You're all right." He holds me until I calm down, and then he kneels on the ground. After kissing my belly, he starts whispering to the boys. "Gotta keep the mothership safe, fellas. Don't let your mama get into any more trouble, ya hear me?"

I laugh and wipe away my snot with the back of my hand. "I think I'm done with the yard for a while. If the city wants to fine me, so be it."

"This is my fault. If I had listened to Amelia's warning a few weeks ago or just cleared the area when you asked me to, none of this would've happened."

"You've barely been home this month. When were you supposed to work on the yard?" I start hiccupping. "God, not this again."

"Are you okay?"

I take his giant hand in mine and place it on my gut. "Wait for it." I hiccup, which is followed by hiccups from Tiny Number One and Tiny Number Two.

"Y'all are all hiccupping?"

"If I'm lucky, this time it won't go for hours."

My belly lurches, and Olly and I look at each other. "Was that the babies?"

"Yes, I'm baking two football players in there, and they're each vying for space."

He pulls me close and kisses me until I'm breathless. "You mean the world to me. You know that, right?" he asks quietly. "I love you, Magnolia, and I just don't want anything to happen to you or our kiddos."

I'm choked up all over again. "Love you too, Michael." I bite my lower lip to keep it from quivering. "Hey, you cured us of the hiccups."

He smiles and wipes my cheek with his thumb. "I'm home now. Don't worry about the yard. I'll take care of it."

"Promise to be careful? What if there are tiny, evil snake babies out there, waiting to bite us on the ass?"

"I'm calling wildlife control first thing in the morning."

We walk back to the house hand in hand. "Tell me about camp. Are you hungry? I was thinking about making enchiladas for dinner."

"Can I take a shower first?"

"Sure."

He pauses. "Want to join me?"

I laugh. "Always."

Wrapped in Olly's big body, that night I sleep so soundly. I was exhausted after our "quick shower," and we decided to make sandwiches for dinner instead of enchiladas.

I crack one eye open to look at the time. Holy crap, it's almost eleven. I've never slept this late in my life.

After I get dressed, I go off in search of my boyfriend. I find him outside with several of his teammates. Half of the side yard has been hacked away, and they planted flowers all up and down the walkway and mowed the front and back.

"Hey, this looks great!" I leap into his arms and give him a kiss. "What about the snakes?"

Olly sets me down. "The wildlife guy went through our whole yard this morning. Confiscated some snake eggs." *Yikes.* I shiver. "He said we should be good as long as we keep this area trimmed. I called for reinforcements so we could get this done today."

God, he's amazing.

He introduces me to everyone. I know Diesel, Billy, and Cam, of course, but there are some younger guys as well whose names I'll never remember. I smile and thank everyone. "Who wants a late breakfast? I can pop some biscuits in the oven, make some eggs and sausage. Whip up some gravy."

"Hell, yes, I want breakfast, especially if you're cooking," Billy says with a wink.

Olly gets in his face. "You better not be flirtin' with my woman."

They shove each other the way manchildren do, and I chuckle. I'm about to have two boys, so I guess I need to get used to roughhousing. "Billy, if you hurt my boyfriend's knee, I'll never feed you again."

He immediately lets go of Olly and backs away.

"You okay, man?" Billy asks.

"I'm wearing my knee brace. I'm fine."

Billy turns to me. "Um... so... breakfast?"

I roll my eyes, but laugh.

After I feed the army, the guys do the dishes, and I take a nap. Olly curls up behind me after everyone leaves.

"You feeling okay?"

"Hmm. Yeah. Just extra-tired these days."

"I'm not surprised. You spackled the holes all over the house and painted the hall last week."

"Work was slow, so I only went into the office one day. I had extra time, and I need this place to be ready for the babies. This is probably what they call nesting. I'm like a mama bird getting ready for her hatchlings."

He laughs. "Okay, mama bird. Before I forget, I have someone coming to look at this ceiling. We need to make sure there's no mold up there."

I turn my head to glare at the ugly water stains. "The first thing I did when I moved in was have this place re-roofed with the money I inherited. The roofer didn't think there was mold. He said that was the upside to having a drafty house."

"Then we'll let the guy paint the room, so you won't have to torture yourself with that ceiling anymore. I was gonna make him spackle the holes, but you beat me to it."

I nibble my lip. "But I don't have the cash for that right now."

He kisses my temple. "Don't worry about it. Since you're so good at swapping services, I figured I might be able to get some repairs done with a few spare football tickets."

"Really?" That's so sweet, I don't know what to say. "Thank you. That would be great."

"My pleasure." He gives me one of those beaming smiles that makes my heart flutter. "The second thing is we need to talk to Sebastian. What about this weekend? He wanted to meet up, and I figure we're overdue on that conversation."

I run my finger up and down his chiseled forearm that's wrapped around me. "How do you think he's going to take it?"

I'm shocked my mom hasn't let our news slip, but Sebastian has been gearing up for law school, so he's been preoccupied.

"Hopefully he won't punch me in the face," Olly jokes.

I don't share his good humor. If Sebastian goes Neanderthal, I'm going to be pissed. My brother had better be supportive. I can't think of a reason why he wouldn't be. He loves Olly, so he should be happy for us. Sure, this happened fast, and in a perfect world, Olly and I would be done with school before we had kids. I'll take what I can get, though. I know a good thing when I spot it, and Michael is the best man I know.

"I feel like this is the quiet before the storm," I whisper. "School and practice and football are about to hit us full force. I'm really glad you're staying here. Worst-case scenario, I'll see you at night." Keeping a room at the football house but sleeping in my bedroom is fine with me.

He kisses the top of my head. "I've been thinking about explaining our situation to Santos."

That's a terrible idea. "But you haven't played in a game yet. He hasn't seen what you can do on the field."

"I've done everything but take a tackle. I'm running full speed, cutting, catching—the works. He's seen plenty. Hopefully he'll give me the go-ahead to play in our first game in two weeks. Besides, I don't like the idea of hiding you. You're not my dirty secret."

Rolling over so I face him, I grab his handsome face. "I don't want to do anything to jeopardize your season. Be it with your parents or coaches or teammates. You and I happened by accident, and I know you've worked your whole life for this kind of opportunity. It would devastate me if I did something that undermined all that hard work."

He rubs his nose against mine. "Maybe we weren't an accident. Maybe this is fate."

"My mother would say it's Jesus."

"God, Jesus, fate, the universe—whatever is responsible for bringing us together, I'm grateful."

"I am too. And in case I haven't told you, I'm really proud of you. Not many people could rehab the way you did after that kind of injury."

"Thanks, Mags." The smile he gives me takes my breath away. "You're pretty amazing yourself."

I take his hand and place it on my stomach. "The boys like the sound of your voice. They're usually asleep right now."

As I nestle in his arms, I start to believe we actually might be able to survive this year in one piece.

46

OLLY

HOLY SHIT, these textbooks are expensive. Even the used ones are ridiculously priced. I try not to freak about the money because Maggie is already stressed out. She hasn't said anything, but she's been biting her bottom lip all afternoon as we shop at the student union. I'm surprised it's not bloody.

We were supposed to meet up with Sebastian today, but something came up and he had to reschedule. I hate putting it off. I already sat down with Billy and Cam and told them about the pregnancy so they could keep an eye on Maggie for me if I'm not around. Maggie and I decided to tell people on a need-to-know basis and keep things low-key, mostly so we don't stir up any drama, which I appreciate. When our quarterback found out he had a daughter the year before last, the whole town freaked out. I'm not the star of the team or anything, just a running back, but around here, anything football-related is fodder for gossip.

And I'm reminded how much I hate drama every time I step outside of Maggie's house and see Amelia's car parked in our driveway.

"I'll see you at home?" Maggie asks, leaning up to give me a kiss.

I like how that sounds. Home. "Just need to stop by the football house to grab a few things." I might also be stopping by Rise 'N' Grind for a giant coffee, but since Maggie can't drink anything fully loaded, I don't want to rub it in her face.

I'm standing in line for my caffeine fix when someone calls my name.

"Olly, hey!" Vanessa charges up to me and wraps her arms around my neck.

"Vanessa. Hi." I'm next in line, so I use that as an opportunity to peel her off me.

I put in my order and shove my hands in my jeans pockets while I wait. Until I started dating Maggie, I never really thought much about how often women touch me. But suddenly I'm aware I wouldn't want my girlfriend's exes to casually drape themselves all over her, so I won't let my exes do that either. Even though Vanessa barely qualifies as an ex.

After she gets rung up, Vanessa turns to me. "Congrats on this summer. My dad says training camp went well for you."

I let out a breath. If she just wants to shoot the shit about football, that's cool. We talk for a few minutes until my to-go cup of coffee is served.

"Listen," she says as I'm about to head out. "I have a favor to ask. I'm doing an article on the football team for the *Bronco Times*, and I wanted to talk about your recovery and what that entailed. Would you have a few minutes to chat?"

I rub the back of my neck. "I really don't want to get ahead of myself. I'm not cleared to take tackles yet."

She waves a hand in the air. "That's fine. I don't expect you to divulge anything you're not comfortable with. But with a new coach and so many transfers to the team, I figured the returning veterans would have some insight about how things are going with Coach Santos and how you're feeling about the upcoming season."

That sounds fairly benign. Although I'm not sure the daughter of the athletic director is the best person to cover the football team, but that's her editor's problem, not mine.

I look at the time on my phone. "Could we do this another time? I'm running late for something."

"Sure! I'm interviewing several of your roommates next Friday at the football house. Billy told me you guys are having a party, so I'll have a good chance of hitting up everyone I need to talk to. Could we do it then?"

I forgot about this, how Vanessa loves going to football parties. At first, I thought she just liked hanging out with me, but now I'm wondering if I was merely her social ticket all along.

"Please." She folds her hands like she's praying. "My dad said you really should be one of the guys I interview since you could speak about the different coaching styles between Sully, Krugman, Nicholson, and Santos."

"Uh... sure. I wasn't planning to go to that party, but I can stop by for a bit."

She gives me a funny look. "Don't you live there? How could you not attend your own party?"

That's an interesting story, one she'll never be privy to. "I'll text you when I get there."

When I get home, I give Maggie the rundown of my conversation with Vanessa. I'm not one of those dumbasses who keep that kind of shit from their girlfriends. "So... would you like to come with me to the party on Friday?"

She laughs. "No, but thank you for inviting me. Go have your chat with Vanessa. When you get home, I'll remind you why you love sleeping in my bed."

God, I love this woman.

I yank her into my arms. "Could I get a down payment on that?"

$\sim$

After a week of training, classes, and trying to get a few minutes to hang out with my girlfriend, the very last place I want to be is at a party. The music is loud enough to make the windows rattle.

Maybe I'm just getting old.

I see Billy at the DJ table, so I grab a beer and join him. After half an hour, the room is packed, and I'm starting to sweat. Finally, I spot Vanessa coming down the back stairs with Cam. She's patting down her hair, and she and Cam are making eyes at each other. I nudge Billy. "What's up with those two? They hooking up? Or is she really here to do a story?"

"I have no idea. For the record, I'm not opposed to boning her. That okay with you?"

Frowning, I shake my head. "I'm the wrong person to ask, bro. Vanessa is the only one who can answer that question. I have no claim whatsoever. Although you might want to check with Cam. If they're dating, he might have something to say."

That's probably a moot point. I have a sneaking suspicion Cam and Billy occasionally share girlfriends, but it's none of my business. I'm starting to think the less I know about people's sex lives, the better.

Billy starts to walk toward them, but I grab his shoulder. "I need to get this interview over, so if you want to mix things up on that front, you're gonna have to wait."

Vanessa smiles when she sees me, but I'm watching Cam to see if me talking to her is gonna cause any weirdness. He just gives me a bro hug and wanders off.

She and I sit out on the back patio. She wanted to talk somewhere quiet and suggested my bedroom, but there's no circumstance that would have me bringing a woman up there who isn't Magnolia.

I answer all of her questions while she jots down notes in her journal. By the time we're done, people are spilling out onto the back patio, stripping off their clothes, and leaping into the pool.

Time to go.

"This is crazy, huh?" Vanessa says as she points at the ensuing nakedness.

"Be careful. The guys try to look out for everyone, but there are a lot of strangers here tonight."

"You're so sweet. Thanks." She hugs my arm, and I awkwardly pat her back.

"No prob. Take care."

On my way out, Samuel calls out my name. He's a six foot, five inch basketball player from Chicago with an infectious laugh. We might have met in an unconventional way, but I'm psyched to call this guy my friend.

"Dude!" I say. We do this dumb handshake we came up with at his party last spring. "Guess what? I won back the girl."

"Shut up."

"I did. She's all mine now, and I have you to thank for telling me about my messages landing in your inbox."

We have a few beers and catch up. I don't realize how late it's gotten until some kid vomits. It's all fun and games until the hurl parade starts.

After I make sure the puker is okay, I go outside to find my truck blocked in by two other cars, even though I'm parked at the end of my driveway. I'm too tired to hunt down the assholes and decide to crash in my bedroom. I text Maggie to let her know I'll see her in the morning. No need for her to worry about me.

Except when I get upstairs, my door is locked, and there's moaning, followed by the sound of my headboard knocking into the wall.

Those fuckers better wash my sheets.

47

MAGGIE

I HAVE TO PEE AGAIN.

Groaning, I roll over, expecting to bump into Olly, but his side of the bed is empty.

That's right. He didn't come home last night.

The neon-blue alarm clock on the sideways fruit crate-slash-makeshift nightstand says it's eight in the morning.

I push my tangled hair out of my face and drag myself to the bathroom. As I strip off my clothes to shower, I take a long look at my swollen body. My belly is pushing out, my hips and butt and boobs are bigger, and I still have at least three months to go. The doctor says anything over thirty-six weeks is considered full term for twins. I'm aiming for the full forty because she said that's ideal for the optimal health of the babies.

Charlie was sweet to tell me I have a pregnancy glow, but the truth is, I feel gross. I'm not hurling as much, but food still hits me funny sometimes, and I feel awkward in my own skin. All those pregnancy videos online are depressing because so many women love being pregnant. As much as I adore the babies and can't wait to meet them, I'm not enjoying being pregnant.

When I stare at my changing body, it makes me wonder if Olly is really attracted to me or if he's just excited about the twins. We have a lot of sex, but I couldn't help feel a niggle of doubt when he didn't come home last night. I thought I made him an enticing offer about what we would do when he got back. Now that I see myself in the harsh light of day, though, I realize I'm probably not so alluring.

Olly wouldn't cheat on you, Maggie.

I tell myself that over and over again. I thought I was being a cool girlfriend to tell him to go meet up with his ex on his own. He said Vanessa wanted to interview him, and I didn't want to sit there like a third wheel and make it weird, but maybe I'm an idiot. Perhaps I should've gone with him.

After I shower and change, I head downstairs, hoping he's home so I can get over the anxiousness that's been swirling in my stomach since I woke up. Peeking out the window, I only spot my car and Amelia's in the driveway.

Needing something to distract myself, I decide to organize my new textbooks, but I left them in my trunk. I grab my keys and go outside, but stop when I see my brother pull up to my house.

"Sebastian!" It's so good to see him that I race down the front steps. Well, as fast as my round body will take me. "I haven't seen you in ages." We were supposed to meet up last weekend, but he had a conflict.

He slams his car door shut and stalks toward me, ignoring my outstretched arms. "Where is he?"

"Who?"

"Olly. Where the hell is that asshole?"

My brother looks so pissed, I back away.

That's when he takes a good, long look at my belly. "Jesus Christ. He did this to you, didn't he?"

Shit. This is not how I wanted to do the big unveiling. "Calm down. It takes two to tango."

"When? *When* did he knock you up?"

"How did you even know Olly and I were together?"

"Mom told me you guys were dating several weeks ago. Been waiting for you two to come clean. But this"—he motions to my gut—"she didn't mention this."

"I'm pregnant. Not infected with the Ebola virus. You don't have to look so freaked out. Women have babies every day."

His nostrils flare. "But they don't get knocked up by my best friend while he's out fucking other women."

My whole body freezes except my heart, which starts to pound. "What are you saying? Olly wouldn't cheat on me."

"No?" He grabs his phone, punches at it, scrolls, and shows me the screen.

It's that damn blog again. I put my hand over it. "They post crazy things. You can't believe everything in the media, Bash. You know that."

"Look at the fucking time stamp, Magnolia. Don't bury your head in the sand."

"I trust Michael. He would never cheat on me."

He lets out a breath. "Where was he last night?"

Ugh. "I don't want to talk about this."

"Where was he last night?"

"At the football house," I say warily.

"Did you know they had an orgy in the pool? There are photos of it everywhere. That's all the local radio station is talking about this morning. Did Michael even come home?"

Angry and overwhelmed, I clench my fists. "No. He didn't. Are you happy now? But just because he didn't come home doesn't mean he slept with someone else."

My brother closes his eyes and shakes his head. "Look, until this morning, I loved that guy like he was my own brother, and there was never any reason to share his dirty laundry with you. But you have no idea what those guys get up to in that house. You would call this an orgy. They would call it a regular ol' Saturday night. Two years ago, a woman dropped off a baby on their doorstep, and they had no idea who that kid belonged to. Do you know why? Because they're all fuckboys. They don't even know these women's names."

"I know who you're talking about, and that is not an accurate depiction of what happened to Rider." Ben and Sienna explained how that all went down. The story came off way more scandalous than it actually was.

While I can't speak about Olly's new roommates at the house, I've never heard bad things about the guys he used to live with who just graduated. Sienna would've given me the scoop if there was someone particularly abhorrent I should avoid.

Sebastian gives me a look. "I'm just saying don't be naive. Because if Michael is screwing around behind your back while you're fucking pregnant, this is worse than I thought."

That's when my boyfriend pulls up. I can't help the rush of tears that fills my eyes when I see Michael. I don't have the answers my brother is looking for. He clearly doesn't believe me.

Sebastian shoves his phone under my face. "Just look. Before he gets out of the car, look, and tell me I'm wrong."

Fine. I scroll through photos of naked people in the pool, but none of them are Olly, of course. "He's not in... any of these..."

I pause on a shot of his bedroom. It's hard to miss the beat-up poster of *Star Wars* he's had since he was a kid. There's a blonde who looks familiar. She's topless. Stunningly beautiful.

Last January at the grocery store. She was with Olly.

And then I see the long red hair of whoever else is sitting next to her on the bed.

Vanessa has red hair.

Vanessa, who he said he was meeting up with.

Before he didn't come home.

My brother is shooting a death glare at Olly as he walks up the sidewalk, but he whispers, "Tell me you see it. How that's his room. And that's probably the redhead he was cheating on last March at the wedding."

What? Why does he think Olly was cheating on Vanessa?

Then I scroll to the second shot where you only see the blonde's eyes. Her mouth is mostly cropped out because it's obviously full of someone's dick.

"Why do y'all look like someone died?" Olly asks just before my brother decks him.

"Sebastian! No!" Maybe I'm dumb for defending Olly, but I don't see how he could tell me he loves me and then bang other women under my nose.

Although he only said it that one time, right after he found out about the snake.

"What the fuck, asshole!" Olly's on the ground, holding his eye, and my brother reaches down and hauls his other arm back like he's going to hit him again.

"Stop!" Without thinking, I grab that arm, and my brother slings me forward as he tries to punch Olly. I topple forward and land on my hands and knees.

Pain ratchets up my body and settles in my belly. Gasping, I hang my head and try to catch my breath.

The guys are yelling at each other, and someone reaches for me, and I push him. "Don't touch me." I don't know if it's my brother or Olly, but I'm not ready to move.

The babies.

Collapsing on the ground, I roll to my side, hold my stomach, and try to breathe.

Please be okay, babies. Please be okay.

"Maggie, I'm so sorry. Are you all right?" My brother kneels next to me, but Olly shoves him away.

"What the fuck is wrong with you?" Olly roars before he turns to me. "Baby, are you okay? Talk to me. Tell me you're okay."

I'm choking on tears when I'm finally able to spit out the words. "Take me to the hospital."

48

OLLY

MAGNOLIA DOESN'T SAY a word on the way to the emergency room. She just holds her stomach, stares out the window, and whimpers.

It's the scariest fucking sound I've ever heard.

What happened to make Sebastian lose his mind? Was it really because Maggie's pregnant? If it is, I've completely misjudged him.

When we get to the hospital, I attempt to follow Maggie, but she holds up her hand. "I can't right now. I need a few minutes."

Stupefied, I stand there and watch the nurse wheel her down the white hall.

Maggie doesn't want me to go with her. That hurts more deeply than I imagined. What happened to us being a team?

Sebastian, that dumb fuck, sits in the corner of the ER waiting room. My vision goes blurry in my right eye from the swelling, and I blink several times. I don't get it. Sebastian comes to our house, hits me, knocks down Maggie, and has the nerve to scowl at me?

I knew he might be upset about the pregnancy, but he's gone full-on lunatic.

After two hours, I'm going out of my mind.

Spotting a nurse, I flag her down. "Is there any update on my girlfriend?"

"No, sir. Not yet."

I don't know what Sebastian said to Maggie, but it must have been terrible for her not to want me in the hospital room with her. She's in there by herself, and I'm freaking out, hoping she's okay.

My best friend is staring at me like this is my fault, and it's bullshit.

When I'm sure I won't commit a homicide, I cross the room in a few strides and yank him out of his chair. "What the fuck happened? What did you say to her this morning?"

He sneers. "Just the truth. That you were cheating on her with that redhead and some blonde and probably living a whole other life behind her back."

His words knock the wind out of me. "What the fuck, Sebastian? When have I ever given you the impression I'm some dirtbag who would treat your sister—or any woman, for that matter—like trash?"

"So you didn't partake in that orgy in your own damn house? Or fuck those girls who were rolling around *naked* in your bedroom?"

"Thank you for your undying belief in my character." I pinch the bridge of my nose, which hurts because this idiot punched my eye. "No, I didn't fucking 'partake' in an orgy. Vanessa was interviewing me by the pool, and we saw it start, but I went inside and talked to a friend for the next hour or two."

He shoves his phone in my face. "Then explain this."

That fucking blog again. I scroll through all the shots, cringing when I see my teammates acting like idiots. Santos is going to flip out when he sees this. He tells us not to be shitheads, and this goes down after the first week of school. Not good.

I stop when I see it.

Sebastian points at the screen. "Tell me you didn't bang that blonde last year. What was her name? Helga?"

The three of us hung out last winter, just before the holidays.

Shit. "Heidi." I might've hooked up with her last December before my surgery. I was bummed out, and after getting betrayed by Amelia, I thought something casual was what I needed, but it just left me feeling empty. That's why I wanted to go slow moving forward with anyone.

"And that redhead next to her? Who also appears naked and rolling around in your bed? Isn't she the one you brought to the wedding?"

I can't see her face because it's cropped out, but if I'm going by the long red tresses, then yeah, it appears to be Vanessa.

And that's definitely my bedroom, which Sebastian would know because he's visited the house a few times over the years. Plus, he was with me when I bought that *Star Wars* poster.

Those might be women I know, but it's definitely not me in that bed.

"You're an asshole. Consider our friendship over. Because friends fucking ask each other before they jump to conclusions and assume the worst of each other." Not to mention haul off and punch each other. "Two of my roommates, Billy and Cam, are living in your sister's house, but they 'borrow' my room for parties."

His brows crinkle. "Where the fuck do you live? Where do you sleep at night?"

Sebastian wants honesty, right? "Your sister's bed. In her house."

He scoffs. "Then why didn't you come home last night?"

"By the time I tried to leave, my truck was blocked in, so I crashed upstairs on that shitty couch on the third-story landing, since my bedroom was occupied. I didn't ask who was in there. I assumed it was Billy or Cam." Possibly both. Who knows?

It suddenly makes sense why Maggie was so upset. Her brother came over and waved these photos in her face, spouting his unfounded theories about my sex life. Maggie knew I was meeting up with Vanessa, and she met Heidi at the grocery store last January. Jesus, she must think the worst about last night.

But she tried to stop Sebastian from hitting me, so hopefully things with her aren't broken beyond repair. Because I've given her no reason to distrust me.

I pull up Cam's phone number, hit dial, and put him on speaker phone.

"It's early," he groans. "What's wrong?"

It's almost noon.

"Did I sleep in my room last night at the football house, or did you?" If it wasn't him, it was Billy, and I'll call him next if I have to.

"You don't remember where you slept last night?"

"I know perfectly well what happened, but I need to prove something. Can you just answer my question? Did I sleep in my bed at the football house last night or not? I have you on speaker phone. Just answer the question."

"You definitely *did not* sleep in your own bed last night. Would've been crowded if you'd been there too." He chuckles.

"Thanks. And wash my goddamn sheets." I hang up and look at Sebastian. "Are you happy?"

"Shit." He rubs his forehead, but then frowns again. "Look, this all started because you were cheating on Vanessa with some chick at the wedding."

It takes a second to process what the hell he's saying. "I always thought you were the smart one out of the two of us." I shake my head slowly, resentful I have to explain myself to him.

"Vanessa and I were casually dating, but it never got serious. And I don't mean that we only slept together, because we never got physical. We decided to break things off after things at the rehearsal dinner were so awkward between us. At the wedding, your sister and I decided to call a truce and, well, one thing led to another."

"You fucked my sister at the wedding?" He has that ragey thing going again that makes me roll my eyes.

"You don't need to be so crass about it. I fully intended to date her moving forward. Although there was some miscommunication and it took us some time to get to that point, we eventually started dating." I don't explain how it took us finding out she was pregnant to detangle our issues. It's none of his fucking business.

Which reminds me. "You gave me the wrong number, didn't you?" It takes him a second, and then his face says it all. He thought I was cheating on Vanessa and didn't want me to make the moves on his sister, so he gave me the wrong number. "Fuck you, Sebastian."

"Mr. Oliver." A nurse waves me over, and I nearly trip over my feet to get to her. "Your girlfriend is asking for you."

Bash is on my heels. I block his entrance to the ER. "No, you don't get to join us. Not after all the shit you stirred this morning."

He swallows, regret in his eyes, and even though I'm pissed, I probably won't be able to stay angry at him long. But he's not my priority today.

"Will you tell her I'm sorry?" he asks quietly.

"Yeah, dipshit. I will."

The sterile hallways are blindingly bright as the nurse and I wind through the ER. Each step closer to Maggie makes me feel more nauseous. Christ, I hope she's okay.

There's a loud beeping coming from one of the cubicles and

several doctors are rushing in and out. It looks like someone's coded. But then it goes quiet and all the movement stops. Oh, shit, I think someone just died.

My heart goes into a full-out assault in my chest as we head closer and closer to that room, but the nurse opens the curtain to the cubicle next to the commotion. I let out a relieved breath that Maggie's situation isn't dire.

At least I hope it's not.

The nurse ushers me in. "A doctor will be in to discuss everything with you shortly."

Maggie's face is splotchy and red. An IV is hanging off her arm, and a wide strap is wrapped around her belly. The frightened look in her eyes guts me.

"Are you okay? What happened?" I will never forgive myself if she loses these babies. Why didn't I just call an Uber last night? I could've gotten my truck this morning. My attention snags on a bloody blanket on the floor. "Is this... are the babies..."

"They're okay. That's from a blood draw. The phlebotomist had a hard time getting a vein and then accidentally popped open the syringe he was using." She rubs the tape around the needle sticking out of her arm. "Getting the IV in was a whole other ordeal, but I'm okay. Your eye looks terrible."

Relief sweeps through me so hard, I almost laugh.

"I'm fine." I brush her sweaty hair out of her face. "Listen, I can explain everything that happened last night. I swear on my parents and everything I hold dear that I was not unfaithful last night. Maggie, I haven't even looked at another woman since we've gotten together."

Magnolia Morales consumes my thoughts, morning, noon, and night. When would I have time to go out and be a dirtbag?

Her lower lip trembles. "I didn't think you were, but Sebastian wouldn't stop. He seemed so sure you'd done all of these terrible things behind my back. That pool situation looked out of control, and then seeing that blonde from the grocery store, the one who looked at me like I was shit on her shoe, in your bed was really upsetting. And that definitely looked like Vanessa rolling around on there too." Tugging on her blanket, she shrugs. "After you didn't come home last night, it caught me off guard."

That fucker. I'm livid all over again. Strangling Sebastian doesn't feel like a good enough punishment. I tell Maggie about the conversation with her brother out in the ER waiting room. "I can call Cam for you if you want to hear it for yourself."

She gives me a weak smile. "It's fine. I believe you."

I sit next to her and wrap my arms around her little body. "I'm sorry for how everything went down this morning."

Nodding against me, she trembles but doesn't say anything. We sit in a strange silence until the doctor enters. He introduces himself to me and then looks over Maggie's chart. "The good news is I don't think you've gone into labor. I suspect that fall, along with dehydration, might've triggered some Braxton Hicks contractions."

Maggie's eyes go glossy, but she's smiling.

"The bad news," he says slowly, "is that I'd like for you to be on bed rest until you can get in to see your obstetrician. So no stairs, no running around, no sex, nothing that would get your heart rate up. Take it easy and give your body time to recuperate. You're getting a bolus of fluids now, but you should stay extra-hydrated because that will keep the amniotic fluid around the babies in good shape. You can always come back here if you don't feel well."

I whip out my phone and take notes. *Extra fluids. No stairs. No sex.* Damn, that last one sucks, but it's a small price to pay for Maggie's health.

49

OLLY

My phone is blowing up with messages, which I ignore.

"Do you have enough pillows?" I ask as I drape a blanket over Maggie's legs. I set her up on the couch in the living room so she can be near the kitchen without traversing the stairs. Plus, down here she can watch TV. I should make her more snacks because I'm not sure how long I'll be gone. She has juice, a sandwich, chips, some fruit. Three bottles of water. Is that enough?

"I'm fine. Thanks." She turns to stare out the front window.

Despite the good news we got at the hospital, she's been surprisingly quiet since she got discharged.

"I'll be at the training facility." Coach Santos called a meeting. I'm bracing myself to get my ass chewed out for a party I didn't throw. "Call me if you need anything. I can feel my phone vibrate in my pocket."

She doesn't say anything, just nods.

I'm not sure what else to say to reassure her. Leaning over, I kiss her forehead. "I'll text you if we run late."

Silence.

She's probably exhausted. The hospital was traumatic. As if

fearing early contractions wasn't enough, hearing that guy code in the room next to hers was terrifying.

When I arrive on campus, half the team is already in the conference room at the stadium. I sit next to Cam and Billy, annoyed I got dragged into this situation because of some dumb photos.

I nudge Cam. "Maybe next time you shouldn't take pics in my bed."

"Swear to God, dude, I don't even remember anyone breaking out a camera. I'm not the exhibitionist type." He winces. "Didn't know you and Heidi had been a thing. Wouldn't have encroached there if I had."

Turning in my seat, I face him. "You know I'm fully committed to Magnolia, right? Which means I don't care if you sleep with every single one of my old girlfriends or hookups or whatever. That shit's history."

Billy leans over Cam. "Who punched you? You have a weird alpha male thing going on right now, and that swollen eye makes you look like a pirate."

I don't get a chance to respond because Santos and his staff head to the podium. The room goes quiet.

The Saint gives us the death glare, which snags on my black eye, and then shakes his head with disgust. Shit.

Coach sighs. "I wake up on a Sunday morning, six days before our first game, to news that half my team had an orgy in a damn swimming pool. Forget for a moment that you're disrespecting your partners by engaging in something like this in a public arena, unprotected sex can change your life in an instant."

Billy coughs. "There were condoms in fishbowls." Santos gives him a look. "Sir."

"I don't care if you personally wrapped everyone's wiener in a prophylactic, nothing about that situation says you're thinking with the big head on your shoulders instead of the little one in your pants."

Billy looks like he wants to challenge the assertion that he has a small dick, but Cam elbows him.

Coach continues. "Trust me when I say you do not want to catch an STD or get someone pregnant. An unplanned pregnancy can wreck your future. And sure, I've heard about Kingston and Rodriguez and their daughters. Those two are the exceptions, not the rule. Most of you have no clue what that kind of responsibility entails."

Having babysat both of those kids, I'm pretty sure I have a good idea, but he definitely has a point about a pregnancy changing your life.

"Get your big heads in the game, gentlemen. I'm calling it right now—no more parties."

A collective groan emerges around me. Personally, I'm relieved. I don't have time to babysit my teammates.

Coach points at us. "You'd better hope all of those girls were of age and consenting, because the ethics committee will be investigating. And just to underscore my point, if you have another party like this one, you're off the team. I'm not here to fuck around. I'm here to win some football games and hopefully mold you into respectable human beings. Looks like I have a lot of work ahead of me."

He dismisses us, and I let out a relieved breath it's over.

But then he calls my name. "My office. Now."

Fuck.

～

Santos slowly taps on his desk while he stares at me. Am I supposed to say something?

I clear my throat. "Sir, I had no idea things were going to get out of control like that. I wasn't even planning to attend the party, which, for the record, I did not throw, but the AD's daughter wanted to interview several of us and asked to meet there."

His eyes close as he lets out a curse. "Are you telling me Liam's daughter was there last night?"

"Yes, sir. But after our interview, I hung out with some other friends, so I'm not sure…"

"… if she got naked and fucked one of my players in the pool."

Jesus, that sounds terrible. "It's possible she left." Or banged Cam in my bed. It's a toss-up, really. I didn't ask Cam if he hooked up with her because, again, it's none of my business. I don't care who Vanessa sees.

"You're the most senior player in that house. I expect you to lead by example. If that means telling your idiot roommates not to throw a raging party the first week of school, then do that."

"Yes, sir."

How the hell am I supposed to keep track of all the shit those guys get up to when I'm staying at Maggie's? Maybe I should tell Santos about my situation. I'd planned on it. One, because I want to spend as much time as possible with Maggie because she shouldn't have to do this by herself. And two, because telling him is the right thing to do.

Santos takes a file, which I suspect is mine, and tosses it on the back credenza. "I was going to tell you that you could start Saturday's game, but first the party, and then you walk in here today with a shiner? I don't condone fighting. Here's the thing— I'm not the kind of coach who plays *just* to win. If I do it at the expense of your character, what's the damn point? You're benched for Saturday's game."

Goddamn it.

I open my mouth, but he cuts me off. "Is there anything else, Oliver? Anything else we need to clear up?"

I sure as hell can't tell him I got my girlfriend pregnant now. "No, sir. There's nothing else."

50

MAGGIE

My phone buzzes with a text, but it's not from the person I need to talk to right now.

Magpie, I'm sorry about everything. Are you feeling better?

When I don't respond to Sebastian, he sends another message.

I've apologized to Olly. How's his eye?

It looks terrible, and it made everything with Coach Santos worse, thanks for asking.

I'm not ready to talk to my brother or really anyone. Olly's parents and sister have called to check in with him, but I think they're worried about his coach not letting him play. I asked him not to tell them about his fight with Sebastian or my trip to the hospital. It'll only prove to them that I'm a bad influence or will wreck his career or derail his focus.

After my brother punched him in the face on my front lawn, I'm starting to wonder if they're right. Because physically, Olly's ready to go. He's worked his ass off to rehab and be in top shape, so him not being able to play tomorrow is heartbreaking. Would his coach have benched him this week for a party that he didn't throw? He wasn't in any of those photos. But him coming in with a swollen eye and bruised face was the icing on that cake and sealed his fate.

And me, well, I vacillate from being strangely numb to feeling terrified I'm going to lose everything—my babies and Olly and this crazy house—in some freak accident or stupid twist of events. I can't explain it. Maybe sitting on this dumb couch all week is making me lose my mind.

At least I have my OB appointment today, and the doctor will hopefully give me the go-ahead to return to class. Then maybe Olly will stop looking at me like I'm a piece of spun glass.

I glance at my phone again.

My appointment is in forty minutes. Olly promised to take me on his lunch break. I keep expecting him to pull up the driveway, but he's not back from class. I text him again, but depending on where he is on campus, it's possible he's not getting the messages.

I could call an Uber, but I don't really have the funds for a round trip to the doctor's. Billy's and Cam's rent checks haven't been processed by the housing office yet, and I don't get Amelia's money until the first of the month.

Twenty minutes before the appointment, I start to get desperate. If Sienna still lived in town, I could call her, but she's in Houston. I try calling Charlie, but it goes to voicemail. I'd ask Billy or Cam, but they're never around except late at night when they stomp through the house.

My eye twitches when I think about asking Amelia. Her car is in the driveway, so I know she's home.

If I miss this appointment, the doctor's office will charge me a cancelation fee, and then I'll have to wait another week or two before their next opening to find out if I can come off bed rest.

I'll do anything to get back to my life, so I tuck away my pride and drag myself to the casita.

Amelia's blasting music back there, and I have to pound on the door for her to hear me. When she opens the door, I gawk at her beautifully trim body that's decked out in spandex. I feel so ungainly and round next to her.

"What do you want?" she asks as she wipes the sweat off her face. I must be interrupting her workout.

"I have a favor to ask."

"No." She starts to close the door.

"You haven't even heard what it is yet. I agreed to let you stay this fall. Isn't that enough? How can you say no?"

"Easy. It's called being selfish."

"I'll owe you!" I shout before she can slam the door shut. "What do you want?"

"An espresso maker. One of those nice ones. I need to be able to froth my milk."

I'd really like to tell her what she can do with an espresso maker, but that won't get me to my appointment. "That's several hundred dollars, which I don't have. What if I buy you one of those handheld milk frothers?"

She mulls it over. "In hot pink?"

Do they even sell frothers in hot pink? Who knows, but I have an online gift card from last Christmas that I can use to get her what she wants. "Done."

"Okay, so what's the favor?"

This is the strangest negotiation I've ever experienced. "I need a ride to *and* from the doctor's office. Right now."

"I want to make an amendment to our agreement."

I blow out a breath. "What else do you want?"

She shrugs. Tugs at her shorts. "Some of those biscuits and gravy that you made those guys who mowed your lawn. It smelled really good, and I haven't had a carb in two years."

"Fine."

We're headed down Main Street when she turns to me.

"Where's lover boy? Why isn't he driving you to your appointment?"

Good question. "He had a conflict." I'm guessing something came up, but it's unusual for him not to text me back.

"Why don't you just drive yourself?" She eyes my belly. "You're not *that* big. Can't you still fit behind the wheel of your car?"

I feel like the punchline of a bad joke. *What's smaller than a house but doesn't fit behind the wheel of a car?* "I drive stick, and the doctor told me he didn't want me driving because it could put strain on—"

"Your vag?"

"That general area, yes. And it's bad for my blood pressure." I sound like I'm a retiree instead of a college student.

We drive in silence. I'm going to be a little late, but hopefully the doctor will squeeze me in.

Amelia drives with one hand on the wheel and one on the radio as she compulsively changes the stations.

It's weird to think that I'm sitting next to Olly's ex. I watch her out of the corner of my eye. Amelia really is beautiful. She has thick blonde hair, stunning eyes, and a killer body. I've tried not to think about her and Olly together, but at the moment, it's a challenge. Deep down I wonder, if she was a nice person, would they still be together? Probably. Now that I know him, I realize Olly's not a love-'em-and-leave-'em kind of guy.

Amelia drives over a vicious pothole that reverberates through my guts.

"Ugh, pregnancy really sucks." I squeeze my eyes shut and wait until the pain subsides.

"Please don't pee in my car."

I squint at her. "You do realize I've been housebroken since I was about two, right? I'll only pee on you if you're particularly evil. Warning—you're cutting it close."

She laughs and gives me the first genuine smile I've seen. "If you weren't dating my ex, I might like you. You're not *so* bad. I mean, you're better than a yeast infection."

"Thank you," I say sarcastically. Being best buds with Amelia ranks up there with re-grouting my bathroom. "I should add that to my resume. 'Graphic design samples available, and according to Amelia Larson, the girl on the Times Square billboard, I'm better than an itchy twat.'"

She howls with laughter, and I reluctantly smile.

When we get to the medical building, she pulls up to the entrance. "I'll just wait in the car."

Great idea. "Thanks for the ride. It hopefully won't be too long."

The office is cold and has that terrible smell I always associate with dying. I've been thinking a lot about my dad lately, ever since the trip to the hospital and that guy who croaked in the room next to mine. I wish my mom had let me see my dad more before he passed. Because now he's gone forever, and I'll never get another chance.

After I check in, I go through the rigamarole of getting weighed. When I see the reading on the scale, I want to fling myself out the window. Some days pregnancy feels like an exercise in humiliation.

When Dr. Perkins enters, she reviews my chart and asks me a million questions about how I fell down.

After several minutes of silence while she jots down notes in my file, I wipe my sweaty palms on the ugly paper gown. "So, Doc, can I go back to class?"

"Yes, but you need to watch your hydration levels, and I want to see you back here in a week. In the meanwhile, avoid unnecessary activities, get plenty of rest, and let me know if you experience any more Braxton Hicks contractions."

I hate that I have to ask this question. "Is sex considered an unnecessary activity?" Not that I'm in the mood because I feel like a beached whale, but thanks to my idiot brother, there's a gulf of distance in my relationship with Olly. Maybe sex would help.

"Let's see where things are next week. Typically, I'd say that should be fine, but you're carrying twins, and I want to make sure you've recovered from your fall."

"Makes sense."

When Amelia and I pull up to my house, I'm surprised to see Olly pacing by his car. He looks up from his phone just as mine dings.

I'm here for your doctor's appointment. Where are you?

He helps me out of the car. "My appointment was at twelve."

"Last night, you said it was at two."

"No, I didn't. I said twelve."

Amelia stands there staring at Olly until he turns to her. "I gave your girlfriend a ride to the doctor's. See? I'm not a terrible person." And then she stomps off to the casita.

"I have to buy her a milk frother and make her breakfast as payment," I say.

He rubs both hands up and down his face. "She was your only option?"

"I don't have enough money to call an Uber if I want to pay my utility bill. Who else am I supposed to call? The guys are never home, Charlie didn't pick up, and Sienna lives across the state. Bubbly person that I am, apparently I don't have many friends, which I never really thought about until I had to beg a girl who hates me for a ride."

I waddle off to the house, and Olly catches up to me. "I'm sorry I wasn't here. I could've sworn you said two."

"It's fine."

"I could've paid for your Uber."

"I don't want your money." Truer words were never spoken.

Ever since his parents flipped out, I'm extremely self-conscious about this issue. The last thing I want is for them to think I'm a gold-digger.

"Magnolia, why are you so stubborn?"

"I'm not *stubborn*, Michael. I'm gestating two children and my feet hurt. None of my clothes fit anymore, and I feel like an overstuffed sausage. *And* I just spent the afternoon with your ex-girlfriend, who hates me, after getting my vagina explored by my doctor. Forgive me if I'm a little surly."

"You're right. I'm sorry. I'm not trying to start a fight." Thank God for small mercies. "How did your appointment go?"

I'm curious to see how he reacts to not having sex. "She said the amniotic fluid looks good, and I can go back to class, but I need to minimize other activities. So no sex. I have another appointment in a week where the doctor will determine if I can bang again."

He nods slowly, his face completely neutral. "Okay, well, that's progress, right?"

I don't know why, but I'm bummed he's not bothered more by the idea of being celibate for the foreseeable future. Why isn't he upset? I'm upset about it because I don't know how else to mend whatever broke in our relationship when Sebastian stormed up my driveway last weekend. "Right. Progress."

"I can make us some lunch before I jet. Make you a sandwich for dinner too, since I'll, uh, be gone."

He's so paranoid after the shit that went down last weekend, he's planning to sleep at the football house all weekend to make sure his roommates don't behave like oversexed monkeys.

"I can feed myself. Don't worry about me." For some reason, I feel choked up. I've barely seen him this week. By the time he gets home at night, I can barely keep my eyes open. I'd rather hang out for a few minutes before he heads back to campus than eat.

"Let me feed you. It won't take long to make some sandwiches." He heads to the kitchen while I curl up on the couch.

I don't realize I've fallen asleep until I wake up to the setting sun streaming through the front windows. My sandwich is on the coffee table, and Olly's gone.

51

OLLY

STARING AT THE CEILING, I lie in bed and listen to my noisy room-mates. Someone's playing video games downstairs. Someone else is having sex, probably on the second floor. Someone else is taking a shower.

How the hell did I ever get any sleep here?

I punch my pillow and flop on my side, wishing I could be at Maggie's. After I finished making us lunch today, I found her completely conked out on the couch. I ate, got ready for practice, and kissed her on the forehead, but she didn't budge. Figured she needed her rest. I called her after practice, but it went to voicemail. Judging by how early she's going to sleep these days, I figured she was fine, but I called Cam to check on her just in case. He said she was holed up in the kitchen, studying and trying to make up for lost time.

Staying here last weekend is literally the worst thing I could've done. I see that now. Maggie doesn't make demands of me, but the less I'm around the house, the greater the distance in our relationship. While she says she believes I wasn't unfaithful, I know Sebastian sowed some doubt. If the roles were reversed and I saw pics of some of her ex-boyfriends rolling around naked in Maggie's bed, it would've flipped me out too.

It didn't help that I didn't pick her up for her appointment. Although I could've sworn I wrote down the time correctly.

Hopefully on Sunday, Maggie and I can finally hang out. I figure Thursdays, Fridays, and Saturdays are the key party nights around here, so I'm planning to babysit for a while until I'm sure the guys can be trusted. My old roommates always took games seriously and didn't get outrageous until afterwards, but a few of the new guys are sophomores, and I'm not sure they've got their priorities straight yet.

Maggie has been strangely unemotional about me staying here. Told me to do what I need to do. That's it.

I have to admit being in this position is unusual. Usually my girlfriends complain I'm never around. Amelia bitched about it constantly. Not Maggie. Taking her to the doctor's is the only thing she asked of me this week, and I'm bummed I fucked it up.

The next morning is a drag. Getting ready for a game I can't play sucks balls.

Cam nudges me on the way to the field. "I feel like shit for getting you in hot water with Maggie and Coach. It's not fair that I did all this dumb crap, but I get to play this afternoon and you don't."

"Don't you dare say a word and make it worse. At least you and Billy will play. I'll take my licks."

It's a tight game. The crowd is insanely loud. I spot my parents, and they wave, smiling. It's cool that they came even though I won't get any time on the field. They love this team, and they'll support it come rain or shine. I look around for Maggie and realize I never gave her a ticket. Fuck.

This week was so busy and intense with classes really getting going, but that's no excuse. It's possible she wouldn't have come anyway. Games are exhausting, and she'd have to do a lot of

The Baby Blitz | 281

walking, which she's not supposed to do. But I would've liked to have given her the choice.

We win by a hair, but a win's a win.

Santos walks by me. Pauses. Turns back. "Be ready for next week."

"Yes, sir."

"And no more black eyes."

He's gone before I can respond, but I'm so relieved to play again, I laugh.

"Michael!" I turn to see my parents and trot over to them. Before this knee injury, I would've leapt up into the stands, but now I can't take any chances.

"Thanks for coming," I yell up to them.

"Want to go for dinner?" my mom asks as she digs through her purse.

"Sure. Give me half an hour." I wonder if they'd mind if I invited someone. "Would it be okay if I asked Magnolia to join us?"

My mom motions behind her. "We saw her a little while ago and invited her. She said she had to get home. I'm afraid she's still upset with us."

She's here? I look up at the stands. They're emptying out, and the crowds squeezing through the exits are intense. If she didn't search me out, there's no way I'll track her down now.

When I reach the locker room, I try to call her, but there's no signal. I can't reach her until I'm nearly to the parking lot. "Mags, hey. You came."

"Of course I went to your game."

"But I didn't play."

"Does that matter? It's your team. Your sport. It's what you do morning, noon, and night."

Is it me or does she sound irritated? "Listen, I'm headed to dinner with my parents, and I wanted to invite you."

282 | LEX MARTIN

There's a beat of silence. "I'm pretty wiped out. It's a hike from the car to the stadium, up those stairs, and back again."

"Of course. Okay, well, thanks for coming. I'll see you tomorrow."

"Yup. See you then."

I want to tell her I love her, but the words get caught in my throat. Just as I cough and try again, she hangs up.

I don't know when things got so awkward between us.

Actually, I do. When Bash got a bug up his ass and decided he needed to defend his sister against my nefarious behavior.

It doesn't help that my schedule is jam-packed. On the nights I'm able to be home, Maggie's always asleep when I get there, so there's no time to talk. Because I have to get up early to weightlift in the gym, she's still sleeping when I leave. I never see her on campus. It's almost as if in the span of one morning, our entire relationship evaporated.

And I don't know how to get it back.

52

OLLY

ONCE AGAIN, I'm staring at my ceiling, but tomorrow is my first game back. I can't afford a sleepless night. There's really only one place I sleep well these days—curled up with Maggie.

Fuck it.

I leap out of bed, toss some clothes in a duffle bag, and head downstairs. The house is relatively quiet. I've already threatened my roommates' lives if they do something dumb between now and the end of the season.

The ethics committee finished reviewing the swimming pool incident. Although we were given a citation for throwing such a big party and have been formally warned that if we get a second, more severe measures will be taken, the guys had the good sense to card everyone who drank. That went a long way to assuaging the committee's ruffled feathers. It also helped that once those videos were reviewed, the committee found those "orgy" headlines to be an exaggeration, because it was really a skinny-dipping situation.

When I get to Maggie's, Billy and Cam are playing video games in the living room.

"Is Mags asleep?" I ask.

"Yeah." Cam points to the kitchen. "She made a killer lasagna, though, if you're hungry."

My mouth waters at the thought of a homecooked meal.

"Actually, I finished it," Billy says. "Sorry. Didn't think you'd be stopping by. It was pretty damn good."

"She made it to celebrate her promotion at work," Cam explains.

I scratch my head. "Is it weird that y'all spend more time with my girlfriend than I do?"

"Yup." Billy fires back at Cam on the screen. "But she feeds me, and really, that's all that matters."

I don't totally understand his line of thought. "She didn't tell me about the promotion."

"You're never around," Billy says.

I look down. It's true. And this distance between us is making me lose my mind. I can't let us go on like this.

Maggie is too independent to reach out to me when she needs help. I know she hates feeling vulnerable. And really, who enjoys that feeling? But if we're going to make it through the season and her senior year, through a pregnancy and twins, I'm gonna have to work harder to prove to her we can be a team. To show her she can rely on me, which means I can't miss doctor appointments or mess up on the rare occasion she asks something of me.

"I'm going to bed. Can y'all make sure I'm up before you leave? I'm setting an alarm, but I'm paranoid."

Cam holds up his fist for me to bump. "Psyched to have you back tomorrow."

"Thanks, man. Night."

Maggie's room is dark. I try not to make any noise as I set down my bag, undress down to my boxer briefs, and slide in behind her.

When I wrap my arm around her, she wiggles backward

until she's nestled in against me. My hand automatically settles on her round belly. Someone thumps my palm, and I smile. Maybe one of my sons will be a kicker.

Maggie's warm and smells so good. We haven't had sex in ages because of those weird contractions, but all I care about is that she's healthy. Sex can wait.

"What are you doing home?" she whispers.

"Sorry to wake you." I kiss the back of her neck. "Couldn't sleep. Needed to snuggle you."

She turns to look at me, her sleepy, disheveled look making me hard. I can't explain why she's my catnip, but she is. "It's nice to see you. Even if it's only in the middle of the night."

"Back at ya, beautiful."

"You're not worried about the guys?"

"If they can't lock shit down the night before a game, we have bigger issues than what I can address. I'm not their father. Although I made sure to threaten them about what I'll do if they fuck up while I'm away."

She rolls over so she's facing me and runs her palm down my cheek. "Miss you. I'm sorry I'm never awake when you get home."

"Babe, you're doing awesome. You're juggling school and a part-time job. Congrats on your promotion, by the way."

"Thanks. My boss said I might actually be able to do more now than just make coffee and take notes."

"So proud of you." I tug her close, and she slides her thigh between mine. She groans when she rubs up against my erection. "Sorry about that."

"That's not a bad thing," she whispers.

I move back so my hips aren't pressing against her. "I can't help it when I'm around you."

"Where are you going? Come here."

"We don't have to do anything. I didn't drive over here to get laid."

"I know you didn't. It's just... it's been so awkward between us since everything happened with my brother. And I thought... I hoped this would help."

"I'm sorry, baby. That weekend was all my fault. If I had just come home, taken an Uber or something, I could've been here to stop things from getting out of hand. I could've explained in time to keep Bash from losing his marbles."

Her brother's been texting me almost daily for updates. I know he feels like shit for what happened. I'm still pissed at him, but I get it. If Maggie were my sister, and I saw the things he had, I'm not sure I would've reacted differently.

"I don't want to talk about my brother."

"Have you spoken to him yet?"

"No."

I rub my nose against her. "Bash flipped out because he loves you."

She sighs. "I wish he believed in me enough to trust my instincts. I'm not a child anymore. I don't need him to beat up my boyfriends or scare anyone away."

"Do you have more than one boyfriend who needs a beating?"

Her eyelashes flutter coyly. "Why, yes. How did you guess?"

"I'll be giving these other nameless boyfriends a beating, no help from Sebastian necessary."

"I've never pegged you as a jealous man."

"I'm not. Except with you." Because I was definitely seeing green when I found out my friends enjoyed my girlfriend's lasagna earlier this evening, as childish as that is.

Her fingers trail through my hair. "I hate thinking of you with other women, so we're even. I want to flip tables every time Amelia hints at her time dating you."

Amelia has not been pleasant to Maggie, and yet my girl-friend always handles herself with class. I really admire that. I wish she didn't need the income and could tell Amelia to take a hike, but we're not there yet.

"There's only one woman in my life right now, and she's absolutely amazing. I love her so much, I can't breathe."

A beautiful smile spreads on her face. Shyly she bites her bottom lip and nods. "I love you too, Michael." Her big, luminous eyes meet mine, then look down. "The doctor gave me the go-ahead to have sex yesterday, so... we could. If you were in the mood. You know, so we could reconnect."

Christ. She feels so good in my arms. But after that trip to the hospital, it's hard not to be apprehensive about having sex.

When I don't say anything, she scoots back. "Of course, I wouldn't blame you if you didn't want to."

"What does that mean? Of course I want to." My cock is a brick up against my stomach. If that's not proof I want to get her naked, I don't know what is.

She starts to turn away, and I tighten my hold on her. "Babe. Why wouldn't I?"

At first she doesn't say anything, but then she shrugs. Looks down again. "Just... I'm so big right now."

That's what this is about? "Darlin', you're fucking magnificent, pregnant or not pregnant. All it takes is one look at you and I go rock hard. You're luscious all over, and I love it." Her tits make me drool. Her ass is so perfectly round, I wanna bite it. I take her hand and place it on my eager dick. "That's all for you."

"Really? I just feel so gross. I'm swollen everywhere."

I jut my erection against her palm. "I know the feeling." She laughs and rests her forehead against my chest. "I want you, Mags, any way I can have you. But I don't want to trigger any contractions. If you promise to let me know if something is too much or too intense, I will absolutely offer my cock to service you."

Her laughter makes me smile. I missed this, the quiet conversations we have in bed when we can shut out the rest of the world.

She kisses up my chest and neck. Slides on top of me. "This won't affect your game tomorrow?"

Fuck the game.

Wait. I don't mean that.

I stop thinking with my cock for a second to consider her question. "Studies show having sex before something athletic might improve testosterone levels." I'm really grateful for those studies at the moment.

"As long as this is a decision based in science," she teases as she grinds against me, "I'm happy to take one for the team."

"I'm happy to give it to you." Ecstatic, really. Reaching up, I tug off her tank top and groan at the sight of her full breasts. Taking her pert nipple in my mouth, I take a little nip that makes her squirm. "Christ, you're a dish."

"Does that mean you're going to gobble me up?"

Great idea.

53

MAGGIE

OLLY STRIPS OFF MY UNDERWEAR, wedges himself between my thighs, and takes a long, slow lick up my center.

"Oh, my God." I arch, and his giant palm rubs my belly on the way to grab my boob. With his other hand, he slides two thick fingers into me, and I tremble. Pregnancy has given me a short fuse, and after just a few minutes of him working me over, I'm close.

"That's it, baby."

"I don't want to come by myself." It scares me how much I need him. And I don't mean for sex. I've never needed anyone the way I need Olly, and that's a terrifying thought.

A second later, he's by my side. He gently rolls me to face him and lifts my thigh over his. His hard length wedges between us as he leans down to kiss me.

I've missed this so much.

I suck on his tongue, run my fingers through his hair. Claw at his back. He pulls me flush to him as we kiss. I can't get enough of his hard body and how it fits mine. My breasts push against his wide chest, and suddenly I don't feel large. Even pregnant with twins, in this moment, I don't feel like a beached whale. I can see the love he has for me in his eyes. It's everything.

He reaches between us. Then his cock is at my entrance, pushing. Squeezing into me. Filling me.

"Jesus, you feel so good." He groans when I press my body closer. "Fuck, you're tight."

It usually takes a second to get used to his size, but I'm frantic to feel him move in me. I ignore the bite of pain and moan when he grabs my ass and moves me slowly up and down his length.

This angle has me panting with the way the base of his cock rubs against my clit.

"Can I try something?" he rasps in my ear.

I nod, because I know he'll stop if something doesn't feel good.

From behind, he parts my ass. Trails a finger around to where he's sliding in and out of me. Then moves higher to circle my back entrance.

Okay, wow, I've never had anything done there, but I'm definitely intrigued.

He slowly pushes into me until he reaches his knuckle. "This feel good?" he asks.

Incomprehensible sounds emerge from my mouth. It's a moan. A gasp. A sound that says *holy hell, that actually feels incredible.*

"So... good." My whole body goes stiff as I come on his cock and finger. I squeeze my eyes shut as I tremble.

He shifts until I'm on top, and he holds my hips and thrusts up. I feel him swell inside me, and that keeps my orgasm going.

"Fuck, yes." It's his turn to arch. His head tilts back, and I lean over to lick his neck.

His muscular arms wrap around my back and hold me to him as he pulses deep in my body.

A few minutes later, his eyes crack open. "I'm about to fall into the best sex coma any man has ever experienced."

"You need a good night's sleep. You have a big day tomorrow." I kiss him softly. "Help me off the ride? I don't have the thigh strength at the moment to disembark."

He chuckles and lifts me off his body and settles me on the bed. After we clean up and curl up together, I'm suddenly at peace. Maybe he and I can actually pull off this relationship despite the challenges we face.

For the first time in two weeks, I see the light at the end of the tunnel.

54

MAGGIE

It's a perfect eighty-five degrees. The sun is shining. The crowd is painted up and ready for the Broncos to race onto the field. I'm anxious, hoping and praying Olly has a great game. He's worked his butt off to play again. I only hope he's able to do it without getting hurt.

"You okay?" Charlie asks.

"I'm freaking out." My lip is raw from how hard I've been biting it.

"It's going to be okay. You said it yourself—he's ready."

I nod. "He's worked so hard. You should see him in our workout room. It's like watching a machine." After a minute, I remember who I'm talking to. "How about you? This is your first time back at a football game since everything happened."

Charlie gives me a sad smile. "Life moves on, right? And it's not like we're playing Jake's team."

Good riddance to that asshole. I don't say the words out loud because Charlotte doesn't look like she's at the stage of righteous anger yet. "After I get a grip on life again, I'm going to find you a great guy." When she lifts an eyebrow, I amend my statement. "A great guy *who's not a football player.*"

"Thank you. My heart can't take that again."

"Have you talked to your sister since you moved here?"

"Not after those first few angry phone calls. I miss my nephew terribly, but at some point, you have to look out for yourself, you know?"

"I do." I hug her. "You did the right thing getting away from that."

When I'm tempted to think I'm cursed with drama, I only have to remind myself Charlie's situation is worse.

"Magnolia."

At the sound of my name, I turn to find Olly's parents headed my way.

Speaking of drama.

They were nice to me when I saw them at last week's game, but I'm still hurt by how they treated me at their house, and I feel like I'm waddling on eggshells around them.

"Hi, Mr. and Mrs. Oliver."

"Oh, honey, aren't we past that?" Olly's mom asks. "We're family now, so you have to call us Wendy and Ted."

I give her a tight smile. "Okay." I introduce Charlie to them and hope this conversation doesn't go downhill.

"Are you free after the game?" Wendy asks me. "We always take Michael out for an early dinner afterward. I know he'd love if you could come, and it would give us a chance to plan your baby shower."

She says it so loudly, I look around to make sure no one is paying attention. Olly hasn't told his coach about us, like we planned, and I'm beyond relieved. Until he makes himself indispensable, I don't think he should make any waves. But aside from a few friends in our tight circle, no one knows about our situation, and the thought of ending up as gossip on one of those blogs turns my stomach.

"Thanks, but I was pretty wiped out after the last game. Maybe next time."

"I understand. Can I call you so we can set up a date to throw that shower? It's a shame you couldn't come to Kayla's."

I sent a gift. I figured going would only make things more awkward with Olly's parents.

At the moment, though, I'm tired and bloated and feel the need to be frank.

I lower my voice, so the whole stadium doesn't hear. "Wendy, it's really okay. You don't owe me anything. I know you're not excited about me dating Olly or the pregnancy or his living situation, and I don't want you to feel obligated to go to any trouble on my account." Besides, I don't need a baby shower to jinx myself. If I can hit thirty-six weeks, maybe I'll consider it.

She blinks several times and sniffles, then covers her heart with her hand. "Oh, Magnolia. Surely you don't think that, do you? I was a beast when I found out about everything, and I apologize for how I behaved, but that had to do with me being caught off guard. Soon, you'll be a mama and you'll understand the fierce instinct to protect your kids. I'll admit I was out of line, and I want to make it up to you. I've always loved you and Sebastian." Thank God Olly never told his parents about Bash going off the rails or she wouldn't be so understanding. "I've had time to process everything, and I think you and Michael are going to be great together."

Her words are so sincere, my eyes sting. "Thanks," I whisper. "That means a lot to me."

She opens her arms, and I stand to hug her, but she backs away suddenly. "Someone just kicked me." She bends over and tells my belly, "Y'all, this is Granny. I'm sure excited to meet the two of ya."

The boys must be doing backflips in there because I have to

sit down again. Wendy smiles. "You call me if you need anything, you hear?"

"Yes, ma'am."

"I mean it."

Ted leans over her shoulder. "Good seeing you, Magnolia. The missus here speaks for me too. Don't be a stranger."

When they walk away, I'm struck by a huge wave of relief.

"That went pretty well, don't you think?" Charlie asks. Without waiting for a reply, she points to the field. "Maybe it's a sign Olly's going to have a great game."

Fingers crossed, she's right.

55

OLLY

MUSIC BLASTS in the locker room. Everyone has their war face on to play Miami. The Hurricanes are a hell of a team to play in my first game back. They struggled last year, but added seven defensive transfers to their roster and revamped their defensive coaching staff as well. It would be wrong to underestimate them.

Case in point, they pummeled Boston College last weekend.

You've faced tougher. I close my eyes and a highlight reel of great matches plays in my mind, times we were down and everyone had written us off, but we scraped together a win.

That's what I need to do today—ignore the cynical voice that's vying for time in my head and focus on what I know I can do. On what I've done before.

Standing, I test my knee. My brace is locked and loaded. ACL rehab is all about controlled power. It means not blasting out of the gates the second your foot hits the ground. Running backs are supposed to be explosive, but my trainers and I have worked a lot on a controlled acceleration that should help me not get re-injured.

I remind myself that I've done the exercises and trained and prepped and stretched and planned. I've done everything in my power to be at a hundred percent. But until I take that first real hit by an opponent, who's not gonna go easy on me because I had ACL surgery almost nine months ago, I won't know whether my knee will hold.

No one has more riding on this season than me. My parents just took out a second mortgage on their farm so they could afford the insulin for Gramps, Maggie's property tax bill went up, and our twins are due in less than three months. I need a win. I need a whole series of wins so I can afford the life I want for my family.

"You ready to kick ass?" Diesel asks me, holding out a fist.

I tap back and nod. "Born ready."

There's no place for doubt in the locker room before a game. I'll go hard or die trying.

As we head out to the field, I spot our quarterback, Ezra Thomas. He may be young, a sophomore, but he's got some decent chops and a great head for the game.

"I got your back, bro," I tell him as we do a little hand-slap-fist thing. "Don't forget to check all the routes." He tends to rush sometimes. As he gets more confident, he'll do a better job of checking the third and fourth options.

Our stadium is packed, and as "Paradise City" blasts on the speakers, the crowd goes insane when we rush the field.

My attention should be on football, but I scan the arena for my girl.

When I spot her, I hold up my fist, and Maggie sees me and holds hers up too. It feels fucking awesome to have her here today.

We needed to reconnect last night more than I realized.

Focus, shithead.

I've never been distracted by a woman before. Usually, when I play, I'm able to shut down everything but the game. Except Maggie's not just any woman.

Coach Santos takes me aside. "Remember what I told you."

I need to speak up if my knee starts to hurt or if I feel off. He doesn't want me to push it my first game back. "Yes, sir."

"I'm proud of you for coming this far. You got this."

"Thanks, Coach."

The whole stadium goes quiet before the first snap. Either that or my hearing shuts down. For a brief moment, I focus on being grateful. Grateful for my parents who sacrificed so much to help me get the surgery and rehab I needed. Grateful that my body has bounced back. Grateful for being on this incredible team with great friends and a coach who cares about us. Grateful for being in a relationship with a woman who understands what football means to me.

When the ball snaps, everyone springs into motion. Thomas jogs back a few steps and surveys the field. Our tight end is open, but in a flash, defenders fill the route. As I sprint by, he hands the ball off to me.

The horizon is filled with the Hurricanes' green and orange uniforms as they shift to descend on me, but I'm determined to make something happen.

I juke one way. Then the other. Leap over a defender who hurls himself at me. Strongarm another one until I shake myself loose, and then blast forward, gaining twenty yards and a first down before I'm tackled.

The crowd roars their approval, and my heart is hammering in my chest, not from the tackle or sprinting downfield or even the excitement of the game.

I'm slow to stand, mostly because this is the moment I've feared since I was injured.

The first hit.

But when I'm upright and take a step back toward the line of scrimmage, my knee feels great.

Fuck yeah. Let's do this.

It's a tight game. Thomas gets his bell rung once, but bounces back after the sack. I get possession several times and ring up some decent yardage. Except I'm not aiming for decent.

After halftime, we get a lead but lose it on the next possession. By the fourth quarter, we're still down. Coach is screaming on the sidelines, but the crowd is so loud, I have no idea what he's saying.

We're behind by one TD and have the ball at the forty-yard line.

On the next snap, Thomas finds me about eight yards away. Diesel sets a screen for me, and I blast around a defenseman, break two tackles, and slip downfield for a touchdown. The whole stadium chants my name when the megatron throws up a photo of me.

We make the field goal, and the win is in the books.

When the game's over, I take a second to soak it in—my family and girlfriend being in attendance, the awesome crowd, how good it feels to be a part of a team like this one.

Thomas is grinning from ear to ear, and we bro-hug. "You made that look easy, dude," I say. "I'm gonna start calling you that. Easy." Easy Thomas has a nice ring to it.

"Back at ya, man."

I couldn't have asked for a better return to the game. Everyone congratulates me, and I'm riding a high like I've never experienced. I'm so damn proud of myself, I feel like a bantam rooster with my chest puffed out. My phone blows up with congratulations from friends and former teammates. Johnny, Ben, Rider, Sienna, and even Amelia—they all watched my game.

I'm walking on water.

Until I get home that night.

56

OLLY

IT'S EARLY, only seven in the evening, but the lights in the house are all off, which is weird because Maggie always leaves a few on for me and the guys.

"Babe," I call out.

I suppose it's possible she's not here, but her car is in the driveway, and she didn't come to dinner with my parents because she didn't want to overdo it. I can't envision why she'd go anywhere else after the game.

When she doesn't respond, the hairs on the back of my neck prickle.

I race up the stairs and fling open her bedroom door. The lights are out, but the blinds are open, and I can see her curled up under the covers. She's so still, it makes my heart stop.

In that moment, I don't give a damn about the game or today's win. The whole world shrinks down to this woman.

With my heart in my throat, I kneel at the side of the bed. Her swollen eyes open.

"Maggie, what's wrong? What happened?"

She sniffles and shakes her head. "I think I overdid it today.

Those contractions are back. My OB is squeezing me in for an appointment at eight a.m. on Monday."

Fuck. "Should I take you to the hospital?"

"Dr. Perkins said if they get worse before my appointment, I should go to the ER, but I'm hoping it won't come to that. I don't know how I'll afford another trip there."

"Forget the money. We'll figure it out." I keep reminding her we're in this together, that I'll do everything I can to help her with the medical bills and the house, but I swear it's like she doesn't hear me. "The most important thing is keeping you healthy. I'll bail on weightlifting and take you Monday."

She grabs my hand. "No, you can't miss anything. I'll be fine. I've been chugging water for the last two hours, and it's gotten better." Four empty water bottles crowd the nightstand.

"I don't know, Magnolia," I say uneasily. "I feel like I'm in over my head here. Taking you to an appointment seems like the least of what I should be doing." I pace the length of the bedroom and rub the back of my head. "We should call my mom or yours and get some advice. They've had kids. They'll know what to do."

Shaking her head, she wipes a few tears that escape. "My mom has her hands full with my sister, and she'll only worry when she can't come up here. And your parents just started to tolerate me again. How excited do you think your mom is going to be if you tell her you're bailing on a mandatory weightlifting session because of me?"

"Mags, who cares what they think? You're more important than their opinions about how we live our lives." I love my parents, but I'm about to have my own family. It's time they realize I have different responsibilities now.

Her voice cracks. "I just don't want them to hate me."

She's breaking my damn heart.

I kneel next to her again and brush a strand of hair out of her bloodshot eyes. "Are you sure you're feeling better?"

She nods, obviously trying to rein in her emotions. "The water is helping. I swear."

Mentally, I review her bed rest restrictions. "How will you get to your appointment if you can't drive?"

She chews on her bottom lip. "Could we switch cars? I could drive your truck, which is automatic. That won't put any extra pressure on, you know, that area."

I wince. "Will you think I'm a weenie if I tell you I can't drive stick?" A laugh spills out of her, and I smile. If I can make her laugh, maybe everything will be okay.

I consider our options.

There's no way I'm asking Amelia to take her again. Once was bad enough. Billy has weights that morning too, but Cam does a later session. "Would it be okay if I ask Cam to take you? I'd feel better than just sending you off in an Uber."

"Do you think he'd mind?"

"He thinks you're better than sliced bread. I'm sure he'll help if he can."

Of course, Cam is happy to take her.

The next day, I make her breakfast in bed, bring her water and juice, and rub her poor swollen feet and ankles. It's hard to believe the game was yesterday because football is the last thing on my mind.

Billy and Cam watch a replay of the game, which is usually one of my favorite things to do, but I have difficulty concentrating.

It's almost ten at night when I remember I have an assignment due tomorrow, so I make a pot of coffee and settle in at the kitchen table to get my shit done.

Even though I have enough credits to graduate, I have to maintain a full-time academic courseload in order to play football and qualify for athletic scholarships. And that sucks because I definitely have the college equivalent of senioritis.

On Monday morning, before I take off to the gym, I say a prayer for the beautiful woman sleeping in our bed.

After the appointment, she texts me that she's fine but on bed rest. I try calling her before practice, but it goes to voicemail.

Cam doesn't know much more than I do. He says she didn't tell him much except that the contractions are better.

When I finally get home at nine at night, I'm relieved to find her awake.

I sit next to her on the bed. "Tell me everything." Leaning over, I kiss her forehead.

She tugs on a loose thread on her blanket. "I'm on bed rest for at least a week, which might extend longer depending on how my next appointment goes, and I have a laundry list of things I can't do from now until I deliver. At the top is sex."

"Sorry, darlin'. It's not the end of the world, though. At least you're here and not in the hospital."

She nods slowly. "Yeah. You're right. That would be worse."

"You're doing great. This is just a small bump in the road. You're juggling so much—classes and your job."

"About that." Her lips tighten. "When I called to tell my job about going on bed rest again, they released me from my position because I'll be missing too much work. My boss said I could come back after I gave birth, but explained I was taking up an opportunity that could go to another student who could actually do the job. He said he felt bad and that it wasn't his decision. He said if it was up to him, he'd keep me on, but since I can't go in for who knows how long, this might be for the best."

Didn't they just give her a promotion because they liked her work? Swear to God, my vision goes red. "They can't fucking do that. It's discrimination."

"Perhaps, but I'm in no position to contest it. And maybe he's right. I'm so tired all the time, Olly. When I'm there, sometimes I'm a zombie. I can barely keep up with my coursework, let alone that job. I knew that promotion was a fluke."

I had no idea things had gotten so bad for her. "Why didn't you say anything?"

"When would I have had the chance? You're gone from sunup until after I'm in bed. You want me to text you to let you know I'm so exhausted I can't see straight? What's that going to accomplish?"

Guilt churns my stomach. Maggie is more than under-standing about the commitments I have with football, but maybe she shouldn't be.

She swallows, her face turning red. "I thought I had turned a corner in the last few days. The nausea finally stopped. You and I finally got to reconnect. You're gone so much, and I can't imagine not being with you like that when we barely get any time together as it is."

I blink, needing a second to make sense of her words. I'm not an expert with women, but I think she just said she's upset we can't have sex. Because if I have to read the tea leaves, I doubt her doctor will give Maggie the go-ahead to bone at her next appointment given how the pregnancy is going so far.

In the same way Coach encourages us to speak up, I need her to tell me when she needs something.

I kiss her forehead. "Mags, I'm not going anywhere. Is sex with you transcendental? Absolutely. Would I give my left nut to do it with you? Any day. But darlin', it's just a few months. Tell me when you need help with something, and I'll do everything in my power to make it happen. I'll move back here full time. Diesel already promised to keep the football house under control."

"Really?" The hopeful look in her eyes kills me. I really need to be around as much as possible, whether she asks me to or not.

"Really. We can get through this. I promise."

It's a promise I aim to keep.

How hard could that be if we love each other?

57

MAGGIE

WILL you be upset if I can't make it home for lunch?

I smile sadly at Olly's text.

No. Do what you have to do.

The guys get fed great food on campus anyway. All I have here are sandwiches. Olly tries to stock my fridge, but really, when is he supposed to go grocery shopping? And we don't have money for delivery.

He's sweet to try to make it home from campus when he can. I appreciate the effort, but it's not going to change my situation.

The last few weeks have been a bummer. Although Olly's kicking ass on the field, which thrills me to no end, I'm stuck at home. Having twins automatically makes this a high-risk pregnancy, so Dr. Perkins said she doesn't want to take any chances given the issues I've had. Since my placentas look good on the ultrasound—which requires drinking a ton of water—I'm able to be on bed rest at home instead of in the hospital. Trying to feel grateful for that bright side.

So far, my professors have been helpful in forwarding my assignments, but I'm definitely going stir-crazy.

Someone knocks on the front door, and I groan. My couch is

deep and super-comfy, but not conducive to launching my big, pregnant self off the cushions. I scoot to the end and use the arm rest to push myself to standing.

The person knocks again, and I yell, "I'm coming! Hold your horses."

When I open the door, I'm so shocked, I squeal. "Sienna!" She pulls me into her arms, and I hug her tight. "Sorry. Am I impaling you on my belly?"

"Look at you!" She reaches for my stomach and pauses. "Can I touch you?"

It's sweet that she asks. So many people don't before they grab pregnant women, which is particularly awful when you don't even know the person. "Of course."

Her eyes are wide as she runs her hand over me. "How far along are you now?"

"Thirty weeks. They're the size of eggplants." Although judging by my giant boyfriend, his boys are probably bigger.

"You're so close now."

"They need to bake at least another month and a half." I explain how twins are considered full term at thirty-six weeks, though I hope to percolate my boys as long as possible. "How long are you in town for? Is Ben here too?"

"We're here through the weekend, since he doesn't have a game. We planned to see Olly play tomorrow. Maybe we could all sit together."

I wish. "I can't go. I'm on bed rest."

Her brows furrow. "What are we doing standing here, then? Get inside and get your ass in bed or on the couch or somewhere comfy. Tell me what you need, and I'll get it."

I laugh. "You don't need to wait on me."

We settle in my living room where I have a few snacks and a huge jug of water. "I have that sports drink you like in my fridge.

Help yourself to one. I'd get it, but I don't think I can hoist myself off the couch again."

She grabs a drink and sits next to me. "If you can't go tomorrow, I won't go either. We'll watch it here together. I'll order pizza, that sausage combo you love, and I'll make brownies. It'll be like old times."

Sienna and I lived together briefly. I miss how simple my life was then. But I didn't have Olly last fall, so I'll take the complications.

Sienna and I chat about Houston and how she's trying to get her new business off the ground and how Ben's doing with his new team. It's exciting to see a glimpse of what my life might be like if Olly makes it to the NFL. I'd say *when* he makes it to the NFL, but I don't want to jinx him.

"I still can't believe you and Olly are together," she says as she munches on some cheese and crackers. "Your fights were so epic."

"Sometimes I can't either."

"So how's it going?" She waggles her eyebrows suggestively. "Is he rocking your world?"

My shoulders slump. "There's no rocking of anything right now. Being on bed rest means no sex."

"Are you serious?"

"Yup. And it sucks." Because not having sex *is* a big deal.

To me, at least.

There's an intimacy that comes from being together like that which isn't easily replicated. If he and I had dated before I got knocked up, I don't think it would be such an issue, but as far as courtship goes, all we have is the responsibility and none of the fun that goes with being in a new relationship.

Kids and pregnancy: check.

House: check.

Bills: check.

Dating and good times: negative.

"How is Olly taking it?"

"He says it's no big deal. That it's just a few months, and we'll be fine, and I appreciate that optimism..."

"But...?"

"But I never see him, and when I do, I'm usually half-asleep. And now I can't even go to his games. It's frustrating." I rub my temple. "I don't mean to complain. He's doing his best."

"I know he is. The season's tough. Ben and I barely made it through in one piece. You were there for it. You know what I mean."

It's so comforting to have someone who understands what I'm going through. Even though Sienna and Ben weren't dealing with a pregnancy, he got custody of his young daughter, who was a toddler at the time, and his ex made his life a nightmare.

"I'm really glad to see you."

She grabs my hand. "We girls have to stick together while the boys are off doing their thing."

True to her word, Sienna lands on my doorstep the next afternoon, decked out in Bronco colors, with an armload of snacks. Charlie joins us, and I'm enjoying having my two friends over when someone knocks on the door just as the game is about to start.

Sienna opens it for me. "Ugh, what do you want?"

My head jerks. It's rare for Sienna to lose her cool, but I can't see who's at the door because Charlie's in the way.

"Where's the roly-poly?"

Amelia.

Before Sienna gets out the knives, I hold up my hand. "It's okay, Sienna. Amelia lives here. Well, not here, exactly, but in my casita." The look of horror on Sienna's face is priceless. "I'll explain later."

Amelia struts in like she owns the place. "The TV won't turn on. Can I watch the game here?"

"Nope, sorry." Sienna points to the door. "You'll have to take your bony ass somewhere else to watch it."

Yeah, Sienna's not her biggest fan. With good reason.

Amelia sniffs. "Pretty sure my rental agreement says something about a functioning TV. Maggie, are you going to honor it, or should I leave that Airbnb review now?"

Sometimes I really hate this girl. "Aren't there children somewhere you need to exsanguinate?"

"No, but that's funny." She tilts her head. "In another universe, you and I could be friends, but now you're banging my ex, so it'll never happen."

Why is she always reminding me that she used to sleep with Olly? I have too much pride to mention that there hasn't been any banging in a while.

Charlie immediately clams up around the new addition to our party, who sits on my couch even though I haven't invited her in. I can see why Charlie is intimidated. Amelia is all loud bravado and snooty fashion. She looks like her NYC billboard —untouchable.

The pizza arrives, and I enjoy how Amelia plucks off all the good toppings so she can nibble on her slice of bread and tomato sauce.

We settle in to watch the Broncos take on the Sooners. Oklahoma has a great team this year.

"Lone Star State has had a phenomenal season so far despite a rough start off the field," the sportscaster says. "Half the team was embroiled in that swimming scandal, to put it politely, but Richard Santos, 'the Saint,' has whipped these players into shape. The ethics committee cleared the athletes to play after they investigated a party that got out of hand. Santos says his boys have recommitted themselves to the game. And no one has had a greater comeback than Michael Oliver. He busted his ACL last November, underwent surgery, and has returned with a vengeance."

My heart jumps when they put his photo on the screen as they discuss his stats. Sometimes it's surreal that he and I are together, especially right now when his headshot is on national television.

They cut to a shot of Ted and Wendy wearing face paint and matching jerseys, and I smile at the fierce pride shining in their eyes.

"Oliver is developing a similar reputation to his coach—as a straight shooter who is dedicated to the game. He's someone the whole team says you can rely on. Oliver started playing when he was eight..." The montage of my boyfriend growing up is adorable. I recognize several photos his parents have hanging in their house.

For some reason, my attention strays to Amelia, and I'm taken aback when I see her eyes glistening.

In that moment, it hits me. She's still in love with Olly.

Is that why she's living here? Is she trying to get back together with him?

I've seen them interact. He barely acknowledges her. It sucked having my brother suspect Olly of cheating, but if anything, it strengthened my belief in him. Olly's not perfect, and we might bump heads at times, but I know in my heart he'd never cheat.

Amelia quickly wipes her eyes, and I have to admit that even though she's a giant twat sometimes, a part of me feels for her. I remember what it was like, being in love with Olly from afar.

"Holy crap, that was great." Sienna's grinning. Until she sees Amelia sitting across from her, and her smile falls away for a second. She shakes her head comically and turns to me. "I bet he gets some endorsements from that piece."

"I thought the rules prohibited that sort of thing."

"It just changed," she explains.

Amelia tosses her paper plate onto the coffee table. "Which is why I suggested he do that photo shoot last year. I thought it would be good for his career. But *nooooo*. That's not how he took it."

I freeze, her words sending a frisson of anxiety through me, but Sienna cuts her off before she says anything else. "Maggie, before I forget, would you have time to help me with some designs for Sunshine Yoga? I need a new logo and a bunch of marketing materials."

"I'd love to help." I definitely need the work, especially since my work-study job tanked.

Amelia turns to me. "You do design?"

"I'm not a graphic design artist or anything. I just like fonts."

Sienna scoffs. "She's being modest. She has a great eye for layouts. By the time she graduates, her portfolio is going to be banging." She juts out her lower lip. "I'm sorry things didn't work out with that first ad agency."

Or the second.

"Where did you work?" Amelia asks.

"Couple of places in town. Evergreen Advertising and this place called Spire. They were both through my work-study program."

She gets a weird look in her eye that I can only imagine is derision. She's modeled for top agencies, so these little local companies probably don't mean much to her. I change the subject before she says anything negative or offensive.

Since Charlie hasn't said much, I ask how she likes living in Charming.

"It's a lot different than the Panhandle, but that's what I love."

"You have to go to the Nut Festival. Everyone sells these crazy shirts about their big nuts. It's hysterical."

Once the game starts, we stop talking. It's a tight match that has us all on the edge of our seats. Now that I'm pregnant, I swear I can feel my blood pressure rise.

Shifting uncomfortably, I close my eyes when my whole stomach tightens and shifts. I don't have to look down to know that my belly is contorting.

"Mags, are you okay?" Sienna asks. "You, um..." She motions toward my stomach.

"I get these weird contractions sometimes. It's what landed me on bed rest. I think the game jacked my blood pressure, and they just started again."

"Do you want to go lie down? I can help you up to your bedroom."

It's a tied game in the third quarter. And I can't watch the end.

I swallow several times and nod.

Even though the team wins, I feel like I just lost something vital.

58

OLLY

I'M STARING at the ceiling again, unable to sleep. Beside me, Maggie is curled up, facing the other way. I try to spoon her, which she used to love, but she groans, "You're too hot," and pushes me away.

I get it. She's thirty-three weeks into a difficult pregnancy and needs the fan blasting in her face so she can cool off. She's been upset we can't have sex, and yeah, that's a bummer, but like I've told her, not the end of the world. For some reason, though, that just makes her more upset, like I'm missing something elemental about our conversation. Sometimes I feel like we're not communicating in the same language.

After a restless night of sleep, I get up for my six a.m. strength and conditioning session. At least today is arm day, and I get out my frustration in the weight room.

Billy is lifting next to me. "Maggie still mad at you?"

I pause mid-lift and set the weights in the stand. "Why do you think she's mad at me?"

He shrugs. "She's usually pretty smiley, but not so much these days. Since it can't be me or Cam because we're awesome, I figure it's you."

"She's been on bed rest. She's miserable. It has nothing to do with me." I don't mention the sex thing because it's none of his damn business. Besides, I don't see how that would piss her off so badly. If she can't have sex, how would that be my fault?

He gives me a look. "If you say so."

His words linger with me all day. *Is* Maggie angry? Did I do something I'm not aware of?

When I finish lifting, I take a quick shower and get to class. I'm hoping to pop home during lunch, but I need to meet with a couple of students about a project, and that meeting goes long. After getting taped up, two hours of practice, a meeting with the team's physical therapist, another shower, and a quick dinner, I hit the library.

Students bustle around me as I work on a paper. I have an hour to write what should probably take at least a few to get it done properly. My grade point average is on a slow downward trajectory, and for the first time in my life, I can't seem to care about it. I have too much shit to do, and not enough time to do it. I'm hoping to get home before Maggie goes to bed, but once again, I'm failing.

It's frustrating as fuck.

I groan when my phone buzzes again with another text from Sebastian, who's still persona non grata in our house.

Tell me what to say or do to get her to talk to me. I feel like crap. You know I do. I want to make it up to her.

I'm really not the person to give him advice. Because all of my problems with Maggie really took hold after he decided to be a shit-stirrer, and I have some residual anger.

Although I suspect it would help Maggie if she made amends with her brother, and what kind of boyfriend would I be if I didn't put her needs first?

I text him a few suggestions and then toss my phone in my

bag. I have to concentrate if I want any hope of getting this essay finished.

I'm finally able to make it home just shy of nine p.m.

Where I find Maggie in almost the exact same position she was in this morning, and I'm starting to worry something's really wrong.

I hate waking her up, but if she's not feeling well, how am I going to know when I'm gone all day?

"Babe," I whisper as I lean over to kiss her forehead. She's sweaty, and in the low light, I have a hard time making out whether she's changed her clothes.

Her swollen eyes open slowly, and my heart sinks. She's obviously been crying.

"What's wrong?"

"Nothing." She shakes her head. "Everything."

I wait for her to explain, but she doesn't say anything, just curls up with her pillow and closes her eyes.

"Are you sick? Are you getting Braxton Hicks contractions again? Did you overdo it today?"

The anger in her eyes when they pop open takes me aback. "Since I've been lying on my ass all fall, I wouldn't say I've over-done it. But no, I'm not having contractions."

Help her look on the bright side, man. "That's good, then. You're feeling okay." She doesn't say anything, so I try again. "Did you eat dinner? Are you hungry? Can I get you anything?"

"I'm fine."

I go to brush the hair out of her face, but she turns away.

Jesus, maybe Billy's right and she *is* mad at me.

"Maggie, what's wrong? I can't help you if I don't know what happened or what I did."

"What happened is I got knocked up by a football player who has to be on campus almost twenty-four seven. And forgive me, but I'm a little pissed about it at the moment. It sucks that we both had a role in this situation, and yet I'm the one on bed rest who can't go to any of my classes. Who can't go to work. Who has to take off second semester to take care of the babies. While you, what? Play football. Get lauded on national TV. Get ogled by women everywhere you go. Have everyone congratulate you when you go get coffee."

I'm so stunned by her outburst, I don't say anything.

She sniffles and wipes her nose with the back of her hand. Her voice softens. "Olly, I know you're busting your ass to make this work. I know you're up at the crack of dawn and hustle all day, and I'm so proud of you. I am. I'm just frustrated I can't do more. My life is a mess. I probably can't afford this year's property tax bill, even if they let me do two payments, because it went up again. I don't have any money to send my mom. I won't graduate on time. I can't even go to your games." Fat tears stream down her face. "No one is ever home. You and the guys are always on campus. It never bothered me before, living by myself, but it bothers me now. I feel invisible. Like I could get sucked into this bed and disappear and no one would notice."

God, she's breaking my heart.

"Darlin', I'm sorry." I take her in my arms and hug her to my chest. "We'll figure this out. I swear it. You're right—none of this is fair. You have the greatest burden by far. I know what it means to have your body hijacked by injury, but even that doesn't come close to what you've gone through this year."

"It's not fair. I can't see my ankles, my boobs hurt, and my ass is the size of the Titanic. And you strut around looking like a Greek god, smiling on camera and being so handsome it hurts to look at you."

I smile against her hair. "You're so beautiful right now. You have no idea. But it's true that I haven't the foggiest what it feels like to have those luscious tits. If I had those, man, I'm not sure I'd ever get out of bed."

I groan in twisted delight, and she snort-laughs. "You're weird."

Obsessed is the more accurate term. "No, I'm just in love with you." I wipe her tears. "For the record, you're the only woman I want ogling me. We'll figure out what to do second semester. I swear you'll graduate on time."

I have no idea how I'll make that happen, but she's right—no matter how important my football career is, her future's just as important as mine.

59

MAGGIE

STARING AT MY COMPUTER SCREEN, I smile. Sienna is going to love this logo for her yoga company. At least I hope she does.

It feels so good to be productive. While I've been doing my best to stay on top of my coursework, I'm not super motivated. Not being in class for the lectures really blows because that's my favorite part of college. I have some great professors who are passionate about what they teach. Reading through lecture notes doesn't compare at all to being in class while they teach.

At least Sienna's project is giving me something exciting to do while I convalesce.

"*Mija*, you need to eat."

My mom's voice jars me. I look up to find her with her hands on her hips. "At least eat your soup. I made it from scratch. You're growing two babies. *¡Dos!* I still can't believe it."

She came over today to check on me and freaked out when I told her I was having a hard time eating.

"You're right. I'm sorry. I'll try." I attempt to scoot to the edge of the couch so I can grab my bowl, but I'm stuck.

"Relax. I'll get it for you." She hands me the chicken soup and a spoon.

"You're so sweet to come over. I know it's a long drive. Who's taking care of Frannie?"

"That nice neighbor. She has an autistic granddaughter, so she has experience, and we've spent a lot of time over at her house in the evenings. And Frannie's been doing a much better job speaking up when she needs something. I'm not worried."

"That's great, Mom."

"The diet you put her on is working so well. Except I need to feed her constantly so she doesn't lose weight. Good thing she loves to eat."

It's not a diet exactly. It's not meant for weight loss, but I know what she means.

"I'm so happy to hear it." I swirl the spoon in the bowl. "Do you need money? I'm working on something for a friend, and I should get paid in a week or two."

"Your brother sent me a check this week. That's enough for now. Frannie has what she needs."

My mouth drops open in shock. "What about those payments to repair his car?"

"He finally paid it off, *gracias a Dios*."

I'm shocked Sebastian thought to help our mom because I know she doesn't tell him when she's having financial troubles for fear it'll make him worry. I only figured it out myself when I came home to surprise her and found her crying next to a stack of bills. "That's—wow, that's great." It would be so huge if he could help her from time to time, especially next semester. But law school is expensive. I probably shouldn't count on his contribution.

It's always better if you plan for the worst-case scenario.

My mom sits next to me, and her attention drops to her lap. Her voice lowers. "Sebastian is very sorry for what happened." She gives me that look. The one that says she knows everything.

"I didn't say anything because I didn't want you to worry."

Oh, shit. I'm doing the exact same thing she does to me and Bash. But come on. Like I really need to involve my mother in our drama. "You have enough on your hands."

"*Mija, eres mi vida.*" You are my life. "Of course I'm going to worry."

My eyes sting, and I wave a hand in front of my face. "Don't make me cry."

She hugs me. "Will you please talk to your brother?"

I nod slowly. It's hard to resist my mom. "I'm still upset with him. He nearly derailed my relationship with Olly, and when I was dumb enough to get between them, I got knocked to the ground and had to go on bed rest. I get furious every time I think about it. I could've lost the babies, Mom. I could've lost everything. I know Bash meant well, but I'm having a hard time working through it." When I see her expression, I sigh. "I'll text him back. How's that?"

"It's a start." She pats my hand. "Do you want to know the real reason I stopped by?"

"No, lie to me."

Reaching behind me, she pretends to spank my ass. "Smart aleck."

We both laugh, and she touches my face gently. I let her inspect me because that's what she does when she hasn't seen me in a while. Doubtless she's wondering when I last washed my hair. I'm not sure, quite frankly. I've been kinda depressed. Showers seem optional.

She clears her throat. "I was curious why you told Michael's parents you didn't want a baby shower. *Explícame esto.*"

She wants me to explain. I shrug. "I don't want to jinx myself. Anything could happen between now and my delivery date."

"But you haven't had any contractions since you went on bed rest, right?"

"That's mostly true, but I'm supposed to avoid any excitement. I can't even watch Olly's games." Which sucks so much. What if he has a bad game and needs someone to talk to? Or, worse, what if he gets injured again? How can I be any kind of support if I don't have a clue what happened? I feel completely cut off from everything important.

Even when he has a great game, like he did last weekend against UT, he comes home in a fantastic mood, wanting to talk about a game I couldn't watch. It's just another layer of separation from him. I listen and congratulate him, but it's not the same.

Honestly, nothing is the same right now. *I'm* not the same.

I look down at a body I don't recognize. I'm bursting with emotions I've never felt before. I have terrible brain fog and can't remember what I said twenty seconds ago.

Who am I? I have no idea.

My mother speaks slowly, like I need extra time to comprehend what she's saying. Maybe right now I do. "What if we had a quiet, *calm* baby shower?"

I shake my head. "I don't know, Mom. I feel like I'm just asking the universe for something bad to happen."

Her eyes grow sad. "This is because of your father, isn't it?"

Confused, I frown. "What are you talking about?"

"When your father died, you went from being a free spirit to worrying about every little thing. Some days, I had a hard time leaving the house. You were terrified something bad would happen to me."

I stare at her. "I don't remember that."

"Because we moved to Heartland Hills to be near your *abuela*. It helped shake you from that dark place, *pero a veces todavía lo veo en ti*." Sometimes she still sees it in me. She takes my hand in hers. "You need to have faith in yourself. I've been saying a rosary every week for you and this pregnancy. Everything will be fine. You'll see."

That's my mother's answer for everything. Say a rosary. And while I appreciate it, rosaries didn't save my dad when he had pancreatic cancer.

I don't tell her that. Just because I'm a cynic doesn't mean I want to make her one. Prayer and the church have gotten my mom through really tough times. I respect that. Heck, I wish I could pray and make everything better, but for some reason, no matter what I do, I can't stop fearing I'm going to ruin everything somehow.

She points to the back of the house. "I did a load of your laundry and folded Michael's clothes."

"Thank you. You didn't need to do that." I swear she has a Spidey sense because I was running out of underwear.

"Please be careful on those stairs. They're so steep. And it's dark down there in the laundry room." She shivers. "It's the only part of the house I don't like." She crosses herself.

I don't tell her I'm creeped out when I go down there too.

She finally drops the issue of a baby shower. I can't imagine seeing people when I'm like this anyway. I see these beautiful Instagram models show off their baby bumps, and the women are glowing and smiling and look so happy, but all I've gotten out of this so far is constipation, cankles, and projectile vomit.

When my mom hugs me goodbye, a part of me wants to beg her to stay. I've never had a baby before, much less two. What if something goes wrong? What if I can't handle it? What if I mess up somehow?

What if Olly is off at a game and can't get back in time, and I have to do this by myself?

But I keep that shit locked down where it belongs. "Thanks for coming, Mom. It means a lot to me. I don't tell you this enough, but you know you're the best, right? I love you."

She squeezes me tighter. "I love you too, *mija. Llámame si necesitas algo.*" Call her if I need anything.

I nod. Maybe I should reach out to my mom more. I do feel better having spent a little time with her.

When she turns around to leave, she bumps into someone. "Oh, you have a friend here. How nice. I'll see you soon, Magnolia."

She steps around Amelia, and I groan inwardly. "Is your TV not working again?" Her flatscreen conveniently seems to go on the fritz when there's a game.

"My TV is fine. I need a favor. Well, not a favor because I'll pay you to do this if you have the time." Amelia looks me over. "What's going on with your hair?"

Dear God, please keep me from strangling this girl. I turn to go back into the house, and she follows me.

"What do you need?" I situate myself on the couch.

"You do graphics and websites, right?"

"Yeah. Why?" Charlie's website turned out great and was much easier than I expected. Amelia must've heard us talking about it during the Sooner game after she crashed my viewing party.

"I need a new website for my modeling portfolio." She sits next to me.

"What's wrong with your current website?"

Her lips purse. "It's all wrapped up with my old agent, who turned into a dick. It's one of the reasons why I'm here this fall and not in New York like I planned."

"Don't you need credits to graduate?"

"Yeah, but I would've blown that off if I'd been offered the right gigs."

My mom would tan my hide if I blew off school to model, but I'm not going to pretend I know anything about Amelia's situation.

I take a moment to consider the job. "How soon would you

need it? I should be able to work on it in the next week or two, but I can't guarantee I'll be done before..." I wave at my belly.

"Before you explode?"

That's one way of putting it.

It grates on my soul to accept this job, but money is money, and I still need to buy a whole nursery of baby crap. "Okay, email me your pics, and I'll start working on it."

She holds up a finger. "Can I see your portfolio first?"

Is she serious? "You came to me for the help."

"But I'd be an idiot to hire you without first looking at your work."

I roll my eyes. She's right, but I'm still annoyed. I unlock my phone and toss it in her lap. "It's the photo folder that says 'portfolio.'"

She doesn't say much as she scrolls. I try not to take that as a criticism of my work. It's mostly signage for some local companies and various invitations for baby showers and weddings. A few ads I worked on from my old jobs.

"This baby shower invite is cute." She shows me the screen, and I smile.

"Kayla is Olly's sister, so I wanted it to be extra-special."

A knot forms between her brows. "You're close with his family?"

"He and I grew up together, kinda." I laugh. "But we fought like crazy when we were in high school and college." I don't mean to divulge anything about my relationship with Olly to Amelia. The words slip out before I can think better of it. I rub my temple, feeling woozy. Maybe I need to eat more.

"Why is that?"

"Olly did something that royally pissed me off, and I swore to get back at him." I smirk, remembering all of the crazy things I did. "My antics drove him nuts. He'd yell at me, but he *definitely* learned his lesson. Revenge is a dish best served cold, and I served it more than once." Closing my eyes, I lean my head back against the couch. "I feel bad about it now, though."

When she doesn't say anything, I glance at her. She has a strange expression as she stares at my phone. I attempt to sit up so I can see what's caught her attention, but she swipes it closed and hands it to me.

"Great. I'll email you my pics, and you can get to work. I'll pay you when it's done." She leaves so quickly, I almost get whiplash at how weird she's being.

But I don't have to like her to do this job and get paid. I have a million things I could do with the extra money.

Deep down, I'd love to get the nursery in order. Put up pretty prints and set out stuffed animals and soft blankets. Maybe I should wait just a little longer, though. Just in case. Thirty-six weeks is only fourteen days away, and of course the closer to forty, the better.

I rub my belly when someone kicks me, and I say a prayer everything turns out okay and that in two to six weeks, Olly and I will get to meet our sons.

60

OLLY

AFTER WE RUN the play for the third time, Santos blows the whistle. "Good practice, guys. Hit the showers."

I let out a sigh of relief. Even though it's the first week of November, we're in the middle of a heat wave, and I just want a cold shower, a massive dinner, and my bed. Except I have at least two hours of homework before I can call it a day.

"Olly," Santos calls out. "Need to talk to you a sec."

"What's up, Coach?"

"Are you familiar with Big Tykes Football?"

"Of course. Great program. I did their summer sessions in Austin for years."

"That's what they told me." He gives me a rare smile. "They asked if you'd be interested in being one of their spokesmen. They've been impressed with your rehab and comeback and think you'd be a wonderful role model for their athletes. It would be a minimal commitment in the fall, but the spring would require several speaking engagements."

"That's so cool. I'd love to do it."

He arches an eyebrow. "Don't you want to know what it pays?"

Sometimes I forget college students can make money without ruining their eligibility. "Sure."

He chuckles. "I like that about you. You're not always angling to get something."

"Thank you, sir. I try to make a contribution to my community when I can." I'm not blowing smoke up his ass. My parents raised me to do volunteer work, which is how I became an Eagle Scout.

"Listen, their only concern was that party in August. I spoke to your roommates, and each one assured me you weren't involved. They said you're in a committed relationship and would never jump in a pool of naked women. So I assured Big Tykes that you're staying out of trouble and are a model athlete in my program."

"Thank you for vouching for me."

"It's a three-year commitment, and since they're nationwide, you can do your required speaking and press engagements with them from whatever city you're at when you get drafted."

My attention snags on the "when" I get drafted part. It's a huge relief to hear him phrase it that way.

When he tells me what the program is willing to pay me, I almost fall over in shock. Holy shit, that's a lot of money. I could help Maggie with the property taxes, my parents with my grandfather's insulin, and afford whatever the twins need and their hospital bill.

Coach gathers his things on the sideline. "Keep your nose clean this fall, because nothing will ruin this deal faster than an ill-timed kegger that gets out of control. One of their reps will be in touch."

"Yes, sir."

The field has cleared out, and only a few assistant coaches are lingering around. This would be a good time to tell Santos about Maggie and how I might need to take off when she goes into labor. Because the closer we get to delivery, the more determined I am to be there.

But would that affect this sponsorship? Will I blow it if Big Tykes finds out I have a pregnant girlfriend?

I shake my head. It doesn't matter. Telling Coach is the right thing to do.

I open my mouth, about to unload everything on him, when one of the NFL recruiters who's been hanging around this week jogs up to us. "Can I have a word, Coach?"

Santos pats my arm. "Proud of you, son." Then he's gone.

I close my eyes, emotions swarming my chest. Deep down, I feel like I'm hiding Maggie from the world, and that goes against every molecule in my body.

When I get home, I'm relieved to find her awake. She's sitting up in bed, working on her laptop. Her black-rimmed glasses are perched on her nose. She's cute as hell, so studious-looking. Her hair is in a knot on top of her head, and she's stretching out one of my white t-shirts with that beautiful belly. I feel like a caveman when I look at my pregnant girlfriend, strangely proud and fiercely possessive.

"Hey, gorgeous." I lean over to kiss her. "How ya feeling?"

Those big brown eyes turn up to look at me. She levels me with a smile. It's the first one I've seen in a while. "It was a good day. Mostly."

I sit down on the edge and run my hand over her stomach. "My boys treating their mama well, or do I need to ground them?"

The sound of her laughter makes my chest tight. "They're kicking like crazy tonight."

She takes my hand and places it where someone's foot feels like it wants to burst out of her, *Aliens*-style. My eyes widen. "Fuck. That's crazy, babe. Does it hurt?"

"Only when they tap-dance on my cervix."

I scratch my head. "I'm not sure what that means, but it doesn't sound pleasant."

"And you're supposed to be the smart one." She gives me another one of those impish grins, and I kiss her again.

"Got some good news. Great news, actually."

"Tell me."

I give her the rundown and relay what Coach told me.

When I'm done, she grabs my hand. "I'm so proud of you. That's amazing. Congrats."

"I'm so relieved, Mags. I can pay for our hospital bill with that money. Afford those meds for Gramps. Pay that property tax bill. It'll carry us until I get drafted."

She frowns. "I don't expect you to pay my tax bill, and I'm not sitting around making plans for your draft payday."

"I know that, but we're a team, which means we should help each other. You're gonna let me help you, right? The same way you helped me by putting together a workout room?"

"That's not the same thing." Her gaze drops to her lap. "It's hard for me to accept help. I just don't want you to feel obligated."

This again? "Magnolia, you're having my babies. This shit all happened backwards. In a perfect world, we woulda dated and gotten married first before we had kids. Then you'd have no problem with this."

"But we're not married." She holds up her hand. "For the record, I'm not asking you to propose."

Is she trying to tell me she doesn't want to marry me... ever? "Why not?"

Her head tilts. "Why not what?"

"Why don't you want me to propose? I knocked you up. Shouldn't we get married?"

Her eyes dim. "That's not why I'd want to get married."

"What's a good reason, then?" Seeing how squirrely this conversation is making her kinda pisses me off.

She slams her laptop shut. "Not obligation."

Fuck. What is it with this woman? "I wouldn't be doing this out of obligation." I pinch the bridge of my nose. Needing to put this fire out before it gets out of control, I shake my head. "I don't want to argue with you. In fact, I need your opinion about something."

The discussion about wedding bells will have to wait. She's not supposed to get riled up or upset, and arguing about the fact that I love her and want to spend the rest of my life with her will have to wait until the subject doesn't jack her blood pressure. Although, honestly? The fact that discussing marriage turns her green makes my heart sink.

She huffs out a breath. "I wasn't arguing."

Sure. Okay. We'll go with that for now.

"I need to tell Coach about our pregnancy. I almost did it today, but then a recruiter wanted to talk to Santos." Coach is known for open practices and letting them watch film, and after our great game against UT, we've had more than usual.

That should be good news. Santos says it'll increase our odds of getting drafted because the recruiters get to know us better. Only having those guys around every corner makes me extra-wary about spilling the beans to Coach about the pregnancy. Now that we're closer to reaching Maggie's due date, though, I have to find a private moment to discuss it with him.

Bracing my elbows on my knees, I run my hands through my hair. "The endorsement with Big Tykes is contingent upon me having a good reputation. They think I'd be a great role model for the kids at their camp. And I'm afraid if I..." Fuck, how do I say this?

"If you tell them your girlfriend is pregnant, that it'll blow the deal."

I try to keep the wince off my face. "Yeah."

"So wait."

"Wait?"

"Sure. Why not?"

Seriously? "Maggie, you're almost thirty-five weeks pregnant. The clock is ticking here, darlin'."

She shrugs. "I haven't had Braxton Hicks in several days, and I'm feeling better than I have in a while. You know my goal is to go forty weeks. I'm taking it easy, chugging water constantly to keep my placentas hydrated. Lock down your sponsorship, then you can worry about everything else."

"What if you go into labor while I'm at practice or a game? Do you think it'll be better to sideswipe Santos with the news then?"

Will Coach flip out if I have to miss a game because Maggie goes into labor? It's something he'll have to live with, because there's no way I'm missing it.

"You want me to tell you to march up to his office and give him our news? Well, sorry, that's not going to happen. I don't want to be responsible for giving you bad advice and messing up your relationship with your coach or ruining your sponsorship. Because if things go downhill because of something *I told you to do*, you're going to resent me."

It hurts to hear that she thinks this. "I'll never resent you."

"You say that now, but what if that sponsorship gets pulled because of my advice? What then?" She shakes her head. "No. I don't want to go back to how things were between us before Kayla's wedding." Those big brown eyes turn imploring. "Michael, it would kill me if you hated me again. I can deal with a lot of things, but I don't think I could handle that."

I wrap her in my arms and pull her close. "I could never hate you, and truthfully, I didn't hate you then. Maggie, swear to God, you're the love of my life." Doesn't she know this by now?

Her face goes splotchy, and she sniffles. "Love you too. With all my heart and soul. And that's why I'm so scared. I don't want to do anything to screw this up."

I lift her chin. "Darlin', there's nothing you could do to mess this up, okay?"

She nods slowly, but the forlorn look in her eyes tears at something in my chest. How will I ever get this woman to trust me and believe I'll be there for her, no matter what?

61

OLLY

GOSSIP SPREADS in the locker room like a wildfire. It starts slowly with a whisper here and there, but if it's a doozie, it burns hot and fast.

As I change after practice, the locker room goes strangely quiet. I look up and find several of the guys standing in tight groups.

"What's going on?" I turn to Cam, and he shrugs.

Billy lopes over and rubs his brow. "So that blog, the Lone Star Stud Report..."

"What about it?" Just the thought of that damn website makes my temple throb.

"Word on the street is Vanessa Fox is behind it."

Cam frowns. "No way. She wouldn't do something like that."

I think about the coolly reserved woman I dated for a few weeks. "She always wanted to go to the parties."

Billy points at me. "And lo and behold, the blog would have pics from those festivities."

"I never saw her take any photos, though. That's kind of a wrench in the theory she's behind it. And we probably shouldn't be making any allegations without any proof. She's given us some cool coverage in the *Bronco Times*, and I'd feel bad maligning her name over false accusations."

Billy leans in. "A guy says she paid him for pics. That she gave him tips on what was going on, and his job was to get the shots."

It's plausible he took some. Maybe Vanessa took others covertly. She and I were never glued at the hip when we attended parties together.

I'm having a hard time imagining this quiet, reserved woman doing these things.

When I get home, I grab my phone, pull up the blog, and scroll down the page. Everything looks the same. Except one image is missing. The one from that wild party at the beginning of the season where you could see those strands of vibrant red hair.

The one that almost looked like a selfie except the photographer cropped out most of herself.

If it was Vanessa, was she trying to get busted? Or get credit for the blog in some strange way?

It's still possible she's not the person responsible for the blog. We're all innocent until proven guilty, right?

I should've asked Cam if he slept with Vanessa that night. It would go a long way to narrowing down what happened, but I'm not sure I want to get any more involved in this situation. Nothing good comes from gossip. A lesson I've learned the hard way.

The next morning, the story is all over campus. I spot the athletic director on my way to practice, and he looks like his head is about to explode.

I almost feel bad for Vanessa until I remember all the shit that blog posted about me. No matter how well I did in games, that Heavenly Hunks billboard is always the first thing people read on that site.

I'm making my way through the stadium to the locker room when I pass Fox's office. He's yelling. Out of the corner of my eye, I see Vanessa's signature red hair through the large, square window. "Dad, there's nothing going on in Charming! It's boring! How am I supposed to make a name for myself in journalism if all I ever cover is old guys who walk their goats? My blog is one of the highest-viewed sports websites in the South. I make bank in advertisements. You told me I needed to do something to stand out. This is coming to light sooner than I would like, but guess what? I've done what you said I should."

How was I so wrong about her?

Shocked, I keep going, but her father's voice carries down the hall. "Vanessa! This is an ethical violation in so many ways. You must realize you're potentially libeling the athletes you write about. Do you have any idea what kind of legalities are involved here?"

The voices dull behind me.

My shock turns into a cauldron of disgust and anger. Was she just using me to get invites to all of those football parties?

What is it with women I date? First Amelia, who somehow managed to get that photo shoot placed on that billboard after we had a heated argument and broke up. Then Vanessa, who only hung around me to get dirt on the football team.

Thank God Magnolia isn't off her nut too. Sure, we've had our issues over the years, and yeah, she's pranked me, but I more than deserved it for interfering in her relationship with Luke. Once we cleared the air, I realized she has a huge heart and is a damn fine woman.

At practice, Coach tells us all to keep our heads down and not comment about the allegations, which I think is good advice. I still can't reconcile the solid articles Vanessa did about the team with the crap on her blog. Regardless, her father has been good to the athletes. You can't criticize one without inadvertently criticizing the other, and nothing positive can come from trash talking the athletic director.

I'm in a surly mood when I head home. But as I pass Rise 'N' Grind, I remember how much Maggie loves their empanadas, so I pull over to grab a few. Thankfully, they're always open late.

"Sorry," the college student behind the counter says. "We only carry those on the weekends."

I lean forward and lower my voice. "Isn't there a code word we can use to get some? I remember my old teammate Rider said we could always use it if we were in desperate need, and I am." I fold my hands together in prayer. "My girlfriend would be so grateful."

The girl rolls her eyes. "All right. But don't tell anyone our secret."

I pretend to zip my lips, and she laughs. The barista disappears for a few minutes, and when she returns, she hands me a bag of apple empanadas.

"Thanks so much. Appreciate it."

She winks. "Anything for our Heavenly Hunk."

I freeze, mortified that's how people are remembering me— as the face of some cheap strip club. But as I make my way out of the coffee shop, I realize several people are looking at me, and for some reason, I get the feeling I'm not garnering attention for my athletic skills.

I'm halfway home when my phone starts blowing up with texts from my teammates.

You shaking that booty again, bro?

I'm saving up my dolla bills for ya G-string!

What time do you go on stage, sexy?

Dicks.

I toss my phone in my bag and turn my truck around. *Please, God, don't let this be what I think it is.*

Dread smacks me hard when I spot that damn billboard and

my stupid smiling face. Although it's dark out, they have the sign all lit up with lights. It's a new ad that says "Heavenly Hunks has hard bodies that go all night."

Apparently I'm that hard body.

Fuck. Coach is gonna have my ass when he hears about this.

I'm so twisted up inside by the time I get home, I crash on the couch downstairs. Maggie's asleep anyway. I checked on her first. She needs her rest, and I'll just toss and turn.

I'm not ready to talk to her about this yet. I need some time to decompress.

They always say things get better after a good night's sleep.

In my case, it doesn't.

62

MAGGIE

I KNOW something is wrong from the moment I wake. Olly's side of the bed hasn't been slept in, and if he came home, he's already left. It's possible he mentioned staying at the football house, and I forgot. I won't jump to any conclusions before we talk.

He's leaving for Chicago later today because the Broncos play Northwestern tomorrow. I stayed up late last night so I could see him. Usually, before an away game, we make a point to touch base. Well, late for me, but when he wasn't home by ten, I couldn't keep my eyes open any longer and crashed.

His bag is still at the foot of the bed, so he'll have to stop by before he leaves. At least, I hope that's the case.

Groaning, I try to hoist myself out of bed, but everything aches. My back has been hurting something fierce since yesterday. I probably slept funny. Being this pregnant means I can't sleep on my back or belly, and I'm not crazy about sleeping on my side.

On the bright side, I'm officially thirty-six weeks today. Thick, hot relief floods me. I still hope to get to forty weeks because that's best for the boys, but this is a huge milestone considering how difficult this pregnancy has been.

I wish my dad could meet my babies. I remember him rocking me in an old recliner, and I think he'd love to cradle my sons and rock them to sleep if he could.

After I drag myself to the shower and get dressed, I settle down to work on Amelia's website. Her hauntingly beautiful face stares back at me. I can't begrudge Olly for dating her. Any sane, red-blooded man would kill to date this girl. I have to admit, when she's not making a special effort to be a twat, she's funny. I count my blessings that she's not sweet because then Olly would still be with her.

When I take a break, I text Olly. He should be at lunch right now. I'm finishing up Amelia's project a few hours later when I realize he never responded.

A sense of foreboding settles over me again.

I rub my belly to make sure the boys are still moving. In answer, someone kicks my kidney, and if it didn't hurt so damn much, I'd laugh.

My phone finally buzzes, and I fumble with it in a rush to answer.

Except it's not Olly.

"Sebastian."

"Hey. You answered."

"Because I thought you were Michael."

"Oh." He sounds sad, and I feel bad for being bitchy.

"Sorry. That was rude. What's up?"

He clears his throat. "I wasn't expecting you to answer the phone, since you never answer anymore. But, uh, I wanted to know if I could bring you lunch tomorrow."

"Aren't you in Austin?"

"So? You're less than an hour away. I can swing it. And if you're not in the mood to talk, I can drop off the food and leave."

My cold heart begins to thaw. "That's a kind offer, Bash. You really don't have to go through all that trouble."

"It's no trouble. I'd like to see you and check on those babies. How you feeling?"

"Like an enormous octopus has made its home in my uterus. But otherwise, I'm fine."

"You and Olly doing okay?"

I think about how odd last night was and how Olly never came to bed. But there has to be a good explanation. I'm sure he'll tell me what's going on when he stops home to get his gym bag. "We're... I guess we're fine. It's been a tough semester. He has a lot of commitments, but please don't jump on his case. He's doing his best."

Sebastian chuckles. "Remember when I was the one who used to defend him to you?"

"I'm sorry about that. I was unnecessarily hard on him. It was childish."

"Aww, you sound so mature." He pretends to sniffle. "My little Magnolia Poo-Pants is all grown up."

"Shut up, fool." I laugh. Maybe it's time to extend an olive branch. "Speaking of poo, have you ever changed a diaper, Uncle Sebastian?"

"Oooh. About that... I'm not really great with anything excremental."

"Hmm. What about vomit? Because I hear babies puke a lot."

"Yeah, no. Frannie puked on me when she was little, and I've never recovered."

"Too bad, because I'm putting you first in line to do some babysitting this winter. By the time you're done, you'll be an expert."

He's quiet for a moment. "Does this mean you've forgiven me

for being a royal ass? Because you have to know that I was only looking out for you. I love you, poopy."

I wipe my eyes. "Love you too, butt nugget. And yes, I've forgiven you. Contingent upon that lunch you're coming here to enjoy with me tomorrow and some twinsy babysitting."

"Deal."

"I really want the boys to know their Uncle Bash."

"Thanks, sis. I'm excited to meet them too. You do realize that if they're anything like you, you're gonna have your hands full with those little hellions."

Laughing, I shake my head. "I beg your pardon. I was an angel."

"Are you serious? You tried skating on the kitchen floor with banana peels tied to your feet when you were four. You attempted to dye my hair orange when you were six. I could go on and on."

When I get off the phone, I'm still smiling. I'm glad Sebastian and I have made amends. It'll be good to see him tomorrow.

But my good mood wanes the later it gets. The sun is almost starting to set, and I still haven't heard from Olly.

That sense of foreboding hits me like never before.

OLLY

"THEY'VE withdrawn the endorsement offer because of that strip club billboard."

I stand there, frozen, not sure what to say to Santos.

The disappointment on his face crushes my soul a little. No one enjoys disappointing their coach, but when the Saint is running the show, it's ten times worse.

He taps his desk. "I expected more from you, Oliver."

"Sir, for the record, I had nothing to do with how that billboard came about." I try to explain how the photographer sold the pics to the strip joint. It's not as though I actually prance around, shaking my junk in people's faces.

He holds up his hand. "Doesn't matter. Big Tykes is out. They want a good role model. Someone kids can look up to. You're shirtless on a billboard for a strip club, so regardless of how it came about, you can't be that role model."

Coach's words knock around in my head the whole drive home.

Plain and simple, I'm devastated. I've been busting my ass almost my whole life to get a chance like this, one that I can use to help the people I love, and in an instant, it's gone. My plan for helping Maggie and my parents and Gramps and paying for the hospital when the twins arrive just got flushed down the drain thanks to those dicks at Heavenly Hunks and that rotten photographer who swore those pics would not be used for anything tawdry. So much for "standard stock images."

I don't know how I'm going to get on a plane in an hour and play football tomorrow. Hell, I don't know how I'm gonna break the news to my family. I couldn't even bring myself to text Maggie back today. She has to be wondering what's going on with me.

When I pull into the driveway, the last person I want to see is sitting in a lawn chair in front of the casita, drinking a cocktail. I get out of the truck and slam the door.

"Olly, I need to talk to you."

"Not now." Amelia has no idea how close I am to losing it.

"Please. It's urgent."

"I said, *not now, Amelia.*" Of all the days to do this, why today?

As I make my way to the house, she grabs my arm. "Michael, seriously."

I turn, ready to tell her off, when I catch a glimpse of her red eyes. Christ. I don't have time for this. Santos will absolutely leave my ass behind if I'm not back on campus when the bus departs for the airport.

"I just have one question for you," she says, her words slurring slightly.

Taking a deep breath as I try to be patient, I nod. "And what's that?"

"Just... I've been wondering why you could never forgive me. How you could forgive Maggie for that ad, but you couldn't forgive me for that thing with Ben. And, well, for the bottle I threw at you."

I think back to last fall. To that night Amelia and I argued and broke up. Ben had given me a heads-up that Amelia told his ex Janelle that he was pretending to date Sienna to get Janelle off his back. I was upset Amelia had involved herself in a situation that was none of her business, and it caused a lot of friction on all fronts for my teammate. It came out at such a bad time that it nearly ruined his relationship with Sienna.

After seeing how callous Amelia was about the whole situation, I broke up with her, and in retaliation, she chucked a bottle of booze at my head and had that billboard done.

That night it really hit me—how wrong I was to involve myself in Maggie and Luke's relationship back in the day. What had I been thinking?

But then my thoughts snag on what she said about my girlfriend.

"What's there to forgive Maggie for?" I ask, confused.

She rolls her eyes. "For Heavenly Hunks. For the billboards. For the one that you yelled at me for last year and the new one that just went up. Even though I explained I had nothing to do with it."

That's not entirely true. "When I first asked you about it, you said I deserved it. From that, I deduced that you had some hand in the matter. Wasn't the photographer, Gerald, one of your 'dearest friends?' If that piece of shit was your friend, could you not have directed him to do this? Why are you backtracking now?"

"I said those things because I was hurt, Olly. I thought you deserved it for being such a prick about Ben and his stupid girlfriend. But that didn't mean I was involved with the billboard."

"Whatever, Amelia."

I turn to go, and she grabs me again. "What about Magnolia? Why aren't you pissed at her?"

I don't give a shit about trying to make peace with Amelia, but why is she trying to drag my girlfriend into this? "You have no shame. Stop trying to fuck up my relationship."

346 | LEX MARTIN

Her eyes soften, and her voice drops to a whisper. "You don't know, do you?"

"Know what?"

"Oh, shit." She blows out a breath. "Now you're going to blame me for this too."

"Swear to God, Amelia, you're talking in circles. Spit it out already."

She stills, and in the silence that ensues, I realize this is going to be bad.

The accusation she lobs shatters my last shred of composure. "Maggie did those ads. The billboards. Ask her. And if you need proof, check her phone. It's in her portfolio."

64

MAGGIE

I'M dead to the world, snoozing on the couch in the living room, drooling on myself, when the front door bangs open. I jump, nearly knocking my laptop to the ground. My heart is racing when I turn to see Olly standing in the entryway.

"Jesus, you scared me." I place my hand on my chest as I laugh. It's a relief to see him. I knew he'd come home before his trip. I wipe the sleep from my eyes. "I was worried I wouldn't see you before your flight. Your gym bag is upstairs by the bed, and I think it's all packed. Is everything okay?"

His nostrils flare. "No, everything is not fucking okay."

My head jerks back. I have no problem with cursing, but why do I feel like he's cursing at me? "What's going on?"

"I lost the endorsement."

"What? Are you serious?" I sit up, and the room shifts. I'm trying to wake up. I don't really know what to say about his news. It's devastating because that endorsement would've changed our lives. "What happened?" I rub my belly. "Did you tell Santos about our pregnancy? Olly, I'm so sorry if I played a part in this."

"Yes, you might've played a role." His words are so cold, I flinch.

I soften my voice because he's obviously upset. "I told you not to say anything until you'd signed the contract."

He stares at me for a long moment. And it's not one of those loving, sweet stares. No, his gaze is hard, his jaw tight, and the anger wafting off him intense. "Magnolia, the endorsement was retracted because of the Heavenly Hunks billboard."

Oh, God. "Why? They took it down months ago."

"Another one went up the other day, just in time to ruin my deal."

"I'm so sorry. That's heartbreaking."

His eyes narrow. "It *is* heartbreaking. For so many reasons."

A niggle of guilt takes residence in my chest, and before he says anything else, I know where this is going. And I know, deep in my heart, that this conversation will ruin everything. Just like I thought it would.

"Maggie, I'm only going to ask this once. Are there photos of the Heavenly Hunks ad in your portfolio? Did you or did you not play a role in that?"

I close my eyes, hating what I have to say. "Olly, let me explain—"

"Answer the fucking question. It should be an easy yes-or-no response."

Swallowing, I nod. "Then yes, there is. But it's not—"

"Not what? Not a complete betrayal of our relationship?"

"That's harsh." My eyes sting, and I blink away the tears. I refuse to break down right now. I need to stay calm so I can explain what happened, but my throat is tight and the words are all jumbled in my head.

I'd planned to tell him about the billboard that day I brought him donuts. I went prepared to clear the air and get everything on the table, but I'm not going to lie, I was scared it would flip him out. Olly's always been so buttoned up—he's a freaking Eagle Scout. I couldn't imagine a scenario where he'd want to be associated with a strip club.

"Harsh? You want to hear harsh? Harsh is having Santos tell me I've disappointed him, that I'm no role model for kids. Harsh is having Amelia waylay me in the driveway to tell me you're behind those goddamn billboards. Harsh is not being able to help my parents buy my grandfather's insulin because I can't afford shit. You and your fucking pranks. You must've had a field day with that one, huh? When are you going to fucking grow up, Magnolia? I had no clue you were so spiteful. Christ. And I thought Amelia was bad." His gaze travels down to my stomach. "Guess you're getting the last laugh and showing me your true colors."

I open my mouth, shocked. "What are you saying? That I tricked you into getting pregnant? Are you insane? Don't be an ass." The tears come now. I can't keep them at bay. "The billboard is not what you think, Michael. Please let me explain what happened." A wave of nausea hits me, but I swallow it back and try to untangle this mess. "The first one went up before we were even together."

"And that makes it okay?"

"No, of course not, but..." I wipe my eyes, wincing because my back spasms. "Remember I tried to tell you how there was one more thing I did, and you said you didn't want to know?"

"That's when I thought you'd toilet-papered my house in high school, not actively sought to ruin my professional life."

I shake my head. "I'm not explaining this right."

The look on his face says it all—I'm dead to him. It's an expression I've seen in his eyes when Amelia's around, and now he has it when he looks at me. "You've said enough."

He storms upstairs and returns a minute later with his gym bag. Without even glancing at me, he heads for the front door.

"Where are you going?" How can he leave right now?

"I have to catch a flight to Chicago. One of us has to give a shit about my career."

Anger like I've never known rises up in me. "You have the nerve to talk to me about 'true colors?' If you leave right now without hearing what I have to say, don't bother coming back."

He shakes his head with disgust brimming in his eyes and stomps out the door, slamming it shut behind him.

65

MAGGIE

I STARE at the front door, shellshocked.

All along I've been afraid that something would happen to make me and Olly revert to the antagonistic relationship we had for so many years, and in one single conversation, all of the headway we made in the last several months goes up in smoke.

I don't know how long I cry, but my eyes get swollen and itchy before the aching sensation in my chest turns back to anger.

How dare he?

Did he actually accuse me of getting pregnant *on purpose*? Or did I imagine that bullshit?

Right. Because I wanted to blow my senior year. Because I love sitting on my ass all day instead of going to class and my job. Because I adore watching my body balloon out until I don't even recognize myself anymore.

As I seethe, it becomes very clear to me how he got so twisted up. That bitch Amelia got in his ear. She must've seen the billboard when she flipped through my portfolio, and rather than ask me about it, she assumed the worst.

And who did Michael listen to? Me or his ex-girlfriend?

I waddle down the front stairs. It takes me a few minutes because that pain in my back is intense. By the time I make it to the casita, I'm sweating and shaking, but I can't let this go.

After I pound on her door, it swings open and I snarl, "You have twenty-four hours to get your ass off my property."

I wish I could storm off, but I can't move that quickly. Amelia calls after me, but I ignore her. "Maggie, wait. Where am I supposed to go?"

"You should've thought about that before you ran to Olly and made false accusations. Stop trying to make 'fetch' happen!" I don't know why I scream this. That line from *Mean Girls* makes sense in my head, but out loud, not so much. "Olly isn't going to wake up one day and miraculously be in love with you. Move on!"

He doesn't love you, Amelia.

And I don't think he loves me anymore either.

The thought steals my breath. One of those Braxton Hicks contractions hits me so hard, I have to sit. Fortunately, I'm by the front stairs, so I hang on to the banister as I sink down.

Amelia comes running from around the side of the house. She pulls up to a quick stop when she sees me. "You look like shit."

"You look like you'd be a nice person. We're both giving off faulty vibes." My stomach contracts again, and I groan. I'm hot and sweaty and nauseous. "Go away. Please."

When I open my eyes a minute later, she's still standing there. "Are you okay?" She waves at my stomach, a horrified expression on her face. "Are you having your Oompa Loompas?"

"Of course I'm not going into labor. I have four more weeks to go." If I have to sit with my legs crossed for the next month, I'll do it. Anything to make sure my babies arrive safely. The doctor said they'd have "optimal health" at forty weeks. That's all I want. The best shot I can give them to live long, happy lives.

"Um. You're already pretty huge. Are you sure you're not in labor?"

"You're really lucky I don't have a firearm. Go pack your shit." I grab the handrail and somehow manage to get myself upright. I hobble slowly up the stairs. When I get to the top, I turn around. "Haven't you done enough damage here? You're a plague, Amelia. Go initiate the apocalypse somewhere else."

I'm opening the front door when she calls out, "I thought he knew."

I rest my forehead against my house. "Sure. Whatever."

"I swear. I just... I thought Olly knew and forgave you, and that's what hurt. I couldn't understand why he couldn't forgive me."

"Well, he *didn't know*, and he's not in a very forgiving mood right now. Especially when it cost him a huge endorsement. But thanks for laying all of that at my feet." As I grit out the words, I can appreciate why he was fuming. If our roles were reversed, I would be too. I would feel completely undermined by the one person who's supposed to have my back. I'm hurt and angry and might take a frying pan to his thick head, but I get it.

Amelia pads closer. "But... you *are* responsible for the billboards. You did the design. It was in your portfolio. Why not admit it?"

Turning, I glare at her. "I wrote the fucking tagline, Amelia." *Wouldn't you like a Heavenly Hunk underneath your mistletoe?* "I wrote the tagline *before* Michael's photo was ever a part of the equation. That's why the photo of the billboard is in my portfolio. I had nothing to do with the photo selection or the design of the ad. I was basically an intern who was fucking around with taglines because I was bored, and my boss saw it and thought it was hilarious and wanted to use it." I'm incensed I can explain it so well now when I couldn't string together two words when Olly was yelling at me.

Her mouth shapes into an O. "Shit."

"Yeah, shit. But thanks for blowing up my relationship! Really appreciate it. Listen, if you plan on giving me something for the holidays, just make a charitable donation instead, because I don't think I can handle you ruining anything else in my life."

When I'm back inside, I slide the lock closed and let out a relieved breath.

Fuck Amelia.

And while I'm at it, fuck Michael Oliver too.

I'll be okay, I tell myself. Who needs him? He'll just be off playing football all the time while I'm at home. Being on my own will be better.

I wipe an escaping tear. At least this way, I'll get the heartache out of the way. Michael and I were never going to work out. In the long term, breaking up is the right thing to do. Because if I feel like death now, how much more would it hurt if we broke up in a year or two or five?

But my relief is short-lived because the next Braxton Hicks contraction takes me to my knees.

66

OLLY

We're somewhere over Oklahoma when I start to calm down. Cam leans over. "You ready to talk about it yet?"

I'm exhausted from not sleeping last night, and my stomach is growling from skipping two meals. I'm a mess. And I have one of the biggest games of the season tomorrow.

My jaw tightens. "You heard about the endorsement deal going south?" His pained expression tells me he has. I debate whether I should tell him what went down today with Maggie. I don't usually discuss my relationships, but I could use a friend right now. "Maggie might've had a role in it."

He frowns. "No way."

"She all but admitted it."

"She said, 'I personally designed the billboard?' Or 'I placed that photo?'"

"Well, no, but she said it's in her portfolio, and she's worked for advertising companies this last year as part of her work-study. I've seen a bunch of her work. Invitations and cards and crap. She's really good."

He makes a sound of disbelief. "Bro, I don't know if you're aware how work-study goes down, but my little sister has one and she has to cold-call donors for some benefit. She says she never gets to do anything interesting. Her duties are usually making coffee, getting lunch for her asshole boss, and if she's lucky, she can proof a press release from time to time. My point being that work-study students never have any kind of big role as far as I've heard."

Unease settles over me. Maggie complained about similar issues at her last gig. I close my eyes as I hear her words play back in my head that there was more to the story.

Only she never told me what it was.

Because you were a giant asshole and yelled at her. Even if she had played a role, you should've heard her out.

"She wanted to explain, but I was upset and in a rush to catch the team bus, and I might not have given her a chance to say what she needed to."

Cam unwraps a sandwich. "Maggie's in love with you, man. She'd probably give her right tit to science if you asked her to."

"Don't talk about her tits."

He snickers. "I'm just saying that she'd never do anything to hurt you. And that woman is not someone I'd want to cross. The other soccer moms out there had better watch out, because she'll go to town on anyone who messes with her kids."

My throat is tight all of a sudden. "I was all fucked up when I got home. I couldn't sleep last night because I was thinking about Vanessa being responsible for the blog that posted all that shit about me, and the new billboard going up, and how everything I want is almost within reach if I don't screw up." I scrub my face hard. "And then Amelia came at me about how I could forgive Maggie for the billboard when I couldn't forgive her for the crap she did last year."

Cam winces. "Please tell me you didn't accuse Maggie based on what Amelia said. From day one, that chick has been out to sabotage your relationship. Why else would she be living in a shed behind your house? Not to mention how she's always asking about you."

That's news to me. "You never told me that."

"You never asked. I figured you knew Amelia was after your nut."

"I don't give a shit about Amelia." Acid climbs up the back of my throat, but I swallow it down. "What if Maggie had a role in that billboard?"

He shrugs and takes a bite of his hoagie. "So what if she did? It was probably before y'all got together, right?"

"I'm not sure. Amelia made it sound like she had a role in all of them."

Shaking his sandwich at me, he says, "There you go again with Amelia. Forget Amelia, bro. The word 'toxic' was invented for her. Let me put it this way, whatever happened, however Maggie was involved, it was not malicious. You have to hear her out."

I nod slowly, his words making so much sense. I've been in a freefall since I heard about the new billboard yesterday, but Cam's advice is finally making me settle down.

As my head starts to clear, my heart plummets.

Amelia leveled me by knowing that Maggie used to work for Evergreen Advertising, which happens to be the company Gerald sold the photo to. And then she said Maggie was joking about getting revenge and how it's a dish best served cold.

I don't know why, but at that particular moment, it felt like she'd detonated a bomb in my life.

But now that I've calmed my ass down, I think Cam's right. Maggie would never do something malicious like that. Plus, Maggie started working for a new company second semester.

"I think I screwed up. No, 'screwed up' denotes something small, like I misplaced my cleats. I think I've just fucked up the best thing in my life. Like, so royally, it'll be a wonder if Maggie ever talks to me again."

"That bad?"

"She and I used to argue constantly. It wasn't until my sister's wedding that we hashed things out and became friends again. I'm worried that I just nuked our entire relationship, and now we're back to our old war zone."

He tilts his head one way and then the other. "Only if she knows Amelia is the reason you accused her of backstabbing you."

I groan and lean forward to rest my head in my hands.

After a minute, he pats my back. "Yeah, you mighta fucked up."

The second we land in Chicago, I call Maggie, but it goes to voicemail.

I check the time. It's late. She's probably asleep, so I leave a message. Cam has gone to the bathroom, so I have a little privacy while we taxi.

"Magnolia... darlin'... I know I said some shitty things, and I want to apologize. I was an utter ass. You didn't deserve my tirade. I want to hear what you have to say about everything. I'm sorry I left without giving you a chance. I was afraid I was gonna miss the team bus to the airport. That's no excuse for picking a fight with you and taking off, though. I hope you'll forgive me for the way I spoke to you and for the dumb shit I said."

Someone knocks into me from behind, and I turn to find Billy. "Let's grab some pizza when we get to the hotel."

I scowl and hunch back toward the corner by the window. "Love you, baby. Please text me to let me know you're all right."

"I luuuuurve you, Magnolia!" Billy howls from behind me.

The guys in the rows around me laugh, and I hold up my middle finger. "Shut up, assholes."

By the time we get to the hotel, I can't shake the feeling that something's wrong. Maggie's been feeling much better since she went on modified bed rest, but regardless, she's not supposed to get stressed out, and I made her cry.

I made my pregnant girlfriend fucking cry. What kind of monster am I?

God, I hate myself right now. Of all the people in my life to melt down on, why did it have to be her? Why couldn't I have freaked out on one of the guys? They would've sat my ass down to chill out. Either that or punched me in the face, and honestly, I probably needed a good beatdown.

I keep checking my phone to see if she's texted me. There are voice messages and texts from a million people, which is typical before a big game, but I only want to talk to Maggie.

She usually knocks out around nine. She's probably asleep.

Except no amount of rationalizing makes the dread in my chest subside. Once we get to the hotel, I call the only person I can think of who would drive over to Maggie's house right now to check on her.

Sebastian answers in two rings. His voice is thick with sleep. "This better be good, Olly. It's late, asshole."

"Sorry to interrupt, Bash, but I need a favor. I got in a huge argument with your sister today before I left for the Northwestern game." If ever I deserved a right hook from my best friend, it's tonight. "I'm worried about her. I called several times. Left a message. It's late, and she's probably asleep, but I'm still afraid. I upset her, and now I can't get a hold of her. I'm going out of my mind. She's had a tough pregnancy. I don't know what the fuck I was thinking. It's like I had an out-of-body experience. She's never gonna fucking forgive me for the shit I said."

"Chill, dude. I talked to her. We made plans to meet for lunch tomorrow. It's all good."

His words don't make sense at first. "Really? You talked to her? Did she sound upset?"

"No, not at all. I'm learning that Maggie's resilient as hell, but if it makes you feel any better, I'll go over there in the morning."

A huge wave of relief hits me. "Thank you. Thank you so much."

"No problem. Kick some Wildcat ass tomorrow."

When I get off the phone, I swear to myself that no matter what storms lie ahead of us, I'll never lose my temper like that with Magnolia again. Because, at the end of the day, she's the only thing that matters.

67

MAGGIE

ONCE I GET off my feet, I feel better, but there's no way I can make it up the stairs again. I snooze on the couch, relieved when those contractions stop.

This has been my whole pregnancy in a nutshell. I stress out over something, those Braxton Hicks come at me with a vengeance, and I have to go on bed rest. This time, I don't even bother calling my doctor. She'll just tell me what I already know. Hydrate, rest, and stay off my feet. If that doesn't make them stop, go to the ER. Yada yada.

Exhausted, I watch the sun come up through my front window. My back aches worse than it did yesterday. Sleeping on the couch doesn't help.

The sound of a car door slamming wakes me up later in the morning. "Magpie Poopy-Pants! Open the door."

Bash.

"Hold on!" I do a slow roll off the couch.

Shuffling those few feet leaves me sweating. I'm sure I look like a mess, but my brother won't care. He probably won't even notice.

I open the door, excited to see him. We're overdue to hang

out and get over our weirdness. I don't want to be this person who harbors old hurts. I may be angry at Olly, but I know it's my bad habit of letting emotional injuries fester that helped turn our relationship into a cesspool of revenge and animosity. That's not the kind of foundation I want to build in my life. I'm ready to bury the hatchet with my brother.

"Bash, hey—" I gasp as a gush of water hits the ground beneath my feet.

My brother's eyes go wide. "What the... Are you... Oh, fuck."

We both stare at the mess and then look at each other. A contraction, a real one this time, hits so hard, I yelp. I would hit the ground except Bash catches me around the shoulders.

"You're gonna have the baby." He sounds terrified.

"Two, actually. Holy shit, it hurts." I let out a wail that probably wakes my neighbors.

That's when the twatwaffle runs up my steps. Amelia sees me, sees the mess, and snarks, "I knew you were in labor!" She whips out her phone and starts dialing.

"Who are you calling?"

"911. You need an ambulance."

"Are you crazy? Do you have any idea how much that'll cost? My brother will take me."

She turns to look at him, like she hasn't noticed the giant man holding me up. "Oh, hi. I'm Amelia." She gives him one of her gorgeous smiles, complete with batted lashes.

"Do *not* flirt with my brother!" He's staring at her like he's starstruck. "Sebastian, this is Michael's *ex*-girlfriend. She will ruin your life and make you rue the day you met her. Please don't take the bait."

He blinks a few times and turns to me. "Uh, what? Yeah, I, uh..."

The man can't even string together a few words. I roll my eyes. "Take me to the hospital."

"Right!" He helps me down the front steps. "Hold on." After disappearing for a second, he returns from the trunk with a gym towel. "For the seat."

He loads me up, and once I'm buckled in, I close my eyes and rest my head against the window. Bash's door slams, but then I hear a second door slam shut. *No.*

"Amelia, why are you doing this?" I talk to the ceiling, knowing full well she's sitting behind me.

"I feel bad, okay? I don't usually feel bad about things, but I do this time."

"That's called being a sociopath. You should see someone about it."

"Just let me help. I promise I'll stay out of the way."

Bash starts the car and pulls out of the driveway. We're halfway to the hospital when he lowers his voice and turns to me. "It can't hurt to have one more person on hand in case you need something."

That's when I realize I don't have anything. Not my purse or phone or hospital bag. Not a damn thing.

Frustration bubbles up in me. I can see my pregnancy bag, which I reluctantly packed the other day, ready to go in my bedroom closet. Lot of good it does me there.

Fortunately, the hospital already has all of my info because I did a pre-admittance and submitted my forms ahead of time. Michael and I also did these online prenatal classes. Separately, of course, since he was always at school and I couldn't get my ass out of bed.

As I squirm on the seat and squish around in that wetness, it really hits me.

These kids are coming.

Soon.

How bad can giving birth be? My water already broke. Soon, I'll be in my hospital room. It'll be fine. I can do this.

But regret slams into me over how much I haven't done yet at home. Olly and I had planned to put the nursery in the room right next to ours. It already has a fresh coat of paint and is ready to go, but I was so afraid to jinx myself, I never bought anything for the boys. No cribs or rockers or onesies.

And now it's too late.

The moment I step out of the car, my water breaks. Again. That's not something my OB-GYN explained would happen, although she did say I had two placentas. I just never connected the dots.

So I stand in another puddle, humiliated, as a family stops to point at me. *Yes, pregnancy is messy, people!* I want to tell their kid to avoid sex at all costs.

A nurse runs out with a wheelchair. Smiling, she looks at my brother. "Is this the dad?"

He cringes, and I respond. "No. Dad's not here."

Michael should be here. He promised he would be.

Our argument comes flooding back.

You told him not to come home.

What possessed me to say that?

Because he listened to Amelia. Because he wouldn't hear me out. Because I had to get in the last word.

And look where that's gotten me.

"Shit, I should call him," Bash says.

I sniffle, resigned about what needs to be done. "What good would it do? Olly's in Chicago. Let him play his game. He'll be back tonight. I might be in labor all weekend anyway."

I'll just have to do this alone.

A nurse helps me change into an ugly hospital gown. "Let's get you on the bed and strapped into the fetal monitor."

Once I'm lying on a bed, connected to a million contraptions, Bash and Amelia walk in with coffee. "We brought you one," he says.

"Thanks, but I can only have decaf." I point to the balloon also known as my stomach. "Kinda pregnant over here."

"It is," Amelia says as she hands it to me. "Cream and sugar, the way you like it."

I squint at her. "You're being... nice. It's creepy. What's going on? And how do you know how I take my coffee?"

"You and Charlie were talking about it one day when you were in the garden. I overheard."

The coffee smells so good, I can't resist.

Bash rubs the back of his neck. "I should call Michael."

"Absolutely not. He has a huge game today. And he already thinks I tried to sabotage his career with that billboard, which messed up a big endorsement. I'm not going to take the blame for messing up his season too."

"What billboard? Oh, wait. The strip club?"

"Yes."

"Why would he think that?"

"It's a long story."

Bash looks around. "We're gonna be here a while. I have the time."

I hate rehashing this, but I guess I should fill in my brother so he doesn't jump to conclusions again. When I'm done, I point at Sebastian. "I'm still pissed at him. That doesn't mean I want you to beat him up."

"Now it makes sense why he called me last night."

My heart stops. "He called you?"

"He'd been trying to reach you, but you didn't pick up. Michael was worried. Called me pretty late. Wanted me to check in with you first thing this morning."

I try to hold back the tears, but I'm too overwrought.

"Michael was so mad at me, Bash. Why would he listen to Amelia instead of me?"

My brother sits on the edge of my bed and hugs me.

"I'm sorry!" she yells from the other side of the room. "I told you I made a mistake. That's why I'm here while you spritz everyone with placenta juice. I want to make amends or whatever."

Sniffling, I look up. "Placenta juice? Really?"

"I realize you don't care what I have to say on the matter, but I think you should let Olly know you're in the hospital," Amelia says.

I'm so tempted to give in. Deep down, I want him here more than anything.

My heart drops when I glance at the clock and reality settles in. "He's about to step on the field. The last thing he needs is to find out I'm in the hospital. Let him play the game. His flight will get home tonight. I'll probably still be here, pushing out two humans."

Bash backs off. "I don't have to stay for the pushing, do I? Because that would be weird."

"Go home, Bash. I can do this on my own." I always do everything on my own. Why should this be any different? "Take Amelia while you're at it."

"Maybe I could just stand by your shoulders. Until Mom gets here at least."

"You called Mom?" That's the first good news I've heard all day. I could really use a hug from my mother.

"She's on her way."

A wave of relief hits me. "Appreciate that." Which reminds me... "Thanks for sending Mom that check. It helped a lot."

"I would've sent it sooner if she'd told me she needed the help."

"How did you know? The only reason I found out is because I came home unexpectedly and found her crying."

"Your boy told me."

Olly. That man frustrates me to no end, except I've always known he's a good guy. An asshole sometimes, but a good person deep down.

I fidget with a loose thread on the blanket. "The women in our family have difficulty asking for help."

"Gee, ya think?"

My stomach contracts, and the sheet moves one way and then the other. I squeeze my eyes shut until it's over.

Amelia points at my gut. "That's fucked up."

Why is she here again?

The door swings open, and a doctor strolls in. "Miss Morales? Hi, I'm Dr. Zavala. How are you feeling?"

"Like I'm about to push out two basketballs through a thimble-sized opening."

He chuckles. "You're not wrong about the dimensions."

Bash and Amelia wait in the hallway while the doctor examines me. When a nurse walks in, I catch a glimpse of them chatting quietly outside my room. They're almost nose to nose with their phones between them, smiling at each other like they're planning a hot date.

Gross. If Bash starts seeing her, I'm going to lose it.

The doctor checks under the hood, so I'm momentarily distracted from the car wreck happening in the hallway. "Good news is you're already dilated seven centimeters."

"Does that mean this will go quickly?"

"You're off to a good start. Contractions every seven minutes." He looks over the notes on his clipboard. "Did they start before you came in?"

"Not that I'm aware of. I've had Braxton Hicks throughout

my pregnancy, and I had some pretty bad ones yesterday, but they stopped."

He scratches his head. "How about back pain?"

"Oh, yeah. So much back pain. For the last three days."

"That might've been an indication you were going into labor, which would explain why you're so dilated." He winks. "This might go quicker than you think."

I should be elated. Kicking my fat cankles in the air with delight. But this means Olly won't be home in time.

I just hope he doesn't hold this against me too.

68

OLLY

THE GUYS ARE in pregame mode. Our usual playlist blasts in the background, but everyone's focused on what needs to get done today—beat one of the top teams in the country. Although we're undefeated at the moment and won a national championship two years ago, we're having to prove ourselves all over again after getting our asses handed to us in the first half of the season last year. Winning today would do that. Prove that we've got what it takes, not only to ourselves, but to the NFL recruiters who are watching.

My head should be in the game. It's not. Sebastian said he would check on Maggie, but he never texted back to let me know how she was doing. I'm not supposed to have my phone out before a game like this. If Coach sees me, he'll be pissed. It's a risk I'm taking.

Bash, is Maggie okay? Let me know.

Because I'm going out of my mind.

"Let's go beat some Wildcats!" one of the assistant coaches shouts, and I reluctantly shove my phone in my locker.

After I'm tackled on the first play and get my bell rung, I

have to shut out thoughts of Maggie before my distraction gets me injured.

We nab a field goal, but Northwestern throws a forty-yard touchdown on their next possession. For some reason, we're just not clicking. I get the handoff from Easy, but the Wildcats are on my ass and take me down. Rinse, repeat.

By the end of the first quarter, we're down nine to fourteen. It should be closer, but we missed that damn extra point after our lone touchdown.

The Wildcats could run away with it if we're not careful.

Santos gives us that look, like we should know what the hell we're doing wrong. "Thomas, you're rushing it. If you start looking for your receivers downfield, it'll open your running backs."

"Yes, sir," Easy pants.

Coach glances at us. "You're ready for this matchup. We've got the power and strength and speed to keep these guys in check. You just have to believe it. We're gonna mix things up this quarter. Get ready to run."

I smack Easy on the back as we head back out on the field. "You got this. Take a deep breath. I got your back." If I spot a sack headed his way, it's my job to try to block for him if I'm able to.

We lose ground on the next two plays, and I can see the frustration in my teammates' eyes.

On the next play, Easy's trying to connect with Billy, our wide receiver, but the linemen are blitzing and headed for us at full force. I sprint to intercept one of them and hopefully give my QB time to get that throw off.

The defender and I go down in a heap of limbs. My teammates peel him off me. For a second, I blink up at the sky, and all I can see is Maggie's beautiful face. Fuck, I just want to win this game and get my ass back home to her.

Diesel gives me a hand up. "You okay? You look like you just saw Jesus."

I chuckle. "All good." Especially when I see that Billy got us a first down. Santos is right. The more Easy throws, the more spread the defense is getting.

We huddle quickly and break to the line of scrimmage. On the snap, I sprint to the fifty-yard line and turn just in time to catch the pass, which gives us the first down. But I juke the defender and narrowly slip past another before I take off down the field like my life depends on it.

My knee feels solid, and that gives me the confidence to power on at full speed.

Another defender appears in my peripheral vision and dives at me. I jump, somehow managing to avoid his outstretched arms, and blast into the end zone.

My team goes crazy. Holy crap, that was a seventy-yard play. I'm smiling ear to ear as we make the extra point, which puts us ahead by two, and that's how we head into halftime.

Everyone's pounding my back in congratulations. Diesel holds out his fist. "ESPN highlight reel material, for sure."

"Thanks, man."

We're headed down the tunnel when I spot Coach talking to Alex Escalante. It's not usual to see Sienna's dad at games. He flies all over the country on business, and since he's our biggest booster, he has unrestricted access to the team. But something about his serious expression makes me uneasy, especially when he and Santos turn to face me.

Santos curls his finger. "Oliver."

Shit. Whatever this is, it can't be good. The man only calls me by my full last name when I'm in trouble. "Yes, sir."

"Great run out there."

That's not what I expect him to say. But before I can thank him, he clears his throat. "Your girlfriend has gone into labor."

Oh, shit.

That's not supposed to happen when I'm at a game on the other side of the country. I'm supposed to be with Maggie when she has the boys. I promised.

"Are you sure?" I ask, praying I have more time.

Santos turns to Alex, who puts his hand on my shoulder. "I just got a call from Sienna, who says you need to, and I quote, 'get your ass home.' Maggie's already at the hospital. Contractions are coming every seven minutes."

My heart pounds harder than anything I experienced trying to outrun Northwestern. "What do I do? We're in Chicago. She's in Texas. Fuck." I tug my hair with both hands.

Alex motions to a man in a suit. "My driver will take you to O'Hare, where you can borrow my private jet. If you're lucky, you'll be back in time."

I turn to Coach. I don't know how to tell him this. I've never missed a game before by choice.

He cuts me off before I can say anything, his expression hard as stone. "This is the biggest game of the season so far. We're only up by two points. What's it going to be? Will you stay and play, or will you go?"

I don't need to debate this. In my heart, I know the right answer. The only answer. "Sir, I need to go. I have to be there for my girl."

If she'll let me in the hospital room. I might need to beg after that argument we had.

Will my decision piss off Santos? Will this affect whether I'm drafted? Will this change how NFL coaches view my commitment?

At the end of the day, it doesn't matter. I only care about getting back to Maggie and being the support she needs. The support I promised to be.

He stares at me a long, uncomfortable moment before he

cracks a smile. "Damn straight you do. Twins, right?" How does he know? "I've been waiting for you to fill me in."

Jesus, I just cannot do anything right. "I'm sorry, sir. I should've—"

"Son, save your explanations. I have a team to coach without my top running back. Go take care of your family. I'll see you back on campus next week."

Speechless, I watch him disappear down the tunnel.

And then I sprint to the locker room.

I have a plane to catch.

69

MAGGIE

PANTING, I brace myself for another contraction. I spot them on the monitor right before those bastards strike.

My mom wipes my forehead. "Hold my hand, *mija*."

"No, I'll hurt you." When Sebastian was in here earlier, he complained I was going to break his fingers. He and Amelia ran for the waiting room as soon as my mom arrived.

"A mother is stronger than you think. You'll learn this with your little ones."

Reluctantly, I take her hand, crying out when the next contraction almost makes me pass out. Fire spreads through my vagina and guts, like I'm being ripped apart. Holy crap. Is every birth this bad? How have humans populated the Earth when you have to endure this kind of pain?

My hair is in a ratty bun, I'm sweating through my gown, and my feet are popped up on stirrups. If I had really thought about what this would be like, I would've found a way to shave my legs because I can't stand staring at the forest sprouting there.

Dr. Zavala taps my knee to let me know he's reaching into the hot zone. After a minute, he nods. "Getting close. Let's get you some more ice chips and water. We'll start pushing soon."

I glance out the window. It's starting to get dark, but Olly won't be back for at least two or three more hours.

"Why didn't I call him to let him know?" Fat tears stream down my face. "I was so upset with him and confused and hurt."

Mom wipes my tears with a tissue. "Michael will be here. You'll see. I've prayed about it."

I wish I shared her confidence. "I'm doing everything wrong. I should've called him to let him know we were in the hospital. To tell him I'm sorry about our argument." At this point, I don't care who was responsible for what. I just want my best friend by my side. I'll kick his ass later.

One of the machines beeps, and it reminds me so much of my dad dying, it takes my breath away. "Mom, if something bad happens to me, I need you to tell Olly something for me."

"*Te prometo, nada malo va a pasar,*" she says fiercely, promising that nothing bad will happen. "You tell Michael whatever it is you have to say when he gets here."

I don't know if my mom is just really optimistic or delusional, but her absurd confidence is reassuring.

She makes a sign of the cross. "*Que Dios te bendiga.*" May God protect me.

I'm not too proud. I'll gladly accept any spare blessings, since my uterus feels like it might explode. A little help from the Almighty is more than welcome.

A knock on the door distracts me from my pity party, and a familiar face pops in. "How's my beautiful butterfly?"

"Sienna!" My mouth drops open. She's the last person I expected to see here. "How did you know I was in labor?" She's been joking she was going to hop a plane and visit the second she heard I was going to deliver, but I didn't take her seriously.

"Oh, a little bird told me."

Bash? But he doesn't have her number. Who else could've told her, though?

I don't get a chance to ask because the next contraction makes me cry out.

She takes one hand, and my mom has the other as the doctor tells me to push.

"No! Olly will be home in a few hours. Can't we wait?" He's going to be so upset if he misses this. Why didn't I call him?

Dr. Zavala pats my knee. "Sorry, the babies are coming. Your boyfriend will understand."

"But Olly's not back yet!" The hysteria rising in me has me wanting to get off the bed so I can press my knees together.

The door flings open, banging against the wall. "I'm here!"

I must be hallucinating, because there's no way Michael is standing in my hospital room, huffing and puffing, sporting his dirty uniform, like he just ran all the way from Chicago.

Another wave of tears hits me as he drops his duffle bag and races to my side. He grabs my face and kisses me. "I'm here. I'm back."

"How?"

He smiles over at Sienna. "Mr. Escalante told Coach what was going on and offered to let me 'borrow' his private jet. It was pretty trippy."

Sienna laughs. "I'm glad Dad's using his powers for good."

I'm so stunned, I just stare at him. My mom and Sienna tell Olly to call them if they're needed and head to the waiting room to give us some privacy. Well, as much privacy as a room with a doctor and two nurses can have.

"It's rare to see you speechless," he teases.

"How did you get back so quickly?" I pause to breathe through the contraction. "Even if you flew back on a private plane, I still... I still don't see how this happened."

The doctor interrupts us. "It's time for liftoff." Motioning to Olly, he says, "I suggest you stand behind her and grab her shoulders if she needs help sitting up."

I grab Olly's jersey and bring him close, until we're nose to nose. "Do *not* look at anything south of the border." Huffing, I add, "I can't handle you watching my lady bits explode."

"Whatever you want." He kisses my forehead and then looks into my eyes. "You got this. You're the toughest woman I know."

My nurse taps him on the shoulder. "Gonna need you to change into these, Daddy."

Olly heads to the bathroom and returns a minute later decked out in blue scrubs. I swallow, the fear receding now that he's here.

"I'm still mad at you," I whisper when he reaches my side.

His eyes grow remorseful. "I deserve that and more, but maybe we can call another truce."

I nod. "Let's table the argument until the boys get here."

He grabs my face tenderly. "There'll be no argument. No matter what you have to say. You did what you had to do, and no matter what it was, I know you'd never deliberately hurt me."

The tears spill over at the wave of relief that hits me. "I'm sorry we've had a shitty few months. I'm sorry I didn't just come out and tell you about that stupid billboard. I'm really glad you're here." I hiccup and wipe the snot away with the back of my hand. "If anything goes wrong today, if it's the worst-case scenario, I just want you to know how much I love you, Michael. I've been in love with you since I was in high school, maybe before that, and I don't want to be at odds with you anymore."

I'm babbling, but what if this is the last chance I get to tell him?

"Fuck, Maggie. Don't talk like that. You're my whole damn life. I need you for another seventy years." Eyes shiny, he kisses my forehead. "The moment I found out you were in the hospital, I knew that as much as I love football, you and our babies mean more."

Oh, my heart. "Did you win your game?"

He pauses. "Honestly, I'm not sure."

"What does that mean?"

"I left at halftime."

"YOU WHAT?"

He chuckles. "I heard my woman was in labor and took off in a private jet."

The nurse hands me a towel that's connected to the birthing bar. I push and groan and grunt and scream for the next two hours. I'm miserable and everything hurts. In between pushes, I make Olly give me the rundown of his game. As he describes that killer touchdown he made in the second quarter, I'm smiling even though my guts feel like they might shoot out my ass.

"For the love of God, get your phone and find out what happened."

He has dozens of messages, which he scrolls through to read one from Cam. **You turned the game around for us, bro! After that TD, we were unstoppable. Tell Maggie we beat Northwestern for her! When we land, a bunch of us are headed for the hospital waiting room. See you soon!**

Olly turns to me. "One win down and one more to go. Let's do this." He sits next to me and wraps his arms around my back. "Push back against me if you need to. I got you."

Teary-eyed, I smile, my heart suddenly full. "I know you do."

And that's when Jude and Levi Oliver decide to join us.

70

MAGGIE

SOMEWHERE, a baby cries.

Crap. That's my baby.

Bleary-eyed, I try to drag myself out of bed, but Michael beats me to it. "I got him. Go back to sleep."

"The milk... it's in the fridge. Next to..." I'm so tired, I can't think straight.

"Next to the juice. Got it."

Olly reaches down to the mini-fridge Bash gave us and pulls out a bottle he pops into the warmer. I mostly breastfeed, but my mom encouraged me to pump extra so I can get a break sometimes.

I glance at the clock. It's almost three in the morning. My attention returns to Olly, who pads to the small cribs we set up next to the bed. He bends over and lifts out our son. "Hungry, little man? Let's take care of that diaper first."

I'm not sure when he became an expert on babies, but Olly can do it all—diapers, feedings, burping. If it can be expelled from a child, he can deal with it. And without the squeamishness I get from Bash, who gags if he smells a dirty diaper.

Honestly, Michael's amazed me. Sienna told me he babysat

for his teammates. I guess I didn't believe it until I saw him in action with my own eyes.

He and I haven't talked about the billboard yet. I've been hesitant to break this spell, the one where we just deal with the boys and try to get a handle on life. His professors are letting him do remote learning for the next two weeks, as long as he checks in with them daily online. And Santos said Olly can weight-train from home for a few days. He still has to attend practice in the afternoons, but it's been a huge relief to have him around more until I get my bearings.

"How are we going to repay Sienna?" I whisper as I stare at all the baby gear.

"When I get drafted, I'll write her a check," he says, not skipping a beat as he swaddles one of the twins. "Although she might fight us on that."

We came home from the hospital to find our living room filled with all the things we would need—cribs, bottles, diapers, wipes, a breast pump, and dozens of the cutest onesies you've ever seen.

Olly has just gotten settled on the rocker when another squawk comes from the other crib. "Sorry, babe. I was hoping to get you some sleep."

"It's okay. Appreciate the effort." Cautiously, I slide out of bed. My parts are still sore, but it's getting better. "Who's this baby?" I can't really tell them apart unless I look at their outfits. We dress Jude in solids and Levi in prints so we can keep them straight.

I peer over the crib to find a pair of big blue eyes staring back at me. It's like staring at a baby Olly, except his hair is dark like mine. It's too early to tell if the boys' eyes will darken or if they'll stay light. Regardless, I'm in love with them.

Picking up Levi, I kiss his precious cheek. "How's my snugglebug?"

After a quick diaper change, I sit back in bed and whip out my boob. He grunts as he eats like someone's going to steal his nipple. It's adorable. I run my finger over his forehead and nose. Over his little ear. "You and your brother were worth every contraction. Worth every time I puked. Worth every single day I was on bed rest."

I look up to see Olly smiling at me with so much love in his eyes, it makes me emotional. "I wrote the tagline." The words come out of nowhere. When he doesn't say anything, I start babbling. "'Wouldn't you like a Heavenly Hunk underneath your mistletoe?' I wrote that."

He nods slowly. "It's clever." After a moment, he chuckles. "My family gave me so much shit about that line. Gramps gave me boxers for Christmas with mistletoe on it."

"That's... weird."

"You're a part of my family now, so you might as well get used to this, but Gramps is a perv. Surprise."

His lightheartedness about the whole thing makes me cautiously optimistic. "You're not mad? I didn't have anything to do with the design or pics chosen. Although... I should tell you that when I realized you were going to be on the billboard, it did cross my mind to make some nice color copies and stick them under your windshield wiper."

"I'm not mad." He stands carefully, never jostling Jude, and sits next to me. "I'm sorry I flipped out on you. I was an ass. There will never be a day that goes by where I don't readily accept that you're too good for me."

"Don't say that." I reach for his handsome face, and he leans close. "You're exactly what I need. You make me crazy some days, sure, but I love what we have."

We talk it out. About how I was half-asleep and tongue-tied and scared he'd be upset with me. How he was sleep-deprived and overwhelmed with losing the endorsement and the crap the blog was posting about him and Vanessa being behind it.

As I think back to all of the terrible stories she posted there, I want to track down that girl and kick her ass.

I grab his hand. "Considering how much stress we've experienced this year, I think we're doing okay."

"It's because you're an amazing woman who can juggle a million things." He laces his fingers through mine. "Before I forget, my parents want to know if they can swing by tomorrow. They want to clean and make us a few meals. Mom and Dad know you can't go to the game, obviously, but they'd like to watch it here with you. If you're okay with that."

"Don't they have tickets?"

"Yeah, but they'd rather watch it with you and the boys. They said they want to split their time evenly between us and Kayla, and the game gives them a reason to make the drive sooner."

Olly's sister just had her daughter. I'm so excited for our kids to grow up together.

"But they've never missed a game before." His mom always brags about that.

He shrugs. "I told them I wanted to check with you first."

"If they don't mind me looking like something chewed me up and spit me out."

Wrapping his free arm around me, he tugs me close. "You're more beautiful now than ever before. I'm in awe of you growing our babies and giving birth. I've never felt luckier than the day we had our boys."

I lean my head against his chest while we cradle our sons. "I can't believe you left at halftime. Football means everything to you." It makes me choked up to say it.

"You, Levi, and Jude mean everything to me," he says quietly. "Football is a sport. It's fun, and sometimes it's work. But it'll never replace my family." Leaning over, he kisses our babies, one then the other, then turns to me. "Thank you for this incredible gift."

"Pretty sure it takes two to tango."

He lifts an eyebrow. "Can I just say I can't wait to 'tango' again?"

I laugh and lean up to nip his ear. "That makes two of us."

But once again, sex is off the table as I heal. While I can't envision doing that right now while everything below the waist aches, I miss that closeness.

In my head, I'm counting down the days.

71

OLLY

I'VE BEEN RUSHING around all afternoon, trying to get everything done. Someone cries from the stroller. I glance down at two sleepy faces, one of which glares back at me.

"Hang tight, Jude." I wheel them into the coffee shop. "Mama needs some empanadas, and then we'll head home."

It's Christmas Eve, so snagging some last-minute pastries might be a pipe dream, but Maggie's been craving them. I'm getting the boys out of her hair for a few hours, and this seemed like a good time to sneak out for a snack.

"Olly!" some guy shouts from the back of the cafe.

I wave. Having an undefeated season has sent fans into overdrive. I'm pretty psyched about it myself, but juggling baby duty has helped me stay grounded.

I'm waiting in line when someone clears her throat.

"Hi, Olly."

And there goes my good mood. "Amelia."

Thankfully, she moved out of Maggie's casita, so we don't have to deal with her craziness anymore.

"Listen, I'm not going to take up your time," she says. "I just wanted to say I'm sorry for any drama I caused you and Maggie."

"'K. Thanks."

"I heard you got to the hospital in time for the birth."

I nod, wanting to keep this brief. "Sienna told her dad, who flew me home."

"I know. She told me."

Surprised, I finally face her. "I didn't think you two were friends." As far as I know, Sienna hates Amelia.

"When I called her to tell her Maggie was in labor, we put our differences aside. Don't get me wrong—we'll never be best buds or anything. But we're over our shit."

My attention snags on that first detail. Maggie told me Amelia went with her to the hospital, but we always assumed that Bash somehow got in touch with Sienna. "That was you? You're the one who told Sienna that I needed to get home?"

"Sebastian and I came up with that plan, but I knew how to get in touch with Sienna." Amelia gives me a sad smile. "See, once in a while I do something right."

Damn. That's kind of a big deal. "Thank you. Really. From the bottom of my heart."

Her smile grows. "Tell Maggie I'm glad she had her Oompa-Loompas." She peeks into the carriage. "Aww. Y'all aren't squishy at all. Look at those handsome faces."

I chuckle. "They were a little squishy at first."

She takes a step back. "Merry Christmas, Olly. Good luck in the playoffs."

"Thanks, Amelia. Merry Christmas."

After I snag the last three pastries, I book it home to find my beautiful baby mama fresh out of the shower. "Hey, gorgeous. Your men have missed you."

She smiles at the little dudes in my arms. "Were you good for Daddy?"

I never get tired of hearing that word. Daddy.

"They saved the exploding diapers for when we got home, so

yes. I changed them downstairs." As I hand her Jude, I mention running into Amelia and my revelation that she's the reason Sienna's dad tracked me down.

Maggie gasps. "Are you serious?" She's quiet for a long stretch. "Now I feel bad for kicking her out of the casita."

"Let's not get crazy. She needed to move on, but helping us like that was pretty cool." My eyes travel over her. Maggie looks more rested than I've seen her in a while. "How was your appointment?"

I'm curious because she didn't want me to go with her for some reason.

A huge grin spreads on her face. "It went well. In fact, I have a surprise for you after we get the boys to bed."

"Speaking of surprises, I have one for you too." I put Levi in his crib, and Maggie puts his brother next to him. "Have you given any thought to your schedule next semester?"

She growls, frustrated. "I already told you. I'm taking a leave of absence. Because there's no way you and I can both get to class while juggling the boys' feedings and naps. I know you don't want to do long-distance next year when you're drafted, but I'm going to have to stay here one more semester to wrap things up."

Over my dead body.

There's no damn way I'm going to be apart from Magnolia. But I don't say that because my woman doesn't like black and white declarations, and there's no need to trigger her to commit a crime before the holidays.

"Well, I have an idea," I say casually.

"I'm all ears." She groans at the wet spot on her t-shirt. "And tits, apparently."

Gorgeous, round tits that I'd love to shove in my mouth, but I don't say that either. "I'm done with classes."

"Ugh, I know. If I have to take one more basic class I forgot to do freshman year, I'm going to scream."

"No, I mean, I'm *done* with classes. I'll hold off on the graduation ceremony until May, but as soon as we wrap up the playoffs, I'll watch the boys and train for the spring combine while you finish your senior year."

She sits at the edge of the bed, her eyes wide. Opens her mouth. Closes it. Shakes her head. "What about your scholarship and eligibility and all that?"

"The last game takes place before second semester kicks off, and I don't need any more scholarship money if I'm done playing." I shrug. "I worked it out with Santos. He gave me some great ideas for getting through the next few months."

I'm a dumbass for not talking to him sooner.

"Oh, one more thing. Ben's loaning me a little money. It should get us through the next few months. I need to help my parents with meds for Gramps, and we can use the rest for the property taxes. I had Ben put it in writing because I don't want him to think I'll fuck this off." Maggie has been doing a lot of freelance work for Sienna, and between that and Cam and Billy renting two rooms that they barely sleep in, we should be able to afford our day-to-day living expenses and some payments on those hospital bills.

I have to hold off on buying Maggie a new car, but that's my first purchase if I'm drafted. I hate seeing her struggle with the twins' car seats in her ridiculously small two-door Ford Focus. I'd sell my truck now to buy her something nicer if I thought I could get anything for it.

Maggie hops off the bed and throws her arms around me. "I can't believe you did all of this. It's amazing, Olly. Thank you."

"I told you we'd figure out a way for you to graduate on time." I kiss the top of her head.

She slips out of my arms to peek at the boys and then back at me. "Think we could sneak away for twenty minutes?"

"Probably have a fifty-fifty shot of pulling that off."

"That's a chance I'd like to take." She turns on the mobile over the crib, grabs my hand, reaches for a baby monitor, and tugs me into the bathroom. "We gotta be quick, though."

It's been so long since I've gotten any action, at first I don't understand why she's unbuttoning my jeans. "You can have sex?"

"Yes! Dr. Perkins says I'm good to go." She pumps her fist. "I bought lube and everything. 'Cause sometimes women can't get wet after having a baby. Did you know that? I didn't."

That sounds like a challenge to me if ever I heard one. I grab her cute round ass and prop her up on the vanity. "First of all, this is gonna take longer than twenty minutes. Second, let's see if I can get you wet the old-fashioned way before we break out any products."

She giggles. "Is there a third?"

"Yup. Gotta be quiet."

And then I throw down a folded towel and drop to my knees.

72

MAGGIE

O<small>LLY STARES</small> up at me with a devilish grin as he slides off my pajama bottoms and panties. "Put your feet on my shoulders."

His deep voice is a growl that sends shivers all over me. I follow his directions until I realize how much I'm putting on display.

As his attention heads south, I put my hand between my legs. "It might look different. I squeezed out two babies."

He nips my finger, and I jump with a giggle. But his antics work, and I start to relax. Slowly, I remove my hand. He returns his attention to the apex of my legs. "Looks like a pretty pussy to me." His eyes go dark. "One I really want to fuck."

Yes, please!

I lean back against the mirror as he takes a slow lick up my center, one that makes my toes curl. "Olly," I gasp.

His hand snakes up my shirt and settles on my engorged boob.

"Careful, I might leak and—"

"Don't care," he mumbles against my damp skin.

"Oh, God. That feels good." My hips gyrate against his face. "Wait. Do we need a condom?"

390 | LEX MARTIN

He pauses. "You have a two-percent chance of getting pregnant while breastfeeding because it works as a natural form of birth control. Condoms also pose a two-percent risk, which goes up to fifteen percent when you consider user error, which... I guess we figured out firsthand." His tongue does something wicked to my clit. "Using a condom while breastfeeding is probably the safest route."

"How do you know all this?" I pant as I wiggle and squirm.

"High school health," he mumbles against me. "You're in the driver's seat, baby. Tell me what you want."

I'm so glad I'm dating a Boy Scout. He really is always prepared. "No condom. Bouncing on latex sounds unappealing right now, and I haven't gotten my period yet, so I think we're good to go."

"Or we can wait. I can finish you off. I might need to jack it, but there's no pressure to do more than you're ready for."

"No, I cannot wait." I jam my hand into his hair and lift his head. "And there will be no finishing off unless I come on your cock. You understand me?"

He chuckles. "Yes, ma'am. Now let's get back to lubricating."

Ten minutes later, I've forgotten all about the 'not finishing separately' thing when I come on his face and fingers with a shriek.

With a grin, he licks his lips. "I'd say you're lubricated."

So much so, I wouldn't be surprised if there was a puddle under me. But I don't get a chance to check because I'm distracted when he finishes unbuttoning his jeans. He's sporting those boxers his grandpa bought him.

"I'm getting *the* Heavenly Hunk under my mistletoe this year. I'm such a lucky girl."

He winks. "You're definitely getting *my* heavenly hunk."

His thick length springs out of his boxer briefs. I wrap my hand around him and give him a long stroke. But as sexy as this is, and as much as I want to pounce on him, the prospect of reconnecting with him in the bathroom doesn't sound appealing.

"Can we move to the bed? I don't think I can sit on this counter any longer."

A split second later, he lifts me into his arms and shuffles through the door. I wrap my arms around his neck and cling to him while he tiptoes over to the crib, where the boys are down for a catnap.

"Let's do this," he whispers. "Berry, berry quietly."

I snort at his Elmer Fudd voice and nip his ear. "You're forgetting the rules. No cartoon voices during sex."

He kicks off his jeans and boxers and slowly lowers both of us to the bed. I glance at the crib again. There's a blanket hanging off the side, so even if the boys were awake, they can't see anything. Not that they would know what they're looking at. Still. I don't want to traumatize my children.

Olly grabs my chin. "They're fine. Cavemen fucked with their kids three feet away."

"Very reassuring." I lick his corded neck and thread my fingers through his thick hair. "Take off your shirt. I want the full 'hunky' experience."

He smirks and strips it off. "This what you want?"

Holy smoke show. Michael has the perfect body. Broad chest and shoulders. Ripped belly that tapers down to a narrow waist. Just the right amount of hair that leads me to that eager part of him I love exploring.

I trace his biceps with a finger and drag it across his chest so I can pinch his nipple, making him yelp. "You know I do, you tease. Get over here."

He laughs and drops down on me. But before he gets to work, he yanks off my t-shirt. I try not to squirm. I know I still have a few extra pounds to go before I reach my pre-pregnancy weight. And now I have those stretch marks, and my boobs feel enormous, but all I see is desire in his eyes.

"Christ, you're beautiful, Magnolia." Our mouths connect as he presses his big body to mine, and his weight feels so good, I groan. "Shh. If the boys wake up, this is going to be over before it begins."

Quiet. Right. I nod and kiss him again and wrap my legs around his waist. His length slides between my thighs, making me light up again.

He nibbles my earlobe and neck, working his way down until he tugs on a sensitive nipple. I'm not sure what to expect. I feed two boys daily, but breastfeeding is the last thing on my mind when Olly sucks me into his mouth. The sound that comes from his chest is so guttural and full of need, I'm desperate to feel him inside me.

Smacking his lips, he breaks out that devilish grin again. "You're so sweet." He takes another long pull from my nipple, and my clit throbs.

"Dirty boy." This is some definite kink territory, but making Olly wild is pretty hot.

He nudges between my thighs, and I spread my legs more to give him room. I squeeze my eyes shut, suddenly afraid it'll hurt, but he stops moving.

"Hey. Mags. Look at me." My eyes open to find the worry on his face. "If it doesn't feel good, we stop. I don't care if I'm balls deep, if something isn't working for you, just tell me."

I forget that Olly's such a considerate lover. "Thanks. I needed to hear that." I kiss his jaw. Lick his bottom lip. Suck on his tongue when he slips it in my mouth.

He takes his time wedging himself into me, but he's right. I'm wet enough to handle his size. Slowly, decadently, he sinks into my body. I lift my knees higher to take him deeper.

"Jesus." Dropping his forehead onto my shoulder, he takes a deep breath. "You feel too good."

Is there really such a thing? "I already came. You don't need to wait for me to go again."

His affronted expression makes me chuckle. "The hell you say." He snakes a hand between us and gently circles my clit while his cock slides in and out.

My head falls back on a gasp. "I lied. I can come again. Don't you dare stop."

"That's my girl." He licks my nipple. Sucks it. Tugs on it. And that slow throb between my legs goes crazy. Shifting, he changes the angle so his dick does a slow tap-dance on my G-spot.

I slap my hand over my mouth as I come, screaming against my hand as I'm filled with bone-melting pleasure. My orgasm has an immediate effect on him. His cock swells so thick, it keeps me fluttering around him. I'm still going when his release hits him, and we cling to each other, sweaty and panting as we give in to the euphoria.

We're about thirty seconds post-orgasm when a little voice squawks from the crib. "That's some damn good timing if you ask me," Olly's deep voice whispers in my ear.

"Amazing teamwork. Maybe we could do some more team-building tomorrow night?"

"Fuck, yes. Let's pencil that in between the feedings and diapers and dirty laundry."

"And presents. Don't forget it's Christmas. Our families will be here by noon." It's not even strange to be having this conversation with him while he's still wedged between my thighs.

His arms snake around me as he leans down to kiss me. "Our first Christmas together."

"The first of many."

Our son yells again, and he's joined by his brother. Michael smiles at me. "Merry Christmas, baby. Love you."

"Merry Christmas, Olly. Love you so much." I rub the scruff on his face. "Thank you for my boys and for our life together. I have a feeling it's going to be amazing."

After all the difficulty of the last year and the pregnancy and us not communicating well, I have a deep appreciation for this blissful, beautiful moment and all the good times ahead of us.

He'd better be ready. Because he's stuck with me now.

And I have no plans to ever let go.

EPILOGUE

OLLY

MY PARENTS' house is filled with people—my old coaches, former teammates, some neighbors, my sister and her family, and of course Maggie and the twins.

In the corner, a camera crew with a local news affiliate sets up to get live footage of us in the event I get drafted.

Sitting here hoping and praying a team calls my name is nerve-wracking.

Sure, I've been positive and saying 'when I'm drafted' anytime the topic comes up, but that's merely me putting the wish out into the universe.

Yes, we had a great season.

Yes, we made it to the championship game.

Yes, we gave it our best, even though we lost by one field goal.

Still, nothing is guaranteed. My knee feels good, though, and I had a great showing at the combine a few weeks ago. But in my mind, I keep wondering if there was anything else I could've done to make myself stand out among the amazing talent in this draft pool.

Maggie laces her fingers through mine. "You got this. Just watch."

I smile at her even though I'm nervous as fuck. The draft isn't the only thing turning my stomach. There's also a diamond ring burning a hole in my pocket.

"You look really handsome in that suit," she whispers.

"Thanks, baby. You look beautiful too." She does. Her thick hair is up in a ponytail and those big brown eyes are lined in dark charcoal. Her lips are plump and shiny. She's wearing a snug black dress that accentuates all her curves. Stunning is the only word that does her justice.

Not only is she gorgeous, she's an incredible mama. Our boys are so lucky. *I'm* so lucky.

She and I have come a long way in the last few months. While I thought I had appreciated how much she sacrificed to carry the boys, I didn't realize the mental toll it took on her.

Now that she's taking classes again and back to her typical kick-ass self, I have a deep gratitude for all the things she put on hold to make us a family.

For a heart-stopping moment, I reconsider my plans for later this afternoon. Because Maggie should get her own day to feel special.

Why did I think it would be a good idea to propose on the same day as the draft? One of my friends should've vetoed this idea.

Johnny plops down on the couch next to me. "You gonna hurl?"

"Hopefully not on camera." I laugh and wipe my sweaty palms on my pants after I covertly let go of Maggie's hand on the other side of me. "Were you this nervous about the draft?"

"I had the shits for three days straight."

"That's... too much information."

He waits until Maggie is talking to my sister to lean toward me. "Ben just texted. He's running late but said everything's ready."

God, I hope she likes what I planned.

Motioning toward Sebastian, who's chatting with Amelia in the kitchen, he asks, "Is it weird he's dating your ex?"

Apparently, sparks flew after they met at the hospital last November.

"More power to them." Yes, it's weird, but it's also kinda funny to watch them bicker. Sebastian doesn't let her get away with shit, and she's always on his ass about something, but I guess it works. He's well informed about my history with Amelia, and if he can handle her drama, I wish him well.

I wouldn't say Amelia and Maggie are friends, although Amelia hustling to get me home for Maggie's labor went a long way to make amends. And if I really have to dig deep, I just remind myself that she saved Maggie from a rattlesnake. That's reason enough to be cordial.

I give Bash and Amelia a year to strangle one another.

Truthfully, I can't be hard on Sebastian. He had an attorney friend review the contract I signed for those stock photos that ended up on the billboard. The lawyer says it has a "no pornography or erotic usage" clause the photographer clearly violated.

I hate being litigious, but if suing that guy keeps those pics from being displayed in that manner again, I'm open to taking legal action.

"What about you, man? You dating anyone?"

Johnny shrugs. "You know me. I like the sampler platter."

Billy sits on the arm of the couch on the other side of Johnny. "Yeah, the sampler platter."

Johnny punches him in the arm. "You don't even know what we're talking about, fool."

"Does it matter? I like tasting a little bit of everything," Billy says as he watches Charlie move around the room, taking pics. Billy motions to Charlie. "Speaking of sampling, what's her story? She's Maggie's friend, right?"

"She's not into football players. That's all I know." Maggie gave me a very clear mandate that I was not to set up Charlie with any of my buddies.

He strokes his chin. "Only 'cause she hasn't met me yet."

I almost laugh. Women like Billy. He's a good-looking dude, but I get the distinct impression Charlie wouldn't find him appealing.

Nudging me, Johnny lowers his voice. "Still can't get over Vanessa Fox being behind the blog."

With so much going on, it's easy to forget how much trouble she caused. "I'm not sure who started it, but she was definitely the one calling the shots by last fall."

After the school investigated, the administration expelled four students for their involvement, including Vanessa, due to invasion of privacy accusations and other legalities. Although I heard she recently snagged a job at a big gossip site in Los Angeles, her legal troubles here are just beginning, as three former Lone Star athletes are suing her for libel. Her father took a leave of absence and likely won't return next fall.

When the draft kicks off, my attention snaps back to the present moment, and my stomach flips. Levi smiles at me from the stroller, and I lean over and pick him up. I sniff the lavender scent in his hair and that baby scent that clings to his skin. He's a chunker like his brother. Jude is sleeping peacefully even though the energy in this room is crazy. But Levi bounces on my lap, curious to see what's going on.

Having my son in my arms calms me.

It doesn't matter what happens today, I remind myself. I already have everything I need in this life. An incredible woman. Beautiful sons. Amazing family and friends. Everything else is icing on the cake.

Worst-case scenario, I don't get drafted. I'm okay with that. Never thought I'd ever feel that way, but I am. I'd be disappointed, sure, but I'll survive. I'll get a job and have barbecues in our backyard with Maggie, and we'll watch our kids grow up. That would be a damn good life.

Not getting drafted would mean I can't help my parents with the renovations to their farm or my grandfather's trailer as soon as I'd like, but I'd be around more to do any physical work they need, and I'd be close in case they had an emergency. We'd have to hold off on the plans we have for Maggie's house. The kitchen is ancient, and I'd love for my girl to have some nice, shiny appliances since she loves to cook and we'd be staying there long-term.

At least Gramps is covered. He just joined a new medical program Sienna's dad developed that helps seniors with the cost of medications. That's been my biggest worry, and knowing that he'll get his insulin no matter what goes down this afternoon is a huge relief.

Ultimately, if today doesn't turn out the way I hope, it won't be the end of the world.

I'm so deep in thought, I don't hear my name being called.

"Olly!" Maggie jumps in her seat as she takes the baby out of my arms. "That's you! Chicago picked you!"

Holy shit. I'm a first-round draft pick.

I did it. Well, *we* did it.

This is a culmination of so many sacrifices. I stand and hug my girlfriend, careful not to squish Levi. "This is *our* victory,

Mags. Not just mine." I lean over to hug my mom and dad. "Love you guys. Couldn't have gotten here without you."

It's one of the best feelings of my life. Not just because I overcame my ACL injury and played again, but because the people I love most in the world are here with me to celebrate.

The cameraman circles us while people congratulate me.

My mom tells everyone to quiet down and points to the TV where there's a montage of me playing football at different ages —from peewee to high school and college. But the photos that make my eyes sting are the ones of me with Maggie and the twins. Of Jude asleep on my chest. Of Levi snuggled in the crook of my arm as I read. Of me jogging down the street with the kids in their stroller. Of my teammates in the hospital waiting room, getting their first glimpse of the boys.

Over the photos, the broadcaster says, "Michael Oliver is not only one of the top college running backs in the country, he's also a dedicated family man. He and his girlfriend had twins last fall, and when Olly's not training, you can find him trying to get his boys to eat their vegetables."

The last photo is of me, covered in pea puree, crouched behind Jude and Levi, who are in their highchairs. Their green, toothless mouths are stretched in wide, pleased grins, since they managed to get more on me than in their stomachs.

Smiling, I turn to my parents. "How'd they get all those pics? Did you do this?"

Mom takes Levi and motions toward my girlfriend. "That was Maggie's idea. She put it all together."

I scoop my woman into a hug. "Thank you. That was amazing."

Her beautiful brown eyes turn up to me. "Wanted to make it up to you." She doesn't have to explain what 'it' is. I know she still feels guilty for that billboard. Hopefully today proves to her I'm over it.

"You've already given me everything, Maggie."

With one tiny exception I aim to rectify this evening.

MAGGIE

"Are you sure the boys will be okay?" I sound like a broken record. "Did I leave them with enough breastmilk?"

Olly squeezes my knee. "They're fine. Remember how well things went last time my parents babysat?"

"Yeah, but your parents stayed at our house while we went to dinner. Tonight, the boys are staying with them."

He glances at me as he drives. "It's been a long day. They're probably already asleep, and you'll see them first thing in the morning. Hopefully not too early."

I nod slowly. "It was thoughtful of your parents to offer. I'm looking forward to having a quiet dinner, just the two of us." Olly's been sporting a suit today, and he is so dang handsome. Seeing his smiling face on television made my heart pitter-patter. "Save some energy for after dinner," I tease.

"Roger that." He winks, and I feel myself blush.

Yes, I'm still blushing a year after we got pregnant.

He taps on the wheel. "Did you really bake me a pie?"

"It's sitting on the counter in the kitchen. To make up for the one Johnny ate and to celebrate you getting drafted."

"What if I hadn't gotten selected today?"

"I had no doubt." Honestly, I didn't. "But if the apocalypse truly descended today, I would drizzle apple pie filling all over my body and let you lick it off to make you feel better." Who am I kidding? I'd enjoy it thoroughly too.

He adjusts himself and gives me a heated look. "Can we still do that when we get home?"

Chuckling, I nod. "A celebratory licking," I tease. "Really, Olly, I'm so proud of you. I can't say that enough."

We have so many things to plan in the next few months. I'm not sure how you move across the country with twins, but I guess we're about to find out. After the draft this afternoon, we talked to my mom and asked if she and Frannie would like to move into our house. Mom can rent out the casita to cover her day-to-day bills, and Olly told her we'll cover the property taxes and utilities so she doesn't have to work so much. That way she can spend more time with Frannie.

I didn't think I could love Olly more, but seeing how generous he is with my family definitely swells my heart. And he wasn't lying when he said he was handy.

When my sweet boyfriend wasn't training this spring, he helped me finish some major renovations, starting with the porch and front steps, which he and the guys ripped out and built from scratch.

Ironically, we found that the easiest way to get the boys to sleep was to rock them next to the dryer in the creepy basement when we were doing laundry. So Olly did a complete overhaul down there too, adding sheetrock to the unfinished walls, attaching a sturdier guardrail next to the steps, bringing down more lamps, and buying a second-hand recliner. It totally changed the vibe down there.

The only things we held off on were the exterior paint job and kitchen renovation we couldn't afford, but my mom assured us she and my little sister don't care about that.

Sienna told me I can continue working for her remotely. She's kept me busy doing design projects for her and her father, which helped me pay for all of those doctor visits last year. Even though that hospital bill was astronomical, Olly's been making small payments. And together, we've been staying afloat. No thanks to my work-study job, of course.

After discussing what happened with Sienna, she encouraged me to lodge a formal complaint since that firm illegally fired a pregnant woman. I'm not looking to win some big settlement. I just want to help protect any other students who find themselves in a similar situation down the road.

As Olly and I head back to Charming, an anxious ball forms in my stomach in anticipation of passing that sign from hell. Olly swears he's not mad about it anymore, that he understands I had no say in what happened, but I still feel a twinge of remorse for the ugliness that went down between us in the aftermath.

Deliberately, I stare out the passenger window so I don't have to look at it.

"Maggie, you okay?"

"Yup." The trees whizzing by start to slow, and I realize there's a crowd of people by that stupid billboard. "What's... going... on?"

After pausing to look both ways, Olly crosses the dividing line in the road and parks the car so we're facing the sign. Then he hops out and runs around to open my door.

I read the giant words on the billboard. Once. Twice. Three times.

Magnolia Morales, will you meet me at the altar? Those giant words are written above a photo of Olly in a tux, holding out a little black box.

He tugs me out of my seat, and I turn to find him on his knee before me.

"Maggie, my life is amazing. Some would say perfect. But I know the truth. I'm missing one key thing—having you as my wife. You keep me grounded in a way I never knew I needed. I love you in a way I never knew was possible. You and our boys possess my whole heart and soul. Would you do me the great honor of marrying me? I promise I will always let you hog the sheets."

Those have to be the sweetest words I've ever heard. Except... "I don't hog the sheets."

He chuckles. "So you say."

I grab his handsome face and lean over to kiss him. "We'll still argue."

"From time to time."

"Just because we'll be married doesn't mean you'll get your way."

"I wouldn't expect to."

Someone in the crowd shouts, "Would you just say yes already!"

I laugh and kiss Olly again. "It was never a question. Of course I'll marry you. You're the love of my life."

He pops open the box and slides a beautiful ring onto my finger.

A flash goes off, and I turn to see Charlie standing next to Ben and Sienna. I gasp when I see my mom and Frannie. They run up to hug me, and I open my arms for my little sister, but she launches herself at Olly. He squeezes her with a laugh, and my mom and I stare at each other, stunned to see her hugging someone.

Frannie stares up at my fiancé with a huge grin. "Mommy says you're gonna be my brother now. Like Bash."

"Sure am, kiddo. That okay?"

Her little lips twist. "Can we have more tea parties?"

"Absolutely."

"Yay!" She wiggles out of his arms and starts twirling, and we all laugh.

After greeting our friends, I lunge at Olly. "I can't believe you planned this."

"More people are meeting us at Lorenzo's to celebrate." That Italian restaurant we went to for our first official date.

"But we should be celebrating *you* today. You got freaking drafted!"

He gives me a tender smile. "But you're the real prize. You're what I want to celebrate."

And that's how I end up with the man of my dreams. The one who made me insane for years. The one who won my heart and soul.

BONUS SCENE

TEN YEARS LATER

MAGGIE

"Mom, do we *have* to go?" Levi whines from the back seat.

"Yeah, Mom. Why couldn't we just wait at home? We're old enough to stay by ourselves."

Ha. As if I'd leave my two little daredevils unsupervised.

I pull into a parking spot, turn off the car, and twist around to face the boys. "The reason we're all going to your sister's dance recital is because she goes to all of your football games."

Levi frowns. "But our games are exciting. Not like ballet."

Jude unbuckles his seatbelt and leans forward. "It wouldn't be so bad if we could get some ice cream afterwards."

Lord, give me strength. "Do you two have any idea how hard those stadium seats are? Gracie sits on those benches for hours at your games *each week*. No, she doesn't just sit there in the stands. She cheers her little heart out for you. Are you going to tell me you don't want to be there to support your sister who thinks you hung the moon?"

Almost simultaneously, the boys slouch, ashamed.

"You're right, Mom."

"Sorry, Mom."

Inside, I smile, but I don't let up my stony demeanor just yet or they might start to backslide. "We're going to march in there and be the best, most supportive family this ballet troupe has ever seen. Do you hear me? Because Gracie needs to know that what she does is just as important as what you two do. Okay?"

They nod.

I'm pretty pleased with myself until the twins cheer like they're standing on the fifty-yard line during a halftime show.

"Boys, sit down." All the other parents are side-eyeing me.

"Shoot, that's not Gracie's group," Levi mumbles.

My boys just cheered for the wrong dancers. I chuckle and reach over to hug him. "That's okay, honey. Those little girls up there need it just as much as Grace."

Finally, my daughter's class lines up on the side of the stage, and I wave.

"When's Dad getting here?" Jude asks.

"He must be running late." I break out my phone and get the video setting ready to go. "I'm recording, so he won't miss a thing."

Just then, the back door swings open, and my husband jogs in carrying our younger daughter Sadie, who's a year old. "Sorry we're late. Someone had poo problems." After he sits next to me and leans in to kiss me, I get a good look at Sadie. She's teary-eyed and sucking her pacifier. I open my arms for her, and she starts to come to me, but changes her mind and buries her head in Olly's neck. Sadie is the biggest daddy's girl, so I'm not surprised. He's a great dad, and you can see it in how much our kids love him.

I kiss her forehead and push the dark hair out of her eyes. "Hang in there, baby. This shouldn't go too much longer. We'll get you home and take a nice bath, and you'll feel so much better."

Under his breath, Olly whispers, "Think Mommy could give me a bath too?"

I chuckle, and when our eyes meet, he winks at me. God, I love this man.

The music starts and all of the five-year-olds walk out, hand in hand. I start my video. The kids are adorable in their little tulle skirts and ballet slippers. Gracie has been practicing her routine for weeks.

She's in the front row of dancers. Only she's not smiling.

Ten seconds into the routine, she stops dancing. Two seconds later, she starts bawling.

Crap. I'm not sure what happened because she's been so excited about this recital.

But before I can jump up to go get her, Olly's already bounding up those steps with the baby in his arms. Next thing I know, he takes Grace's hand and starts dancing right alongside her.

I smile, loving that my husband knows the routine. Because we both helped her practice it.

The audience is chuckling, and two moms behind me quasi-whisper something about Michael being a sexy beast.

I almost turn around to point out that he's *my* sexy beast, but I don't. During the years Olly played pro football in Chicago, I learned to tune out the way other women made eyes at my husband. He and I had too much on our plate to worry about all that noise. I knew I was the only woman in his bed, just like he was confident he was the only man in mine.

Now that life has slowed down a bit and we're back in Charming again, he's a huge hometown hero. Restaurants post his photos, and he gets stopped everywhere we go. I'm glad he's getting that adoration. He's a standup man and deserves the appreciation after years of crisscrossing the country to get banged up every weekend by three-hundred-pound linemen.

Don't get me wrong. I'm grateful for his time playing pro ball. I'm just glad it's over.

On stage, he twirls Gracie and sways and pliés just like the other kids. All while holding Sadie. It's freaking adorable and so sigh-worthy.

I lean over to the boys. "See how Daddy doesn't mind doing ballet? He's not worried about what other people think about him. He's only thinking about Grace. I really love that about your father." And I plan to show my appreciation tonight.

Once we're home and the kids are in bed, I grab my husband's hand. "Want to do a load of laundry with me?" I waggle my eyebrows. Next thing I know, he's dragging me down the stairs at a speed I can barely keep up with. Because he knows what 'laundry' is code for.

After Olly retired from football, we moved back into our old house in Charming and bought my mom and sister a place a block away.

When we're down in our renovated laundry room, we kick off our clothes at record speed, and then he props me up on the washer. The kids are scared of coming down here even though they all spent so much time next to the dryer, trying to fall asleep, as babies. It works for us since this is the only place in the house where we can find a little privacy. The kids joke about how much laundry their parents do, and I have a hard time not laughing whenever one of the twins mentions it.

I take my husband's handsome face in my hands. "You set everyone's ovaries on fire with those dance moves."

He snorts. "I'm sure."

"No, really. A man holding a baby while dancing with his daughter?" I fan myself. "So hot."

As he takes a lick up my neck, he chuckles. "I can give you a private dance next time."

"A private dance from my Heavenly Hunk? Sign me up." I thread my fingers through his hair.

His laughter grows. As does one particular appendage that he nudges against me. I don't know if it's the stress of the day or the fact that he's going on a business trip tomorrow, but the fireworks go off in record time. Of course, having kids means you learn how to get to the end zone as quickly as possible before someone bangs on your door.

We're panting and sweaty and clinging to each other when I whisper, "I miss you already. How long are you going for again?"

"Just two days." Even though Olly lost that first endorsement deal, once he made it to the NFL, he became widely known as a family man. I was always posting pics of him being adorable with the kids. Like that time he duct-taped that singing bass fish to Jude's diapered butt to help him fall asleep. Or him carrying the boys in shopping bags when they were toddlers. Or running football drills with the twins and their friends in the backyard when they got older.

Shortly after we moved to Chicago, that horrible photographer agreed to discontinue using Olly's pics rather than get sued. As for the strip joint, Olly snagged the owner a few tickets to the hottest college football team in Texas, and he promised not to use those photos anymore.

After a while, people forgot about those billboards, and the business offers rolled in at record speed—for tandem baby strollers and carriers and clothes. And by the end of Olly's time playing in Chicago, that Big Tykes football program made another offer. For three times the original amount. Of course, it didn't hurt that Michael was Chicago's best running back.

But sometimes that means he has to travel.

"I'm glad you could make it to Gracie's recital before you left."

He kisses my forehead. "You know I wouldn't miss it. I missed enough when I was playing."

As much as Olly loved playing football, he hated how it meant less time with me and the children.

I'm so blessed I've always been able to work from home. I eventually learned calligraphy from YouTube videos like Olly suggested and have made a whole business from it. So I still do those wedding and baby shower invitations but now with custom hand lettering. And the best part? I'm always around if our kiddos need anything.

Grateful for this quiet moment together, I graze my lips against Olly's. "Do you think you'll take that broadcasting job?"

He sighs. "It's an amazing offer, but it would mean road trips every weekend. I'd miss so much. The boys' games. Gracie's dances. Sadie's first everything. Not to mention how much I'd miss you."

I rub the scruff on his handsome face. "You know we'd support you, right? If you wanted that job, we'd be your biggest fans. The kids would understand. It would take some adjustment, of course, because we've been spoiled having you around lately. And it wouldn't be as bad as when you played because you wouldn't be training incessantly on top of traveling. I'd miss you terribly, but I'd hate for you to make a big sacrifice if you wanted that job."

"It's no sacrifice." He brushes his lips against mine. "I already have everything I want."

I lean my forehead against his shoulder, beyond grateful for everything in my life. Starting with this amazing man. "I have everything I want too."

In spades.

WHAT TO READ NEXT...

Thanks for reading! If you enjoyed The Baby Blitz, I hope you'll consider leaving a review. I try to read each one!

To stay up-to-date with my new releases, be sure to subscribe to my newsletter, which you can find on my website, www.lexmartinwrites.com.

Next up in the series is Charlotte and Jake's book, SECOND DOWN DARLING! (You haven't met Jake yet, but he's dreamy!)

And if you want to start at the beginning of the VARSITY DADS series, be sure to check out THE VARSITY DAD DILEMMA, which is a USA Today bestseller. Keep flipping to read the synopsis.

THE VARSITY DAD DILEMMA

SYNOPSIS

What's worse than having Rider Kingston, the star quarterback, give you the big brush-off because he doesn't want to get serious? You'd probably think living across the street from him where you get a firsthand view of his hookups, right?

That's what I thought. Until someone drops off a baby with a note pinned to her blanket that says one of those jocks—either Rider or one of his roommates—is the father. The problem? Baby mama doesn't mention which of these numbskulls is the sperm donor.

I wouldn't care about their paternity problems—not the slightest bit—except my brother lives there too. Which means that adorable squawking bundle might be my niece, and there's no way I'm leaving her unattended with those bumbling football players.

They need my help, even if they don't know it yet. Once we solve this dilemma and figure out who's the daddy, I'm out.

I'll just ignore Rider and those soul-searing looks he gives me every time I reach for the baby. He broke my heart three years ago. He won't get a second chance.

Check out THE VARSITY DAD DILEMMA, a USA Today bestseller, to find out what happens!

ACKNOWLEDGMENTS

This book was such a joy to write, and I'm so grateful I get to share it with you! The best part of this gig is being able to draw on first-hand experiences when drafting a story, and I used several for The Baby Blitz.

When I was a kid, my dad and I renovated my grandmother's house. We re-roofed it, leveled the foundation, yanked out the porch, and built a new one. Just the two of us! I have the stitches on my shin to prove it—because I was a klutz who fell through the rotting floorboards one rainy afternoon. Despite that slightly traumatic event, my dad and I had a great time. He's always telling me you can learn anything from reading a book or watching a YouTube video, and he's the inspiration behind Maggie's can-do DIY attitude.

The other experience I drew upon heavily was my difficult pregnancy with twins. Seriously, I was so preggers, I couldn't fit behind the wheel of my car. While not every pregnancy turns you into Linda Blair, mine did, and when I wasn't hurling, I had major Braxton Hicks contractions. Of course, I'd do it all over again to have my girls, but I'm still a little jealous of people who've had easy pregnancies. Dragging poor Maggie along through my own misery was quite therapeutic.

I hope you feel I approached Frannie's condition with dignity and respect. If you're interested in the meal program that helped her cognition, it's called the Special Carbohydrate Diet, and a dear friend of mine had great results using it for her autistic son.

I'm particularly blue about finishing this book because I'm going to miss Olly and Magnolia! I banged out the first draft in two months. Honestly, it felt like the planets aligned. I loved the characters and everything just felt magical. None of that magic would've happened, though, without the support from my husband Matt, who never complained about all the nights we did take-out. He and my girls are my whole world, and I'm so grateful to have them in my corner.

I also need to thank my friend Tish for her suggestion to do a surprise baby book next. (You were so right!)

A huge thanks to my team who helps me get to the finish line: my agent Kimberly Brower, editor RJ Locksley, proofer Julia Griffis, photographer Lauren Perrywinkle, designer Najla Qamber, and Kylie and Jo from Give Me Books. Thank you for everything you do for me!

My beta readers are worth their weight in gold. Serena McDonald, Leslie McAdam, Victoria Denault, Kelly Latham, Kristie White Bivens, Jan Cassi, and Amy Vox Libris—thank you for helping me write the best book possible!

Serena McDonald gets a second shout-out for also being an amazing PA and helping me keep the wheels on this bus! Serena, thank you for your friendship, your daily support, your unwavering enthusiasm, and for kicking my ass when I need it.

And hugs to my cousin Lisa for checking my Spanish and my dad for always making sure my football is tight.

Lastly, thanks to my ARC team, everyone in my Wildcats

Facebook group, and all of the readers and bloggers who've picked up my books and shared them with friends!

Next up is Charlotte and Jake's book! Their story kept shouting in my head while I was writing The Baby Blitz, and I can't wait for you to read SECOND DOWN DARLING!

xo,

Lex

ALSO BY LEX MARTIN

Varsity Dads:

The Varsity Dad Dilemma (Gabby & Rider)

Tight Ends & Tiaras (Sienna & Ben)

The Baby Blitz (Magnolia & Olly)

Second Down Darling (Charlotte & Jake)

Texas Nights:

Shameless (Kat & Brady)

Reckless (Tori & Ethan)

Breathless (Joey & Logan)

The Dearest Series:

Dearest Clementine (Clementine & Gavin)

Finding Dandelion (Dani & Jax)

Kissing Madeline (Maddie & Daren)

Cowritten with Leslie McAdam

All About the D (Evie & Josh)

Surprise, Baby! (Kendall & Drew)

ABOUT THE AUTHOR

Lex Martin is the *USA Today* bestselling author of The Varsity Dad Dilemma, the Texas Nights series, and the Dearest series, books she hopes readers love but her parents avoid. A former high school English teacher and freelance journalist, she resides in Texas with her husband, twin daughters, and a bunny named Dandelion.

To stay up-to-date with her releases, **subscribe to her newsletter** or join her Facebook group, **Lex Martin's Wildcats.**

www.lexmartinwrites.com

Printed in Great Britain
by Amazon

60266912R00241